THE GENERALS OF OCTOBER

JOHN T. CULLEN is a writer and editor with many years of experience in publishing and technical documentation. He was the editor, with Brian Callahan, of the world's oldest professional web-only magazine of speculative fiction, Deep Outside SFFH, from 1998 to 2000 and now continues the magazine on his own hook under the name Far Sector SFFH. He continues to innovate in new ways to present original and exciting fiction to discriminating readers on the web, through such venues as Fictionwise. He has degrees in English (University of Connecticut, BA 1972), Computer Information Systems (National University, BBA, 1984), and Business Administration (Boston University, M.S., 1980). He lives in San Diego.

AVAILABLE NOW

THE GENERALS OF OCTOBER

John T. Cullen

ibooks

new york

DISTRIBUTED BY SIMON & SCHUSTER

A Publication of ibooks, inc.

Distributed by Simon & Schuster, Inc.
1230 Avenue of the Americas, New York, NY 10020

ibooks, inc.
24 West 25th Street
New York, NY 10010

The ibooks World Wide Web Site Address is:
www.ibooks.net

ISBN 0-7434-9338-9
First ibooks, inc. printing November 2004
10 9 8 7 6 5 4 3 2 1

Editor: Dwight Jon Zimmerman
Cover Design: M. Postawa

Printed in the U.S.A.

PROLOG

U.S. Vice President Louis Cardoza and the man licensed to kill him actually once came within 25 feet of each other. This happened at a reception in the White House, a year before the option needed to be exercised.

There was nothing accidental about this near-meeting.

It was a cold, calculated exercise by the Second Service, the shadowy intelligence arm of the equally shadowy government-in-waiting in Washington, to show that they could penetrate what they called the Rots at any level, any time, at will.

A preppy-dressing man of 35, Cover had a bland, unmemorably youthful face that could belong to any serious but impish graduate student, and could blossom into a warm if somehow distracted grin. His blond hair was cut short around the ears, and was already receding from his bulbous temple ridges. Only the thinning hair, a certain slouch when he relaxed, and hard lines around his eyes, gave away his real age. He preferred to wear custom eyeglasses with thin steel rims, because he could kill a man with them if all else failed.

At a reception in the East Room for diplomats and their wives, Cover posed as a Swedish correspondent. The Swedes were naive and open, and he slipped in among their party as they left their embassy for a row of limos. The Ambassador's wife wore a leather coat and smelled of a faint, expensive violet perfume. Cover hovered by her side, speaking sufficient Swedish to impress her. When the Ambassador noticed, Cover smiled disarmingly, and the man nodded and smiled back with a bit of a confused look—was this an old friend whose name would come back to him? Cover nodded and smiled, and the Ambassador smiled back.

At the reception, Cover held a sturdy saucer in one hand and a steaming coffee cup in the other. A waitress in black, with white apron, offered miniature blintzes from a silver tray, and Cover accepted one. Behind the thin lenses, his eyes twinkled cornflower blue, and his cheeks dimpled in a smile. The woman gave him a lingering look of appreciation before moving on.

Cover sized up his man. The Vice President, Louis Cardoza, was a former boxer. Light-skinned for a Mexican-American, and sandy-haired with gray sidewalls at 48, Cardoza was movie-star handsome. Cardoza's beautiful wife stayed by his side, a smallish brunette from immense old Anglo wealth, with a model's picture-perfect face. She looked stunning in a little black dress that complemented her tanned, firm breasts and well-exercised thighs. Cover could easily understand the charm these people had upon a nation mired in the Second World Depression, with all its poverty, homelessness, crime, and despair. A nation waking up from nearly 200 years of uninterrupted rule by a two-party cabal that used billions of dollars of taxpayer money as a reelection slush fund each year—roads to nowhere, bridges over nothing, ships the Navy didn't need, planes the Air Force didn't want, to bring tax dollars to one's district, and get votes—grand larceny, felony theft in Cover's dictionary. He was reminded of the Romanovs—300 years in power, and nobody had believed there was any other way to rule the country. Soon, America would awaken from its long sleep.

Cover was a moral man. There was a job to do. Actually, these people were so pretty, he hoped they would not get in the way, because then he'd have to do fearsome things to them.

Wiping sugar dust from his lips as Louis Cardoza moved within 25 feet of him, Cover beamed. The Secret Service Rots hovering out of earshot from their man had no idea the Second Service was at all times moving among them, as Cover's ideological archenemy Chairman Mao had said, 'as a fish swims in the sea.'

One of them even brushed Cover's sleeve, and mumbled, "Excuse me."

Cover shrugged matter of factly, waving a napkin, and said: "think nothing of it."

PART I

PRELUDES: THE GATHERING STORM

CHAPTER 1

IMPERIAL BEACH, CALIFORNIA

Terrified, Brandy ran along the Pacific seashore just after dawn on a summer day.

She was 14 years-old and alone, except for her tormentor.

She ran on long thin legs, wearing faded pink pajama shorts and her much-older brother's olive-drab T-shirt. Her thick dark hair, glowing with reddish-amber highlights, bobbed as she raced over the flat wet sand of Imperial Beach, just north of the Mexican border.

Her mouth was open, sucking desperate gulps of air, and her dark blue eyes fluttered as she heard every breath and curse of the man who pressed close behind her.

Offshore, a gray island loomed, swathed in sea fog—an aircraft carrier, and beyond that a line of smaller gray shapes. The sky was the lightest of powder blues, the sun a cold silver coin in the mist. The ship turned her bow into the wind, with a fighter plane roaring aloft every 40 seconds or so. The aircraft carrier churned up a distantly visible bow wake as she sought advantage in her practice for battle. Oblivious of Brandy's struggle on shore, the carrier battle group was assembling to race toward a new confrontation on the other side of the globe.

Brandy stumbled and fell with a shocked yelp.

Mr. O'Brady coughed a mixture of sputum and triumphant laughter. She glimpsed him barely 20 feet behind her: white haired, red faced, wearing only dingy gray boxer shorts and a stained green tank top that showed off the middle-aged flab on his arms and breasts. He smelled of whiskey and cigarettes—the horrid musky animal scent that had helped awaken her, gagging, in her bed in the mobile home barely four or five minutes ago.

She was deep asleep, dreaming in movie color of a great vegetable patch in which teddy bears marched around with hoes, perhaps because of the marijuana haze coming from the livingroom. She felt rough hands on her bare legs, pulling off her pajama bottom. He swayed drunkenly from side to side, each sway pulling the fragile, worn fabric further down her legs. The bottoms were easy anyway—the elastic had long given up, lost snap. She blinked numbly, wishing he'd stop and she could pull up the covers because her thighs had goosebumps as the cold morning air wafted over them from the open window. When she realized who he was and what he was doing, she screamed, for she'd heard rumors he killed people.

"Jeremy!" she screamed over and over for her brother.

She screamed: "Stop that, Mr. O'Brady!" but the groundskeeper of the mobile home, who'd spent the night drinking and playing cards with her brother and his friends, was the only one who could hear. His eyes were maniacal buttons of sexual hunger, his grin idiotic and festooned with spittle—from early evening she'd seen him staring after her with a kind of mean speculation, but it had taken a night of hard drinking to remove the last thin veneer of false decency.

She palmed him in the face as hard as she could, as her brother had taught her. The bony pads near her wrist caught him full on the nose and he let go of her legs. She dug her fingernails, with dirt showing where the red polish had chipped off, into his eyes, and he bellowed, but luckily his eyelids had closed reflexively at the strike of her palm, or she'd be blinding him. Instead, she felt the soggy meat in his wrinkled eyelids turn bloody under her fingernails. He bellowed again and she slipped past him, running.

In the livingroom lay five bodies. Not dead, just drugged out. The place smelled of marijuana smoke and spilled beer. And food, lots of food, when the boys got together for cards. She was street-wise and saw the picture in a flash: Mr. O'Brady must have had money, and they'd cut him in, hoping to skin him. Instead, he drank them under the table, probably had all their money in his pocket, and for good measure thought he'd help himself to a piece of Brandy.

Mr. O'Brady staggered out of her bedroom calling her dirty names.

She kicked the door open in an explosive run, and jumped. With one bound she landed on the tiny landing, with a second bound hopped on one arm over the railing, sailed over the bushes, and hit the driveway of the battered 60-foot single-wide mobile home running. Mr. O'Brady chugged right behind her, chuckling and breathing raggedly. He knew he would catch her, and she read the triumph in the noises he made. His grunts telegraphed the violent, lurid, angry movie of what he planned to do once he caught her. Jeremy and his biker friends had mentioned him in conversation, with some bravura awe, not to show they were intimidated, but legend had it Mr. O'Brady had spent ten years in a Navy brig for beating a man to death. The bikers also spoke of O'Brady taking hookers up into the Jacumba mountains, and coming back alone.

As she ran, the thought of those dark, deep forests of pine growth—dark green, almost black, a color of terror—made the skin crawl up and down her back. Mr. O'Brady was so close she could not stop to gather breath to scream. It was early and nobody was out. She could stop to bang on doors, but that would let him catch up with her—and the first thing would be that dirty, cigarette-smelling hand, hard as steel, closing over her mouth, the other hand digging vicious knuckles into her unprotected ribs, and then would come the ride into the mountains. Brandy could rely on nobody now—just herself. They raced down beachside back alleys and then out onto the sand.

She picked herself up from the stumble on the beach and continued running. Not far ahead, as she ran north along the sand in Imperial Beach, was the pier. Surely there would be fishermen there. She thought she spotted the thin whisps of their poles, but she couldn't be sure. Mr. O'Brady was getting angrier now, and he kept closing. How did he summon this superhuman energy? Was it all the sugar in the booze? Was he on speed? She wished she had the fleshed-out body of an adult so she could run more effectively. She felt awkward in her growing frame—legs long but not long enough, skinny and not very strong, torso just budding, narrow-shouldered, not packing enough oxygen to make the whole apparatus run well.

She knew well enough what he was after. She'd been having sex with a succession of Jeremy's friends during the past year. Jeremy's attitude was: "Just be cool, girl. Go to school, keep the heat off me, I don't need that bullshit. And remember, I love you and I'll take care of you."

Yeah, right. Like now.

They had a pact of survival. Their dad was in Long Beach at the federal prison, serving 25 to life on a third conviction for embezzlement, forgery, and confidence crimes. Their mom had lasted a bit, but raising children alone on welfare had been too much for her, and she'd taken off with a flashy fellow from Vegas who always had rolls of C-notes in his pockets. Actually, besides that, mom hadn't been so bad. The flashy guy—Brandy had blocked out his name, hated him for taking her mother—had liked to pinch Brandy's butt and check her breasts with his thumb and index finger. Mom had seen that, and Brandy had seen the look of pain and realization in her mother's eyes, the way mom rolled her eyes up knowing that she must go away with this man so he would not molest her daughter. And mom had stolen two grand from her lover, by way of getting even, and given it to Jeremy, making him promise to take care of his little sister. That had been over a year ago. They hadn't heard from her since. Jeremy, by now 18, was out of school and running with the Imperial Beach Foo Klan Angels, a biker club that wholesaled street drugs and occasionally carried out a hit—all out of town, of course, quick in, quick out.

Maybe, she thought as the cool sand grabbed her ankles time and again, if she went full circle, back to the mobile home, maybe they'd be awake by now. They'd take Mr. O'Brady out of town, maybe to the Jacumbas, and they'd come back alone.

But there he was, panting along behind her.

The aircraft carrier wheeled in glory, her bow wake gleaming white as laughing teeth. The jets banked one by one and howled in low over the beach across the inlet at Coronado. Sun gleaming on their wings, they would land at North Island Naval Air Station for a final checkout before the fleet sailed to the Iranian Gulf.

Brandy barely noticed. She only wished the sailors could come to help her. Though Jeremy and his friends spoke badly of it, the military was supposed to be a good thing. Brandy carried secrets in her heart—of long ago, when mom and dad had been together. They'd had fun times, always easy, with money flowing past, and she'd get whatever toys she wanted. So long ago. Dad sitting her on his lap, mom laughing as she spoon fed her little girl, Jeremy yelling as he ran outside with his new toy rifle. All gone. Just in the corner of her room, where Jeremy would not notice, was a picture of a stern ageless man in Army officer's uniform. He had kindly eyes—she'd never met him, because he'd been killed in Vietnam many, many years ago—Dad's dad. Somewhere out in the world, Brandy vaguely knew, was a strict old lady with bluish-white hair who always wanted to make Jeremy and Brandy come live with her. While the old lady offered good things to eat, the rules were strict like in a prison, and the weather back in Iowa sucked big frapping weenie balls. Jeremy and Brandy lived in fear that the old woman would find out mom had split, and come to take Brandy away. For that reason, and because she liked the orderly, tidy world in school, she marched off to the school bus every schoolday morning. She tried hard to keep her mouth in check, and she'd had some detentions, but the teachers mostly liked her and felt sorry for her, and kept her out of the principal's office. She did her homework, even sometimes if her brother and his boys got her high by blowing jay into her bedroom through a cracked door. "Stop that!" she'd say, and get up to kick the door shut. She'd girlfriended them one by one, liking the affection she got. Jeremy was the leader, and kept a sharp eye out for her. "What are you doing this for?" he once asked as she sauntered by after making love with Rafer; she had a cigarette dangling from her mouth, and wore only a large bath towel. "What's wrong with you, girl?"

"Nothing wrong with me," she said tossing her chin back and using both hands to fly her hair back in a bundle so she could turban it with a second towel lying on one shoulder. "That's what it's all about, right? You get love where you can find it and don't worry about tomorrow, like in those old hippie songs."

He'd shut up after that, as long as she went to school and kept him and herself out of trouble. He said once: "I don't give a damn if you act 14, or 34, as long as you keep us out of trouble. And go to school. You're the only one with brains around here."

Someone got her drunk once, and there was this attractive picture on the bottle. Still she was drunk, her boyfriend at the time paid a guy down the row to tattoo a peach on her belly, with 'Peach' written above it, and 'Brandy' underneath, just above the v between her belly and right leg. She'd had mixed feelings about it. They'd nicknamed her Brandy. She found she enjoyed having a man at her side—a young man, a boy, not an old animal like Mr. O'Brady. She enjoyed hanging out, feeling a boy's hand on her waist or hip or butt. She liked the anger, the possess- ive rage, the jealousy she made them feel. She knew how to control a situation so she brought her boy to the edge of a fight with another boy, and then ease off. Jeremy's boys had a reputation, and the other guy was usually happy to back out of it. Once, though, Eric had bloodied a good-looking young boy's face, and she'd reconsidered the sport. The boy had looked so neat and trim, like some of the goody-goodies at school that she didn't belong with. She hated them at first, then realized that she wanted to be like them. Now she kind of resented them, not hated them, but was angry because she could never fit in there. Jeremy's motto was "live and die young, it's the only damn way." She had a sort of sick feeling deep inside that she'd die violently, and maybe now with Mr. O'Brady the moment had come. She remembered church and offered an Act of Contrition for all her many sins, all the fights, the stoned nights, the sex she knew she should not have had. She swore she'd give it all up if God let her survive. Not the forest, she pleaded, not that! She remembered the pleasure of belonging, of intimacy with those big boys, their smooth hard skin rippling with muscle like steel inside rubber, their breath delicious on her lips, their arousal full inside of her. She thought it odd that now she wished she hadn't. She was done with them, she thought; her last gig had been a few months with Eric, but he was 20 and married, and the wife had showed up banging on the mobile home door with a baseball bat at 3 in the morning. Jeremy had gone out with a .38 and told her to shut up before the cops came. Eric had wrestled his wife to the car to take her home, and the cops came anyway, but it was like that most nights at the Happy Dell Mobile Home Ranch.

This whole fractured movie, this trembling mosaic of her life, flashed through her mind in millisecond bursts inbetween squeaks of terror and frantic looking toward the pier.

Odd, now, that she didn't hear Mr. O'Brady anymore.

Glancing behind her, she saw that he had fallen. He lay curled on one side, one arm over his head. A hand dangled over his forehead, twitching. Was he having a heart attack? She hoped. Would he croak and leave her alone? She made a wide turn and jogged back toward the mobile home. She ran on the side where she could see his face. His eyes glittered as if he were crying. His face was blue, and his mouth was open, round, like the end of a fat hose, as he vomited. Out came little bits of grits or something ugly, like he was counting them out, whup!, one two three, urp, there went another one. Gross!

"Asshole!" she yelled, realizing in a wave of relief that she'd won. "You asshole! Fuck you! Wait until my brother finds out about this, you old smelly idiot!

You better move out of this state, or your ass is gonna go one way and your nuts the other!" She picked up a wad of wet sand, spit in it, balled it up, and dumped it on his head as she jogged past. He cried out feebly but didn't move.

"Die of a heart attack, you stupid asshole! Go ahead, make my day, you pie-ass son of a bitch!"

She sprinted toward the water, whooping, skipping and jumping up and down in great strides. Seeing the magnificent aircraft carrier heeling smartly, she waved her fists in the air and whooped repeatedly. Its white bow wake grinned at her. She did a cartwheel and ran home.

The boys glowered over breakfast. "Where you been?" Jeremy asked. "Been out all night?"

"What are we, married?" She took the o.j. from the fridge. "Where friggin' are you when I need you?" She let the door swing shut as she drank from the carton. "Freakin' toked out on the floor, and me hollering for you." Juice dribbled down her front and she wiped it with her wrist as she tore a plate from the cupboard. "O'Brady tried to rape me. He chased me down the beach." She scraped a wad of eggs and bacon onto the plate. She slammed the drawer open and shut, and a fork appeared in her hand as if by magic. "I was asleep, and he was pulling my pants off."

Jeremy listened with darkening face, exchanging glances with the other men.

"And I'm sure," she rubbed it in, "I'm sure you guys don't have a dollar left between you. He cleaned you out, ain't that right?"

"Where is he now?"

"I think he's dead on the beach. If you want your

money back, better go now before he starts to stink. I mean, he already reeks, but that ain't quite the stench of death yet, you know?" She gulped o.j. and wolfed down her eggs. She enjoyed being thoroughly in charge at the moment. "What the hey? No money, no girls, no dope—you guys are in sad shape."

"Shut up, Brandy," Jeremy said. Nobody else dared say it, with Jeremy there.

As Brandy walked out the door a while later, showered and dressed and carrying her schoolbooks, the boys were combing down the beach in a row, hands in pockets, their gait ominous. Brandy had to run to catch the school bus as it started to snort and roar away from the curb. Mr. O'Brady never did show up at the mobile home park again, and she never wanted to ask what happened to him. Sometimes at night she woke up shivering, thinking he was coming to pull her pants off again, and she'd wander out of her bedroom holding her teddy bear, half asleep, to snuggle with whoever was sleeping on the couch. The picture of the man in Army uniform never changed—always self-righteous, shit-don't-happen-to-me, except shit happened when he died in the war—and she revered him the way other people kept religious icons on their dressers. One day, Grandpa would come back and make everything be normal the way it was supposed to be.

Nothing was as it was supposed to be. They had an old tv, whose control wand was stuck on CNN. Every time she turned it on to watch MTV or Discovery or something cool, she had to distastefully watch the ugly world of adults playing itself out. If that was Congress, she thought, those were a bunch of fools. Grownups in business suits, attacking and accusing each other, lawyers sharpening points of law to impale each other—especially that one man with the smug face and bullying attitude, the one with those mean beady little eyes whose fat head always seemed to be in the middle of everything. What would Grandpa have said if he knew he'd died for these morons? It was really hard to have any respect at all. It was hard to feel, as a teenager, that all of life was not a mean, dirty cesspool created by the adult population who seemed to have no brains.

Some detectives came around after Mr. O'Brady disappeared, and they asked Jeremy some questions, but Jeremy was smooth, real real smooth, and they left, giving him their cards and asking Jeremy to call them if he learned any more about Mr. O'Brady's whereabouts. Jeremy was real slick—he didn't throw the cards away, but kept them taped to the cracked door window, in case they ever came back; then he could say he'd kept them in mind. But Brandy had a feeling he was laughing inwardly, and the cards were like trophies. And Mr. O'Brady was a reeking, grinning skeleton under the pine trees in the mountains.

Brandy began throwing up every morning.

On a Saturday afternoon, she sat with her best friend Rosie on the sea wall near the Hotel Del Coronado. They were smoking cigarettes, high up on the one-ton boulders that had been brought to keep the ocean and Coronado money apart. Each girl had a 16-ounce beer stashed in a nook between the rocks in a plain wrapper. They picked up their cans, sipped quickly, and then hid them again. The wind ruffled their hair, and the sunny afternoon air was balmy, with just a hint of moisture as an offshore breeze started toward land. They absently flicked their cigarettes, blew the smoke up high to one side so it wouldn't linger in their hair, and watched the young men heading down to surf.

Brandy felt dazed.

"Does Jeremy know?"

"Not yet. Men can't figger this kinda shit out on their own."

Rosie nodded. She was small, with smooth dark skin and dark eyes and long black hair that turned mahogany at the ends, where it was a year or more old. She wore gang sister clothing—black canvas slip-on shoes, white socks, gray work pants rolled up at the cuffs, a clean white t-shirt, a gold chain and crucifix given by her boyfriend who was doing time for armed robbery. Rosie was a good soul.

"I gotta do something though. Problem is, I don't know which one of Jeremy's friends is the dad."

"You could have the baby. Get welfare. Ain't much, but what you got now?"

"I want to stay in school."

"I know," Rosie said softly, with deep regret. She'd dropped out over a year ago. Didn't look like she'd go back. Maybe do her equivalency one day. "But better be quick—they'd had this conversation many times—'cause when Junior gets out, look out. A kid every year. Well, there's always the different clinics."

"Can't," Brandy said. She was thinking of the old white haired lady. Sure way to bring the county down, the cops, the whole bureaucracy, and wind up in a house full of rules. No smoking, no drinking, no—no way.

"Okay," Rosie said, knowing Brandy's situation. "My sister knows somebody."

"How much?"

"Two hundred. Cash. If you don't got the cash, I can help."

"Thanks, Rosie, you're a bud."

"Done, girl."

They high-fived.

But things didn't go smoothly at all for Brandy.

First, Jeremy got shot in Riverside. Brandy was home alone, the day after her illegal abortion, feeling terrible stomach cramps and unable to get comfortable. She kept spotting her pads with blood. She was alarmed because she seemed to be bleeding more, not less. She kept groaning at this deep, rolling, twinging pain. She kept doubling over and sometimes the pain made her cry. Where was Jeremy? The phone rang and the minute she heard the authoritative, invasive, curt voice on the other end, she knew something terrible had happened. Tears sprang to her eyes and she absently pulled tissues from a box, dragging the box toward her as the tears rolled down her eyes and she dabbed them with a fistful of tissues. "Your brother is in critical condition. He has one bullet wound to the head and two to the abdomen. I'd like to talk with you about what he was doing where he got shot."

"Is he gonna live?" With a bullet wound to the head...

"They don't know yet, honey. I hope so, okay?"

She started crying loudly, uncontrollably. She heard the detective say "Go ahead, I'll wait," and she dropped the phone and threw herself across the couch wailing. Her gut seemed to have huge pliers turning in it, and it hurt to sob, but she couldn't control her tears. In the back of her mind the thoughts rolled by: call Rosie. get a car. somebody who can drive. what's the address? Will we get lost? Will he be alive?

In the ICU on the western side of the second floor of the University of California San Diego (UCSD) Medical Center in San Diego, equipment and sheet-draped bodies competed for cramped space with racks and stacks of electronic monitoring equipment. Male and female nurses in blue smocks sidled among their patients, fingers constantly busy at the exacting task of maintaining lives that lay on the edge of existence.

One of the patients was smaller than the others. She was a scrawny girl of 14 with thick dark hair with amber highlights. Her skin color was a pasty yellow, and her eyes were closed and shadowed as she lay dying. Her caretakers were slowing that process down and trying to reverse it. But she was dying.

By the bedside stood a tall, thin, angular woman of about 70 with white hair tied severely back. The woman wore a plain wheat-colored coat and an equally simple brown leather purse with hand straps. Her face, which looked young for her age, was stony, impassive, as she hovered over her granddaughter. She wished she'd known that her daughter had run off. She'd known about her son-in-law being in jail. She hadn't known about the conditions under which her granddaughter had been living, or she'd have come sooner. A little Mexican friend of the child's had called. Wild little girl, Rosie, whose scary brother had picked the white-haired lady up at Lindbergh

Field in a souped up car and took her to the hospital. Tattooed kid with gang clothes, somber and polite.

The stern lady reached out and touched her granddaughter's wrist. "I will be praying for you," she whispered. And for your brother, she thought, as a nurse led her outside. She was tired from her flight, and grieving because her other trip, today, would be to a morgue. And she had so much to prepare for Jeremy's funeral. A doctor waited outside the ICU, extending a hand. "How are you, Ma'am?"

She shook his hand and looked away, unable to answer.

"I know this is hard for you. Your granddaughter is gravely ill."

"Will she live?" she whispered.

The doctor looked distressed.

CHAPTER 2

YEARS LATER: MONTECITO, CALIFORNIA

As he began his vacation, California Governor Louis Cardoza, 49, centrist Democrat, had little more on his mind than making love with his wife later in the morning—probably after a swim and maybe before a rub-down—he'd decide later.

On this first morning of his vacation, he'd already once sated his appetite for her firm, smooth skin. Still glowing from that and what she'd told him, he sat by the pool reading The Wall Street Journal, sipping black coffee, and munching hot buttered toast with a sprinkle of sugar and cinnamon. He felt great. The morning air smelled divinely of leaves and flowers, birds twittered, and the day was still full of promise. Louis had lined up a round of golf with his old law partners this afternoon. Meredith had just this morning told him, in the middle of their wake-up sex, that she was pregnant with their first child. He felt a deep sense of pride, almost—well, use the word, he told himself inwardly, go on, you're a Latin lover—machismo.

Meredith, wearing a fluffy white jacket over her black bikini, walked out of the tiled entrance of their mansion. A medium-height brunette, she was a tanned Girl Next Door. Louis watched with pleasure as, back straight, she strode on firmly muscled legs. Her long straight hair glowed with a mahogany warmth. Her stomach was flat; her breasts were firm and round, her gluteal muscles tight handfuls, her thighs trim and dark like forest honey—almost Latina, he thought lovingly. Despite her athletic buffness, her face had a delicate, finely proportioned beauty. Her lower jaw was full and strong, while her lips and nose were delicate and expressive, her eyes large and dark, her forehead high and clear. She carried herself proudly, with a quiet happiness, and Louis never tired of her.

Meredith carried a big red towel as she walked on cork heels toward the bar cart. Today was the staff afternoon off, which meant the Cardozas had to look after themselves; it also meant privacy. The gates and windows of the mansion were electronically guarded.

Off came the white robe, and up went Lou's appreciation. She had a glow today—she was finally, after years of trying, an expectant mother. She stepped to the diving board and favored him with a fond, conspiratorial smile—like, wait until I get you into bed again. She executed a sharp dive into the deep end. That was Meredith for you—sharp moves, and never afraid of the deep end. Of course, she came from old wealth, unlike himself, and she understood perfectly what she must do. It was bred into her. She came from a long line of senators and millionaires. Her extended family had vinyards in Napa with designer labels; newspapers in several Midwestern cities; stables in Kentucky; department stores in Hartford, Manhattan, Boston, and Philadelphia; a truck factory in Michigan, and so on.

As Meredith swam up and down the huge pool in graceful strokes, Louis put down his newspaper and watched her. Unlike so most men he knew, he did not cheat on her; well, not any more. He loved her deeply, and he could not understand why other men, married to women even more beautiful than Meredith, would risk their love casually. At 35, she was a junior partner in Cassoli Johns Jenkins Mackensie and generally worked out of Santa Barbara.

As he watched the tanned skin on the backs of her legs glisten wetly, and her glutes twisting as she cut strong strokes in the water, the phone on the table interrupted Lou's reverie. Now what the hell could that be? He'd issued strict orders not to be disturbed except in a great emergency. Usually he carried either a lapel com button, or a pocket cell, or a wrist appliance—but today he wanted to be out of touch, tethered to the world only by one ancient cordless telephone. Irritated, he picked up.

It was his chief of staff, Meredith's cousin Teddy Warington, calling from Sacramento. Teddy's voice was rapid fire, anxious: "Louis, John Dunstan has been killed in a plane crash. Hamilton called here—he's looking for you; flying down from Chicago to see you."

"What?" Louis sat bolt upright, swinging his legs around to place his feet on the firm concrete. Dunstan was the opposition Middle Class Party's white knight, their best shot at the White House this election year. Dead? Teddy didn't know that he, Louis, had met several times with Hamilton over the past year or two. Hamilton had dangled various offers if he defected to MCP, and Louis had listened.

Teddy repeated: "Hamilton's flying down to see you. He'll be landing in Santa Barbara any time now. If I can guess what he's after, don't do it. For God's sake, Louie, I beg you, don't."

"What do you think he's after?" Louis said absently, while his mind raced ahead of his cousin-in-law's words. Robert Lee Hamilton had founded the Middle Class Party just a few years ago, and people who'd stopped voting for the Democrats and Republicans were flocking to the MCP. Already, MCP had ten state legislatures and nine governorships—and more were expected to fall to them in the next midterm elections. "All politics is local," House Speaker Tip O'Neill had once remarked—and Robert Lee Hamilton, a billionaire industrialist with a vision for America, had taken that to heart. Unlike the abortive Perot campaigns of the previous century, RLH (as his fanatically loyal people, and many of his enemies, called him) took that to heart. He was building his way to Washington, he liked to say, on a highway of governorships and local offices. State legislatures were his bread and butter. A shy, reclusive man, he stayed out of the limelight while hordes of enthusiastic Joe Sixpacks went door to door talking up the Middle Class Party. No more one party pretending to be the party of the poor, and the other pretending to be the party of the rich—this was a party for the taxpayers on whose broken backs generations of waste and fraud had been carried. America had numerous "third parties," but only MCP was racing out in front, challenging the old pols. It was all but official that, to beat a coalition of MCP and Greens, among others, the Democrats and Republicans were floating a new idea: a combined ticket called the Old Constitution Party. Open primaries in numerous states smoothed the path in that direction. It was the only way, Louis and many like him thought, to keep the White House and the Congress. The scheme troubled him deeply, though he saw its logic. As a Latino, an outsider who had worked his way in, he didn't see the urgent need to preserve his own or the other ancient cadaver of a party. He'd won handily because of the population mix, but the traditionals were slipping badly in most other parts of the country.

Louis listened to what Meredith's cousin had to say, but firmly, though warmly, refused to make a commitment. "I'll just wait to see what Hamilton has to say."

After disconnecting, he walked to the pool in several crouching steps, and dove in. He swam up under Meredith, captured her in his arms, and smothered her squeals with a kiss.

After a moment, she gripped his shoulders. "What is it, darling? Something's up." In a lightly tanned face dotted with water droplets and fringed by wet dark brown hair, her dark eyes glittered with calculation that mirrored the rapidly winking chessgame going on in his stimulated mind. He was shocked by the politician's death, felt bad for him, but had no time now to dwell on it. Time flowed, life moved on, and some opportunities came only once in a lifetime.

There was a time when Luis Cardoza did not have enough to eat, and he forced himself never to forget where he'd come from, because that was the root of his power and success as a politician. One of eight children, he was playing hookey from school by eight and selling drugs by 10. At 12 he'd been in his first serious fight, a rumble in which a 14 year old girl was paralyzed from the waist down by an errant gunshot by an older boy in Luis's gang. At 13 he was acting as a lookout for two men robbing a convenience store, when someone threw a brick at the two men as they fled, but hit the boy instead. Luis, with a head injury that took years to heal, was sent to live with his protective and conservatively religious grandmother in Houston. Away from his crime-ridden home turf, he became an excellent student. Sheltered and cared for, he became an avid reader. He also developed a formidable interest in boxing. By the time he was 18, he was in competition for the regional Golden Gloves. Then his grandmother died and the time of sheltering was over, but he emerged from that period a changed person. He dropped out of school and started working by day. At night, he began boxing semi-professionally and then professionally for money. He married a young girl named Roberta and by the time he was 22, had two little girls. They were hardscrabble times, and he and his trainer often drove overnight in an old black car that spewed smoke—sometimes returning victorious from a bout, with a few thousand dollars, cheering and slapping fives; other times silently and broke, with Luis in the back seat, sulking, holding an icepack to his puffy jaw or bloody lip.

One day, Luis noticed the two blind men who came every day to sit in the shady corner of the gym while several dozen young men, most of varying shades of dark skin, worked out. There were a few whites, but mostly it was half black, half Latino. They might not get along on the streets, but in the gym it was all cameraderie, business, professional. The blind men were like saints. Both were blacks, white-haired in late middle age, but of a light skin color as if they had been transfigured. They smiled, sometimes like the light of wisdom, at other times like cackling children as they twisted their heads one way then the other to hear. Their smiley teeth shone in the gym's hazy light. Their milky eyeballs were wide open and staring into infinity. Both men had been boxers. Both had been blinded as young men, in vicious bouts, with poorly maintained equipment—old gloves whose cracked backs could tear the cornea off an eyeball when they connected with the force of a thrown rock. Neither of them betrayed any bitterness—it was their joy that made Luis's stomach turn. He turned away, resentful that any man would let himself become so helpless and then revel in it. He walked away and beat his sparring partner into a pulp, for which he was exiled from the gym for a month.

When that month was up, he and his trainer went on the road for a week. He won a thousand dollars fighting in Las Vegas and then drove to San Diego, where they'd lined up a fight at an old American Legion hall in the tough Southeast district. There, Luis slipped on a sweaty patch and took a right jab, left hook, right cross combination that left him unconscious for three days in a hospital.

When he awoke, and drove back to L.A. with his trainer, he returned home to find that one of his daughters—Mariela, 4, had died suddenly. Roberta was silent and immobile with grief, and aunts were caring for the younger daughter, Ana, 2.

The child—his daughter, his love, his future—lay in a drawer in the morgue, ice cold, oh God how cold, as he laid his face and his fists on her and cried from the heart out. How could they let her be this cold? And wearing only a thin paper cover? He held her thin face between his palms and begged her to open her eyes, to speak to him, to say goodbye, to forgive him for not having been there when she needed him. She was still expressionless when the morgue attendants gently but firmly pulled him away and pushed her back into the wall.

Luis flew into a rage of grief and anger, storming through the hospital overturning inboxes on desks until the security people arrested him. A doctor who had helped treat Mariela offered to speak with him.

—*Why did my little girl die?* Luis demanded.

—*She had a high fever and secondary infections brought on by the adenovirus*, said the doctor.

—*Then why did she not receive medicine?*

—*She did, but it was too late.*

—*But my wife came to the hospital with her five days before she died.*

—*They were turned away because they had no insurance.*

—*In this country a child can be left to die because she don't have insurance?*

—*I'm sorry, don't yell at me, I didn't make it so.*

—*This is one sick country that lets children die.*

The security people were going to send for the police, but the doctor had pity and walked with Luis to the side door. The night was like a great bandage, wrapped around the hole in Luis's heart. Luis and the doctor spoke in whispers for a few minutes, as if time stood still, and why should it not upon the death of a princess, a girl with bright lively eyes and teeth like little porcelain squares?

—*I wish we could have done more.*

—*I wish I could at least have been here, but I was on the road.*

—*You work in sales or something?*

—*Boxing.*

—*That's a nasty gash on your ear.*

—*I just spent couple days in the hospital.*

After a silence he added, thinking of the blind men smiling up into space:

—*I'm going to find a way. I'm going to fight this system all the way to the top.*

—*I'm sorry.*

—*They let my little girl die because we didn't have ten bucks. And they think this is okay…people who tip the shoeshine boy ten bucks without thinking about it.*

The doctor did not offer to help, but made understanding body language. Of course they took courses in how to do that. The doctor shook Luis's hand and walked away, like a ghost in his long white coat, shoulders hunched as if burdened.

Luis could not stand to be still, so instead of calling a cab, he walked over ten miles to get home. During that ten mile walk he was like a drunk, staggering through intersections, not hearing the shouts of drivers who'd had to brake hard. He still had nagging headaches from the fight—same kind of headaches he'd get as a kid at his grandma's after getting hit on the head with the brick—and he knew there was no future for him in boxing. He remembered the blind men, and shuddered. He wanted to wage war on the system, the nation, that had done this to Mariela. He lived in the only industrialized nation without a civilized health care system. He wanted to tear the walls down, to kill the mean-spirited white men who clutched power to themselves. But the country was already tearing itself apart, with militias battling in the woods, and depression making people desperate. He thought about joining the Muslim faith, because a man named Jamal Mustafa was in the process of toppling the corrupt kings of the Middle East and taking the oil away. Good. Take the oil from the Americans, he thought. I'm too poor to even own a car, so what do I care if they all walk? But he'd seen too much violence to not know the hopelessness of the violent path. There had to be some other way to honor his little girl.

It was never the same again with Roberta. She was consumed with grief, and later more and more with self-pity. During the next year or two, Ana stayed with one of Roberta's sisters, and Luis lived briefly with her because he had no place else to go. He still loved Roberta, but not in the same way. He had brief flings with other women and stopped thinking of himself as married. But also during that period he rediscovered the joy of reading. And some higher agency took him past the local community college, where the very scent of books lured him into the administrative offices and to the realization that he could have an education almost for free. Given his mixed scholastic background, the school officials were amazed that he could read fluently, and that he easily challenged the entrance requirements because of his many hours of reading.

Luis vowed to change the system from within. He

was Anglo-looking enough and handsome; he made his way. More and more Latinos voted these days—a formidable force to reckon with in the Southwest. Even before finishing his degree in business administration, majoring in health care delivery, he changed his first name to Louis, to be less scary to white people, and ran for a small office—health inspector—and won.

During those years he'd teamed up with the beautiful, aggressive, and determined young Anglo lawyer from Montecito, Meredith Warington. Their affair began as a fling, he taking her as a trophy, she likewise bagging him for his power and eloquence. They found they couldn't walk away from each other. They were intoxicated by one another. Against her family's wishes, she married the poor boy from the barrio; she was his wife, his lawyer, his strongest partner, his right hand, his Friday. Together they reached the governorship.

In twelve years he'd gone from that little rickety house in Southeast San Diego, where they couldn't pay for medicine, to living in a mansion where he could swim in a pool with this woman who could be a fashion model.

His former wife had married a taxi driver in Pomona and taken Ana there to live. One of Luis's regrets in life was that he did not spend more time with Ana as a child—she was now 14 and estranged from him. He tried to see her sometimes, but it was always depressingly uncomfortable, even politically embarrassing. Roberta had gotten heavy, had more kids, gotten dumped by the taxi driver, and was now living with some guy who brought home decent pay as a foremen of laborers—Carlos, his name was, silent guy, treated Roberta and Ana okay. Louis often invited Ana up for a weekend, but she had never agreed to come.

But Meredith would bear him a new family. In the pool, he embraced Meredith passionately, and she responded. In the privacy of their garden, in the warmth of their jacuzzi, he stripped off her lower garment. She helped him, kicking her bikini bottom off, and eagerly pulling him into her hollow where life began. He pushed, pushed, pushed, and she held the hair on his head in her fists. Eyes closed in concentration as if she were counting, she let him lightly rock her, as if she were riding a horse. She did not let go of his hair. Aroused, rising in passion, Louis held her by the thighs while she sat on the rim. Louis closed his eyes too, and listened to the slapping of the water between them, and the whispered slapping of their firm, flat bellies together. When she moaned softly, he held her tightly against himself while lifting one of her muscular thighs and rotating it smoothly so that in a second she stood with her back to him, resting her face on folded hands on the brick-red pavers while he rocked on, enjoying the sight of her tight buttocks quivering with each impact. Her cries became hoarse, outraged, repetitious. He turned her again so that they stood in the water face to face. Her smooth, perfect face was against his, her tongue in his mouth, her fingers in flashes of red nail polish alternately pinching his nipples and hers. He climbed up on the pavers and leaned back so that she was riding him, her face contorted in ecstasy. Thrusting groin to groin, moaning, they climaxed together. She fell limply upon him and he held her close, running his hands over the fullness of her breasts and thighs.

They would make babies together, this beautiful way. Louis lay back and smiled happily into the sun-filled, shady magnolias while Meredith lay beside him on a towel, drying in the sun and catching her breath.

The years of Louis's rise had been eventful for the United States.

First, there had been the continuing, endless squabbling between the nation's two super-parties. Clinton had been payback for the endless hearings on Iran Contra, the indictments of seemingly everyone on or trying to be on Reagan's cabinet at one time or another—Ray Donovan, Ed Meese—and even more piquant as a payback for the Nixon impeachment vote. The 2000's had seen efforts by both parties to bring each other's leaders to every conceivable court of justice. National politics had become chess among lawyers, threatening to supplant Sunday football as a blood sport.

Second, Robert Lee Hamilton had begun challenging the national budgets created by his enemies in the Democratic and Republican parties. "No wonder," he said one evening during a MCP rally in Atlanta, "that no third party can get elected. The Republicans and the Democrats have the biggest illegal and unconstitutional reelection slush fund in the world—taxpayer dollars, and the Social Security trust fund, which has been drained of every last penny in each budget for so many years that everyone thinks this is normal. One Senate Majority Leader caused $1.5 billion to be embezzled to build, in his home state, in support of his reelection, naval vessels the Navy did not need, did not want, and begged not to have built. A House Speaker likewise embezzled nearly $400 million to build C-130 airframes in his home district, for his reelection, that the Air Force did not want, did not need, and begged not to be built. This happens all the time and has been going on for generations. This, in a nation whose ships often can't sail and whose planes can't fly for lack of funds for spare parts. This theft and pilferage can actually affect our combat readiness—but the generals and admirals are essentially powerless—all they can do is beg, and hope to get. These are the kinds of situations we want to change. How can our leaders steal ten or fifty billion dollars, when one third of our children have absolutely no access to health care, as do a similar percentage of pregnant women?" Hamilton's pointed and relentless legal attacks, fronted via the MCP Congress members, as well as MCP governors and state legislatures, crippled the two superparties. But more than that: there was serious talk of a Second Constitutional Convention. Things were so serious. With the shock in world oil markets, with the stubbing of U.S. toes around the world, the country had slipped into a long and severe recession. Crime, poverty, rioting, disintegration of law and order, all out war among some militia groups, bombings—these became the commonplace of headlines. Many Americans had lost faith in the system; many had stopped voting in what they felt were sham elections for an antiquated political dynasty of two 19th Century parties that had generations ago lost any meaning or edge or mission, and only fought to maintain their hold on power, much as the PRI had held its morbid hand on the neck of Mexico for generations.

Third, there had been Gulf II—a war in which two

ships were sunk, a thousand sailors died, and the world's surviving superpower was demoted from that role. Jamal Mustafa, protege of Moammar Khadafi, had been elected ruler of Libya. Mustafa, a profound hater of the West, a fervent Arabist, and one who found it convenient to wear the mantle of an Islamist, immediately conquered Sudan and Tunisia. Educated in Egypt, and wise in the ways of history, he adapted the better methods of the last Islamic empire to rule the Arab world—the Turks. But he was an Arab, not a Turk, and he did not come as a foreign oppressor. He fostered national governments rather than destroying them, and thus, as Great Chieftain in the manner of a desert conqueror, he was welcomed first into Algiers, where he promised to bring relief from years of civil war, and then in Morocco, where he paid obeisance to the king. Soon he got a similar welcome in Cairo—and, momentously, the Islamic Arab Republic (I.A.R.) was born. By now, every western-supported king, emir, and sheik in the oil countries was trembling, eyeballing Jamal Mustafa in terror—and with good reason. Soon he attacked Saudi Arabia, in a skirmish capturing a string of U.S. made missile armed PT boats. It was clear that another row of dominoes was about to drop, and the President of the United States, while drumming up the ghosts of the Gulf I coalition, sent two carrier battle groups to scare Jamal Mustafa. Instead, the American ships were surprised by two fleets sent to aid the I.A.R.—a Chinese battle group, and a Iranian battle group. Both of the latter were armed with very high second tier equipment, and their announced purpose was to support Jamal Mustafa and level the playing field. Both China and Iran had made momentous oil finds, and did not need Arab oil, while the West still pathetically craved it.

Tehran, in particular, wanted to scare the Americans, so one of their ships launched a nuclear-tipped missile over the U.S. fleet, aimed to fly over the U.S. supply station on Diego Garcia, and splash down harmlessly in the Indian Ocean near the 15th parallel. The gesture would clearly demonstrate that a U.S. carrier battle group could be wiped out by, say, a megaton blast in its proximity. The gesture not only sent that signal, but the missile's trajectory was short, and the detonation occurred within a mile of a missile frigate, the U.S.S. John Hampton, approaching Diego Garcia. The Hampton vanished without a trace—vaporized.

The U.S. Navy went into first class battle standby, as did the entire U.S. defense forces, and those of many U.S. allies from Australia to the U.K. to Germany.

For several days, while U.S. ships withdrew to put distance between themselves and the Sino-Iranian fleet—and therefore more time to blast incoming missiles from the sky—the President wavered on the verge of retaliation by which a Chinese ship would be sunk. The President, weakened by attacks from the House and the relentless inquisition of the press over various scandals, including the budget, took the issue to Congress. Should the U.S. declare war on China and Iran?

Congress—already paralyzed with divisive hearings, allegations, and counter-allegations—argued for two weeks while Jamal Mustafa sat openly laughing on Tripoli television. The Iranians and Chinese remained in place and did not back down.

The bitter reality sank in that the U.S. could well continue to deploy its forces all over the world—at the risk of having those forces nibbled out of existence. No longer could it be said that the sun never set on America's commitments around the world. The world's regional powers, armed with high-quality second-tier equipment from Brazil, South Africa, China, Iran, and India, were capable of dealing heavy blows to the qualitatively superior U.S. forces. The President made a somber speech, saying that Congress had no "will" and he had no "mandate" to risk U.S. service members and ships in ill defined wars, especially fights picked by formerly Third-World upstarts.

U.S. Navy planes sank the flagship of the Chinese fleet. Then, as the Chinese and the Iranians made ready to attack and escalate, the U.S. fleet sailed home to CONUS. The Chinese and Iranians stood down.

The press had the final word: The U.S. had ceased to be a superpower. The U.S., they said, was now a regional power.

The President then enumerated a new "doctrine," in which he declared that the U.S. could no longer pay the lion's share of defense costs anyway, and would now remain just as strong as before, through a system of east-west alliances (ANZUS/European Union) and north-south alliances (CANUS/Latin American Union).

Gulf II was over—and everyone in the world knew that it was only a matter of time until Gulf III began. Jamal Mustafa could be expected to linger as Saddam Hussein had in a previous decade—with a difference; where Saddam had been a brutal clown, Jamal was a brilliant tactician, strategian, diplomat—and conqueror.

The outrunners came through Montecito around noon, two square-looking sedans full of men and women in bullet-proof business suits—Hamilton Industries' praetorian guard, the cream of the billionaire industrialist's private security forces.

The security detail got out while Louis and Meredith watched from a high, secure balcony. Louis let the garages open electronically, and the two cars slipped inside. There, he knew, they would fan out with assault rifles and gas masks, checking every corner to make sure it was safe for America's king-maker to enter.

Soon, a dark motorcade of six armored black limousines rolled up the narrow streets of old Montecito, windows darkened so no assassin could see which car contained the prize. One by one the cars passed by. Then, in a surprise move, one turned suddenly into the garage and the steel security door swung down, almost clipping the car's rear bumper before locking into the concrete floor.

Meredith and the security guards left Louis and Robert Lee Hamilton alone in the kitchen.

A bar of sunlight fell through heavy muslin curtains and gleamed on the yellow enameled tea service Meredith had lovingly left on the stylish plexiglass table with chromed frame. Louis poured them each a cup. The other man accepted lemon, but not sugar.

Robert Lee Hamilton was a sparse man of 60—thin, energetic, looking more like 40 except for the ring of closely shorn white hair around a gleaming yellowish skull surmounted by the white whisps of what must have been a shock of dark hair in his youth. He had a large forehead, with still-dark eyebrows that were like scabbards under which fiercely intelligent, dangerous, almost scarily brilliant eyes burned with energy and ideas—and with insight. People said the billionaire seemed to look right through one. There were both a piercing coldness in his gaze, and a soothing toleration for those less gifted. RLH had earned a Ph.D. in Physics at 20 from UC Berkeley and gone to work for engineering companies, first as a novice employee, then as a consultant. Soon he'd had his own company, and the rest was history. Forty years out of college, he commanded a world-class fortune. He still sat on the boards of over 40 companies, more as a hobby than anything, but his consuming passion for the past decade had been politics.

"We lost a great man," Hamilton said.

"Yes." Louis could see the obvious. He himself still reeled from the shock as he thought about this upstart party's most charming and charismatic hero, the comer on the stage of presidential politics, burnt beyond recovery in a flaming airplane crash.

"We have to act fast," Hamilton said. He had not touched his tea, which steamed unseen under the incandescence of that gaze.

"We," Louis said, feeling an aura of unreality.

"We've talked before. This time, I come with a concrete offer in hand. I want you to run for Vice President. I don't see any problem about us getting it. I think the Old Constitution Party is the last hurrah of the Democrats and the Republicans. They're ending their sham and joining up because it's the only way they can capture the White House. Even at that, they need MCP's votes, and the only way to get those is to run a split ticket."

Louis was almost breathless. "Isn't that risky?" he whispered.

"Life is full of risks. As a politician, you know that."

"Yes. But I have always been grounded firmly—"

"Yes, I know—national health care. We'll deliver that. Louis, we want a Second Constitutional Convention, but not the way the militias want it. Not a dramatic rewrite, but ten amendments, under very controlled conditions—get in, do the job, get out. The only way we can get it done is to offer five amendments to the Left, five to the Right, things they can tolerate of each other. That's the only way to get the ¾ majorities we need to ram it through. One of those amendments will be universal health care. Your life's dream. Your promise to your little daughter Mariela."

The floor seemed to sway under Louis's feet. "Why me? Why not any one of the hundred great men and women of your party? Why a Democrat?"

RLH's radiance increased as he beamed with humor at the beauty of his insight. "It's not good enough to be good, or even great. Politics is the art of building, tediously, shaking hands, door to door." He gathered his fingers together and pounced them from spot to spot on the table top "...but that's not enough. There has to be the art of keeping everyone off balance. The great gesture. Yes, you're right, I could nominate Thurow of New York or Fassilli of Michigan or Landers of Lousiana. Great governors. But think. Our party has no presidential, no national experience. We have to transcend."

"I have no national experience. Never been in Congress."

"Yes, but think, Louis, think. First, we get the California governorship. Plus, a major defection. You are one of what, 100 guys your parties might run for prez or veep one of these decades?"

They'd been over that before, but never in this context, Louis thought. They'd talked about how, even though he and Meredith were voted most likely to create the next Camelot, he really had little or no shot at the big ring. John Dunstan's death earlier in the day had changed the equation completely.

"You are my pick," Hamilton said. "I'll go to Fasilli next, probably, but I stand here before you, so to speak, with my hat in my hand, asking you. Please, do it for yourself , for Mariela, for Meredith, for me, for my party, for your new party, your country."

The clock in the kitchen ticked. And ticked.

"Yes," Louis said. "I have no choice. This is an opportunity I can't let pass."

RLH beamed as he reached out to shake Louis's hand. "We'll make the announcement together this afternoon. Will Meredith understand?"

"We talked about it before you came."

"Then you knew. Good. I want you both in conservative business attire, and looking your best. You'll be our movie star couple. We'll sweep the dinosaurs from power."

CHAPTER 3

COLFAX, KENTUCKY

Cover's assignments came in regular succession in these busy times.

He owned ten acres in the Appalachian Mountains, not far from Colfax, Kentucky, paid up by someone he'd never met. He had a woman here, commonlaw under Free State law not recognized by the U.S. or Kentucky, who kept up the five bedroom, two-bath, two-garage house. The only part of the house she was not allowed was in the basement, where he kept his office, his communications center, and his armory. That part of the house was booby-trapped with enough exlosives to send the entire house an cighth of a mile into the air. The woman knew this and had been instructed to leave the house if the Rots raided.

The woman was quiet and didn't seem to mind his being around. Of course he was gone most of the time on one mission or another, and she didn't seem to mind that either. She'd been thoroughly checked out and found to be loyal, if somehow broken inside, for she was the widow of a militia officer from Idaho, shot in the line of duty while liberating illegally minted dollars from a federally insured bank along with two other patriots. There'd been a standoff, and she'd lost her two children besides her husband. Sometimes she wandered about the ranch in a daze, but at other times she kept up a furious pace of housework. She could not bear to be around children, but she was like a Francis of Assisi with the animals around the former farm. Kept a couple of thoroughbred bitches who regularly bred pups that she sold around town to farmers and hunters. Once in a while, Cover had sex with her. Usually he kept his distance, and she seemed grateful for that.

Cover had several names. One was the phony one on his land deed, which was the same on the Free State paperwork on the woman. The oldest was the one by which he'd been born, which he never thought about. He'd been orphaned as a child, and the name was the only thing he had from his folks. Nobody got to know that, only he. He'd been shuffled around between foster homes and orphanages. Usually that lasted a while and then something happened, like the cat. He'd been 13, and the family's daughter 15. The family had let him adopt a cat, because they thought it would make him happy, and therefore normal. He hated the cat, feared its malign stare and its poker-faced, predatory gaze. Perhaps, he thought, he is too much like myself. One day the cat threw up on his bed. He tried to snatch him up and run to the door. The cat scratched him bloody down one arm. Next thing, he was in the back yard swinging the cat by the neck on a rope. He swung him in a great circle for at least a half hour, and he must have been long dead, but he kept swinging him in that steady, silent circle, probably 30 feet in circumference, curled up with his head tucked and his paws limp like a passenger sleeping on a jet, until the screaming from the door brought him out of his reverie, screaming from the door way all together like a chorus, and of course that was how that ended.

When he was 18, Cover tried to enlist in the Marines and was rejected after some pencil and paper tests. The I.Q. thing went fine, and he was tops in physical, but something about his attitude on things prevented them from needing him just then. So, being alone in the world without a hook to hang his hat, he'd hitched a ride out to the Cascades Mountains and walked into the woods until he ran into some mountain men who directed him to the nearest militia post—ironically, in a suburb of Boise. There his life had come together. He did a three-year stint with what they called the Regular Militia, or Well-Regulated Militia, which was kind of like a real Marine Corps not ordered and twisted and mucked around by Liberals and Rots. There he distinguished himself and was sent for officer training at Cable College in western Montana.

The years at Cable were the high point of his life. In with hundreds of like-minded young men, he'd played football and studied hard. He loved the pomp and ceremony, marched ardently in parades. They had a way of playing "The Stars and Stripes Forever"—in fact, any patriotic song, in a kind of heavy, brooding, slow manner that made you ball your fists and nearly cry as you marched. That music had tragedy rather than joy in it, but also grand uplifting energy that made you love your flag and country and be willing to die for them. He'd come out with a B.S. in Engineering and a commission as a Second Lieutenant in the Montana Free State Militia (Regular). The Regular part referred to the word "well-regulated" in the Second Amendment of the Bill of Rights. Cable was proud of its sons—no daughters here, no Liberals, and nobody with dark skin or weird eyes—and its sons were proud of Cable, none more so than Cover.

Not far from Cable was a Federal Military Reserve that was actually under militia control. At the John Brown Militia Reserve, in the freezing mountains where dark-green pines clung to life under heavy folds of snow in winter, Cable's young officer cadre did maneuvers and exercises with the growing NCO cadre of the First Service, drawn from disenchanted young patriotic men all around the country. It almost seemed sometimes difficult to think the Rots didn't know about the John Brown Military Reserve, as the First Service called it, but it turned out there were just enough of the right people in the Pussy Army to keep it under wraps. Wouldn't need to go on forever, anyway—the Second Constitutional Convention was just around the corner and things would be set right.

The call came when Cover was riding on his old horse. He sat on the horse, lost in thought, dreaming ahead into the years when he would wear his uniform proudly and openly on the streets. Wrapped in a frayed nylon poncho and cowboy-style hat, he was oblivious to the cool rain that came down in long gentle strips and ever so softly hissed on his poncho, like a woman trying to get his attention. He thought about the woman a little and wondered if she'd laid in a good oak fire in the main room. He wanted her to lie on the bearskin with him, both of them naked, while the dogs slept in the kitchen, on the tiles by the kitchen hearth. She would lie on her back, her eyes lost in some dream, while absently rubbing her mound with her two index fingers to make herself wet so it would be easy on both of them. When the feeling aroused him, he would make the slightest gesture and she would roll over to take him into her. He had never lost his temper with her, though she feared him a little. But the first time, she'd put her palm against his chest and held him away. Communicating without words—though she could speak with her mouth, she spoke powerfully with those flat, bitter eyes—she taught him to fondle her gently for a few minutes. She taught him to rub tongues with her and when he did that he could feel her breathing change. Okay, so that was how it was done, he thought, and it wasn't much to ask. He was thinking about these things when his cell phone warbled.

"Yeah."

The familiar voice of his handler, whom he'd never met: "Got mail for you."

"Okay."

He drove all thought of the woman from his mind, wheeled his horse around, and headed for the house.

In Gary, Indiana, a highly secret meeting took place at the Condor Hotel, in a bridal suite on the fifth floor. Unknown to most of the participants, the Second Service had each of the four rooms bugged and under surveillance the entire time.

Behind shuttered windows and guarded doors, the paramount chiefs of seven major militias met for the first time ever under one roof, all together. They represented a force of over 35,000 armed and trained patriots from four corners of the 48 contiguous states. It was, an undercover officer of the Second Service thought while watching and listening, the first time he'd ever seen such a thing—remarkable all the more for the absence of weapons. These guys loved and worshipped guns and munitions, and no meeting was ever complete without a veritable arms bazaar. Not this time. Even the bodyguards carried only licensed concealed handguns. It was even fairly certain that none of the chiefs had the next best thing—a fleet of cars filled with soldiers and rockets, machine guns, and grenades. The stakes here were too high. Nobody wore camo—it was a strictly dark suit and modest tie affair.

At the heart of the matter was Robert "Strack" Bennett, 49, a retired Army Infantry colonel and now a self-proclaimed general in the shifting and murky waters of militia affairs. The Second Service, an entity unknown to the militia movement, in no way opposed the operations of these people, as long as they did not get out of control.

The men running the Second Service, and the rest of the dark machinery waiting in the shadows, had been around a long time. They represented some of the oldest money in America, some of the quietest and richest ultra-conservative Christian churches, and some of the most dutifully serving flag officers. As long ago as the Franklin Roosevelt administration, they had considered the country to have been taken over by Communists. They considered the man in the

Oval Office to be the Reigning Red, and some of them—among the most famous names in America—put sums of money toward marching an army to the Capital and taking back America. That plan had foundered in a sea of weakness, liberalism, and betrayal. The current effort would not.

Bennett, the "coveree," was a formidable force in the militia movement. He had the stature, the guts, the bullying power, the persuasiveness—in short, the charisma—of a national leader. He had managed, through outreach from his Kansas Militia, to bring together the hopes and dreams of angry, disenfranchised men all around the country.

The Second Service had good reason to think that the F.B.I., and the rest of Pussy law enforcement, had no idea this meeting was taking place. That was just as well, for the Rots would take the full brunt of whatever happened here.

Bennett, a big man, graying around the temples but still physically robust, did most of the talking. Whether he sat or stood, he towered over everyone in the room. His voice was firm, strong, and convinced. And convincing. After four hours of conversation, the men agreed to take certain actions. They all rose to pledge allegiance to the flag in the now famous Flag Salute: left hand over the heart, right hand raised, right hand held in imitation of a pistol aimed at the sky.

Afterward, Bennett took a side trip known to almost nobody.

He had a mistress in St. Louis, and at odd times he'd slip away from his guards and visit this woman. Accompanied by only one close bodyguard, Bennett slipped out of his hotel room in Gary. Together the two men drove to a small private airport at the edge of town, where they hired a pilot and his plane for the slightly over 2 hour trip to Missouri.

It had rained lightly, but a fresh wind had scoured the runway dry but for some puddles here and there. It was mid-afternoon, and the sky was darker than it should ordinarily have been. Huge ashen cumulus clouds made mountains on the horizon.

In the airport's small lounge area, about 20 persons of all ages had gathered for one of the commuter hops to Indianapolis. Bennett and his guard moved through this crowd unrecognized, except by one individual they did not know: Cover.

Nobody noticed the lean, preppy young blond man in his blue blazer, white shirt, school tie, gray slacks, and black loafers. Cover waited with a newspaper rolled up in his left hand, and a tan raincoat thrown over his arm. He had a briefcase near his right leg, and in his right hand a can of cola that he'd just bought at the concession stand.

Cover looked passive and disinterested as the small plane taxied down the runway. The plane cranked up its engine to a loud buzzing pitch and lifted off with a drone like that of a giant insect. The powerful engine echoed for two or three minutes and then dwindled out of earshot.

The commuter plane rolled to a stop, having just landed, and the passengers trouped out to board. Cover tossed his empty can into a trash can, picked up his briefcase, and joined the crowd.

A man came running from the control tower and spoke to the pilot, who stood near the open side door of the DeHavilland Twin Otter. The two men nodded.

The captain kept up a passive face, while the other man dashed back to the control tower.

"Did you hear?" Cover overheard one passenger tell another. "That plane that just took off? Crashed a few miles from here. Everyone on board is dead."

The Cessna was making good headway, flying with an easterly wind, and climbing to 5,000 feet, when the engine began to sputter.

"God damn!" the pilot yelled in a loud, scared voice. There was genuine terror in his eyes as he gripped the stick.

The plane began to lurch.

The pilot frantically pumped his hand instruments, trying to keep fuel flowing, trying to unblock the fuel lines, but the sputtering got worse.

Bob Bennett had been a soldier all his life. He'd fought in battle and been decorated. He'd been scared with the rest of them, and he'd faced death before. Each time, he'd been grateful of reprieve. Now he prayed to the powerful God of his Judeo-Christian heritage for another reprieve. He had so much good work to do in a country that needed him badly. He'd had the blessings of a dozen ministers before setting off on his mission to Gary. If now was the moment, well, God had his reasons. Still, he sat terrified, white as if he'd been bleached, his knuckles bloodless as he clutched the armrests with shaking hands. His body guard began to cry.

The pilot held the radio mike with one hand while working his instruments with the other. "Tower! Mayday! Mayday! I think I got water in my gas. We're going down!"

The plane abruptly grew peaceful as the engine died.

The pilot did his best to steer as it plunged ever faster toward the ground. He simply did not have the power required to move the plane fast enough to generate a laminar airflow over the tops of the wings.

In the last two or three seconds before impact, the plane was spinning along its yaw axis. The impact, when it came, drove the shattered pieces fifteen feet into the earth in a farmer's yard. For a few minutes, the field was enveloped in a hot ball of burning aviation gas from the full tank, and everything—the seats, the bodies, the luggage, was scorched on the surface, but enough would remain for dental I.D.'s. The good soldier Bennett had failed to win his last reprieve.

The DeHavilland Twin Otter was grounded for an hour while specialists checked its fuel and found it to be pure. Cover waited with the other passengers, trudging patiently from the tarmac into the lobby. The concession stand did a brisk business in candy and popcorn and soft drinks. Cover had not counted on being stuck here, but an hour or so would not hurt him. Even if the militia goons showed up, they would not know to go after him. He considered dumping his briefcase, and thought better of it. Why panic? And sure enough, in just over an hour, the De Havilland Twin Otter was checked out and cleared for takeoff. Aboard as it climbed into the darkening sky was Cover, straining like all the passengers to see any signs of distant wreckage or burning—and sure enough, there was the remnant of a dissipating cloud of ugly dark smoke to the east, soon lost in a marvellous orange and black marbling of sunset. Cover kept his briefcase firmly between his ankles, containing a baseball cap, one set of medium-sized tan-colored flight mechanic's overalls, and two tall, empty Evian bottles.

CHAPTER 4

WASHINGTON, D.C.

At first, Washington seemed to be in love with Louis and Meredith Cardoza. The President and his wife, Clifford and Edith Bradley, were old-fashioned wallpaper, two faded grandparents in their late 60's. After years of grinding poverty on the streets, and grinding meanspiritedness in Congress, the badly wilted social set in Washington went wild over an infusion of new life. The glamorous couple were old hands at this sort of thing, especially Meredith, and they moved with a quiet easy grace through the stellar flares of flash bulbs.

Louis quickly became uneasy, though.

The first issue to hit was the business of the Secret Service. From the first day, it became clear that the Secret Service, whose personnel could be subpoenaed to testify against the object of their services, could not be trusted to be loyal to two masters. Neither the

President's party, nor the Vice President's party, was willing to accept shared protection. Accordingly, the Treasury Department had to create a new hierarchy—in effect, two separate Secret Service units that hardly spoke to one another. Service One, consisting of 72 special agents, was assigned to the President. Service Two, consisting of 36 special agents, was assigned to the Vice President. Treasury felt they could draw upon a pool of alternates and uniformed personnel if they were needed for some special function. Certain military commando units were also available in case Louis traveled overseas, so he agreed that his needs were well covered. However, everyone felt the sense of competition, the lack of trust, the palpable sense of something being missing. There was a lack of elan. There was a guardedness throughout the Executive Branch, indeed also in the Congress after a quarter century of increasing rancor.

On a rainy evening, Louis and Meredith were alone in the family room of the Vice President's House at Observatory Circle. The grand old house, formerly used by a succession of Navy admirals, had the look of a bastion of sorts. It was certainly roomy enough—by now, there were two small children—and Meredith had the central heating redone to keep off the damp Potomac chill. With the fireplace crackling as three-years cured oak burned with a clean, light flame, and rain washing down the windows, Meredith sat in her green terry bathrobe. She had her feet up, tucked under her behind, with just the toes of her thick socks peeking out. Wearing a towel around her head, fresh from the bath, she trimmed and polished her nails one by one. "What's the matter, honey? You've been on edge all day."

"I didn't think you noticed." He clutched a whiskey and soda in one hand, and rubbed his damp hair with the other. He'd tossed aside his raincoat and briefcase, but he still wore his suit. He pulled his tie loose as she replied.

"I noticed it first thing as you got out of the car."

"Yeah... well, you know, RLH told me it wouldn't be a picnic working with a President of the opposition party. Cliff's not a bad guy personally, but those old OCP politicians know how to play hardball."

"What did they do to you?"

Louis hesitated. So much of it was subtle mind play. A lot of mental touch football. They were good at it, the politicoes, even for a former governor like Louis.

"What did they say?" she insisted brightly, lowering her hands into her lap.

"Well... it's not what anyone said, exactly. Let's put it this way. Bradley has on his Cabinet a mix of old Democrats and Republicans. The Democrats of course are furious with me for dumping them. That's okay. But they shut me out of a Cabinet meeting about the situation in the Middle East. Bradley kept me waiting for two hours afterward before giving me a half-ass briefing. Jamal Mustafa is getting ready to make his move on the oil fields, and we've got to stop him, whether those weak sisters in Europe help out or not. We're heading into a crisis, and Bradley's basically telling me that if they need me, they'll call me, but not to hold my breath. He's pretty straight, but some of his staffers are like real vipers. One of them actually said to me, as I was leaving, half under his breath, that I should get plenty of practice on my golf game while I'm vice president." He held up his hand quickly to signal that he wasn't stung by any of the pettiness.

"Oh honey," she said, slipping away from her chair and walking over behind him. She kneaded his shoulders and kissed his cheek. "I'm sorry."

"It's okay. What frustrates me is that I made Mariela a promise, and here I am in Washington, wasting my time with these idiots. I need to get more done."

"What about RLH?"

He pulled her down into his lap, welcoming the familiar roundness, the softness, the light weight of her rear, and the feel of her curves. "Honey, RLH does not run me. RLH does not run this country. I'm the elected Vice President. I think that gives me some say, even if these old-style political hacks still don't get the message. It gives me a mission. To help out. Not to warm my chair like those guys did in the old system. We need a new system. A people's system." He actually had his fist lightly balled.

She captured his fist in her hands and kissed it. "I love when you talk strong." Her towel came loose, exposing heavy wet strands of mahogany hair. "I know what you need, darling, and I need the same." She slipped a small, strong hand behind his ear and pulled his head close so her tongue could find his.

After a few more weeks of this, Louis agreed with Meredith's reluctant judgment—she went back to Montecito with the children, and Washington's social couple were no longer available at Moderate affairs where Centrists came to socialize. The Vice President's House became a dark, cold, lonely place.

CHAPTER 5

GULF WAR III

Undermined by Mahdi Jamal Mustafa's united front of Islamic zealots and Arab nationalists, a major Arab kingdom fell. Hundreds of lower ranking princes scattered throughout the country fled, while others were burned in their palaces by angry mobs. Most of the National Guard went over to Jamal. Remnants of the Army fought a rear-guard battle at a military airfield while a C-130 carrying the royal family lumbered down the airfield into the night.

In a magnificent show of lights, the C-130 was enveloped in fire as its jet assisted take-off (JATO) rockets kicked in. Climbing a thousand feet almost straight into the air atop a golden shower of light, the plane then tilted belly-down into normal flying attitude. The JATOs fizzled out and the plane could be heard droning away. Over the horizon, however, a rocket caught up with the plane. Buckling in a blinding tangerine flash, it fell to earth in a scattering of glowing embers.

At the airfield, the remnants of the royal palace guard were massacred in place by Mahdists, or Jamalists, who unleashed relentless rocket, machine gun, and mortar fire into their positions. The era of the British mandates was finally over, its last chapter written in blood and gunfire as it had begun over a century earlier as the British Empire devoured the servant states of a dying Ottoman Empire.

Today, the name Arabia was on the tongue of every Middle Easterner like a precious perfume, making the people drunk with pride and patriotism. Along the southern and eastern moon-edge of the Arabian Peninsula, tiny medieval monarchies slept on for now. Jamal Mustafa would turn his attention there after securing his greatest prizes: the holy cities and the oil fields. Jamal was the intelligent, moral, courageous, and generous hero of every Islamist, every Arabist.

Non-Arab Islamic states like Iran, Afghanistan, and Malaysia pledged neutrality, in return for which he promised them immunity from the terrible blow he was about to inflict on the corrupt Western world as soon as he captured the oil fields: instant economic collapse due to a shutoff of oil. No amount of North Sea or Norwegian oil could offset the vast wealth of Arabia.

Mustafa had already taken Kuwait, and now he was poised to go after two things: the oilfields around Basra, and that crown jewel of cities along the ancient Silk Road: Baghdad.

As Operation Desert Eagle kicked off, the elements of a million-man United Nations Expeditionary Force came ashore on the coast of Kuwait.

European and U.S. naval forces cleared the area of Mustafa's missile-armed patrol boats. Capturing Kuwait City back from the Jamalists was a relatively easy task, since the Kuwaitis hated them and cooperated with the Allies. Still, 2000 U.S. and Allied soldiers died in some pockets of house to house fighting. Within two weeks, the former Emirate of Kuwait, recently the Islamic Republic of (Mustafa's) Kuwait, was liberated to much cheering in the ruined streets. The Free Republic of Kuwait was quickly proclaimed with a secular, pro-Western president and parliament. The first ambassador to arrive in the new nation was from Turkey, a similarly oriented nation.

David Gordon, 25, was a first lieutenant in the First Infantry Division out of Ft. Riley Kansas, the first fully composed major military unit to arrive in theater. It was a race to build up sufficient forces to prevent Mustafa and the Iranians from even launching their attacks. David and his platoon of 40 men slogged ashore from a Navy landing craft near Kuwait City. The entire coast line, as far as he could see in either direction, was crawling with the most massive buildup since Desert Shield a generation ago. Cranes and derricks turned, unloading dark shapes—tanks, trucks, hummers, self-propelled howitzers. Air Force and Navy planes circled overhead, bullying their way into air superiority over the region—not an easy feat, since the Jamalists and the Iranians had the latest, most sophisticated second-tier avionics and planes in the world, made by China, India, and Brazil.

Every half hour or so, on the horizon, David could see a 10-20 cruise down to a landing. The 10-20's were unmanned ships launched as rockets that turned into powerless gliders like the old space shuttles. A 10-20 could deliver ten tons of cargo anywhere in the world within 20 minutes.

Huge C-401B's carried the really heavy stuff, like Eisenhower Main Battle Tanks, or "Ikes."

Everywhere he looked, David saw helmets, backpacks, and rifle muzzles. He was in a moving sea of men. David's platoon sergeant was Staff Sergeant Ed Montoya, the chief enlisted member of the platoon. Together with their corporals, they assembled the men on a small rise. A long line of mixed Kuwaiti civilian and U.S. Army buses crawled along, picking up platoons of men and their personal gear. A small knot of European and Japanese officers with maps and flashlights oriented each driver toward a destination ordered by the U.S. Army's planners in Al-Kuwait. The Supreme U.N. Commander of Expeditionary Forces (SUNCEF) in Kuwait, U.S. General Billy Norcross, was a dashing and popular figure who inspired hope and endurance by his leadership. Norcross was a seasoned soldier, a hero of both Gulf I and Gulf II. The men and woman of Desert Eagle clung to his pronouncements, which appeared in Stars and Stripes, and which could be heard on Armed Forces Radio.

On their night trip through Kuwait, 3rd Platoon, A Company, 1st Battalion of the 3rd Regiment, passed through alternating scenes of hell and normality: brightly lit, stylish downtown streets, and bombed-out piles of rubble in neighborhoods where fighting had gone on. They left the city, they passed rows of fresh equipment stretching across the flat desert in all directions as far as the eye could see. Several dozen buses turned south toward the border with Jamal's (Saudi) Arabia.

David, who was from Connecticut—the son of a well-to-do shoe manufacturer—felt slightly carsick but didn't let on. A West Point graduate, he'd been through rougher stuff than a plane trip followed by a bus ride. Besides, he suspected most of the silent men hunched in the crowded bus were feeling some pangs about the great and terrible battles they knew must surely come. They weren't up against the same lame and unwilling recruits, led by a generalissimo who was a murdering idiot, that the previous generation had faced. They all knew they were up against a fanatically zealous, disciplined, motivated force numerically superior to their own, and probably just as well armed.

"Yeah, we're getting ready," David heard Ed Montoya mutter, more to himself than David who sat beside him in the front of the bus. Montoya was from Los Angeles, a former tough gang cholo, with tattoos of knives and crosses on his brown arms. Now he was a proud infantryman, and a happily married man with three little children.

"We are ready," David half assured, half jibed.

"Yeah, right, Lieutenant." Montoya had a low, growling voice and a slow, deliberate way of talking. With his jet-black hair in a buzz cut, and his hard round face, he still looked dangerous. "I'll make sure we get this over with and send you back home to that blonde lady."

"You better, Mo."

David had kissed the blonde lady, Kristy Brindisi, goodbye at Kennedy International Airport less than three days ago. She'd driven down from Boston to meet him as his 160-man company joined the throngs of service personnel from all over the U.S. heading out on Operation Desert Eagle. It was hot and muggy on Long Island, and flashes of light jagged here and there amid ash-colored, apocalyptic skies. The airport, like every spot along the various routes to Kuwait, was jammed with military passengers and cargo. Delays were normal. Tractor-trailer trucks sat on the major approaches to JFK, backed up for miles, waiting to get to the cargo bays. David had been sitting on his duffel bag for at least two hours. He had a full canteen of water, which he drank sparingly to avoid long lines at men's rooms, but he was bored and thought he'd get a candy bar from a vending machine. As he sought one of the concession areas, he heard his name called out. "David!"

He whirled, for her voice was high and thin and aimed at him. He stared in amazement as she ran toward him, a thin blonde of medium height, wearing a burgundy raincoat and holding a plaid purse and a flowery umbrella. Heads turned to stare, for she was striking. Her blonde hair, a short pageboy, bobbed in rich swirls as she ran. Her hair was cut slightly longer before the ears so it could slash across her small, high cheekbones. Her skin was faintly brown, and her features were Mediterranean. Her blue eyes and small, rouged mouth were slitted with desire for him; she almost looked distraught. Immediately, he knew the answer to the question he'd asked when he'd last seen her a week earlier. As she reached out, he plucked the engagement ring from his shirt pocket and put it on her finger. He'd pledged to carry the ring everywhere until she said yes.

So far, the war was anything but eventful.

David worked hard to contain his own frustration, while keeping his men's spirits up. They were not being properly used as trained Infantry. Instead, because of snafus bringing in support troops, David and his men were shuttled from one ammo dump or supply depot to another, two days here, three days there as the buildup continued.

At the supply depot, David's platoon were connected to their company command by ten miles of a single thread-like road, unpaved, distinguishable only by its shallow wheel ruts. The sand was unlike the fine, silky American beach sand the troops were used to—it was gritty, unpleasant, and hard. In some places it had the texture of gravel; in other places it more resembled roughly crushed glass. Very little vegetation grew anywhere, though the country had a few oases. The nation had virtually no water, since rain was almost nonexistent, as were lakes, ponds, and rivers. Therefore, all drinking water had to be trucked in from outside or desalinated from ocean water. The Americans, in time-honored fashion, got bulky plastic containers of water air-dropped at their outposts, and had to drop in purification tablets, since the water often had a greenish slime floating in it.

David and his platoon were finally assigned to guard a small supply depot in southern Kuwait, where they stayed put. The supplies had been brought in by large helicopters; the quartermaster troops were not yet in country, and there was no telling when they were due, given the controlled chaos of the logistics network. The supplies consisted of six trailers filled with general items—blankets, sleeping bags, first aid kits, tents, that sort of thing. One of the trailers contained a company level field headquarters, complete with a small arms room in a cage at one end. David installed himself in the future company commander's office at the opposite end, with Ed "Mo" Montoya taking over a desk that would soon belong to an E-8 First Sergeant. They put up a cardboard sign with black marker lettering: "Platoon HQ. Take A Number."

At night, the stars would blaze overhead while, to the south, blazed the exhaust flames of the huge Al-Manageesh oil fields. South of there lay the I.A.R.'s positions, as well as east and north in the former Iraq.

With time on their hands, they found a massive camo net, which they slung over the entire six trailers. They set up tents between the trailers to further shield themselves from the direct sunlight. If the humidity let up, late at night, it might be cool enough to actually sleep in the tents. On other nights, it seemed freezing cold.

Fat, black flies buzzed in great numbers, and the men had to swat them from their faces. A never-ending wave of diarrhea seemed to go around, and there was a well-worn track to the four chemical potties broiling under a camo cover 300 feet away. The men had to watch out for snakes and scorpions. They trained hard, they played volleyball and softball after dark, and they learned to rest in the noon heat. It was almost acceptable. Somehow, David felt, in this quiet outpost, with the silent weight of the sky, and the occasional whisper of wind, and the drone of the flies, you could almost get used to this life style.

David conducted standard training—protective mask, blister agents, nerve agents, first aid, enemy hash marks and rank insignia—there was plenty to do. Still, for a large group of rowdy infantrymen, the enforced sitting was tempered only by the sober realization that soon a war might begin, and each man's fate depended on how well he was prepared.

A further element contributed its own dimension of uneasiness: the gangs and militias back home. The officers and NCOs were taken aside by traveling U.S. Army education squads and taught to recognize signs of simmering tension. Racial confrontations between rivals often signaled gang violence down the road, as these tough boys right off the streets were often ready to rumble at the slightest annoyance. These were tough times on the streets of America as the world-wide depression continued with no end in sight. Not surprisingly, there were covert militia elements scattered throughout the military, learning all that the regular Army and Marine Corps had to teach, and then taking those skills home to the woods and mountains for use in defending against imaginary enemies. In one unit on the coast, several militia members had assassinated their company commander during the past few weeks and attempted to commandeer a civilian airliner to return home. The incident had resulted in their deaths and the destruction of the empty 757 cargo plane in a pitched battle on the ground. General Norcross, under fire from all sides about the reliability of U.S. troops, instituted an R&R policy so that, at any time, ten per cent of any unit's troops could ride by bus to massive recreation centers on the coast. This was to keep the troops happy and also to reduce the ratio of troops to officers and NCO's, presumably making the units easier to manage.

David and Ed found new problems in their small, isolated unit, though they kept a sharp eye out for signs of trouble.

There wasn't, as yet, a front. As the operation built, so did the territory the Allies were prepared to defend. At the moment, David and his company were pretty much at the edge of the Allied Zone. When the quartermaster troops arrived to relieve them, David expected he and his men would push farther forward.

After two weeks, Company pulled two squads away to complement a combat service support unit halfway between Company HQ and David's location, and David had to make a daily trip there. His men were doing little more than pulling guard duty, but they understood the meaning of their larger mission and only complained in a light-hearted, ironic manner. Mail call was a near-daily event, with hummer from the nearby Army Post Office (APO) making frequent runs along a circuitous route through the desert. Because they carried Official and other low-level Classified mail, the mail hummer was accompanied front and back by two other hummers with turret machine guns.

David's men had no television, only a couple of pocket radios around which the men would cluster each evening to hear the BBC or Radio Luxembourg. They knew about the divisiveness among the world's powers. They knew about Jamal Mustafa's blustering threats—somewhere beyond the shimmering desert horizon, in the black of night, lay a force of one million devout Muslims recruited from around the world to win a holy war.

There was little to do at night but think, and David's mind always wandered back over the same lovely scenarios.

He'd met Kristy at West Point, one rainy April evening near the end of his senior year. He was hurrying across campus on the innocent mission of returning a library book. As he hurried down the wet and shiny walk in the darkness, he barely noted the warmly lit windows of offices and residences. As he passed the library windows, which were partly open and emanated the familiar smells of books, he heard a commotion to his right and saw several laughing young women surround a large passenger car. One of them was a striking blonde, and he slowed in his tracks. She was still smiling from some joke she'd just heard, and her glance at him was interested and warm.

That Friday evening, at a special coffee hosted by the Commandant's wife in the Commandant's residence, he saw her again. David, as a cadet captain, was one of about two dozen cadet leaders invited to meet a group of Vassar seniors to plan a special dance and fundraiser for the local unemployed and homeless. At the civilian coat and tie/evening dress affair, David managed to seat himself beside her. He was determined to get to know her, and he was not at all disappointed. Her name was Kristy Brindisi and she was 21. She was an Art Appreciation major at Vassar and she did not have anyone serious in her life at the moment. David didn't either, so that went well. Her father was an English professor at Boston University and her mother was deceased.

Now that he sat in the sweltering desert at night, he rested his head back, closed his eyes, and went back to those long, cool, rainy walks after dark. Sometimes they met at the Point, other times across the Hudson and north a few towns at Vassar. Kristy had warmth and intelligence. She was understated in her demeanor, but she had that winning smile in a beautiful face. David was proud to be seen with her. She was fun to be with. They went to Cape Cod on a warm Spring weekend, and she raced him to the water. She drove an older Ferrari convertible, usually too fast, wearing driving gloves and sunglasses. At those moments, David thought, she looked like someone out of an ad. When she looked at him with her slightly crooked, mischievous grin, he knew she felt the same about him. They made love in a tiny cottage not far from the lighthouse at the tip of the Cape. She was lithe and passionate, surprisingly strong, and sometimes inclined to fight before yielding and welcoming him into her groaning pleasure. He loved to lie beside her and stroke the golden curve of her thigh, or to laughingly try to count the million peach-fuzz hairs in the gully of her spine as she wore a bath towel around her wet head and ate an apple while reading D.H.Lawrence's *Etruscan Places*. Kristy was also an excellent and passionate cellist, and David would lie on his side, while she sat in a chair and played dark, moody pieces that whirled slowly through the air like hot, melting chocolate. At those times, her eyes would close, and she would turn her face slightly down and away, as if looking and listening in another world. Her music sometimes saddened David, at times even frightened him, and he wished she'd stop, because it brought up the crushing panic anxiety of the night he'd been told of his dad's death, and he would feel his chest contract. One time, when he couldnt' wait for her to finish, and when she finished, she asked: "Sweetheart, what is the matter, darling?"

"Your music makes me sad. I was remembering…" He remembered his sister Mary, who had died of leukemia when he was 12, and she 10. Mary's giggle, her new permanent teeth, lips rumpled in a smile, eyes happy and mischievous, floated up out of a blur of blackness and pain at the memory, the loss of her.

Kristy laughed, a warble of mellow joy that seemed to rise from her stomach and fly upward like the flutter of her blue eyes. "Whatever it is, I can fix it, my darling!" She rose, took off her dress and flung it to one side, dropped her bra on the floor, kicked her panties off, and sat down again, a slender and perfect body. With a teasing grin that lit her eyes, so that the ends of her hair hung banging against her cheekbones, and her small breasts and pink nipples swaying with her elbows, she grasped the cello and bow in strong fingers, tapped one foot up and down, and ground out a throaty Gaelic jig that brought laughter to David's soul.

This particular night in the desert, the mail convoy was late. At about 10:30, David heard the whine of sand-filtered engines and stepped out onto the road holding a cup of hot decaf coffee. It was a warm but tolerable night, with the humidity under 40%. The quarter moon hung like a scimitar in a cloudless blue-black sky cut from dark silk. The three hummvees hove into sight, mail vehicle in the middle. The men in them took turns standing up with the turret machine gun to feel the night air move across their faces.

Mo Montoya and several other guys quit a slow game of softball and walked over. David hung back so his coffee wouldn't get jostled. There was a chorus of hey's and whassup's. "You guys are late tonight," Mo said.

The passenger in the mail hummer was a little round-faced, bespectacled farm boy from Indiana, wearing an olive drab wool watch cap. His name was Jimmy Herman Schweigel or Sweegel, David wasn't sure. Jimmy Herman, who could hardly see over the door ledge, handed a small nylon bag of mail over, and the unit mail clerk, Oberley, a black kid from Atlanta, handed yesterday's bag back empty. Someone snapped on a flashlight, and Oberley began to call names as he handed envelopes out.

"Yeah, we made a lot of stops today. The operation sure is growing. Got ten new stops today, got lost in the freakin' desert, almost ran over some towel-head's friggin' camel, got yelled at"—he glanced at the driver, a silent Hispanic guy hidden in shadows, who spoke in shrugs and grunts—"what else did we friggin' do today, Darby?"

Darby uttered a few syllables and yawned.

Oberley stepped over and handed David a letter from whose fluffy softness David could guess it was another of his almost daily little notes from Kristy.

Jimmy Herman turned to Mo and his spectacles glinted. "We drive around like spazzin' robots all day. I should have joined the infantry, Sergeant Mo."

"Right," Mo said, "we're just havin' a ball out here. I wish they'd put cranks on the clocks so we can make them turn around faster."

"Hey Lieutenant!" Jimmy Herman greeted.

"Hey yourself, Jimmy Herman. Whassup?"

"Nothin' much, Sir. When's the war gonna start?"

"Wish I knew, man."

"Yeah…" Jimmy Herman said, running out of thoughts.

"Hey, let's go!" hollered a staff sergeant from the hummer in front.

"Yeah, quit shootin' the shit, Jimmy Herman. Let's go home, such as it is."

With some final cheering, the three vehicles executed separate u-turns and started back up the road toward Company. David's men drifted back to their ball-throwing, except those who had received letters split off and found lighted spots to read and think about home. There weren't many lighted spots, so there was a cluster of men in the office.

The six trailers were shielded by eight-foot high berms from view of the main east-west highway a few hundred yards north of their position. The main road was four-lanes of concrete slabs, elevated about six feet above the desert floor. On the sides of the berms grew desert flowers imported from the U.S. Southwest by successive Al-Sabah nobility in Kuwait. In the past few days, combat engineers had stopped by and graded the area around the trailers. They had pushed up a C-shaped perimeter of gravel and sand, six feet high, surrounding the trailers on three sides and making them almost invisible from the highway. Still, on any clear night, they could see the distant blaze of lights from Al-Manageesh oil fields some 20 miles to the south.

Sitting on the harsh desert gravel on top of the berm, David slowly ran a wet towel around his sweaty skull as he wished this sitzkrieg or sitting war were over.

Kristy, so stylish and bohemian and thin that she seemed to come from wealth, had gotten a job as an assistant curator at Sotheby's. She loved David deeply, but seemed unable to commit. She'd several times almost accepted his ring, but couldn't. Then she'd pursued him to the airport, and in a flurry of wet and stirring kisses, promised to wed him as soon as he returned from the Middle East.

Kristi seemed skittish about the Army. She brought out in David a love of the arts he'd never strongly pursued. "You study war," Kristy once said in a dark moment; "I'll make you study peace." She could be temperamental at times, running out of the room, slamming doors, weeping in the bathroom, yelling in the yard and throwing handfuls of grass. In that way, she was not unlike her father. David's mother did not like her. Neither did David's sisters. But they didn't say much.

As David sat thinking about cool rain, about walking with Kristy, arm in arm, he could almost feel the strong tug of her thin, muscular forearm against the crook of his arm.

David was pulled from his reverie by a shout and a noise.

There were three distant flashes of light far off in the west. Then there was silence. The flashes dissolved into a slowly darkening haze. Even as the light in the west faded, hot dry wind rolled across the desert. "Nukes!" David yelled. "Nukes! Everyone suit up!"

For two long minutes, the men were enveloped in an oven of dry, prickly heat. David gasped and held his sleeve over his mouth for fear his lungs would be sucked out. Then the pressure waves passed.

David, and everyone else in the world, now understood the meaning of Jamal's long silence, and the slow nature of his buildup in the face of overwhelming U.N. power: Jamal had the Arab Bomb. The Middle East equation was forever changed.

The men raced to their NBC suits. Their breath rasped as they pulled on the baggy charcoal-lined garments. Fingers trembled as they hastily pulled zippers shut. M17K10 masks went on, hands patted cheeks to make sure the fit was snug, and fingers twisted the new external chin-filters in place. David grabbed a radiation counter from the trailer and swept each man—luckily, minimal.

"Must have been small ones. Kilotons," someone said.

Then came a shout from Oberley, who had belatedly gone out to pull in the small U.S. flag, and now ran toward the compound. "Hey! Hey everyone, douse the lights, man! Quick!"

David rose from his perch, where he'd been leaning against the wooden leg of their one prized picnic table. "Whassup, Oberley?"

At the same time, he heard it clearly: a sound like highway at home during rush hour.

Mo stepped forth and pointed south. "Look, no lights!"

David's heart raced. Indeed, there was black night where the lights of the oil field usually blazed.

At that moment erupted sounds of gunfire and explosions that would be with them throughout the night, and David felt a rip of fear. He was so scared his knees shook and his teeth chattered. He felt as if someone had loosened the strings on his bladder.

"Lights off!" he shouted as men scrambled in the dark. Men stumbled over one another looking for helmets, protective masks, flak jackets, that they'd treated with growing casualness until this moment. "Masks!" David yelled.

"Masks!" Montoya echoed. There was a clatter of breeches as men jammed ammo clips up into their weapons.

Thank God for the berm all around, David thought as he and others race to crawl up and peer over the rim.

The sight amazed them: a column of dark pickup trucks roared in out of the desert, some with lumps in the back that might be weapons, each truck carrying at least two passengers in the back. "Must be a hundred of them," Mo muttered beside David.

The trucks passed into the night with the mufflered whisper of souped-up four cylinder engines. They came out of the night in a whisper, roared by briefly, and were swallowed up again like a whisper.

"Those are not ours," someone said.

"Yeah, and they ain't gonna be good for us," someone else said.

"Mo, keep an eye out. Let me know if any come this way. I'm gonna call Company."

"Yessir," Mo replied. "Oh shit, here's another hundred. How many them dookers is there?"

David ran to the office, fumbling in the dim moonlight. In order not to send any air signal, he did not immediately use his lapel com button. He tried the powered land line, but the desk phone was dead. He tried the green-nylon covered field phone, which was battery powered, but again there was nothing. At last he tried his lapel com, but they were too far from a relay cell; it was dead. Last, he cranked up the radio and called: "Second Platoon to Charley Company, over." He repeated this, listening to the hiss. Finally a voice came over, with a crackling background. The voice was agitated: "This is Charley Company. We're getting hit by something. Who are you?"

"Third Platoon, Lieutenant Gordon speaking. Who are you?"

A frantic voice responded: "Sergeant Medavoy, Sir. Captain Cardiff took a bullet, Sir. I'm scared and I don't know what to do."

"Who's left?"

There was no answer.

"Sergeant Medavoy, are you there?"

No answer.

David put out a call to his other position five miles away.

No answer.

David put the phone down. "Mo!"

Montoya ran in. "Whassup, Sir?"

After a brief consultation, David had Montoya gather the two squads together.

As they fell in, David explained the situation. "Company just got wiped out and I can't reach the rest of Second Platoon. There are eighteen of us, at last count. We have two old vans. I think we have plenty of gas and water. We can either sit here and wait to get hit like Company just got it, or we can make a run for the back lines, less than forty miles.

We could make it in an hour, and I've decided we're going to make a run."

"You heard the Lieutenant, guys," Mo bawled. "Start loading the vans. We travel as light as possible. Keep the lights off. No smoking. No talking. Keep your eyes and ears peeled in all directions. Oberley, you drive the van with the three hubcaps. Myers, you drive the one with the two hubcaps."

The men laughed nervously. Boots grinding on sand, they trotted to the vans shadowed in a corner under the camo net.

Oberley couldn't resist. "Anybody want to stay here?"

"Shut up," Montoya said.

Nobody answered.

"Just jackin'," Oberley grumbled.

David climbed on top of the berm with binoculars and scanned the horizon in all directions. Al-Manageesh to the south was black as a tomb. The skies west, north, and east were dark. The night rattled with gunfire and explosions. Suddenly, terror lurked in every direction. David felt chills crawling up and down his spine. He felt fear so vivid it hurt him like a physical pain. But he was responsible for forty lives; 38, not counting two men on sick call at Company; oh God, what of them? For the first time in a long time, he thought of the lost gold coin, which his ancestor had carried for good luck in a war not far from here. He wished he had it; oh how he wished he had that coin! Not out of superstition, but simply because it would be right for the coin to be here.

For a moment, all was silent, and the night mocked him with its innocence.

He might as well be a child again, on a summer

night in Waterbury, Connecticut, looking up at the constellations.

Or he might be one of many men about to die. Death would come suddenly tonight for many men and women. Will I ever see Kristy again?

The distant sound of massive explosions signaled the loss of ammo and fuel dumps.

The vans were old but reliable. Each carried nine men. David and Mo rode in the front van. Both vans had their windows and rear doors open so the men inside could breathe and listen, but there were hands on those doors, ready to pull them shut at a moment's notice if there was a need for speed. David's plan was to take the most direct route feasible, starting with the dirt road back to Company. He'd see what could be done there, and then they'd follow another back road eastward toward Al-Kuwait. In an hour, they could be in the safety of the supply depots. Or what might be left of them. There was no place else to go, except into the sea, into the desert, or into Jamal's hands.

As they approached Third Platoon's other position, they heard distant gunfire and saw fires blazing nearby. "Drive as close as you can, but be ready to bolt if we see any IAR's," David instructed the driver. David had brought along the one 50 caliber machine gun from their host unit's armory, and one of his troopers had it set up inside the other van. They carried all the ammo they'd been able to find, and David had found an Uzi undoubtedly meant for the company commander.

Cautiously, the two vans crept up to the small

depot. Unlike their own just abandoned position, these guys had not been hidden behind a protective wall. David gave up counting at the twenty-fourth body. The IAR's had come and gone. Some IAR bodies lay strewn around, and one of their pickups lay on its side, smoldering. David briefly examined it. Looked like they had a heavy machine gun mounted on a center tripod in back; boxes of ammo; and what looked like the carrying cases for several anti-tank missiles.

"Anybody alive?" David called out. He waved the radiation counter—minimal roentgens. He and his men searched the area, but all they found were hideously contorted and burned bodies, most of them American, many known to David.

David felt sickened. His fear turned into revulsion. Here was Corporal Berry, from Wyoming, blackened almost beyond recognition, his skull split, his brains boiling out. Here was the upper half of Private Wallace, who was twisted with his eyes open as if looking for the lower half of his body. Everywhere were loose arms and legs and feet. Somehow, the boots always seemed to come off and fly separately.

"These guys took a couple rockets," someone said.

"Oh God." David felt his gorge rise. Vomit projectiled away from him in a brown, ropy, twirling stream.

He felt tears on his face, but remembered that he had work to do. "Come on, you guys, let's move on to Company!"

"This is war," Montoya said in a voice without resonance. "Come on, guys, pull it together, this whole night's gonna go like this. We gotta pull back so's we can fight tomorrow and the next day."

"Right on," Oberley said, suddenly a man of determination as he hopped in and fired up the first van.

"Everybody in the vans, let's go!" David yelled.

They drove at a steady clip. Mo offered David a canteen. David sipped and spat acid mouthfuls out the window. "Thanks."

Ten minutes later, they found Jimmy Herman and his companions.

The three hummers sat smoldering in the middle of the road. Oberley pointed a spotlight on them. David and Mo got out to inspect the damage. Nobody alive. "They never had a chance to get out," Mo said.

Jimmy Herman was a blackened mass that had become part of the bare seat springs. Darby's door was gone, and Darby was in pieces all over the road outside. There was an actual fantail as if someone had used orange and white and black markers to paint an explosion on the concrete, radiating out from the hummers. The area was littered with shredded pieces of mail.

"These guys don't stop," David said. "They hit their target and move on."

"What do you figure, Lieutenant?"

David led the way back to the van. "I dunno. Might be a suicide operation. Couple of thousand commandos in these little trucks, making enough of a mess to slow us down. The nukes screwed everything up big time, and they can move around."

Twenty minutes later, after driving through the blank night that rumbled with distant gunfire and explosions like a dry summer storm back home, they came to the burning ruins of Company. The sprawling camo tents had burned to the ground. In one place, a charred corpse sat in a steel chair at a desk. Its head was gone from the jaw up. David and Mo walked around with flashlights. The stench of burning flesh and other debris filled the smoky air.

"Okay," David said, "let's move on. We have no choice."

The two vans wound through the semi darkness. The weak moonlight gleamed off the glassy desert floor, giving just enough light to see by. They must avoid the main roads at any cost, David knew. Oberley had driven this route so many times that he must remember it somewhat. The other van followed blindly about ten feet behind.

"What the hey?" Oberley came to a stop about fifteen minutes after they left Company.

"What's the matter?" David said.

"Look!" Oberley pointed.

David and Mo used their binoculars to gaze ahead a half mile into a slight depression. There, sprawling by the road, was what looked like a wealthy villa. Like an oasis, it had palm trees, white walls going this way and that, even a small minaret inlaid with blue tile. Parked in front were a half dozen enemy pickup trucks. Over the far horizon, they could see the flashes of huge explosions toward the coast and the capital.

David asked Oberley: "You never saw this villa before?"

"Seen it, yeah, but look—there's IAR trucks outside."

"I'll bet you those folks got visitors," Mo said.

"Yeah," David said, "and we've got to get by there fast."

"Make a run?"

"Not a chance."

"What do we do, Sir?" It was a question David knew he'd be asked many times in his career.

"We take them out," David said. "They've killed a bunch of our friends. Let's make it count. Let's maul these frigging bastards. We can't sit here all night, because there will be more of these trucks coming by. Let's see. I count six trucks down there. What do you figure, maybe fifteen twenty guys?"

"Be about right," Mo said. "Why do you figure they're down there instead of shooting up the depots?"

David said: "Maybe a command post or something."

Mo grinned. "Yeah, old Mustafa rednose is here."

"Nah," David said. He studied the place through his binoculars. "Battalion HQ, probably. They've got to have at least one or two men guarding the trucks. The rest won't be scattered all over that huge complex. They'll be together in one area."

"Right, Sir. A com center. They must have some follow-up coming. Big invasion."

"Oh Jeez, well, we don't have time to worry about that now. One thing at a time. Oberley!"

"Yessir!"

David gave instructions, and Oberley hurried off.

David left Oberley and three men in the first van.

He ordered eight men plus Montoya to stay with the second van.

Then he, Corporal Diem, and five men trotted across the landscape in an airborne shuffle. He checked the radiation—slightly higher here, but still tolerable. The wind was blowing north-northwest, taking whatever fallout in the direction of Basra and into Iran. In fifteen minutes, they came around the back of the villa. David stopped and listened. All was quiet. David told Diem: "They'll have at least one radio or something. We've got to find that and knock it out first so they can't call for help."

"Right, Sir," Diem whispered. Diem signaled to the five men behind them, and they began crawling up the embankment that surrounded the villa. The villa must have a perimeter of several thousand feet, David thought, and it was a hundred feet to the steel rod fence on top. In some places the embankment was even higher.

They climbed through deep, well-watered pickle weed.

At the top of the grade, they listened. The night was still full of distant explosions. Nearby, they heard only silence.

One by one, David and his men slipped over the six foot steel fence.

They were in a grassy back area between two stucco buildings. Between the buildings, David spotted a huge swimming pool. Around it were picnic tables and umbrellas. This must be the center of the complex. Identical white stucco structures were piled around the edges of the hill, home for some large family or clan with lots of oil money. Everything looked as if recently abandoned, and suddenly.

From the silence, it appeared all of the princely family were gone. There were no bodies around, so they must have fled. Cautiously, David and his men advanced in two groups, Diem ten feet away at the head of three, while David led two.

Then they heard laughter. Somebody was telling a joke in Arabic in a very excited voice, mentioning Allah often, and David nodded to himself. They were congratulating themselves. That was understandable, for the moment, until he gave them bad news.

They backed away, keeping in the shadows of the ominously silent buildings. They worked their way around the back walls, until they again heard voices.

David signaled to Diem: stop. look. there. wait for my command.

Diem nodded.

Ahead, one of the buildings was ablaze with light. Men in dark green uniforms milled about, smoking cigarettes and making happy, boastful body language. That building must be their command post. Okay, he wished he had a rocket. Just one. No such luck.

He noticed the electrical switch box on the side of the house.

Through the windows, he saw a massive field radio set up on a table and two soldiers talking into phones. Yup. Might be a battalion HQ or so.

He told the two men behind him in turn: "On my signal. Your job is to cover him, okay? Your job— that switch box over there—I want you to empty your gun into it. Make sure all the lights go out. Got that?"

David slipped through the darkness until he was next to Diem. "Wait for my signal. We're gonna wipe this group out." He called Montoya by lapel com. "Get over here fast. Come up the back. I think we can secure most of this place. They're in one building on the east side." He called Oberley: "Drive by, stop, back up, open the doors, and shoot up the trucks and everything in sight. When we hear you, we'll start up here."

As they waited, David wondered if he was still scared. He was numb, he noticed that much. As he rifled through his feelings to see which ones were noticeable, he only found itchiness and anger. The itchiness was from not having had a bath or a change of clothes in a week. The anger was from having just lost two dozen friends.

Somewhere in the distance, he heard a shout.

He heard the crunch of a vehicle sliding on gravel after its brake was applied.

He heard a squeal of tires, the popping open of the old van's rear doors.

The heavy machine gun began to rattle, loudly and steadily.

David listened for a few seconds more—not too much return fire; good; Oberley had a chance. He could probably wipe out some of the IAR's down there.

David signaled the two men he'd just left.

One of them stepped forth and threw a grenade. It crashed through the window. Men yelled. David and his people started firing. The grenade blew the hell out of the radio inside, shattering glass and dropping at least two men. The door came off, walked ten feet upright, and fell into the pool. As another grenade took out the electrical controls, the building went dark.

"Let's go," David told Diem and his men. Together, they started firing, and all the men on the patio dropped, some just as they began to run. One pulled a revolver, but collapsed in a hail of bullets.

David heard firing behind him, and told Diem to take three guys and cover the rear.

IAR men came running out of the darkened building. Some jumped out of the windows. David and his men picked them off.

As the firing died down, David jumped up. "Let's

get in there and make sure they don't have any more transmitters going."

A room to room search revealed nothing surprising. The owners of the buildings had left quickly, probably a few months ago when Jamal Mustafa conquered Kuwait. From a few remaining pictures, it was evident they were the family of an Al-Sabah prince closely related to the ruling emir. David found a few bodies on the first floor, all IAR.

Oberley came racing up the steps, holding an Uzi in each hand. "We finished them off, Sir. Six guys guarding the trucks. Grunts. Probably just drivers."

"Okay. Hide the bodies. Bring them in the house here and put them in a room, secure. We don't want to advertise too much."

Diem appeared, having linked up with Mo and his group. The Americans had suffered no casualties in this go-around.

"So far," Mo added.

"Right," David said. "We've still got enough gas, so let's get back on the road."

"Lieutenant," Mo said, "it's pretty near dawn. We'd be dead meat out there in daylight."

"Dammit, you may be right."

Mo shrugged. "We could be cooked here too."

"I don't know." The soldiers all looked toward him uneasily, awaiting what to do next.

"Let's load up the vans and head east," David commanded.

"All right!" "Yesss!" "Right on." The men murmured assent.

Shortly, the two vans pulled out, David and Mo in the lead as before. It was still dark out. They had not gotten a thousand feet, lights off, when Oberley cursed and slammed on the brakes again. The van behind nearly hit them. David didn't need to ask this time—he could see the five or six pickup trucks flying westward toward IAR territory at well over 100 miles per hour.

A U.S. Army attack helicopter corkscrewed in overhead, discovered the trucks, and headed for the nearest hill to hide. But there were no hills, just flat desert. The chopper turned in desperation to shoot its missiles at the trucks. The trucks were faster. A missile streaked out from one. The chopper disappeared inside a fizzling cloud of gray smoke. The cloud lit up with repeated electrical sparks as it dropped to the ground. There, its fuel tanks exploded.

The pickups hardly faltered in their flight.

"Back to the villa," David ordered.

"You got that, Sir," Oberley said spinning the wheel. The old van lurched around and built up speed.

"Head around back. Maybe we can hide." He was hoping the pickups would continue heading west—
—and they did.

Everyone in the vans breathed a sigh of relief.

"Tell you what," David said. "Let's get back into the villa. Give them until nightfall. By then, our guys will have secured the whole country."

"Good plan," Mo said.

"At least, we hope so." David noticed some garage doors nearby. "Open those doors. Push those trucks out of sight. Hide the bodies. Then let's check the whole place out," David said. It would keep the men busy, and it would give them an idea of where to hide if they must.

Shortly, Diem discovered a pantry full of canned U.S. and European foods. The men ate heartily, even using a microwave oven. The villa, David thought, must have dozens of kitchens.

A lookout saw sporadic pickups zooming past on the dirt road, headed into IAR.

"We'll continue to lie low," David said.

"Sir!" a man yelled. "Come and look!"

David and Mo followed the soldier down a series of winding outdoor stairwells and into an underground hallway. It was a bare, concrete hall with light bulbs overhead in simple cages, all very utilitarian.

"You won't believe what we found, Sir." They turned a corner and emerged on a platform. Leaning on the railing, David had to laugh in amazement. He was on the upper level of a large underground garage, probably two hundred feet by a hundred feet, and fifty feet from floor to ceiling at the deepest point, the wall where he stood.

Several black limousines were parked off to the left, but the star of the show was the brand-spanking candy-apple red two seater airplane sitting there like a child's wonderful toy. On its tail, wings, and fuselage it bore Kuwaiti flags and some sort of royal ensigns. It was parked and aimed toward a large roll-up door. The concrete floor sloped upward noticeably, as if it were a ramp to assist take-offs.

"Is it working?" David yelled to the men below. His voice echoed.

"Don't know, Sir. We can check it out if you'd like." Their voices echoed back.

"Can anyone here fly?"

Oberley waved.

"You're kidding."

"No, I'm not. I was a licensed pilot by age 16."

"Think you can fly that thing?"

"Looks pretty standard inside. It's American made. A 2005 Cooper Joy. Sporting model. This dude probably does... did... his own private air shows with it."

"Get it running." As he walked idly down the stairs and to the plane, David debated—should they just lie low and make a run for it by night? Would it be worth risking Oberley's life? What if he were shot down by friendly fire? Though, not in that candy apple red plane. Especially not with those insignia.

As David neared, the plane fired up. The propeller became a spinning disk, and the air moved briskly around. David's uniform made snapping sounds, and the air smelled of burned aviation gas.

Oberley poked his short Afro-cut head out the window, grinning. "She's loaded up and running like a charm."

David leaned close, putting his hands on the red metal windowsill. "Will you volunteer to get a message to our people back there? We're here, we've secured this place, and we're awaiting relief?"

"Sure, I'll do it," Oberley said, putting on a pilot's hat with scrambled eggs on the visor.

Within minutes, they had a second volunteer, who sat in the backseat. The doors rolled up revealing a long clean stretch of new concrete.

Daylight had just broken fully, and the sun lay over the horizon like a boiling yolk.

The engine noise was earsplitting as Oberley expertly maneuvered the small plane up the ramp. He drove the craft—too fast, David thought, crossing his fingers—down the runway, and then, with a sound like a bee, up into the air, rolling to starboard, climbing, rolling, rolling until he cleared a distant range of hills... By now he was little more than red dot, but by God the man had the plane in the air and heading east and looking good. All the men cheered.

There was water to drink, thank God. They had food. They had ammo. They kept a watch on the road outside. Every once in a while a pickup would come hauling by. No U.S. vehicles. It was eerie. David supposed that the Army would first secure the main roads and then worry about the back roads.

The men were all exhausted. They took turns standing watch and sleeping.

Darkness fell, and they sat about with the lights out. David was worried about Oberley. Help could not be more than a half hour away by helicopter. Maybe everyone was too busy putting out fires and such.

David felt groggy. He'd rested pretty well, gone to the bathroom, cleaned up, almost like home; but the events of last night left him drained

Then, about eight o'clock that morning, David and his men heard chopper noises. They were sitting in the main entrance building of the compound, outside which the pickups had been parked.

Men cheered.

David held up a hand. "Hang on. That sounds strange for a chopper."

Indeed, it was a deep, booming sound. They crowded at the window to look.

"Holy shit," someone said.

There was indeed a chopper landing, but not a friendly one. Several helicopter gunships swarmed around the horizon in the line of fire to protect a huge

Brazilian-built five-rotor Aero-Boi K-56 "Air Bull," capable of carrying a huge load of men and weapons. The chopper was as imposing as a dirigible, probably 100 feet long. It was painted dark green, almost black. Landing lights twirled underneath and on top. The only markings were the IAR flags under the cockpit windows. Dust kicked up as its two dozen heavy rubber tires clawed toward the ground for a footing.

"We're in trouble," Mo said.

David nodded. "That thing's probably full of commandos."

"It can carry about sixty guys in full gear," Mo said, "and throw in a small tank."

David thought fast. What to do? If they did nothing, if they even hid in the bowels of this complex, those guys would find the bodies, find the vans, and figure out the score. In an hour, it would be over. Best to attack rather than be attacked.

"Let's head for the big garage," David said. "Then we can either run for it, or we can attack if we must."

As they jogged through corridors with their weapons at ready, they could see the Air Bull through passing windows. The chopper hovered in the air, checking out the grounds as it drifted in lazy circles.

"We could shoot the pilot from here," Mo suggested.

David shook his head. "We don't have any sniper rifles. We'd have only one or two shots before he got wise and pulled back. If they can field that thing in the air this close to Al-Kuwait, it means they took out a lot of our stuff. They can clean this joint out looking for us. I have an idea."

They came to the garage and bolted down the stairs, all 19 of them. David had lost two of his squads. He wanted to get these two home in one piece.

As the Air Bull slowly descended to the ground in front of the palace of Prince Mohamed Al-Ahmad al-Sabah, six black limousines careened around the far end of the embankments surrounding the property.

Waving from the lead car's antenna was an IAR flag that David had found in one of the pickup trucks. As David, sitting in that car, drew near, he looked up at the huge black sausage shape. In the lighted cockpit, he could make out the pilot and copilot laughing, waving, giving a thumbs up.

David's and four other limousines drove under the helicopter and stopped. The last limousine stopped about twenty feet away from the chopper. A window rolled down, and Diem waved.

The pilot waved and grinned.

On the horizon, the gunships had either taken off or settled down. Engines feathering, they waited to resume operations at a moment's notice.

The 50 cal slid out, snake-like, as Diem pulled away, and began firing. Glass flew everywhere in the Air Bull's cockpit. The pilot and co-pilot twitched and slumped, still strapped in, but dead. The blunt nose of the chopper became full of large ugly bullet holes. Diem's gun traced the fuel lines along the skin of the ship. Black oily smoke poured from the wing engines, gray smoke from the instrument panels in the cockpit. Diem ordered the firing to stop and the driver to take the car around to the fuel tanks.

David waited. They'd have to be careful of their ammunition, and he expected the '50 to run out shortly. He eyed the horizon nervously. Any minute now, the gunships might lift off. If they did, the cars would have to bolt for the garages and then there would be a room to room fight to the death. Also, he had to be ready to bolt if the Air Bull showed signs of lying on its side. If it came straight down on its landing gear, the belly would be about ten feet above the limo roofs. Under here, they'd be relatively safe. The limousines were heavy armored models designed for a run to the border; which hadn't been necessary, but they could take a firefight and keep rolling.

A hatch dropped from the center belly, a rope dropped down, and a number of commandos slid down with lightning speed.

David's men were ready, picking them off.

Then a ramp door dropped down with a thud. A small, low Chinese-made Butterfly army field car skidded down, studded with weapons, and tried to run in a circle to attack the limos. The driver took a shot to the head and the vehicle spun out of control, flipping on its roof. Nobody crawled out, but David fired a few shots at it anyway.

Then the side doors slid open, and more commandos piled out. David's men fired away until there must be twenty bodies out here, David figured. When would they run out of soldiers? "Diem, take out the fuel tanks."

"Yessir."

"I got some tracer rounds," a trooper said.

"Good. Shoot 'em off," David said.

The '50 opened up. Tracer bullets streaked through the air like fireflies.

Black smoke began to engage the rear of the helicopter.

"Let's get out from under here," David ordered. All six cars pulled out and lined up behind the chopper. By now flames were visible in the tail engine.

More tracers rose up, and the side fuel tanks erupted in great orange gouts of flame.

On the horizon, the supporting gunships were flying away. What?

A white cloth waved from a rear window.

"Cease fire," David said. "Keep your eyes open."

A ladder dropped down, and a group of men in various types and colors of flight suits ran down to escape the increasingly embroiled chopper. They gathered on the ground and held their arms up.

"Cover me," David said. If any one of them does anything funny, shoot him."

The limousines cruised up. David got out, waving his 9 mm. side arm.

The IAR, some of them older men, kept their arms high and nobody tried anything. They looked sullen and ashamed.

"Look!" one of David's men cried out.

Coming over the horizon were a row of U.S. Sheridan tanks and hummers, all proudly flying unit pennants that snapped in the moist air. Oberley jumped out and came running. "Lieutenant, we took three tactical nukes. Small H-bombs! 10 kilotons each. Wiped out a mess of people and stuff, but we're regrouping and pushing these jerks back into the sand!"

David thought with stunned joy he'd get to see Kristy again after all.

Diem nudged. "Sir, two of these guys are generals. We bagged a couple big ones."

More and more U.S. military units arrived. Waves of choppers flew by overhead.

"What's going on?" Mo asked quietly.

"Not sure," David said as a couple of U.S. choppers landed. "Ah! I get it. Photo-Op!"

Out stepped General Billy Norcross and his staff. Norcross was easily recognizeable as the most flamboyant U.S. military officer since Patton. He carried an object that resembled a riding crop, but was actually an ivory-handled, telescoping lecture board pointer. He wore twin, pearl-handled 9 mm automatics, one at each hip. On his cap, effective the President's executive order this very morning, he wore a dark blue baseball cap with five glittering silver stars in a circle: the nation's first five-star general in the 21st Century.

As Norcross and his staff approached across the desert, Mo whispered: "This joker gonna claim he captured these bad boys here?"

A gaggle of press ran behind the general, filming every move as the general was shown toward David.

David choked down a wry grin as he whispered back: "You got it. A major photo op! If we're lucky, we get to be in the picture!"

CHAPTER 6

COLFAX, KENTUCKY

Cover liked the ranch well enough, and the woman was okay, but he most liked the excitement of a job. For the moment, though, he had to lie low. The hit in Gary was a major flap, and it was best to cool off for a while in case someone could make him.

So Cover rode his horse around the estate in solitude, enjoying the stillness, the occasional tang of charcoal smoke from some mountain shack on the ridge lines beyond his property. He kept a sidearm under his shirt, but he carried with him a small caliber birding shotgun. He wasn't exactly pressing it, but at times he'd overcome his lethargy, dismount, and pursue something into the dark fringe of the woods. A pair of mountain hens, almost the color of brown leaves, waddled quickly away and vanished. "Bang," Cover said as he followed them with his gun but didn't fire. Sometimes, it was relaxing not to take life. Sometimes it was relaxing to let something live.

The cellfax beeped. He took it from the horse's saddlebag and put it on the saddle. A strip of accounting tape peeled out in four inch segments, each time with a whine from the machine. He knew the routine, but the name coming out made even Cover raise an eyebrow: "Louis Cardoza."

What an honor, he thought as he eagerly collated the little sheets into a pocket-size information brief—everything he'd need to know to cover his new subject in case that person needed a treatment similar to the one he'd just given "General" Bennett. His eyes lit up, and his boredom with peace quickly evaporated. Bennet had been the type of job on which Cover prided himself. There was usually time to come up with something really good that required detailed knowledge of the subject's movements and habits. Was there a mistress in Cardoza's life? In his past? Start there, Cover thought, stuffing the papers in his pocket and walking back toward the house. He led the horse by the reins. His mind was suddenly so awash in thoughts and plans that he forgot to remount. In any case, the mountain air and the crisp wind that came with the falling night would do him good, put color in his cheeks, give him an appetite for the woman's beef stew that she'd been fussing over all day.

CHAPTER 7

WASHINGTON, D.C.

V ice President Louis Cardoza had become something of a hero in the eyes of the opposition press. He forced his way into White House and State Department meetings at will. The President generally tolerated this; the venal rabble of left-over old party bureaucrats loathed him. Their eyes radiated wishes for Byzantine punishments upon him, because they knew that if ever OCP were fully out of office, there would be a housecleaning in which they would be the first to go.

For his own, Louis began to despise OCP more and more, and generally was glad he'd left the Democratic Party, even if he'd put himself out on a limb.

The insults they publicly heaped upon Meredith did less to humiliate her than to convince the voters finally that there was no merit left to the old regime.

If anyone were still holding out against CON2, that changed with the announcement in the early 2000s that Social Security was broke. For generations, citizens had believed the system was some sort of savings account. Yet, every year, the politicians had offered tax breaks to get elected, and had used the slush fund of pork projects to get themselves reelected in their districts. Louis could well agree with the system's harshest critics, even if he did not buy into the politics of the militias or the radical conservatives. He still held to his one simple premise—a solemn promise made to a dying child that he would campaign that children could get health care. It was a simple, sweeping, glorious, and true premise. He found it almost unbelieveable that a nation so founded on high moral principle could preach to the world, and yet be the only industrialized nation with nearly half its citizens unable to get even rudimentary health care.

With the collapse of Social Security, the nation was electrified to learn that Senator Charles Carberry of California had resigned from the Senate to coordinate an independent drive for a Second Constitutional Convention that relied heavily on MCP support. Just starting out, he already had a third of the state legislatures required to provide a two thirds majority to call a convention. Hamilton and Carberry's initiative would simply bypass Congress. Louis was almost entirely left out of the planning, which was typical of how he was being treated in Washington. Hamilton offered little solace, and Louis was quickly becoming suspicious about Hamilton's plans for him, indeed for the party and the country.

When the going got rough, as it frequently did in this capital of crime and slime, Louis often would meditate on where he had come from, his roots, his promise to Mariella. He no longer visited Ana for fear of embroiling her in the ugliness that whirled around him—arcane committees of Congress calling for his impeachment, calling for investigations, bringing to the table spurious witnesses to crimes and misdemeanors so outlandish that only specialized lawyers could parse the layers of innuendo. Hate radio was in full swing, lambasting him day and night, ridiculing his wife and children, calling him a sleazy criminal who should resign, calling him an enemy of the people. How many tens of millions of old wealth dollars were going into that campaign, he wondered.

"I know the going is tough," RLH told him in one of their monthly meetings, "and we're doing everything to smooth the road ahead for you."

By that, Louis assumed he meant the next term in the White House.

"With Social Security broke, and people's checks being shorted, or people who were planning to retire being told they have to work five or seven more years, the American public has awakened to the reality of where we went these past fifty years or so. The people are angrier than ever before, and many are listening to the extremists. We're trying to stop that, Louis, by taking control of the ball. Anarchists on the left, and Libertarians on the right, are trying to dismantle all government so that we have chaos. Rule of every man by his own gun. The militias want to break up the Union—first time that's been discussed since Lincoln's time—and look at the bloody Civil War we had. Everyone's talking about sending delegates to Washington, Louis, and amending the Constitution. Article V, they're saying. The solution to all our problems!

Amend the Constitution. Why stop there? Let's just rewrite the whole thing."

"You're joking."

"Of course I'm joking." Water runnelled down outside the windows of Louis's office. "I've come up with a compromise plan to make the whole country happy. We have a majority of the states sewn up at the grass roots level. We can push through a call for a Second Constitutional Convention and make it stick. We can have the delegates in Washington next year. We can have your national health care plan—a good mix of common sense and good medicine without running it like a cutthroat business—we can restore some form of old age security—we can put something on everyone's plate and get the country happy again."

Louis nodded. "I'll campaign on that when I go for President."

RLH got a funny look on his face, and a chill ran through Louis.

"Louis, it's time we talked."

No, Louis screamed inwardly, don't do this to me.

"I have a party to run, and a lot of people to look after. We have to look at the polls, Louis. We have no choice."

The polls are fine, you lying sack of shit.

"The polls are telling me that people like you. They like the health care message. They're past the point of being brainwashed that having health care is a form of communism or socialism. They want health care like people have in Germany or France or England or just about anywhere that people no longer eat with their hands. I can give them health care, Louis, but I can't give you the Presidency. I'm sorry."

I want to kill you.

"Maybe in another four years, Louis. Right now, the strong ones are Bartoletti from New York and Cadney from Arizona. Those governors are the two strong horses that are going to pull this party's wagon in the next election."

You have betrayed me.

"The people see you as ineffective in bringing around Cliff Bradley and his OCP hacks. We can't sink into their mire with them, Louis. I know what you're thinking."

"I bailed out on my party and political future to join MCP..." Louis finally managed, in his rage, to push out through gritted teeth.

"Yes, but you were at the end of your day, my friend. The Democrats had other plans than to offer you national office. You might have moved to the Senate and tried it that way, but for Chrissake, what were the odds? Slim to none? Remember, that is why you bailed."

Louis jumped up, and two of RLH's body guards materialized out of the shadows.

"Don't do or say anything rash," Hamilton said, rising and ducking toward the door behind the big bodies of his guards. "We'll have plenty of time to kick around more ideas. I'm not giving up on you, Louis. I'm just giving you some time to cool off."

Meredith took the children back to Montecito. They were still very small, but the climate in Washington had become more corrosive, vindictive, and destructive than ever. One leading senator compared the climate in the nation's capital with being in a hurricane—"any part of you that's exposed, anything about your private life, your past, your little stumbles in life, and you are spun out of control and dashed to your death in this maelstrom of press, lawyers, special interests, and morally bankrupt politicians."

Louis flew with his family, and vacationed with them for a few days behind closed gates and tightly guarded walls.

A leading militia general had just been assassinated in a plane crash, and the militia movement was threatening to fall apart into open regional warfare, one group against the other, all groups against the government.

Jamal Mustafa had been brought to a cease-fire in the Middle East on his own terms, giving the West a bone in the form of promises to keep oil prices under $20 a barrel. All the oil companies were expelled, their plants and equipment confiscated, and the revenues going straight into the Islamic Arabic Republic's coffers.

Immediately, Jamal tightened the screws, raising prices "temporarily" to $30 a barrel. World commodities markets fluctuated wildly. The flow of oil continued in some places, but came to an abrupt halt elsewhere. The U.N. threatened another expeditionary force to internationalize the oil fields if Jamal did not back off.

There were long gas lines across the U.S. and Canada as reserves of North American oil were used up. Grocery prices went through the roof. People were begging on street corners. Winter was here in full force, and people were freezing in their houses in the northern states. There were rashes of house fires as people tried to burn their backyard trees in jury-rigged ovens. The mood of the country was getting bleaker.

One state after another signed off on Robert Lee Hamilton's plan for a Second Constitutional Convention, or CON2. Better to do this now than risk violent insurrection a few years later, he said publicly. He and Louis were no longer on speaking terms. RLH no longer needed Louis, and that was clear to Louis.

In Montecito, an old friend visited, one of the few people permitted access to the inner sanctum—Teddy Warington, Meredith's cousin and Louis's former Democratic Party chief of staff. They hadn't spoken since Teddy resigned following Louis's joining MCP. Now they shook hands circumspectly and kept their distance. Meredith broke the ice for them by declaring: "Well, it's good to be away from all those nauseating people in Washington. You wouldn't have liked it there, Tedddy. Louis is finding it pretty awful, aren't you, dear?"

Embarrassed by his poor fortune, Louis was annoyed by her, and looked at Teddy ready to trade angry words.

Teddy's respectful and sympathetic silence made him realize these were his family members. "Sorry," he muttered, "I guess I'm getting used to being surrounded by people who want my hide."

"I understand," Teddy said, "that MCP is pushing for a CON2 with ten or twelve amendments—strict agenda—get in, get the job done, get out—"

"—that's right—"

"—and health care is one of them."

"That's right."

There was a silence. Teddy was a tall, commanding presence, florid-cheeked, short tight curls of blond hair fading into white as he passed 50. "So you've accomplished your goal."

"I suppose I have, Teddy. Somehow I thought there would be more." He remembered Mariella. "Sometimes there isn't. That's all there is." He was in shock, with the wreckage of his political career strewn all around.

Teddy stayed on another day or so, and they talked about old times. They talked about the Democrats and the Republicans. They talked about how things might have gone differently. And then Teddy mentioned an old mutual friend in passing, Nadia Kinman.

They were walking along the beach in Santa Barbara, with oil derricks visible in the distancel. Louis stopped: "What did you say?"

Teddy looked surprise. "I was talking about who's in Sacramento and San Francisco these days, and I mentioned that Nadia Kinman's husband is getting remarried."

"Why?"

"Because she died in a car accident a couple of years ago. Why?"

Louis felt confused. "I don't know. I was just—surprised. I didn't know she had died. When was it?"

Teddy couldn't remember. After he and Meredith had dinner with Teddy and waved as Teddy drove off for San Francisco in his heavy black car, Louis went to the computer room and got on the Web. A few searches brought up all the information he needed. There it was—a newspaper spread in one of the local papers, eulogizing the socialite who had done so much for various communities in Los Angeles. She'd been a bright, attractive young Jewish girl from New York, married to an eminent cardiologist in

Beverly Hills, and a big Democratic donor. God, she'd been pretty; and that smile...

The cause of death had been massive injuries from a car crash. The police had never resolved why it happened, and the answer remained open that someone might have tampered with the brakes—motive unknown.

Louis went for a long walk outside, up and down the quiet lanes of set-back mansions of Montecito. It was a full moon, and a steely light seemed to pursue him. Like the errant dry leaves circling on the ground, he had no rest. Her death had come the day after Louis had met with RLH and agreed to jump parties. How odd, how odd!

It was a secret Meredith must never know, nor could Teddy—her family, after all. Louis had always been crazy about Meredith. He'd had plenty of come-ons from attractive young women, but that kind of playing around was political suicide anymore after the '90's. But there had been one slip. Allison Miranda, then a beautiful young up and coming newswoman from Los Angeles, movie-star beautiful with her long black hair, wide mouth and angelic smile, and dark lively eyes. Allison and Louis had a crush on each other for a few weeks. The only person on earth who knew was Nadia Kinman, because Nadia had left her Los Angeles apartment available to Allison so that Louis could stop by. After a few weeks of heady, breathless love, Allison and Louis both realized this would destroy not only his marriage, but potentially both of their careers. It had been a sensible thing to do, Louis thought, not mercenary, not calculating, really an act of love on his part for Meredith. Allison had briefly been the way not taken—the Latina, the woman he might have married, perhaps even Roberta, had the baby not died. It was a private matter, honorable people involved—certainly not fodder for sleazy talk show hosts. Louis feared and hated the rape of privacy almost as much as he feared the pain he might inflict on his wife. He passionately kissed his mujer, Allison, goodbye one last time in Nadia Kinman's apartment, and they had never seen each other again. The Allison he saw almost daily on television was an older, more mature woman happily married and probably never recalling for a moment her fling with the current vice president. That had been ten years ago—a lot of water under that dam.

Louis walked with furious speed, shuffling leaves and stiff grass with his feet. The moon shone down like a relentless inquisitor. Was it possible? Had RLH found out about the affair and killed Nadia? Was it possible that his sin with Allison long ago had been a death sentence for his friend? The coincidence of dates would not let go of Louis. There could probably never be an answer to this question, but RLH must be looked into. RLH was the shadowy czar who called the shots and would soon be making or unmaking U.S. presidents. This wasn't about local politics anymore.

Louis had time on his hands, but he did not know where to start digging.

Back in Washington, he started by reading the two biographies available. Pablum, all—nothing critical of the great man. Born Minneapolis 1949, educated Yale, Harvard—brilliant—on the boards of corporations by age 30... that was what RLH did—he had been a board member or a CEO most of his adult life. He was royalty, a kingmaker. And possibly dangerous.

Am I obsessing? Louis thought. Yes of course. Should I be? Probably.

He asked himself those questions more than once as he turned his study at the Vice President's House into an investigative lab. Nobody could go in there, not even his Secret Service team. He kept the door locked, and even had a special deadbolt installed with an alarm if anyone tried to force it. Since the split ticket administration had arrived in Washington, the Treasury Department had decided to split the Secret Service into two details—Tiger Detail for the President, Puma Detail for the Vice President. That way, the detail members could be loyal to one person. Even so, Louis had his doubts about whom he could trust. He began to feel paranoid, like a King Lear who would soon be wandering the streets of Washington... but no. He was a strong man, and he got hold himself. At some time he'd have to trust his personal guards, or what hope was there?

He began to compile biographies, locked in his study, working almost entirely from the Internet. Names, names, names... members of Congress... people who were known to associate with RLH... what boards did he sit on? What boards did they sit on? Louis became alarmed at the large number of prominent families and commercial brands tied to RLH by one bond or another. And another thing: among military officers of high field grade (colonel) and up into the flag grades—if they weren't from one of the service academies, some were from places like Virginia Military Institute. A name began to recur: Cable College. Now where was that? Louis pulled down his old dictionary, which had very quaintly for generations listed things like Biographies, Geographical Places, Commencement Colors by Academic Area of Interest, and U.S. and Canadian Colleges and Universities. Cable College... hmm... nothing.

He got on the Web and searched—ah, there it was, a smallish sectarian college in western Montana, located in the mountains near a U.S. Military Reserve. Degrees offered were exclusively B. Div., M. Div., D.D.—accredited by the Western Association of Colleges and Universities; high academics and entrance exam scores required. There were pictures of it—a forbidding cluster of sandstone architecture dating to the late 1800's. This was situated in some icy cold looking pine forests in the Rocky Mountains, elevation one mile... Very strong military officer training but not ROTC rated. What? Now that was strange. Louis studied every word he could find about Cable College. There were only two or three websites with any mention. Cable had existed since 1991 in its present form—ah, that would exlain why no mention in his old dictionary. Founded by a group of conservative clergymen interested in the Protestant Fundamentals and strict Biblical literalism, the college was funded by various foundations, mostly with the word Missionary in them... blah blah blah... when he got the feeling he'd come to a dead end, Louis put a virtual bookmark there and continued his investigations along other alleys.

Nowadays, there was not only a primary in the Spring of the election year, but a pre-primary in which the parties eliminated some of their more outlandish contenders. It was an ugly new wrinkle in U.S. politics because it took much of the color out of the election stumping process. Gone were the Paul Simons with their bow ties, the Lamarr Alexanders with their checkered shirts, the Clintons and the Gores with their tour buses... there was really too much at stake for a party's best candidate to be running in a field with a group of clowns, so went the professional politico thinking. The pre-primary was where the party put its support behind a team that could then go into the primaries well-defined and armed—others could still challenge them, but at a disadvantage. The newspapers said unfair, un-Constitutional, and the smart money said CON2 could fix this, too. The smart money also said, hell, if the Constitution's been working so well, why are we in the mess we're in?

The MCP pre-primary was held on a snowy day in Manhattan, New York. The Democrats and the Republicans used their pre-convention in Chicago to formally announce the continuation of the Old Constitution Party as a sign that they were opposed to the growing support for CON2, and that they supported solving the nation's problems under the real Constitution.

The Middle Class Party announced its support for the nomination of Gov. Bartoletti of New York for President, and Gov. Cadney of Arizona as his running mate. The millions of voters energized by the new party were expected, in the Spring, to endorse these candidates overwhelmingly at their convention in Miami. Louis showed up only briefly at their victory celebration, shook their hands, avoided RLH, and left with two Secret Service guards.

On the steps of the Federal Court House in Manhattan, a mob of reporters briefly slowed the three men down. "Mr. Vice President! How do you feel about tonight's nominations?"

"It's a great moment for the party," Louis said, smiling and waving.

"We haven't heard you say yet why you were not forwarded by your party."

Louis stopped. It was a question he'd been dodging for the past few weeks—his situation was an open secret in Washington's lake of leaks—but he recognized that this was a decisive moment for him. He could let this opportunity slip by, or he could make history of it. After all, there was life beyond RLH, just as RLH had proven there was life beyond the Democratic and Republican dinosaurs. "Well, let me answer that." He gave it a moment for everyone to crank up their lights and microphones and position themselves for the best shots. He felt very genial, and he thought of Mariella. "I made a promise to my dying daughter almost 15 years ago that I would go all the way to the top so that no American citizen would be without health care. The brutal and unequal system we have lived under for over a century is today dying a well-deserved death. As you know, one of the proposed amendments in CON2 will be just what I have been fighting for all these years—a universal statement on the basic human right of every American citizen to equal and unrestricted health care, regardless of income. Equal health care will not cost more, but less—preventive medicine will predominate over interventive medicine. Just by eliminating the insurance layer, we can save over 20% of the annual health care dollar. All of that is going to happen very soon. I feel I have achieved what I came here to do. I am a team player, ladies and gentlemen, and my party and

I decided that the best candidates next time would be Governor Bartoletti and Governor Cadney. I will continue to support the party in whatever way I can, and I wish them well."

Good, Louis thought—he was creating a bookmark for the future to find him. He had an ominous sense of the extremism buried in this so-called Middle Class Party, which was nothing but a Trojan Horse for the most extreme right wing to get into power. After Bartoletti and Cadney were finished screwing up, and the American people turned their backs on RLH, there would still be a future beyond going back to the dinosaur days. And Louis, after a nice four year rest, would bound back in good form to run for President.

"Mr. Vice President, do you support the Second Constitutional Convention that is all but certain to happen in Washington next year?"

Louis froze. What? He wanted to mouth some mealy platitude about trusting and believing in the Middle Class Party—but hold it, that was the opposite of what he felt. Whatever RLH touched was slime. If he wanted to be remembered, he must say something really meaningful right now—he almost laughed at himself, politician that he'd become, that when the time came to tell the truth, the truth itself was one of several options. "No," he said, throwing much of his reserve aside, and feeling somewhat bold and reckless about it—the old Louis, the boxer, coming from the bottom, gloves up at his temples, cut, slash, jab jab jab... "I personally feel that the politicians of this country should have been solving our problems Constitutionally for generations. Instead, they have consistently lied about Social Security, robbing from the American people's retirement plan to make up for deficit spending. Instead of planning for the future, they slimed each other for some brief partisan advantage. I think that CON2 is just another smoke screen to fix something that isn't broken, in order to cover up for things that are badly broken. I would have preferred that we did it under the existing Constitution that we have cherished for over two centuries. Thank you, that's enough."

They broke into a babbling mob. "Mr. Vice President, are you refuting your party?"

"Mr. Vice President, is it true that you are on the outs with Mr. Hamilton?"

"Mr. Vice President, would you consider running as an independent?"

Louis felt he'd said enough. Anything more, and it might be too much. He tugged the sleeves of his guards, and together they formed a wedge to push through to the Secret Service car waiting by the curb. "Thank you, thank you!" he shouted, waving, as the door closed and the car shot away into traffic.

Louis had found a stance that worked for him. He was transforming himself into a new politician. This wasn't state level—this was national; this was world class.

Meredith stayed almost entirely in Montecito with the children, and was thinking of getting a law degree to practice locally and perhaps run for local office. During one of his monthly visits she laughed at him, waving a newspaper. "Honey, what are you doing? What are you saying here? You never finish a sentence. You say one thing on Monday, and another on Friday."

"It's my new piece," he told her, embracing her Valentino-style, making her shriek with laughter. "Dah-ling, I flitter about like a butterfly, alighting on this flower, then that… always I keep those slime balls off balance. It's the only thing that works. And I beg your pardon, I don't contradict myself. That would make me look foolish. People would scratch their heads and want to impeach me all the more. I'm now the quintessential politician, saying more but meaning nothing. I don't say," he clarified, "I imply. It makes me quotable and makes me sound vague and wise… the kind of man the American people will want to elect after RLH is done slashing and burning the country." He added, in a whisper, "I'm also fishing."

"For what, darling?"

She looked so pretty when she was confused. "I'm fishing for the truth. It's buried deeply someplace in Washington, probably in a drawer with a woman's red shoe, a middle-aged senator's used condom, two champagne glasses, and a whole load of dirty money."

"Be careful."

"I am always careful."

Louis returned to Washington and put in the appearances Cliff Bradley thought he should. The economy was in desperate straits, but holding steady—not getting any worse—that at least was good news. Unemployment had actually dipped below 20 per cent for the first time in two years, and there were signs that the world was ready to get back to work. Jamal Mustafa, while still in control in the Middle East, understood that if he made a move to tighten the flow of oil, he'd be at war with the entire world.

Clearly he was building up his arsenal, and Arabia would be a world power within a generation, but the signs were that moderates would be running the show—there was too much at stake to let a bunch of wild-eyed medieval clerics run amok in the streets; and with Arabia (or the I.A.R., as Mustafa called it) solidified, the Arabists had what they wanted. The leading players in Europe, the U.S., and Asia were quite sanguine about this and considered it a smart play. Louis was inclined to go along with it—the radical religionists and nationalists were split off from the mainstream of Arabs who simply wanted their own nation, and a rapidly emerging middle class would stabilize the situation. That meant renewed economic stability and growth, and a positive atmosphere in the U.S.—provided MCP put the damper on CON2—which it did not look as if they were going to do. That became more and more apparent to Louis as he talked his way around town. He was marginalized; he was a gadfly; he was already a senior statesman like Richard Nixon but without having committed any crimes; people were more willing to talk with him; and he went around talking with people. He was fishing... and soon, he hoped, it would pay off.

He'd made the decision to trust the leader of the small group of Secret Service agents, a tall, slim Afro-American named Archie Cooper. Special Agent Cooper was 42, olive-complexioned, with acne-pitted, sunken cheeks and a scarred chin that made him look tough. Which he was, having served as a Green Beret during some covert Central American operations. Cooper also had some of the darkest, most penetrating, and analytical eyes Louis remembered ever encountering.

He asked Cooper to step into his studio one evening and close the door. And sit down. Which Cooper did, defensively, eyeing the room, which none of the agents had yet been allowed into. After a few brief pleasantries, Louis said: "I have kept you guys at arms' length because I don't trust the other party and I don't know which ones of you are spying for them. For that matter, I don't know who is in Hamilton's pay."

Cooper stared impassively, processing every word with lightning speed.

"I've decided I have to trust somebody or I'll go mad. Can I trust you, Special Agent Cooper?"

"Yessir." Cooper steepled his fingers carefully and reached for more words. "I think you're right—I wouldn't trust all these people either."

"Do you know which ones?"

"I might have some idea, but it's just my guesswork, and don't make me go there please."

"I won't. See, I'm outta here in a little over a year. I'll probably never be back. Quarter billion fine American people out there, and surely they can send better people to Washington than the trash they've sent in recent years. Don't you think?"

"I don't get paid to offer political opinions. I'm trained to think around them. Like what do you want—Sir?"

"I'm not trying to put you on the spot, Special Agent Cooper. I'm totally isolated because I haven't been able to trust anyone, but I'm working on something and I need help. I'm taking a chance on you. You have a good record and you seem like an honest man."

"I'll do what I can within the limits of my position, Sir."

"That's fair enough. Here's what I think. This CON2 that's going to be held next year is going to fall apart. The old constitution will be just another piece of paper, by virtue of being challenged so rudely—when it took over 200 years to create just 17 amendments beyond the Bill of Rights, and one of those amendments took over 200 years to be approved. The new constitution won't happen, because once you open the floor to debate, there is no law in the Constitution that says debate can be limited to one or ten or x number of amendments. More and more radicals will propose outlandish amendments be added to the agenda, and the whole thing will fall apart. That's when a group of civic minded middle aged white men with lots of money will step in and provide a constitution convenient to their interests."

"That's a frightening scenario, Sir."

"Well, maybe I'm paranoid, but it makes sense. I have lots of time on my hands inbetween tea garden parties."

Cooper's face crinkled in a smile. He really seemed a pleasant fellow. "We have been wondering about that, Sir. We have been getting tired of guarding you from all those little old ladies with blue hair."

"You have no idea how much I wish someone else could handle the tea parties."

They laughed together for a moment or two.

"Coffee?"

Cooper shrugged. "Sure." He rose. "I'll help myself, Sir. Thanks. You?"

"Just a little tea."

The first grit of snow pressed against the windows on Observatory Circle.

"Gonna be a cold winter," Louis said.

"You think so?" Cooper traipsed over with two cups and saucers. "How about you move your office to Florida, since you aren't too involved in politics here?"

"Thank you. Well, that's a good idea, but I can go back to Montecito, which is also very pleasant." A black cloud of depression whirled up. "I could just resign, you know. This whole thing is a charade. I've been impeached without any ink being spilled."

"Oh, Jesus, don't give them what they want, Mr. Vice President."

"I've been telling myself that for a long time, Archie. May I call you Archie?"

"Please do."

"You could call me Louis, but that would be against regulations, I suppose. I was a feisty guy when I was young." He made fists, brushed a thumb against his nose as if flicking sweat away. "Used to box."

"I heard you were pretty good."

It was good to joke with another human being in Washington. He hadn't realized how alone he was, especially with Meredith and the children away for their safety and well-being. "I won twenty out of thirty. Six TKO's on top of that. The last four were the bad ones. Last one put me in the hospital and I knew I wasn't going any higher. Just like here today."

Archie stirred his coffee, balancing the cup on his knee. "Well, Sir, you bailed out at the right time and made a magnificent career for yourself. Now maybe you'll bail out here and make another magnificent career for yourself."

"Doing what?" Louis snorted lightly. "Why don't you run for office or something?"

"Me?" Archie's turn to laugh. "I'm a steady, regular guy, Sir. Get up, stare in the mirror scared, shave, march off to work, collect my check, have fun with my family. I have a lovely wife and three girls."

"No boys?"

"Three girls."

"I have a boy and a girl. Babies still, really. My wife is still quite young and we could have another one." He had a brief vision of bliss—in the garden of their home, with several children crowding around him, and Meredith as wonderful as ever.

"There you go, Sir. Lighten up."

"Thanks, Archie. You just made my day. There is life after this hell hole after all."

"There sure is. I've seen several presidents come and go, and several vice presidents, and I can't seem to remember any of them that weren't happy as hell to leave here and never come back when their time was up."

Time was up... those words lingered in Louis's mind, clogging his further thinking. Maybe he'd write some books. Sure... about children's and pregnant women's health. What a great idea.

"Sir?"

"I'm fine."

"You were staring into space."

"Yes I was. I was seeing something nice. That still leaves me with this problem, Archie. I think there is a conspiracy, and my party has a hand in it. Have you ever been to Cable College?"

It wasn't Louis or Archie who went to that frigid wasteland in western Montana, but an old Green Beret buddy of Cooper whose name Louis did not want to know.

Archie was extremely tense and upset as he detailed the findings a few days later: "My man happens to be caucasian, so he had no problem in that regard. They're sort of like the KKK mixed with Bible fury up there. Anyway, they have a strong military officer program, not ROTC, but it's recognized for credit with the National Guard, where they get commissioned, and then they transfer over into the regular Army or whatever."

Louis whistled. He said: "Ah! A trick for every problem. Clever."

"My friend learned a few other things from talking to the locals. Seems Cable's cadets are half the population, the other half being seminarians who have little contact with the military side. The cadets have regular contact with militia groups in the area, with whom they train several weeks a year."

"Train for what?"

"To defend themselves against the United Nations which is supposedly taking over the country."

Louis grinned. "Oh, that. Then they must be relatively harmless."

"You haven't heard the rest, Sir." Archie's eyes had a stressed, hooded look. "My friend did some more checking. He found out from the yearbooks that a large number of these turkeys wind up in special infantry and other combat arms occupations, and some of those have already been tapped for CON2 duty."

That alarmed Louis. The Composite was a military

command of 20,000 reservists who were to be stationed near the convention center to protect the convention—already, thousands of death threats had been received by the FBI against the delegates who had not yet been chosen, to a convention that had not even been formally called.

"Not the Composite, which you are thinking," Cooper said, "but the units directly inside the convention center which are under a totally different chain of command but are in effect the nerve center, its command and control, its life line for everything from first aid to sandwiches to bomb squad protection."

Louis digested this. "So you're saying the military safety ring that's been designed is already being penetrated."

"I'm afraid so. What are we going to do, Mr. Vice President?"

"What else? Forget politics. Go to the President. Lay everything on the line. Tell him Hamilton may look good but he smells like three day old fish. Bring whatever evidence we have—a list of names of Hamilton's connections—I've been working on that end—bring the Cable College connection—let the FBI do their jobs so we don't have to. Hopefully before it's too late—before CON2 kicks off next year."

CHAPTER 8

DAVID GORDON

The Gordons and the Brindisis did not like each other, so the wedding was held on neutral ground in New Haven, ten days after David's return to CONUS after two years in Kuwait. He was now a much-decorated first lieutenant.

When David stepped off the military transport plane at the former Fort Dix, N.J., on a gray, cloudy day, he felt like throwing his bags aside, kneeling, and kissing the ground. Instead, for the sake of decorum, he let himself be swept up in the tide of other men in various uniforms and of various ranks, most lugging carry-on bags, all looking about with hungry eyes and then breaking into broad grins as another tide met them: their women, their children. Meanwhile, a National Guard band played Stars and Stripes Forever on the tarmac nearby.

David heard her voice clearly: "David!" as she flew

toward him—Kristy, blond hair flying, smile ablaze, eyes delirious for him as she reached out her arms. She wore a white raincoat, a light tiny-flower print dress cut just above the knee, white hose that showed off her thin legs, and white high heel shoes. She wore a light, fragrant perfume redolent of citrus blossoms.

David closed his eyes, absorbing the gentle shock of her body against his. He had dreamed of this moment for over a year, but he hadn't known it would feel this good. He hugged her to himself, feeling the soft, firm reality of her. He'd almost forgotten how it felt to hold her, though he'd dreamed of her touch every day in the searing heat of Gulf III. Her hands softly worked their way across his face and neck. Her lips sought every inch of skin to kiss, to taste, to drink thirstily. She moaned, pressing her soft thigh around his leg, pinioning his hard, muscular thigh against her bony mons. Even the hard parts of her were soft. David could not get enough of holding her, could not let her go, kept tasting her nearness as his hands, like things that had become crippled without her, learned all over again to touch each part of her in wonderment.

There were hundreds of such reunions going on at the same time on that cold airfield. The weather was more like autumn than spring, and the miles of forest all around rustled emptily. After the heat of Kuwait and I.A.R., after the desert and the flies and the stench of bodies and things burning, but most of all after that miserable conspiracy between a sweltering sun and the oven-like, waterless desert, it was good to feel a light drop of rain on the tip of his tongue. The abundance of green leaves added a scent to the air that he'd forgotten. Kristy laughed, holding his arm tightly in hers, as they hurried toward her car. David did a little jig, dancing this way and that, trying to catch more rain drops on his tongue. He heard laughter around him, and knew nobody minded, not even the colonels and sergeants-major who'd turned out in greeting.

"I feel like I've just come back to life," David said.

"We have each other now." Her eyes were serious.

"I'd forgotten what you feel like."

She handed him the car keys. "I'll help you to remember, darling."

When they were in the car, she darted across from the passenger seat, put a hand over the seat to brace herself, and attacked him again with kisses. Her free hand roved down to the hardness between his legs, rubbing, squeezing, caressing. Her tongue tip wandered through his ear. He laughed. "My God, I'm going to come right here and now."

She blew in his ear. "You come all you want. Just never go again."

"I won't." He held her at arms' length. "I promise." Their eyes met. He looked into her eyes and read, in her steadfast gaze, the same feelings he had for her.

"My dad hung up on your mother," she said as he started the car.

"I don't need to hear this."

"I'm sorry."

"It's not your fault. Look, I'm not going to let anything spoil my homecoming." He felt her hand squeeze his on the throbbing gear shift knob. "We love each other. That's all that counts."

"You're right, darling. We are all that counts. After we're married, they never have to talk with each other again."

Marriage. David looked at her. She stared impishly, mysteriously, hungrily back.

Using his lapel com, David called home as he sped north on I-95. "Mom? I'm back."

"David!" his mother cried, somewhere between tears and laughter. "Da—" she started to repeat, but the final syllable seemed to stick in her throat.

"I love you, Mom, and I'll be home soon. Can you make a pot of coffee?"

On the way in, David had noticed the rust on the metal highway signs, the papers blowing on the streets, the potholes, the beggars…nothing had changed. If anything, there appeared to be more boarded-up shop windows, more lean-looking prostitutes of all ages. The police, short on budget, wore cheap baseball caps instead of the traditional cola-cap hats. What police cars there were looked dented, and many cops seemed to have walking beats.

Dora and her husband had added a room addition in back for Mom, jutting into a leafy green yard that overhung a hill. Their house reminded David a little of their magnificent home when Dad had still been alive. Dora's husband Joe, who owned a small tool and die making shop in Bridgeport, had done okay the past year with government contracts. They were getting by, as the lucky ones were apt to say.

The porch light was on and the front door popped open as David turned the corner into Dora's driveway. Several neighbor kids on bicycles appeared out of nowhere to watch and wave. Several adult neighbors came out to clap and cheer. David waved to them all. David's sisters Dora and Elaine rushed down the stairs amid a gaggle of boy and girl children, David's nephews and nieces, the oldest two now approaching ten years old. Some adults took photos and videos.

David's sisters had made a complete turkey dinner with mashed potatoes, sweet potatoes, green beans, dark and light gravy, a 22 pound bird whose stuffing aroma filled the house. David found himself being clasped, patted, punched, poked, stroked, kissed, laughed over, and cried over. It hit him really hard, in a major pang all at once, how much he missed his Dad and wished he were here. He wiped a tear away and sniffed, and it was just as well, he thought, they all thought he was only touched by their happiness. Only to his mother did he whisper, sitting beside her and holding her arm, while Kristy sat on his other side holding his arm, "I wish Dad were here." David's father had died a few years ago.

From the depth of one soul to the depth of another, she mouthed: "I know. I do too."

Out came the camera. Elaine instructed loudly: "Everyone, let's get some shots with Mom and David. Come on, crowd in behind them." And David felt the weight of their combined bodies pressing against the back of his chair. He tried to shake off his moment of sadness, laughing with everyone.

That evening, when Kristy and Dora's family had gone upstairs to get ready for bed, and Elaine and her family had left (after hearty hugs), Dora took David aside. "Um, Mom wanted me to talk with you."

David took a deep breath. "Dora, don't spoil the occasion."

"I'll try not to." She sat down on the sofa, flounced her dress, and patted the seat beside her. David sat down. Dora had always been the diplomat, the messenger, the facile of tongue. "David, honey, we all love you very much, and we like Kristy. She's a beautiful girl, well educated, kind, and so forth. Mom and I and Elaine and, well, let's let it go at that, we had a talk—because we love you, mind you—and we agreed to say one thing, and just say it once, and nobody will ever say a word about it again. Okay?"

"I guess."

"Here's the deal, David." Dora put her strong, firm hand on his knee. "This is a one-time shot, okay?"

"You're breaking my knee."

She ignored him. "This is from all of us, because we love you." Tears brimmed in her eyes. "Will you just wait a year before you marry her?"

"Oh, Sis—"

She burst into quiet tears. "I know you can't and you won't. It's not that I hate her or anything. I've been your sister for all these years, Davy sweetheart, and I know she's not right for you." She began to boo-hoo, having come to the end of her skills.

David hugged her to him, torn by her expressed feelings, equally torn by his love for Kristy. "There, I love you and I know you mean well." He stroked her head, holding it against his neck, and felt her tears soaking through the shirt on his back. He hugged her sturdy, familiar, beloved frame close.

She composed herself. Blew a red nose. "There. I did it. It's over and nobody in this family will ever say another word about it. You know I'll always be there for you if you need me. And Mom. And Elaine."

"I know that. You know, Sis, wasn't there a story Dad used to tell?"

Dora frowned, trying to remember.

"Wasn't there a story Dad used to tell about Mom's parents—that they threatened to shoot him if he didn't stay away?"

Dora rolled her eyes up. "I do remember something about that, but honestly, David—well, I promised —I'll never talk about this again." She rose and held out a hand for him to take in his hand. "C'mon, let's go in the kitchen and have a beer. You can tell me some war stories."

David was in a car, driving. The back of the car was on fire, and no matter how fast he drove, he could not escape the flames, which became hotter and hotter. Up ahead on the road was a sofa full of bed springs. As he drew closer and closer, he could see that embedded in the sofa springs was Jimmy Herman. From the neck up he was flesh and blood. The trapped face looked at David, unable to speak, but he mouthed the words: "Please kill me."

David screamed and clawed his way out of the car, to land in a heap of bed sheets on the floor. He lay half on the hard wood floor and half on a thick woollen throw rug. Covered in sweat, he gasped deeply and and realized he'd had the dream again. It had been like this, at least two or three times a week, since Gulf III. After a minute or two, he looked up and saw Kristy. She stood by her side of the bed, holding the bed sheet to her chest. Her eyes looked terrified.

"I'm sorry, this has been happening to me since the war. I need time to—"

Someone's fist pounded loudly on the door. "David? Kristy? What's going on?" It was Dora's voice.

"It's okay," he told Dora as he rose, "go back to bed. I had a dream."

For days, David tried to figure out why Kristy so alarmed his family.

"Why are you looking at me like that?" Kristy wailed. They were in the large spare bedroom on the side of the house, overlooking the slat fence. It was a dry, sunny day, almost warm, and the first buds were visible on the small black trees outside the window. She sat by the bay windows, combing her straight blond hair as she looked in a small round mirror. He lay on the bed, legs crossed, arms behind his head as he stared at the ceiling, at her, and back at the ceiling. "David!" she added in the same wail.

"Just admiring how beautiful you are."

"Oh shit!" She slammed the mirror down and jumped up. "I feel like everyone is watching me. Even you. I can't wait to get out of this house." She sped away into the bathroom, leaving the mirror broken on the little brown table between the bay windows.

David followed her and stood outside the bathroom door, leaning against it with his shoulder. "Honey, I'm sorry. I can make it right."

She sobbed stubbornly behind the door.

David was by nature temperamental, but had learned to keep himself well in check. Kristy was a musician, an artist, her father's child. They had no more than anyone else's share of arguments. David could not call them fights, because, aside from Kristy throwing a thing or two, not at him, but aside, there was nothing physical to them, and they blew over. Kristy was much like the weather in New England—changeable. Reasonably sunny most of the time, she got upset, not by big things, which she took in montane, glacial stride, but little things, like a lost paring knife or a misunderstood word or a splashed skirt or a forgotten date. Usually it was a combination of these things when they built up on a day when she wasn't feeling right. Then Kristy's clouds came out, and the rain beat down. She'd run out of the room, slam doors, be silent for an hour. Then she'd go to her easel. Or David would hear the black tones of the cello, gradually lightening into broad scrapes of joy plastered on top of one another like yellow and white and orange paints. Then she'd come out, smiling, seductive, and the mood meter was reset to zero. Sunny. Okay.

The wedding was in the beautiful, large St. Mary's Church in New Haven. They came down the steps on a sunny, dry day with small, puffy, high clouds in a baby-blue sky.

From the clamor of relatives rushing about in Sunday best, from the throwing of rice and the playing of bagpipes and the cheering of children, David and Kristy thankfully drove away as quickly and gracefully as possible in her Ferrari.

Several blocks away, David pulled over. He and Kristy each took turns holding up a blanket so the other could change. The suit and the wedding dress went into the trunk. Clad in jeans—in pants, she in a short skirt—and T-shirts, they stopped at the beach in Woodmont. It was too cold to take a swim, but they bought sandwiches and colas and sat on the rocks, watching seagulls fight over shellfish and thrown bread crumbs. For the first time in days, Kristy seemed herself again. They laughed and ran around and played.

For their honeymoon they drove to Manhattan, where they roamed museums and art galleries, libraries and restaurants, malls and galleries and bookstores for five days. Sated on culture, they drove the heavily packed sports car up to Cape Cod. There, for another five days, they lived in a spare wooden cottage by the sea. The sand stretched for miles. It wasn't tourist season yet, so the seaside motels were mostly empty. The off-season prices were low. David and Kristy rented bicycles and pedalled up and down sand-strewn, deserted roads near the beach. At night they made love long and passionately in their simple bed with its gray sheets, that smelled of sand and sea-salt. On their first day here, the bedding had smelled of mildew also, but Kristy had taken it to the beach, within walking distance, and used bar soap to wash it. "All that old sweat of people," she muttered while making a face. After a good drying in the wind and sun, the sheets had a slight stiffness, almost like starchiness, but they were clean. At night, she and he held hands and walked together under a full moon while the inky sea by their sides murmured in white phrases like bubbling milk.

David's orders were to report to Fort Lewis, Washington. He rented a small moving van, which they loaded with their mix of new and old possessions. "I feel like I'm being uprooted," Kristy remarked, carrying one of her large potted philodendra to the back for David to lift it in and place it amid books, a cello, a large potted areca palm, his easy chair, her lamp. They each had a toaster, a microwave, a powerful radio; and pillows enough for several people.

"Uprooted?" David slowed in the act of lifting the plant from her hands.

She shrugged and grinned. "Well, unlike these plants, I suppose it's good for us to climb out of our pots and move around the landscape."

David set the pot aside. "You'd be pretty spooked to see palms and rubber trees walking around on a foggy morning."

She shivered, crossing her arms and rubbing her elbows.

They trailer-hitched the Ferrari and rode the 3000 plus miles together in the cab. The greenery of the Northeast gave way to the flatness and increasingly yellowish, wheat colored aridity of the Midwest. Then came the rising grade into the Rockies. Snow still drifted across the high-up highways of Wyoming. In Idaho, the land was potato-brown, lumpy, cramping even the rich blue sky. Then, as they headed further into the Pacific Northwest, it got green again. The Cascades Mountains rose up before them and fell back behind them, as they entered into heavily wooded lands. Tree crowns stretched from horizon to horizon, visible at moments when they crossed through the higher passes. The forest surrounded them in surreal gloom as they dropped down into the lower valleys. The deep forest, with its dapples of sunlight, was as turbulent and moody as any of her cello compositions.

The dream of Jimmy Herman still came, but not so often. Sometimes it was the charred officer sitting sitting at his desk. Or it was women in black veils, moving like creatures from another world. Sometimes it was the two I.A.R. generals, looking at him with accusing eyes while their big helicopter burned amid black smoke. Sometimes it was Mo, just talking. The dreams were getting less and less with time.

David and Kristy Gordon lived in Company Grade Officers' Quarters at Fort Lewis. They had a small ranch-style house, a small yard—"a small everything," as Kristy put it. The rainy weather that constantly moved in from the North Pacific was hard on her, but she tried to make the best of it. David worried about her, particularly when he was away on maneuvers, which was often. His primary duty now, as a First Lieutenant, was as Executive Officer of a 180-man mechanized infantry company. That meant the captain, or company commander, delegated to him large part of his responsibilities, including personnel actions, personnel management, courts martial, nonjudicial punishments, and so on. David also was the company's motor pool manager, overseeing the maintenance and repair of a small fleet of assorted cars and humm-vees, three mobile field guns, and six Bradley fighting vehicles. The company's bubble of operations also included a field communications platoon, two squads of artillery specialists to man the field guns, and two large NBC scrubbers (nuclear, biological, and chemical). David was also the unit finance officer, though he had a second lieutenant and a staff sergeant to help with budgetary matters.

David's duties kept him from home for days at a stretch. He missed Kristy terribly, and he worried about her being alone. It pained him to spend a night without her passionate love making. She was hungry for him, and when he could, he'd sneak away for an hour or two from an overnight duty to reassure her, to comfort her when she was lonely, to hold her while she cried, to roll on the floor with her while she breathed hard and grappled him to her and wrapped her legs tightly around him so he could hardly make the rocking motions that would bring them both to climax.

She brought something new into his life. He wasn't sure what to say it was, but when he'd risk punishment by leaving his duties, he knew part of it was a strange intoxication and danger. As he slipped out of his responsible, controlled mind and into her stormy, turbulent world, he actually felt a perverse thrill at taking risks in order to gratify himself sexually.

As they passed the two-year mark, David had had several speakings-to by his company commander. He'd been late for duty several times, and he'd been caught leaving his post as weekend Officer In Charge. Nobody wanted to paper the file of a West Pointer and war hero with reprimands or Article 15's, and he, who had always excelled, began to feel guilty. He felt like an addict. He wanted her but began soberly to realize that she was taking him along a path to ruin. Maybe not death-ruin, but something just as bad—mediocrity. David knew he was not a perfectionist, nor an over-achiever. He'd managed to live a balanced life, enjoying his pleasures, working hard where it was appropriate. Bringing home medals and trophies had always seemed natural to him. He'd enjoyed boxing and running so much that they hadn't seemed like work.

Now, the woman he loved was taking the edge off him. No, he must not blame her. He'd stand by the window at night and stare into the runneling rain and punch his palm with his fist—no, dammit, he blamed himself for blaming her. He must somehow figure out how to manage a situation that was coming apart at the axles.

After two years at Fort Lewis, and the prospect of more years in places even farther away, Kristy announced that she was going home for a while. About a year ago, she'd left a note unexpectedly, saying she was going home to visit her father. Shocked and hurt, David had waited as the hours dragged by, every minute an agony. She'd driven the Ferrari back to Boston. Her dad had driven her to the airport and bought her return ticket to Ft. Lewis. She'd returned to him beaming as if she'd been on a wonderful vacation. She was more energized and sexy and creative than ever, and David had quickly forgotten the two-week nightmare without her.

But she'd begun making a steady succession of trips back to Boston over the past year. She flew home on average once a month for a few days, and it seemed this commuter marriage relieved a lot of her tension. David was so busy he did not have time to think about her and worry and pine for her. She seemed to be maturing, also, becoming a little more settled and thoughtful. David felt that, although their marriage had its difficulties, they were slowly heading in the right direction. She'd steadily remained on birth control, so at least there was not the specter of an unexpected pregnancy, which he felt would have added stresses that neither she nor he could take just now. Sometimes her father flew out to get her, sometimes a cousin, sometimes her aunt Rosa; sometimes she flew out by herself, though she was morbidly afraid of flying alone and took a small stuffed animal in her coat pocket. She liked to also take her cello bow for good luck, whenever she could sneak it through security; once, she'd gotten in a violent fight with a security matron, whom she'd hit with the bow, and David had had to call the airport police and beg to get her released with a warning. The matron had hit Kristy first, it turned out, and no charges were filed on either side. All this, during furious battalion maneuvers in a muddy, rainy forest, David riding on a tank, blinded by rain, poncho slick with water, while he spoke on his lapel com.

Suddenly, on a cold night in December, she called from Boston, on her way back to Fort Lewis, to say that she'd turned around at Logan International Airport and taken a taxi back home to her father's house. "I love you for all the world," she said, "but I need some time to ground myself again. I can't stand all the rain and the trees and the people and the whole thing. Being alone in that house, waiting all day for you to come home at night and make love and then leave again. It's not your fault, darling, and you can come see me here whenever you want."

"But Kristy—"

She'd cut the connection. Staggering, David walked out of the kitchen, where he'd taken the call. His knees were wobbly. The Christmas tree sat blinking on and off, half constructed. A few ornaments were on the tree, but most lay scattered on the carpet in and out of their boxes. An unopened packet of glitter sat to one side. Two empty packets testified that she'd hung all the silvery tinsel streamers. The lights were half up, though two cords of lights streamed across the floor where she'd probably worked to untangle them.

A half-empty tea cup sat by the tree. A squeezed-out tea bag lay in the saucer. An unopened pack of cigarettes lay within arm's reach on the night table. Ah yes, she didn't smoke, but once in a while succumbed when she was under great stress, but she never smoked more than one because they made her vomiting-sick. David studied every inch of this scene, imagining her tension, imagining the tears rolling down her face, the memories of Christmas back home.

She never returned, and one of the most difficult things he'd ever done in his life was forcing himself to stay put, to continue grimly and devastatedly on with his duties, day by day. They spoke one more time, a half year later, a bitter and irrational conversation that ended with her crying hysterically for several minutes while he waited, until he heard the phone rattle into its switchhook as if she'd dropped it with a shaking hand.

David let the phone slip into its cradle. "Sir," he called out.

"Yes?" the captain called from his office across the room.

"If you don't mind, I need to take a walk over to JAG."

The captain stepped out holding a coffee cup. Very military looking in his fatigues and combat boots, he was a blunt paratrooper with a sharp eye. "I know it's none of my freaking business, Gordon, but let me be the first son of a bitch to cheer you on. I only heard your end of this verbal rumpjumpin' just now, and I guess you're the one that's gonna be pregnant from it. I watched your face, man, and I don't think you're ever gonna let that broad muck you up again. If you do, you're not a tenth the man I take you to be."

David took a minute to gasp for words. "Thanks, Sir."

"If you get any notions about flying back to Boston, you'll have to desert, because I'll burn the blasted leave request form on my desk in front of you."

"Actually, I'm going to file for a divorce in the next hour or so, and then I'm going to go check on the spare U-joints for the track vehicles."

"I figured you'd go and get good and drunk."

"I already did that a few months ago. No… If I ask for leave, it's going to be to go camping in the mountains for a few days." He added: "I used to have really bad dreams after Gulf III."

"You too?" the captain said.

David Gordon, 29, was promoted to Captain and reassigned back to the First Infantry Division at Fort Riley. He was jump qualified, but it was time to make a few jumps to renew his certification, and for that he would attend a three-day refresher at the Airborne Training Center in North Carolina, culminating in a jump on the last day.

Proud of the double silver bars that took up much more real estate on his uniform than had his lone lieutenant's bar for so many years, and resplendant with a chest full of awards from his Gulf III service, David reported to Headquarters and Headquarters Company, Ft. Bragg, North Carolina. He was fresh from a two-week leave in Connecticut with his mother and sisters. Though he still longed for Kristy at times, he knew there was no going back. David thought of her sadly each time he saw a famous painting. He could not bear to hear cello music; once, in a coffee bar in Kansas City with a female friend, when a trio of musicians had played, and the cellist in turn had played his solo, David found tears running down his cheeks. The cellist noticed and played all the harder. David's girlfriend, an exchange student from Indonesia, who knew the score, gently ribbed David until he laughed about it, and they tipped the cellist handsomely before leaving. David bet it was an evening the cellist would tell his grandchildren about.

On the third and last day of training, David stood on the flight line with twenty other students, a mix of officers and enlisted, some gray older men and women, others still kids. It was a beautiful spring day. The sky was clear and blue, with smatterings of high cirrus clouds. The sun was bright but did not yet have the piercing heat and crushing humidity of summer in the Southeast. The air was exhilarating to inhale. A wind snapped across the tarmac, making pennants rattle. Several troopers blinked as dust blew in their eyes. Some held their arms up ward off grit that got in their eyes. One small female sergeant bowed her shoulders as if hiding behind her front parachute pack. It was she that David would always remember.

It was fun to be around the big planes. The Air Force kept a fleet of C-130's on hand for training. In the distance, painted gloomy green and surrounded by a haze of blown dust, loomed larger C-141's, C-5's, and C-7's. The change from Fort Lewis was just great, David thought, inhaling the air the smells of mowed grass and aviation fuel.

After a half-hour lecture on safety and procedures, the jumpers trooped aboard double-file. They sat on benches along the inner walls and hooked up. Soon the C-130 taxied down the runway, made a snappy turn in the hands of a cowboy pilot, and roared into the sky. David did a last minute check-out and was satisfied with his equipment. As he waited, he felt the plane buffet in the wind. He frowned. If the winds got too severe, all jumping would be canceled. Evidently, the authorities didn't feel the wind was too severe at this point. Though he'd jumped about a dozen times before, he always felt a little pang in his gut. "Okay, go, go, go!" the jump master said in a calm voice, touching each soldier'shoulder as he or she went out the door. David felt the tap and stepped out into empty air with his arms crossed on his chest. He was rather proud of the fact that, for the first time, he had not flinched, though it was a change like diving into cold water.

That instant of not blinking told him something was wrong.

Seriously wrong.

He heard the jump master shout: "Abort!"

At the same time he saw the plane buck in the air as if a giant sand bag had hit it.

He felt himself spin dizzily as the demon fist of turbulent air whacked him. One more person had come out the door after him, and that person was spinning head over heels out of control.

David fought to stabilize himself. In the silence and freedom of free-fall, with the wind in his ears, he watched the giant plane recede. No more bodies spilled from its bay. The plane majestically banked right, pitching the left wing up in a marvelously graceful gesture for a whale that size, and headed back to Pope Air Force Base.

David was ready to deploy his main chute, but he hesitated. The woman who had ejected after him had already popped her chute, but it didn't seem to be deploying right. He recognized her as the small sergeant who'd been bowing her shoulders against the wind. She did not recognize him—she was screaming, eyes filled with terror. He and she were headed on a collision course. If he opened now, they would tangle and perhaps both be killed.

Heart beating—now was no time to lose control—he looked down. Already, the green hills with their brown tops were getting closer.

Seconds.

He had seconds to do something.

There was nothing to do but lie back, waiting for her to pass.

Then, her reserve chute opened. From about two hundred feet away, David saw her terrified face as she clawed at her equipment. The reserve chute might have yanked the lines on her main chute straight. That did not happen. It slowed her, though, and pulled her into a different trajectory.

Already the brown mountain tops were getting closer and closer.

David popped both chutes and felt the yank throughout his entire body, the swinging, the sudden thank-God slowing. Dazed from the deceleration, he shook his head and saw he was headed into the fringes of the jump zone. Struggle as he might, he could not avoid the trees that drew all too rapidly close.

As he threw his body and kicked to steer the chutes, he heard a snapping or popping sound. Whirling helplessly, he saw her, seconds after impact. Her body was like a rag thing thrown under the billowing nylon and tangled lines of her crippled chute. He glimpsed her oddly twisted legs and arms, and the way her helmet was pushed into her back, and he knew with a sick feeling...

The tree limb was about a foot thick and David barely glimpsed the scars and warts on its silvery bark as he crashed through a sea of leaves and snapping twigs. Horrified, he arched backwards so that he would not hit his face as he came down.

His lower half wasn't so lucky. He felt the breath knocked out of him and darkness swallowing him up as his feet came down on the limb. His body continued downward unchecked, but his legs snapped upward and then followed his body as he plunged head-first toward the ground.

He—a being that was dimly conscious of itself—had been here before, in this swimming red and yellow blur, where sharp pain alternated with drowsy, nauseous blackness filled with lights. He, this being, dimly remembered something about swimming up to a light. It was called being born. He was being born. This being swam upward to the light and the voices. At times the voices spoke loudly, at other times softly.

Before he opened his eyes, David knew he could not move. Not even his fingers. Not his head. Nothing. Dread made his skin crawl. Am I quadriplegic? Am I finished? He kept seeing that helmet pushed into the woman's back, severing her spine. Why am I not dead? He was afraid. No, terrified to open his eyes.

He withdrew, tried to swim back down into the sea of narcotics, went back to deep sleep.

A loud bang made him open his eyes before he could remember to be scared and now it was too late.

A stream of sunlight came into his room where everything was white. A plump woman in a blue jacket, with dark curly hair, had just filled the towel dispenser over the sink and slammed its door shut.

"Ah—"

She turned. "Oh, you're awake. Well, it's about time."

David was about to ask where he was, when the pain slammed through him and he closed his eyes. He strained his body as the pain continued. This wasn't just a sharp pain. This was a continual, mangling agony that came in waves, as if a giant were wringing him out like a towel.

He heard several pairs of feet come running. The bars on the side of his bed lowered with a crash as hands reached out to do things. A lovely blonde nurse reached up and adjusted the IV bag hanging over his bed, and soon he felt a soothing, relaxing numbness in his legs. "Where am I?"

She turned to him, and she seemed to have a halo of sunshine around her head. For a moment he thought it was Kristy, but no. This woman had similar flingy, heavy, straight blonde hair, but it was cut differently. Instead of an exotic Mediterranean face, this woman had a crisp, fresh Englishy beauty. She had a light dusting of freckles along a sharp, delightful nose, and she spoke with a faint Southern something... "I am Captain Maxine Lee Bodley, and I am the head nurse on this ward. Welcome."

"What's wrong with me?" He felt terrified.

She looked at his chart. "You have two broken legs, four broken ribs, a sprained back, a broken collarbone, a sprained arm, a lot of bruises, and probably a genuine case of fright that will turn into an extreme gladness to be alive once I assure you that you'll be just fine in about six months."

"Thank you," he said, wishing he could crawl out of the bed on his knees and kiss her hands. "Thank you."

She stroked his head. "Now, don't thank us yet. Your legs are the big worry. We may have to re-break them at some point if they aren't healing right. You're going to be a very sick fellow for a while. You're on morphine, which is going to make you—" (she poked a cute little finger in her lipsticked mouth) "—yuckie, barfie." The way she said it, it just seemed natural that a woman like this would say something like that without being ridiculous. She had quick, busy arms and hands as she folded sheets and tucked pillows around him. I hope you weren't leading a busy life or anything, because you're going to be doing a lot of reading here on your back."

David tried to remember. It was a blur. The tree. Before then—a lump on the grass, tangled chute writhing over still body... "There was a woman..."

"Dear, there always is a woman."

He shook his head. "God, I think she was killed."

Captain Bodley frowned, realizing he was serious. Her freckles drew near. Her skin had a faint, marvelous rose blossom smell. "When you jumped?"

He nodded.

Her eyes widened. "Yes, I remember reading something in the paper. There was a parachutist killed, a woman. My God, you saw it?"

He licked his lips. "Just a second after. Then I hit the tree."

She rubbed his lips with a kind of lollypop—a stick with a wad of material wet with some sour lemon concoction that made his mouth water. "I'm sorry you saw that. It must have been awful."

He flashed back to Gulf III. Saw again the melted remains of Jimmy Herman embedded in the seat springs. Saw again the bodies lying around where his platoon had been. Saw again the woman's flattened body under the chute. War was one thing. Civilian life, even on an Army post in peacetime... no place to die.

He felt Captain Bodley stroking his cheeks as he fell asleep. Her touch was soft and healing. A warmth like sunshine glowed from her baby-soft palms. This warmth filled his body like a reliquary of light, a burning oil lamp, a peaceful leaf blown upward by the wind into the sun. He was so grateful that he was alive, and that he would walk again. He thought, also, that he was falling in love with his nurse.

Patients came and went, but David stayed. He took two courses offered in the hospital through the University of North Carolina at Chapel Hill, one on Elizabethan Poets and the other on World Geography. He was still a patient at the hospital, but now lived at the BOQ and only spent three or four hours a day at Womack for doctor visits and Physical Therapy. His wounds were healing nicely, bones all knitted together, but he was permanently disqualified from service-connected parachute jumping. For a worrisome few weeks, he waited for a determination about his future in the Army. His slot at Fort Riley had been filled, and he was subject to medical evaluation over his injuries. The doctors had reassured him he was 95% likely for retention, especially with his West Point background.

David dated Captain Bodley, kind of. At 29, she was two years his senior. She was from a very wealthy Virginia family. There was absolutely nothing sexual about their friendship, and somehow he accepted this, knowing it was a part of him that needed mending. She was a healer, a nurturer, and he felt his trust of women being restored.

Maxie, as she refered to be called, also loved to have a good time. She was a beautiful woman, and he was not ashamed to be seen with her. David sensed, and she had hinted with weary resignation, that there was someone in her life, but since she spent so much time alone, David could not at first figure out what lay at her core. She thought nothing of wrapping herself around his arm and pressing close to his side as they jumped laughingly over rain puddles on their way to an evening movie. She thought nothing of going swimming with him at the Atlantic shore 100 miles from Ft. Bragg, and she was indeed a turn-on. She was smallish, and thin, but athletic, wiry, with twisty muscular legs and tight small buttocks. The blue and white striped bikini she wore that day left little to the imagination—small firm breasts, a flat belly with almost invisible silvery peach fuzz hair, smooth vanilla skin, that pinewood-yellow hair that twirled as she walked. She was a good sport, and much fun. But no sex. Just a dry brush of the lips at the end of a date. One evening in the doorway at her rented house in Fayetteville, they'd started kissing. He'd felt the tip of her tongue hungrily pressing into his mouth. She was breathing audibly, and pressed against him. Nobody could mimic Kristy's wild expressiveness, the fire with which she burned and branded her lover, so he did not expect it from Maxie. And it wasn't there. On most days, Maxie was cool sunlight. She reminded him of clean linen, always cool to the touch, fragrant, reasonable.

David had just one moment when he felt her passion, and that was still cool by Kristy's standard. During a doorway kiss goodnight one evening, David was startled by Maxie's hard breathing, her little moan, the tip of her tongue between his lips—and no leg wrapped around his leg—he was just as startled by her pushing away. "No!" she whispered distraughtly. She turned back to him, huddled in her coat, and fumbled with her key.

"I'm sorry," he said.

"It's not your fault. I'm sorry." She turned ruefully. "Good night, David. Call me soon." With that she stepped inside.

He did call her next day, to apologize again, but she rambled brightly on about the movie they'd seen last night. And he went out with her again, but did not even try. Somehow, it was just great to be with Maxie. It was just enough to be near her, to feel good. He was still healing—his legs, his ego, and she was good for both those things.

David was called to the Adjutant General's office at

Ft. Bragg a few weeks after starting to walk again. He was directed to the Career Management Office, and made his way along semi-dark corridors with some misgivings. After asking civilian and enlisted clerks for directions, he found himself knocking at a door marked CMO/OIC. A voice hailed for him to enter, and he did.

"Close that door behind you, Captain." He faced a graying light-skinned black lieutenant colonel, small and bony, with a crooked nose and a lot of paratroop-related decorations on his Class A uniform jacket. He stuck out his hand. "Richard Sutcliff, West Point Class of 1985. Sit down and get comfortable."

David shook the hardened paw."Thank you, Sir." He sat on a hard wooden chair.

Sutcliff sat back in a huge brown leather chair too large for him. He was surrounded by bookcases full of Army Regulations, D.A. Pams, Technical Instructions, and so on. "How are the legs?"

"Getting better, thank you."

"They treating you all right at Womack?"

He thought of Maxie. "It's been a great experience."

Sutcliffe raised an eyebrow. He had bright, inquisitive, and somehow tired or skeptical eyes. "You are an enthusiastic man, given why you are there."

"I was lucky to make a few good friends."

Sutcliff sat forward. "One Pointer to another, son, I'll do my best to take care of you." Sutcliff shook out a pair of regulation black plastic eyeglasses and put them on. He looked as if he'd only recently begun wearing glasses and couldn't get used to them. "Here's my problem, son. Hear me out, and don't storm out of here, okay? You will not be allowed to stay on active Infantry duty."

David's heart sank. He'd had some worries and doubts on this score, but hadn't believed his luck could actually be so bad.

"We have the medical board's determination. Were you planning to be a great battlefield commander?"

David reddened. "I wasn't counting on it, but I didn't want to rule it out."

"Don't worry about it. This isn't the end of the world. I've been on the phone a good deal today." He flickered a faint smile for the first time. "One Pointer to another."

"Thanks. I really appreciate it." Whatever the man was doing.

"You're a captain and you don't have the requisite time in grade or service to merit special relief under today's regulations. I looked through all your very impressive Gulf III awards and decorations, and I couldn't quite make them work for you in this situation, although the combination of West Point and distinguished battlefield service will always count for you. Now, how attached are you to those crossed Infantry rifles on your lapels?"

"I would rather stay Combat Arms than anything, Sir."

"That's what I figured. Technically, the only way I can keep you on active duty under today's regulations is by reassigning you to another specialty or corps, outside Combat Arms. That rules out Armor, Infantry, Artillery, and Air Defense Artillery. I can put you just about anywhere else except Chaplain, Medical, Nursing, those sorts of things. How would you feel about, say, Transportation? You can be part of the battlefield."

David swallowed hard. This was not where he'd hoped it was going.

Sutcliff made a brief pointing gesture. "Hang on. I may have a solution yet. See, if you were a major, I could get you on some general staff as an Infantry officer. I mean, shit, you've done your combat time. And now the legs. You're one banged-up trooper. But here's what I think I can do. There's a new circus in Washington. It's called the Composite Force, and it's brand-new. It's being fielded to support the Second Constitutional Convention, or CON2. The Composite will have 20,000 troops and officers from all branches of the service, including large Army Reserve components. The Pentagon seems to think that, with the riots that keep flaring up, and the controversial nature of the convention, it will be best to over-protect it. Here's the great thing. The Composite is expected to be disbanded after six months, because the Convention won't go on that long. At least we all hope it won't. So, what I can do for you is buy you time. I can get you assigned Temporary Duty, TDY, to the Composite, starting soon, so you might buy a year of time. Who knows. You get to keep your Infantry status at least that long, and maybe you can do the mile in four minutes or some shit by then and take a poke at a Combat Arms assignment. You'll have more time and grade and that might work for you."

"What kind of job did you have in mind for me, Sir?"

"I'm gonna recommend one to you, but there are others, and you can take your pick. I'm gonna recommend an I.G. assignment, and let me tell you why I think Inspector General Corps would be best for you. Most of those poor bastards are either going to be sitting in tents in Rock Creek Park, or else they'll be cooped up in the Atlantic Hotel and Convention Center, which will be packed to the gills and you'll have to wait in lines a block long just to find a urinal. With the assignment I have in mind, you're independent, which is the nature of Inspector General. You'll have an off-post housing allowance. In other words, my man, you can commute to work and live like a human being in a city that will be even more insane than usual while they destroy our Constitution." He flipped David's records shut.

David held up his arms. "You've convinced me, Sir."

Sutcliff looked grim, or bleak, or cynical, or whatever; he appeared to be a complex man, with a cross on his back and a chip on his shoulder. "We've gotta get approval from D.A. That could take two weeks, and they can still say no."

One evening, Maxie came to meet David at Physical Therapy. He had just finished his exercises, had his jacket on—civvies—and was on his way out. She met him in the hall, wearing her white nurse's uniform with Army insignia and captain's bars. Cap rakishly tilted over one eye, she swung her purse and looked mischievous. "Hi, David."

"Oh, hey!" He was glad to see her. It was shift change, but for propriety's sake, they never met at the hospital (as if there were anything to hide). "What are you grinning about?"

They fell in together, headed for the door. "I got something for you," she teased sing-song. She grinned from ear to ear.

"Okay?"

"But you gotta pay."

"I'm not paying until I know what you got."

"Fair enough. We'll make it an even trade. You buy me dinner this evening, and I'll give you what I got."

"I'm not paying until I know what you got."

"That's fair. After I give you what I got, you'll want to pay."

"You drive a hard bargain, lady. Luckily, I'm a soft touch."

"You are indeed a soft touch, and I'm very glad about it." She slipped her arm around his. They walked down the main steps, David still a little stiffly and holding the rail. "I'm gonna run home and change. Meet me at Tammie's? I'm in the mood for a steak and a martini."

"Uh-oh, red meat and hard liquor, huh? This sounds serious."

"See you there." Her parting glance, in a glitter of blue eyes, under a rakishly tilted green garrison cap, was at once mischievous, calculating, sad, and happy.

In keeping with their buddy relationship, they took separate cars.

Tammie's was a big steak house on the edge of town, with couples and families taking numbers and waiting in line. David and Maxie had eaten there before; he liked the New York steak. She liked the Roast Beef with sour cream and horse radish. Both orders came with baked potato and sour cream, a vegetable, and a length of French bread. As they sat waiting in the bar, she had a martini. She liked to drink, he noticed. The martini was too strong for him, and he preferred a beer. She handled it well—and oh

Jesus, for a nurse, she smoked! He was almost glad they weren't into French kissing.

She grinned with square little white teeth visible between thin glossy rouge lips in a wide mouth. "So, David, I got."

"You got, and presumably I want." He touched her nose with his fingertip. The freckles were invisible in the bar light, and he admired the delicately curved crest of her nose.

She made a half-shrug, half-laugh, exhaling smoke, and flicked her cigarette ash in an ash tray. "Okay, I'll tell you. If you don't like it, you don't have to pay for dinner. I'll pay, just as a way for apologizing."

"I may make you pay just for teasing me along so much."

"You know that I know people, right? I mean, my family is connected everywhere. We had colonels in both sides in the Civil War, for Chrissake—"

"—Never generals—"

"—Never generals," she said, fielding his teasing without missing a beat. "In the South, Generals become famous, but Colonels own land. We had officers in the Revolutionary War. Colonel Francis Lee Bodley stood right next to George Washington at the surrender of Cornwallis. Anyway, so I have an uncle who is a Navy Admiral who knows the Brigadier General and Chief of Staff of the Adjutant General's Office. I was having dinner with my uncle a few days ago, so I mentioned you, and—"

"Oh no."

"I'm sorry, I couldn't help it. I like to help people. Anyway, so I found out that your TDY to Washington has been approved."

"Oh wow!"

"Congratulations, David." She held out a small hand. "I'll miss you."

"Wow. I'll miss you too." He stared at her, mystified. "Jesus H. Christ."

She thought for a moment. "I'd like to explain about last week. The kiss."

"Oh, yeah. That."

"I—" She halted. "—Don't discuss these things with anyone, because people tend to get mad at me. And I don't often really like someone the way I like you." She cleared her throat. "Anyway, here goes. I have never been married, David. And I'd like to get married more than anything else. But my parents are very wealthy and I'm an only child, and they programmed me so that I can only marry a certain type of man. I am attracted to men with money and power, but I don't think I've ever met one I loved. What I mean is, I love them and then they dump me. Oh dammit!" She stubbed out her cigarette in little furious motions. "I am actually engaged to one right now, but he calls me about once a week, and I'm sure he's having affairs right and left. He's the CEO of a magazine publishing company, probably worth fifty million. I'd be nice hood ornament for him, that's probably all."

David felt mortified for her. "Maxie, dump the scumbag. Now."

She shook her head. "That's the kind of men we have in our family. They may be scumbags but they are rich, powerful men. I know this sounds terrible and I hope you won't hate me and I do pray you'll forgive me. It's not my idea. It's just how I am and if you're really my friend you'll accept me for who I am." She looked ready to cry.

He started to take her hands in his. "Maxie, if this is too hard, don't—"

"No!" Her eyes were glittering, determined points of liquid light. She rubbed shaking fingers across her face as tears twirled toward the ground. "I need to tell you, because you are my friend, and I was so worried that I might have hurt your feelings."

"Well—"

"I did, didn't I?"

"No, you puzzled me. Yes, no, I just stubbed the big toe of my ego a little, maybe. Or maybe I lusted for you. And I think you lusted for me."

"I—" She looked down, seemed to collapse inwardly. "All right. I did lust for you." She pawed in her purse, laying various things on the table—worn platinum lighter, hankie, lipstick, driver's license, pencil stub, key ring with a million keys on it—"aha!" until she found a fresh pack of cigarettes. "For about five minutes in that doorway." She lit up and waved the smoke away. "No, honestly, all that evening. I could have, er—" she paused—"I would have gladly lit your candle for you, but I can't. I think too much of us as friends to do the cheap thing. I couldn't just casually—well, I don't know if you can see it, but our friendship would never be the same again. I'd hate myself and run from you. I really, really need to deeply love the person I sleep with, and I've never met anyone like that. I'm afraid my early experiments with sexual liberation were—well, very nauseating."

"That's sweet. I like that about you. I'm pushing back the wolf part of me."

"You're not ready," she said. "You are one hurt man, David." She knew all about Kristy. "You need time, David. You don't need a lay—well, you're a

154

man, and so I suppose you do—but what you need much more is a friend. A woman who is your friend. Whom you can trust. Who won't hurt you or let you down. And that's me."

"Aw geez, Max, that's a goddam speech." He felt a little misty himself.

"I'm sorry."

"No, no, you're absolutely right. The Colonel asked me why the hell I was so happy about being at Womack, and I told him it was because I made some good friends. I didn't tell him it's one friend, and that it's a woman."

"He might not have understood."

"Maybe not. But I'm glad you understand."

She held his face between her palms, which were soft and warm. "I hope you'll write to me. And maybe we'll be stationed somewhere together one day."

He put his hands over hers. "I hope you find the right guy."

"It's going to be lonely here without you."

CHAPTER 9

COVER

Cover waited on a sodden, windy street corner in Albany, New York. It was a city he'd chosen because he was familiar with it from several visits—and because he wanted this meeting on neutral ground. His new assignment was on, and he had a good plan. He just needed the right help.

Light snowflakes drifted past street lamps above. Everywhere, people were doing a little more shopping before Christmas and hurrying home. The buildings were mostly 19th Century style, and already little snowballs had accumulated on a thousand little cornices and gargoyles and pointy window frames. Nasty weather, this, with the dampness soaking into one's bones. Cover smelled tar and fresh air alternating with auto exhaust; he smelled a whiff of cigarette smoke and another whiff of perfume, a whiff of leather coat or purse as he kept a lookout—there. Cover's hand went to the small .35 automatic in his pocket; at this range, it was the best weapon for his purposes.

A black car slid to the curb. Cover recognized Albert, his handler—all handles, no names here. Albert nodded, and the rear door popped open. Cover looked inside, ready to spray the occupants with light ammo that would sound like innocent popping to passing pedestrians. The car would sit there for five, ten, 15 minutes with steam billowing from the exhaust before someone thought to look inside at a pile of dead bodies. But it was safe, he saw.

Cover showed his hands as he climbed in. He pulled the door shut and the car drove off. Albert, an older white man, rode in the front passenger seat. The driver was his regular man, Ronald, which reassured Cover. Albert said: "I want you to meet your new partner. Shake hands with Trend."

Cover recoiled at the word partner, though Albert had already softened him up at the farm in Kentucky—this job was too important for any lone wolves, and Christ, man, you've proven you're no cowboy, you're the best there is, and this is your big chance to top out and become chief of section...

Still Cover recoiled. The man extending a beefy gray hand looked like some racial gumbo. He had a pasty grayish brown complexion, mud-colored buggy eyes that glittered like those black bumps on beetles, and a small mouth and pushed-in nose. Trend withdrew his hand.

"It's okay," Albert said. "He is of fine Norwegian stock. He has a little melanin problem, and this is as good as plastic surgery could fix him after the fire. They did a good job, I'd say. I think he's downright handsome. Trend, shake Cover's hand. Come on, boys, get along."

Trend spoke in a thick, slurry voice: "Uh-uh. He's got a gun in that left coat pocket. I can smell the oil on his left hand. You're a leftie, aren't you?"

"You ask too many questions."

Trend chortled. "Let me have three minutes in the ring with you, bud. I'll make you a believer."

Albert said: "That's right, get to know each other. Duke it out if you must, but in the end you've got to be buddies. Our management has several juicy jobs lined up for you. I hope you guys like museums, because you're going to spend a lot of time around Washington."

Cover sized his neighbor up and thought, this will be an enjoyable challenge. He stuck his hand out. "You'll get your three minutes."

Trend chortled—the sound of a big man who was used to controlling a situation—stuck out a hand seemingly made of iron. "I can't wait."

CHAPTER 10

LOUIS

Unexpectedly, Louis's fishing and baiting paid off.

Louis received a visitor late one December evening at the Vice President's House on Observatory Circle in Washington. The Secret Service detail did not detain the visitor long: Senator Donald Lomax, Middle Class Party, Virginia. Lomax was Minority Chair of the Foreign Relations Committee.

Meredith and the children were in town—at the moment, the house was in an uproar because the Cardozas were getting ready for their annual vacation in the Cascades Mountains, courtesy the Middle Class Party. Robert Lee Hamilton had donated a large chalet there on private land to the Party Steering Committee, to be used for VIP vacations and various planning functions. It was three p.m. as Senator Lomax rolled up in his black limousine. Meredith was chasing around the house after one or another of the children while maids scurried about and butler-types carried suitcases down into the garage. Archie announced the visitor.

Louis, wearing sweats and thick fur slippers, stepped down into the entrance way wiping his hands on a kitchen towel; he was making applesauce pancakes at his daughter's demand.

Lomax was a heavy set 70ish man with straight white hair that hung just over his ears without seeming messy or too long. As always, he wore conservative clothes—a dark suit and a white shirt, neither of which seemed to fit very well, and a dark red necktie. Louis watched as the Senator lumbered through the light dusting of snow on the asphalt driveway. Lomax had a strange look on his face. "Mr. Cardoza," he said in a strong voice, extending a hand. He seemed in a hurry, and there was something unpleasant in his demeanor, Louis thought—not unpleasant, but not pleased. Unhappy? "Can we talk?"

"Of course." Louis led him upstairs into his small library on the second floor. He waited until Lomax was inside before closing the thick, sound-proof door.

"I know this is unexpected," Lomax said, shifting his bulk uncomfortably in a large, ugly brown leatherette easy chair that Louis hated and never used because it made his skin sticky.

"Not at all, Senator. I appreciate your visit." He sat down and waited.

It became clear after a minute that Lomax was under some great stress. His skin was flushed, his breathing was thick, his eyes seemed wide and glazed. "Can I get you some water, Senator?"

"Yes, please."

Louis felt puzzled as he stepped to the wetbar, went through the motions, and handed a clean glass full of ice cubes and water, veiled in condensation, to Lomax. He noticed Lomax's hands were trembling as he coaxed a sip to his mouth.

Lomax nearly dropped the glass. He set it down abruptly and wiped the back of his hand across his mouth. "Well, I'd better get to the point of my visit."

Louis plopped into his chair. "Take your time."

"There isn't time." Lomax took a pair of heavy-rimmed glasses from his inside suit pocket. He fumbled with the glasses, opened them, propped them on his nose. "You have to do something." He pulled some folded papers from his other inside suit pocket. A small recording disk fell out and rolled across the carpet.

"You keep that," Lomax said sharply. "It's priceless information, but only if you act in time."

"Senator, this is very puzzling."

"I know. Look at these papers." He extended the oft-folded sheets to Louis—three of yellow legal pad paper, three of standard letter size laser printout paper.

Louis glanced at the documents, some written, some typed. "And this is—?"

Lomax stirred in jerky motions, unable to settle down. "Important enough, I think, that you go patch things up with your old party and get to the President. I think you're the only one who might really make an impression on him. He likes you even if his party has you roasting slowly on a spit." Having spoken, the Senator fell back in a tired slump.

Louis read the documents slowly, and sat gaping as their significance became apparent to him. "I have to say I agree with you, Senator," he said after a long silence.

Lomax said: "I envy you, because you have been kept in the dark. You're not part of this. I'm in over my head, and I didn't realize how serious this was until I found out that I'm marked for retirement. Hamilton's not giving me another term. I'm out the door like a worn out shoe, and it makes me pretty bitter. But I'm beyond that now." He pointed to the documents. "I got that through another member of a committee I belong to. My source is unimportant, because he was killed in a car crash this morning, and I don't know if it was an accident."

Louis gasped. "Senator, are we down to—?"

Lomax nodded funereally. "I'm afraid it's come to that."

Meredith was pregnant again, and never looked lovelier.

Louis wanted to spend a day or two with her in blissful enjoyment before all hell broke loose, before he had to act on the Lomax papers and the recording.

Louis and his family played on the snowy slopes around the MCP chalet. Meredith's cheeks glowed and she was full of energy. She was eating well, and she had stamina. In a snowball fight, she actually made him cry uncle. When he was out of breath, she was still running circles in the snow. Louis Jr., Annie, and Albert yelled as they tried to catch their mother.

A couple of times she asked: "Are you okay, Louie? Are you okay, sweetheart? Is something bothering you?" and he'd deny it each time. Then she'd look hurt, and he'd comfort her. He smothered her with cocoa and love and love making.

"You are a real romeo," she said laughing one time as he pulled away from her.

"I've got it all under control again for the first time in a long time, that's why."

For two and a half wonderful days, Louis almost forgot the hell that was Washington. Archie had done his best to surround them with hand-picked, loyal Secret Service staff. Louis had made it clear he wanted no public exposure, and stayed out of view, except for a brief turnout each morning where Meredith and Louis did a smiling, waving walk along the fence to satisfy the rumor mongers in the media that all was well.

On the second evening of his stay, Louis and his family stood sight-seeing on the helipad, watching the black ocean of an Arctic storm wheel in. Dark gray snow clouds rolled silently across a brilliant tapestry of stars. A fog reached the helipad and crept around their ankles. The temperature dropped a few degrees, and the fog was replaced by thick, whirling snow flakes. The Cardozas went inside.

Archie signaled. It was time. Louis had briefed Archie.

Louis sat with his family by the roaring fire. He held Meredith in his arms, while Louis Jr. demonstrated his guitar playing skills and Annie fought with Albert. To tame the situation, Louis laid out a Monopoly game from the Ready Room downstairs, and for several hours the family lost themselves in a game. Louis Jr. and Meredith were the last ones in the game, until Meredith landed on Boardwalk, where Louis Jr. cleaned her out.

4:30 p.m. The sun, a swollen marble wrapped in frosty breath, winked out. The baby blue sky turned black, speckled with a million points of light. There were so many stars that one could not recognize any of the constellations. They might as well be someplace a million light years from home.

High in the Cascades Mountains, Bryson Airfield had gotten a foot of new snow during the past 24 hours. As long as the Vice President was in town, the airfield had to be kept open. As long as it snowed, a special Air Force detachment kept snowplows, sanding trucks, and hummers running up and down the main runway. The Vice President's twin-engine jet sat in a hangar awaiting his command while he spent what was supposed to be a two-week winter vacation with his wife and children at the Middle Class Party's secure chalet.

Five p.m. At Bryson Airfield, argon aviation lamps sketched lines of light across the valley floor, growing more noticeable as night fell. High above the airfield, cliffs towered from horizon to horizon, topped by pine forest.

At a point on the edge of the cliffs, the Middle Class Party's chalet glowed like a cozy yellow lantern. The chalet's upper floors gave the illusion of being airy and light, though composed of bullet-proof glass, and of missile-deflecting steel beams made to look like wood. The lower structure was an undisguised concrete redoubt anchored in mountain granite, capable of sustaining a small army of Secret Service personnel and military advisors. All day long, wind-borne snow looked like white fog over wooded ridges. Snowflakes plummeted past mountain walls, past pines at the edges of cliffs, down into a black abyss, into valleys that were not only the lair of wolf and bear, but also of humans with a relentless hatred of the Government—and the means to strike. In the concrete redoubt, narrow slits covered in thick glass formed observation windows. Telescopes oscillated back and forth all day and night, sending streams of visual data to the chalet's central data processing unit, where pattern recognition engines churned the pixels at multigigahertz clock speeds, looking for predetermined threat patterns—anything from an incoming missile to a human figure approaching from where it shouldn't. On top of the chalet, by the helipad, in a glass cube, were two other lookouts—human, with powerful wide-field binoculars, backing up the machines.

5:30 p.m. As evening deepened into night, the snow storm passed by leaving blanketed and stunned silence under a night sky.

Louis sat back and inhaled the cedar fragrance coming from a closet, the freshness of mountain air leaking under an unlocked window, the very leather smell of the new wallet his children had given him for his recent birthday. He pulled the wallet out to look at it, and found it drenched in sweat. History would remember him as a man who had done the right thing.

6:00 p.m. The storm outside had died away. Louis stared through the second-story office window across a pristine landscape of pine forests and rugged mountains smothered in snow. Like the passing of the storm, his anguish evaporated.

He spoke into a collar com button, asking Archie

to order a jet from Bryson to Seattle, and thence Air Force Two to Washington D.C. within the hour.

6:30 p.m. The storm blew away into Idaho and points East. The clear night air was crisp and still like ice water. A full moon's mercurial light glowed on snowy mountain peaks which in turn illumined surly cloud bottoms. About nine p.m., the helipad atop the chalet received a phone call from the Secret Service chief special agent on station. The Vice President wanted to fly out immediately. The helipad control center replied that the helicopter would be grounded for several hours because water had gotten into the fuel. Could another chopper be flown up from Bryson, the chief special agent asked. No, was the reply, because there was only one helipad, and the disabled chopper sat on that. Next, the chief agent called the motor pool. Yes, he was told, two vans would be available immediately. It was five miles to Bryson by the winding, switchback road, which could be done in less than hour, provided the road were plowed.

In a sky the color of blue ink, a few stars seemed dipped in silver and left to float. A stray snowflake drifted down, but the rug of clouds was moving east. From the chalet's garage, a county snowplowing truck started down the winding road to the airport.

7:00 p.m. A plow scraped as the truck crawled along, piling snow on top of older snow to one side, while the sander left circles of grit on the road. The truck's headlights and red warning lights looked lost amid mountains of piled snow.

7:30 p.m. Louis finished speaking with Meredith in

their family quarters, telling her as much as he could of the situation. She was visibly shaken, but determined not to reveal her fear to the children, who played in another room. "Do you want us to come with you?"

"No," he said. "You'll be safe here. I want you to stay here the whole week. By then this will be over one way or the other, and we can return to Montecito."

He returned alone to his office, locked the door, turned on a microphone, and walked to the window. Looking at the clear black sky, he wished it would snow again. He remembered snow sleeting down silently and constantly like a cosmic morphine, and he wished time would stand still. But it didn't, and he began to speak. His hands were cold, and trembled as he held the mike. "Mr. President, I must speak with you about a matter so grave that I am going to fly out from Bryson tonight to see you. I cannot call ahead because I don't know who is listening. I am going to forward this message to my personal computer in Washington so that I can be sure it's there. I'm also going to carry the message on disk in my pocket. We must talk tomorrow. It's about CON2. I believe there is a grave conspiracy in the air, and I have documentation about it, plus a list of names of men who are involved. These men must be watched closely. And, Cliff, the coming constitutional convention must be stopped. I know you all see me as a defector, and we both understand the atmosphere. That is not important anymore. This is not about my party or yours. This is about the country, and it's very serious." He finished the message and forwarded the file to himself at Observatory Circle.

As Louis sat on the couch putting on his winter boots and ski parka, there was a knock on the door. "Come in!" he shouted in a fresh voice.

Archie Cooper stepped inside, holding an Ablass 414 Spider assault rifle pointing up, the frame-only stock resting on his hip. He wore an olive green wood watch cap, and white winter warfare camo and gear. "We're ready, Mr. Vice President."

No more time to waste. Louis zipped up his heat-retentive middle garments, and pulled white camouflage overall over those. "Let's go."

As they rattled down the huge circular staircase into the main lobby, Archie said: "I've got two vans out front and two six person details including myself. We are fully armed and ready to roll, Sir. Airport's open, and the Lear Tandem is being warmed up on the runway."

"Good work, Archie. Keep slugging."

"We'll wait for you under the portico, Sir." Cooper clomped out the door, the assault rifle looking toy-like against his long frame.

Meredith, wearing jeans, a sweater, and jogging shoes—she'd primped a little, knowing she'd be seen, bless her—ran out holding something. "Honey, your hat!" She pulled the wool watch cap down and zipped his overalls up. He kissed her passionately, then hugged Louis Jr. and Annie. Albert was already in bed, asleep, and Louis took the time to go plant a kiss on his sleeping son. Then he ordered the two older ones: "Go to bed, kids. I'll see you in Santa Barbara next week. Have fun sledding in the morning."

"Yay Daddy!" the children said clapping. "We'll miss you. We love you."

Meredith gave him a desperately tight hug and

whispered through gritted teeth: "Please be careful, darling."

He squeezed her and whispered: "I will."

In the horseshoe drive stood the two vans to take him back down to civilization. A dozen Secret Service men and women waited for him, dressed similarly to Archie. Looped over their snowsuits were added nylon ammo belts and quick-loader ammo cylinders. They carried assault rifles with night scopes and flash suppressors. Running engines blew milky vapor from trembling tail pipes.

Archie stepped close. "We go in Van Two, Sir."

"Okay." He climbed up into the spacious van, knowing it was the shell game—nobody must know until the last minute which vehicle the VIP would be in.

The ride down was slow but smooth, in contrast with the numbness and chaos in Louis's mind. Snow muffled bumps in the road. The van smelled of machine oil, upholstery, leather, aftershave. It was warm and dark with glowing green and amber dash displays. Layers of plowed snow formed walls on either side of the narrow road. Louis sat in the middle seat of the rear van, flanked on all sides by agents. Archie sat in the other aisle, his rifle between his knees. His eyes were on the road behind, scanning for any signs of danger.

The agents around Louis kept a wary watch. The heater was on, and Louis was a little drowsy now from all of his frenzied deliberation. He felt worn out from worry, and was glad this would not go on much longer.

It was quiet in the van as it crunched gently down the dark slope, blackness enveloping them on the sides as the cones of the headlights probed on ahead.

The red lights of the van in front flicked on and off as the driver feathered his brakes on slippery spots.

Suddenly, Louis was stunned by a bang and a flash on the road.

"Rocket!" shouted an agent.

"Mountain men!" Louis heard Archie yell into his lapel com. "Base! Base! We're under attack!"

Louis cringed amid a rattle of gunfire.

Louis heard another bang, saw a flash as a second rocket found its mark and the front van exploded. Louis's eardrums rang, and his head felt as though he'd been punched. In a daze, in a dream, he noticed the agents snap into blurring motion around him. One agent jumped to his feet, Colt AR-115 in the air. Another agent sprang forward, speaking into his collar button. Several agents clicked the safeties off on their assault guns and formed a wall crouching around Louis. Archie stood towering above them, shouting orders, holding his assault rifle ready. "Get down, Sir. Get these doors open, on the double. Let's all bail out."

All around, it rained dark, heavy objects that turned out to be car parts, guns, shoes....

Archie kicked open the door and jumped outside, swallowed up by the darkness. "Come on!" he yelled to Louis.

A rear half-axle from the front van, with the wheel and the tire still attached, came down and hit Archie in the back. He went down fast, eyes closed, and did not stir.

As in a dream, Louis felt the cold coming in.

Streams of assault rifle bullets made pinging noises as they streamed into the vehicle from all sides, even through the thin metal skin.

Louis tried to move, but he couldn't. He felt the weight of four or five dead agents pinning him down. He could hardly breathe.

Louis heard a shouted command, everything got very still.

The air smelled sweet and cold, like a candy made of fresh snow. That was how winter had smelled during his childhood in the Laguna Mountains. It was a smell as wonderful as freshly baked bread.

Figures in white snow suits advanced out of the forest. With their helmets under white covers, and black, round goggle lenses, they resembled aliens. Their boots crunched on the sanded snow.

The air began to smell of things burning. Of gun powder. Of singed flesh.

An owl hooted in the surrounding pine forests and mountains.

Louis breathed peppery gunsmoke as he lay with his cheek on the freezing cold steel floor. He still could not move. He realized that he must have taken several bullets in the lower spine, because he had no feeling from the waist down. And the warmth on his face was the fresh blood of the dead men on top of him flowing together in a metallic, sticky river, over Louis's cheek, down his nose, and onto the metal floor where small droplets began to haze over in freezing.

Louis's left eye seemed to be hazing over, also, and his right eye felt blurry. He was able to focus about a foot away on a pair of black combat boots that stood on the gleaming, scuffed floor of the van.

Louis saw snow melting on scuffed toes, making

tiny puddles amid the grit. The owner of the boots squatted down. The man wore white, an angel of death.

Louis looked into the muzzle of an assault rifle. He knew that now for him the universe was a space exactly as big as the span between his head and that muzzle. It was a universe whose age could be expressed in seconds, free now of the objects and energies that cluttered space and time in larger universes. The man who hunched aiming, squeezing the trigger, looked surprisingly young, like a preppy law school grad with a wide friendly smile, prematurely thinning blond hair, and steel rimmed glasses.

Louis's thoughts turned to God, then wandered to Meredith, and Louis Jr., and Annie, and Albert. They smiled at him like a family portrait. He was smiling when the assault rifle bucked and the muzzle flashed and the sun went nova before everything collapsed into nothingness.

Snowy surfaces flickered red and yellow as the vans burned, each twisted chassis with a wheel or two still attached. Rubber, upholstery, clothing, and bodies soaked with oil and gasoline burned. Vietnam War era rifles stopped popping like strings of firecrackers, leaving the silent air acrid with gunsmoke. Shadowy men in black goggles and white winter camouflage moved off into the wilderness, swallowed up just as mysteriously as they had appeared. Every detail seemed authentic, pointing to mountain men and garage militias, mimicking their hatred of Arabs, Jews, Feminists, Catholics, Evolutionists, and other agents of the U.N. who were taking over America.

CHAPTER 11

DIRECTORY Z

Senator Donald Lomax, after leaving the Vice President's House on Observatory Circle, had his driver take him home to his ten room house in Falls Church. A widower whose children were grown and long gone from home, Lomax lived alone. He had only his Senate seat to live for, and now they were going to take that from him. It wasn't right, any of what they were doing. Lomax took great care to feed his three little old rheumy-eyed dogs, the oldest of which he'd had for 15 years. He and they grown old together, so to speak. Somehow, old age had come quickly after Lomax's wife had passed. He went about the quiet house, puttering, fussing, making sure all the doors were locked and bolted. He mashed up their dinners in three little bowls, as they'd been accustomed since his wife had still lived. Senator Lomax, wearing slippers on the cold tile floor, and wearing his bathrobe, stood in the kitchen waiting until the little dogs stopped twitching, one by one, and lay still on the kitchen floor. He took his .38 special from the kitchen drawer. He walked through the pantry and into the solarium in back. There, across a wintry landscape, he could see the many stars winking in a clear black sky. He was in no hurry, but in time he brought the gun up and put the muzzle up against the roof of his mouth. He breathed evenly and calmly, almost as if asleep. Staring into the lovely innocence and purity of eternity, he pulled the trigger.

Before dawn, U.S. Government police in plain clothes knocked on the door of the Vice President's House at Observatory Circle. Displaying a court order and their badges, they sent the distraught Secret Service agents packing and took over. By noon, they were still going over the house an inch at a time, looking for evidence. The Vice President's computer had been searched minutely, but not even a shadow or a pointer remained of any of the files the experts thought might be on his hard drive. To be sure, they used magnets to degauss all drives and floppies in the office, and then reformatted what they did not haul away in evidence boxes that would be conveniently stashed and forgotten in some Justice Department basement.

The only fly in anyone's ointment was the message Vice President Cardoza had sent to himself. The Vice President's message and the attached list of names traveled at light speed from the mountain chalet to a relay in Bryson. There they joined other data routed to a fiber-optic relay station in Missoula, Montana. The storm system had knocked out a power station in Missoula, so amid a burst of other data the e-message streaked to a com satellite rolling 38,000 miles above the earth. The solar powered moonlet mirrored the data down to a transponder in Gander, Newfoundland. Cruising along a fiber-optic stream through New York City, and Roanoke, the memo flashed into the nation's capital and joined other traffic heading into the computer network linking the Vice President's (Admiral's) House to the Government info net. Just as the Vice President stepped out of the chalet and hugged his children, the e-message joined a queue in the local data stream. Somewhere in the capital, a squirrel gnawed on a cable, killing itself and forcing a switch to close. For two seconds, parts of the net browned down, running on minimum power in backup mode. The system did a self-check at a million terraflops per second and made a backup copy of every file, including the Vice President's message, to store in a temporary database. By the time the Vice President stepped into the van outside the chalet, the browndown was over, hardly noticed, little more than a brief flicker of lights. The Washington net resumed full operation. The original message streaked into the Vice President's computer in Washington, which would be accidentally, perhaps not, cleared of all files the next morning when Federal police began to shut down the building as part of the investigation. In an underground bunker near the Library of Congress was the city's temporary backup database. There, 125,000 ceramic super-chips, each the size and shape of a piece of writing paper and with its own read/write interfaces, hung stacked pagoda-style amid power and relay buses in mid-air. The atmosphere in the bunker was chilled to near zero degrees to prevent overheating the circuits; it was heavy in nitrogen to prevent condensation. Technicians walking the catwalks wore silvery atmosphere suits with oxygen tanks on their backs. Articulated tubes carried their exhaled breath to a plastic bag worn on the belt; here and there steam leaked from the breathing apparatus. The walls were lined with ceramic composites to block outside electromagnetic fields. In this eerie and inhuman environment lived the backup copy of the Vice President's memo, amid bank records, personnel files, department store transactions, military purchase receipts, payroll ledgers, every recordable transaction in modern life. The backup of the Vice President's memo sat in a storage chip whose virtual address was Carousel 49, Directory Z.

ANN Breaking News with Allison Miranda

ALLISON: We have this breaking story from Washington State. The Secret Service confirms Vice President Louis Cardoza has been killed in a savage assault by an unknown private militia, who ambushed a convoy carrying the Vice President from a vacation home to a nearby airfield. Rescuers at the scene say there are at least a dozen bodies—nobody is alive. Hundreds of Federal investigators are heading to the area. U.S. Forest Service rangers at a nearby winter camp said they heard explosions but thought it was part of an avalanche control program by state authorities. The Vice President's widow and three small children are reportedly devastated but composed, and will be flown out of Seattle on Air Force Two bound for Washington. President Cliff Bradley has canceled his appearance at a Middle Class Party fundraiser to meet Mrs. Cardoza. MCP backer Robert Lee Hamilton is preparing a statement of grief and outrage. General Billy Norcross, Chairman of the Joint Chiefs of Staff, has offered assistance by U.S. Armed Forces, but so far the Governor of Washington has only called up a National Guard battalion of helicopter infantry trained for mountain rescues. We will keep you updated on this breaking story.

PART II

THE SECOND CONSTITUTIONAL CONVENTION (CON2)

CHAPTER 12

Late on a lazy Sunday afternoon on the cusp between summer and fall, Captain David Gordon, 28, crossed a tree-lined street in Alexandria, Virginia. The Little River subdivision had in recent months blossomed with short-term leases for military officers, paid for by the Government as the Second Constitutional Convention got underway. David's condo was a few blocks from where he now walked. He carried a bottle of wine, a handful of long-stemmed red roses, and a crisp new white plastic throw-disk. He wore a crisply ironed white shirt with rolled up sleeves; light blue jeans; and mahogany loafers. As he walked in that evening sunlight, time seemed to stand still and it seemed to take forever to cross the street. The humid heat of Washington summer had finally collapsed in a brisk, windy autumn. Though a distant plume of smoke rose from some street fight in Virginia, the massive presence of tens of thousands of troops was keeping the nation's capital quiet as if no depression, no poverty, no violence, no calls for revolution were sweeping the land. The trees were turning cathedral colors, and rustling as if filled with important messages. David smiled at those chatterboxes. What could a bunch of leaves have to say to each other? Then again, they were old leaves, wise leaves, dying leaves, and perhaps he'd better listen to their gossip.

Parked cars lined the sidewalks, and not a vehicle seemed to be moving anywhere. The air was smoky with barbecue. The street, still warm and smelling of tar, seemed to point straight into the huge sun that quivered yolk-like in a reddish haze on the city horizon.

Hard to believe that CON2 had already been underway for two weeks, and there were serious signs of chaos as the 1,000 delegates disagreed more and more on the simplest points. Congress, which had called the convention after receiving the mandate from two thirds of the state legislatures, now sat helplessly by while its creation threatened to go amok. Neither the Judicial or Executive Branches had any more power than the Legislative to intervene. And the delegates had full immunity from prosecution for their actions.

Hard to believe all that turmoil, David thought, on a sweetly pensive day like this. He passed a group of young officers playing football, barefoot and shirtless, on a lawn. He walked through a long shady hallway ("The Palms," a sign read, "Condos 2-3-4 BR/Good Rates") and rang a doorbell.

"Why hello there," said the smallish blonde who opened the door—Maxie! Her condo contained shoulder to shoulder people laughing, talking, holding drinks, yet she seemed to have waited only for him. But it was an illusion, a shared gesture, the remembrance of a special relationship. She'd been his nurse.

For a moment he was almost disappointed. He'd come such a long way since his disappointment with Kristy and the bad luck breaking his legs in a jump that killed another person. He felt his old red-blooded self again, more robust than ever, and Maxie was a shadow from a sorry interlude. It had been well over a year since he'd said goodbye to Maxie at Fort Riley. He'd changed, bounced back, and she still seemed caught in that time warp. He knew she hurt inside, but the exterior kept right on going like a full-screen motion picture. And maybe nothing would ever make her turn the projector off and face the reality that she was getting older and was not doing the right things for herself. He shrugged—can't do anything about that, he thought—and relaxed, almost laughing at the ghost he'd been back at Fort Bragg, and the ghost of a relation he'd carried on with his beautiful woman who kept saving herself for some wealthy guy who'd please her family but neglect or even abuse her. He wouldn't stay at her party long—just enough to renew his acquaintance. She was so spunky, though, that he couldn't really feel sorry for her. He really was glad to see her. "I told you I'd bring that throw-disk."

"Come in, I'm glad you came, the throw-disk is great, oh look at the wine, the roses are so-o-o lovely, thank you." She stood on tiptoe to kiss his cheek. Briefly he held her slight, firm frame. She wore a white summer dress, and he smelled a subtle citrus perfume on her bare back. She was not sweating at all despite the population problem between there and the refrigerator. "You did promise," she said cradling the wine and the roses, "and you are a man true to your word."

"And the throw-disk."

"Close the door. Yes, and the throw-disk. We'll all throw it later. Are you hungry?" She situated him in a comfortable corner chair between two Air Force pilots arguing about landing F-23A's. The pilots held their beer bottles like joysticks and made repeated landings.

Maxie came back minutes later carrying a tray with hors d'oeuvres, southern style chicken pieces, and plastic cups of rosé spritzer. She chased the pilots away and sat on a folding chair beside him. "How are your legs?"

"I run five miles a day."

She frowned as she served. "There's no table surface free. Napkins and laps will have to do."

"That smells great and I could eat a horse. Napkins and laps are fine."

"If you have that kind of appetite you must be feeling okay." She smiled, which was a sunny crinkle in a wonderful face. She had small, white, perfect teeth. Her face had a clean almost boyish squareness, with ash-blond hair flying as she moved.

"I'm feeling just fine. And I want to thank you for being a friend when I really needed one."

"It's my job." But she glowed, searching with small, square hands and greasy fingers for just the right chicken breast. "Aw hell, David, I enjoyed your company too. I missed you after you left."

"I've missed you too. So what's this about you being a combat flight nurse? You promised to tell me all the details."

She sat bolt upright, a little leap from the tush sort of, and folded her hands in her lap as if sitting for a portrait. Her face lit up in a proud, excited smile. She made fists. "I decided I couldn't be an old maid anymore, so I broke off with the man I was seeing. I applied for this combat flight nurse school, and I got in—on my own, with no help from any uncles—and I just graduated a few weeks ago with honors! Can you believe it? So now I'm stationed here at Walter Reed. We spend most of our time up on the flight deck—on the roof—or flying around town."

"What unit are you with?"

"55th Aviation Battalion (MAES)."

"Which means?"

"Medical Air Evacuation Service." She added with a hint of pride: "I'm in Flight 1. We have three flights, each with four completely equipped and staffed helicopters."

"Sounds exciting, Maxie. I'm thrilled for you."

"It is exciting. One chopper can act as a complete field dispensary, or carry six stretchers."

David frowned a little. "So the military has extra MAES units in town. They're ready for a war, sounds like."

She shrugged. "We're training to evacuate sick people from the roof of the hotel, or if someone is in an accident. I doubt there will be anything more than that." She frowned a little.

David changed the subject. "The papers came in a few months ago. I'm a single man again." He chomped down, enjoying a mouthful of fried chicken followed by a wash of rosé. The divorce was final. Kristy had sent him a little hand-lettered note of apology and goodbye, with a heart in one corner, and a not very happy Happy Face with a tear coming out of one eye. He'd written her a thank-you note. Other than that, he didn't expect to ever hear from her again. Which was kind of what he preferred, because he still felt the loss of her passion that had been like an addiction. Often, he thought there could never be another woman like her in his life. He still felt like a bomb crater inside. It was best to just move on.

Maxie studied him. "Should I say sorry?"

"That's behind me, along with the broken legs and the airborne corps."

"But you want to stay in the Army?"

"Yup. I'm taking it a day at a time. I've seen all the combat I want. I'm just not ready for a desk job quite yet. This little assignment here with CON2 can't last more than three months. Just enough time to build up time in grade so I can apply for a waiver and move back to Infantry. I want to be a company commander for at least a year or two. Got to have that experience under my belt."

"I see you are still the same never-give-up hard charger, David."

"I'm afraid so. Maybe a little more selective about where I'm charging."

Maxie laughed, apparently reading his thoughts. "Army people shouldn't marry civilians, huh?"

"Not if they're nutty civilians. Oh God, this chicken is good. Did you make this?"

"You always made me laugh, David."

"No, I'm serious. I'll bet these were all first-born chickens with references."

She gave a demure smile that seemed to light up a few freckles on each cheek. She'd confessed once that she felt very self-conscious about the freckles, and spent a fortune on all sorts of creams and salves from around the world. A hint of Southern Lady crept into her voice. "Actually, I had it catered in from a little specialty house in Georgetown, sorry. My little fingers just ache from all that telephoning and debit carding."

He wiped his mouth and fingers with a warm, wet

terrycloth towel scented with lemon. "Maxie, you're first class. How do you do it? Have you met Mr. Right yet?"

She sighed deeply, and her slight bosom hove. "I'm afraid not. Those are the first roses I've received in about two weeks."

"Two weeks, huh? So there is a guy." So she'd finally dumped Mr. Wrong in North Carolina, and it sounded as if she'd found another Mr. Wrong in Washington.

"Yes," she said looking down and folding her hands in her lap. The sun was going down outside and some of the sun was going down in Maxie's eyes.

"A doctor," David prodded. She must be getting the run-around again.

"Yes."

"A brain surgeon."

"No, a proctologist."

"Oh." David held up a chicken leg, making poking gestures with its thin end.

She laughed. "Stop it, David."

"I haven't teased a woman since I irritated my two sisters when I was home on leave. That was last Christmas."

"Well you're quite good at it. I'm very irritated." She rose, running her fingers along his cheek. "I have to speak with my roomie. You stay put and rest your legs."

"I jog five miles a day," he said but she ignored him. He watched her walk away—small rear; narrow hips; perfect calves under knee-length skirt.

The Air Force guys floated in again This time they were trying to impress two nervously smiling women, who nodded a lot and made fluttery, wide eyes. The pilots waved Little Smokie Weenies and foreign beers as they made takeoffs and landings, and it was clear they wanted the women to come fly with them.

David ignored them as his gaze roved. He made his way to the front door, plotting his escape, and then back to his seat in the corner. Another half hour, he thought. Time to move on.

He noticed a tall, dark-haired young woman speaking with Maxie as they walked in his direction. The roomie wore a black dress and was bare-shouldered. David's interest perked up, and he forgot about the half hour thing. The roomie was attractive in a sultry, mysterious way. Somehow, in his first impression, he got a sense of something not happy about her somehow, but he brushed it off. She walked in long, languid steps and, when she smiled, her features lit up with mischief and self-assurance. And yet—ah, but how white her eyes and her teeth gleamed, ivory-perfect, against the smooth texture of her skin. She carried a black purse that looked small against her long frame. Maybe because she was tall, she let her shoulders stoop a little and move with the rhythms of her walking.

By the time they were halfway to him, he realized that Maxie's roomie was gorgeous. Of course she would be. Everything Maxie did had class. Take the plastic cups. Anywhere else that would be kitsch. Better glass, or even crystal. But in Maxie's matter of fact world, that would be overdoing it. Plastic was just right, the simple, elegant solution. Less was more. It wasn't that Maxie was affected or snobbish; things just always went that way. And of course Maxie's genes dictated that she act as social glue, rescuing people from being loose ends or third wheels. Maxie was to wallflowers as fresh water was to droopy house plants. David rose.

"David, I'd like you to meet Lieutenant Victoria Breen. Tory, this is Captain David Gordon." David and the roomie shook hands. She had a dry, warm grip; long arms; honey-tan skin with butterscotch freckles on her shoulders.

"David promised me roses, and look over there."

"That's nice, Maxie." Her gaze avoided David's but he sensed she might be interested. Maxie kept chattering, and then she was gone and David was alone with this Breen woman who sat quietly, comfortably leaning her chin on her fist, watching the pilots and their quarry. She seemed to have a playful inward smile, as if she had a secret. And she didn't appear to be in a hurry to go anywhere. She carried herself almost regally, though in an unassuming manner, he thought. She had cute eyebrows, too, that seemed knit up in some undefined discomfort which he immediately longed to understand and soothe.

Ah Maxie, you planned this all along.

"Have you lived here long?" David asked.

Breen turned to look at him for the first time. She had rich dark hair piled neatly around her head. On each bare shoulder was a small galaxy of brown-sugar freckles. Her skin was lightly peeling, and the circles of new skin were pinker, but still not entirely fair-complected. Her answer was direct and soft and aimed right at his heart without intending to be, and he didn't even hear the answer—she could have lived here a month, a year, a thousand years—because they looked in one another's eyes—hers teasing and dusky like a forest—and he totally forgot his half hour was up.

They talked about nothing and everything for a while. "Would you like another spritzer?" she asked, looking away, breaking the spell. Her tone had a hint of teasing: "Your legs—"

"No thanks." He added in protest: "I jog five miles a day. Six. Sometimes ten."

"Oh really."

"I'm serious. Airborne."

"I'll be right back." She had a way of closing up, of withdrawing, and then she seemed darker somehow, as if she had something on her mind. Was there a guy? She rose to open a window, long-limbed and graceful, then wandered toward the kitchen. He watched her as she nodded and smiled, first here, then there along the way. She moved with an unpretentious stride. She was indeed pretty, her white smile dazzling. Her head rode gracefully on a long neck. Her features were delicate and even, and her jaw had a brittle china-cup strength.

David and Tory sat talking all evening, most of it on a love seat where they sat close, face to face, gazing into each other's eyes.

"What do you do?" Tory asked.

"I'm working for the I.G. detachment assigned to the Composite." He was sure she'd find that boring, but she actually looked startled, and he wondered why. Some dark wink or thought or other moved in the liquid depth of that dark gaze: an involuntary blink tightening her pupils. The Inspector General's office existed to inspect everything from blankets to burros, from tarps to tanks, from boots to bullets, and make sure it was according to regulations; the I.G. also listened to soldiers' complaints and tried to make right where right was due. Did she have a complaint? The Composite was the 20,000 member military joint command assigned to guard CON2 in these violent times, with so many bomb threats and shootings related to nutty causes. "What about you?" he asked Tory. "What do you do?"

"I'm the Executive Officer of a data security unit. I'm afraid it's kinda hush hush." She looked regretful, signaling she couldn't say more about her job.

They turned from topic to topic. She was from Iowa. Her grandpa had been an Army officer killed in Vietnam. Her parents had a home in Davenport. Her dad was in real estate, her mom a housewife. She had an older brother and a younger sister.

David liked to read and had read some of the same books Tory had. He was sportsy—liked biking, hiking, martial arts, swimming, soccer. Funny, so did she. She laughed. "You're making all this up, aren't you?"

"Yes. I read minds, you see, and I just parrot whatever you're about to say, so that you'll be impressed."

She threw her head back in a cascade of soft laughter. Light gleamed on her teeth, the pink of her palate. It took her a moment to regain control. "Maxie said you could be really funny." She looked as if she were having fun.

People began leaving. Maxie opened some windows and a wonderful breeze came through.

The Air Force pilots left silently and slightly tipsy by the back garden gate, without passengers. Maxie brought two frosty rosé spritzers, and handed David and Tory each one. "Thanks," David said, hardly noticing Maxie's triumphant look.

A while later, Maxie signaled from the kitchen and Tory strode away. David sat with his eyes closed, enjoying the cool night air, and wondering how to make sure they saw more of each other. Maybe dinner? Or lunch?

More people left. Maxie was in a battle of goodbyes at the door, shaking hands right and left, smiling, hugging, encouraging. A man and a woman in white smocks appeared and began cleaning. David went out into the garden and inhaled a scent of trees. The city loomed darkly all around, sleeping, glowering.

Leaning on a wrought iron railing, he glimpsed the two women inside. Unseen, he watched Tory, trying to figure out how she had managed to tug that one note on his heart's strings that no woman had in years. He was determined to have her. Under the thick hair with reddish highlights, she had a wide, sure smile. Her eyes seemed to throw off light when she smiled, but at moments she looked sullen and mysterious, almost hurt, and then her mouth took on a sultry pout, lower lip full. Was there a man in her life? This all seemed too easy. Maybe she was getting the proctology treatment from some other geek, and Maxie was trying to fix her up with David as a mercy thing. Everyone is getting the shaft from someone, David thought in a moment of alkaline despair. The world is full of proctologists. Actually, they are an alien race, invading the earth, and killing us off by ruining our love lives and frustrating us until we become extinct. We shall be as dinosaurs. Then the world will become one gigantic rectal exam populated by these people with huge gloves. But how long will they rule? How will they fare before other aliens—endodontists, perhaps—take over by a fiendish ploy? David set down his spritzer, and with it the childish thoughts. Courage, he thought. He went back inside to mount his attack.

Already, the white-smocked man was vacuuming, and the woman cleaned plastic cups and plates from every surface. Maxie exhaled a puff of breath, and a few straight blonde wisps fluttered over her forehead. "David, I'll invite you again. I'm having a cookout in a few weeks."

"I'd love that." He looked over her shoulder, and saw Tory in the kitchen with a broom and dust pan. Her hair looked frizzled from effort, her look preoccupied. How neatly drawn was the outline of her face, how warm her lightly-rouged lips, how neatly arranged her features seemed, crisp and just right.

"Tory," Maxie said to her, seeing his look. She put her tools aside and walked toward them. Though she bore faint impression of pleasure, there was something dark in her eyes; not something cold at all, but warm and defensive, a beast that could be roused, a wall that might have to be climbed over.

The two women walked him out to the street. They swatted mosquitoes and talked for a few moments under the bug-chased lights. "Maybe my unit will fly around your building one of these days," Maxie said.

David laughed, teasing: "Don't tell me you wear a flight suit?"

"Bigger than Miami. Helmet, boots, this suit with all these pockets full of medicine packets. I also carry a great big gun on my belt. It's just so cool. Beats doing blood draws and emptying bed pans. No offense—you were a fun patient."

David told Tory: "I would really enjoy having lunch with you. Maybe a movie. We can talk some more about my mind reading and your interests?"

She thought darkly for a moment. Then, as if a sudden breeze had blown those thoughts away, her eyes sparkled and her red lips pleasured in a smile. "I'd like that."

"You have our number," Maxie told David with a dig in the ribs. The women waved and said goodnight as David drove away.

ANN Breaking News with Allison Miranda

ALLISON: Washington in this pre-election year has a kind of nervous energy that borders on psychosis. Grinding poverty for half the population since the third collapse of the world economy in less than ten years; international humiliations of the U.S.; armies of homeless people on the streets; terrorism; scandals; rioting; the collapse of Social Security; the relentless bickering of hate radio; the endless partisan impeachment struggles between armies of lawyers; these are just some of the complex factors that have brought us to this Second Constitutional Convention. Here is our political reporter in the field, Peggy DeMetrio, for a convention center update. Peggy, can you give us a complete update and analysis of what's at stake, and where the Second Cosntitutional Convention is right now?

PEGGY: Sure. I'm standing before the Atlantic Hotel and Convention Center, near the Islamic Mosque and Cultural Center along Embassy Row. It seems hard to believe that CON2 has been in session now for two weeks. Remember how, when the first bus loads of delegates rolled in, everyone was so upbeat and excited? To quote one delegate I spoke with, "We're tired, we're angry, and we're going to do something about it. The Constitution is over 200 years old and needs to be amended. We're going to take our country back from the criminals, the foreigners, and the liberals. We're going to stop the constant sniping, the impeachments, the censures, the stealing of our money." That sentiment may still be there, but the exhilaration has faded in the midst of gridlock. The convention has been stalled for two weeks now on procedural issues. Radicals of the left and of the right, as predicted, are pushing the center to allow for more amendments. The limit of ten very carefully predetermined amendments so far still stands firm, but one has to ask for how long. People here are beginning to talk not about amending, but about rewriting. People are saying that it was a long, arduous road to this point, and they want to make it count.

There are signs that the American people's confidence in this convention is slipping. Polls show the support level is down to just under 50% today, down from 75% six months ago when this movement roared through the state legislatures like a brush fire. This convention was approved by the legislatures of 45 states as a handshake with the American people—a carefully crafted compromise of positions on abortion, creationism, gay rights, a balanced budget, and other positions—designed to resolve a number of long-standing conflicts without tipping the game to either extreme.

The majority agree on what are called the core amendments—balancing the budget, eliminating the Federal debt, creating a replacement for Social Security, joining every other civilized nation in guaranteeing full medical coverage to every citizen regardless of class differences. Then there are the so-called special interest amendments, designed to mandate positions on abortion, creationism, gay rights, furthering the separation of church and state by taking away the right of clergy to create marriage contracts, and so forth. This is only the first such national convention since 1787, and there are a lot of questions about what to do next at every step.

There is a strong swell of support for the notion that CON2 should dictate what, but not how—in other words, we want universal health care, but it will be up to the Executive and Legislative branches to work out the details—for example, can we eliminate the health insurance industry entirely, thereby saving 20% of the annual medical dollar up front as some argue?

There is another swell, however, in support of dictating both what and how, in the frame of mind that the people don't trust Congress to get it right—after all, we're here, those delegates say, because the two lawmaking branches failed to get it right decade after decade, so why should we trust them now, especially since they reached such a low point in the 1990's?

The most dire warnings were that this convention could not possibly be such a big tent and hold together so many opposing views; that the convention would fall apart, resulting in no new document. That would leave the United States without a new Constitution, but the old one, the 1787 Constitution, would be tarnished. It would be seen as just another piece of paper now that its glory had been poked through. Those warnings have not come true so far, Allison, but we are holding our breath.

The key to the whole thing is if the limit of ten amendments is breached. Right now, the Procedures Committee is deadlocked as extremists of the left and right want to remove the limit, and centrist moderates are fighting desperately to keep the limit, get the convention rolling, finish the business, and go home. The extremists don't want it that way. They want a whole new piece of paper, and they've got to eliminate the center before they can go at each other's throats.

ALLISON: Is there any progress in the committee at all?

PEGGY: The next vote in the committee should tell the tale. Right now, we have 50 committee member delegates wrangling in a room off the side, while the other 950 are engaged in arguments in the main hall. Those 50 are going to hold one final vote in the next few days. I cannot over-emphasize how critical this will be. If the center holds, the number of amendments will remain at ten; the convention will do its business and go home. If the committee again deadlocks, the extremists have promised to walk out and hold a floor fight. If they have the numbers, they can open it up, and then we could have a hundred amendments, a thousand. The entire Constitution might be rewritten.

CHAPTER 13

During that fine half summer, half autumn weekend in September, a graying Coast Guard specialist sat in a restricted, gloomy basement at the U.S. Naval Observatory in Washington, D.C., working with the world's most powerful computer. His name was Ibrahim "Ib" Shoob, and he was a head walker. He caught hackers who broke into secure data bases, civilian or military, and got their hands on sensitive information. It was all in a day's work, as Ib smoked cigarette after cigarette in the Secure Room of the National Systems Security Office (NSSO).

Ib was away from his family for long stretches. By day when the observatory's silvery domes made flashbulb shots of the noon sun, or by night when the domes glimmered in moonlight, Ib was usually at work stalking his targets. Ib lived for his wife and children, computing, and the Coast Guard, not necessarily in that order. He was grateful to the nation that had sheltered his immigrant parents from the ravages of wartime Beirut during the 1980's. They were an industrious family of merchants and bankers, but proud of their middle son who'd chosen military service instead. Now Ib was on the verge of retirement. His three children were well on their way, two of them in college. He'd earned his degree while in the Coast Guard, and the service had helped him discover his genius for computing. He had just been admitted to the doctoral program in computer science at Boston University, and was to matriculate after his retirement next year. He looked forward to relocating with his wife Hala to some picturesque New England town with brick buildings and winding little streets. Meanwhile, he used his technical finesse and moral zeal to chase electronic wrongdoers. He felt privileged to be working on the CloudMaster computer system, of which only four machines existed.

CloudMaster had originally been developed for the Navy as a weather modeling system. It was so powerful that it could reliably micro-read the weather over a huge footprint of land and sea. It could predict the number of raindrops or balls of hail that would hit a square yard of aircraft carrier flight deck during a given segment of minutes or hours, adjusting constantly as realtime information in the system drifted through changes. In its guts, each CloudMaster created a tiny universe complete with pulsing stars, whizzing comets, and rotating planets—cyber fantasies. On the rotating planets were seasons, latitudes, weather pinwheels, storm systems, high and low pressure areas, rain fronts, snow levels, tornadoes, nights and days. CloudMaster worked on the principle of a fuzzy network—over a million processors shuffling information at near light speed, sharing registers, floating data streams. To prevent the machine from burning up, its insides were, like outer space, chilled to near absolute zero and nearly a vacuum. Photon bit streams streaked across each other's luminous vapor trails, racing between golden logic gates. To keep the machine from collapsing under earth's tremendous atmospheric pressure, CloudMaster resembled a deep-ocean bathyscaph with an egg-shaped, massive steel hull. The machine had been developed as a weather modeling system for the U.S. Navy, but it could also model a nation's economy in a thousand dimensions, or predict the fate of a nation. Just before CON2, all four CloudMaster machines in Washington were yanked from their jobs and linked together in a secret net. This puzzled Ib. And he was not one to let go of a puzzle.

At the moment, Ib was tracking an intruder. The hacker was somewhere in Holland and went by the handle Flying Dutchman, though head walkers at NSSO quickly dubbed him Salty. He'd pop up in a Navy parts list or an Air Force flight schedule, and flaunt his icon: a wooden warship under full sail, with a cannon blowing smoke. Gotcha, a sign in the sail read, and he'd be gone.

You just wait, Ib thought. This afternoon, Salty had shown up in a top secret personnel data base of Metro Power & Light, groping into sensitive information about people's salaries, ages, that sort of thing. The phones to NSSO flooded with frantic calls from system administration at MP&L. Like a Texas Ranger, Ib hopped into the saddle—or rather, his office chair while wearing V-goggles—and entered a parallel reality. Ib was the ultimate pro. He had no working icon, just a symbol he displayed at the moment when he had his man and the police were breaking doors down in Tokyo, Rio, London, or Mombasa: a cross with R.I.P. above, and Thank You underneath. Most head walkers liked to use the effects provided by manufacturers and software enhancers—a walking or running man complete with clicking footsteps, or a race car with roaring engine, a thundering rocket, a clanking knight—but Ib preferred to be a silently floating, invisible eye. He left almost no signature. He glided in and out of forbidden places like the truncus of a flashlight beam moving flat along a wall. He was a ghostly manta ray in the cyber ocean, barely flicking a wingtip. With CloudMaster running in background, dissecting thousand digit numbers to find their two unique prime factors that were 500-digit entry codes, Ib could break any lock on cyber-earth in seconds.

Head walkers traversed a pseudo-reality of high-ways, roads, bridges, skyscrapers, underground metropolises, long halls—a virtual city peopled with the icons of its population, millions of workers and players around the world like Ib. When the call from MP&L came, Ib put on his goggles. The presentation of V-world sites varied. Some places were monochrome black on gray. Many were cartoon-like. Some achieved oil-painting artistry. Most were interesting. But Ib never dallied among other people's silly games. Blending into the raging river of raw photons that was the net, he sidestepped knights or cowboys challenging him to fight. He avoided beautiful females luring him, with winks and waggling fingers, to flash credit cards and step into shady side-rooms with a promise of more to be seen. These were often just roll-joints; your session was relayed to some casino town in Africa or Asia, maybe to a ship in international waters, where such billing was legal, and presto—you'd be billed 100 bucks a minute on the plastic you flashed to get in.

Ib entered MP&L's General Area Network. It was

a simple, elegant environment, a monochrome reminding Ib of an architect's rendering of a future airport: spacious, floors dotted with meandering stick figures, its walls numbered with access ports to data bases. In the middle of this imaginary lobby floated a 1500's Dutch warship with cannon blazing. Of course it was too late to catch Salty entering. Ib could only hope to follow him, link him to the trail he'd left, have him arrested based on that evidence.

"Alert, Ib. Subject on site," CloudMaster's unisex voice whispered.

Ib's heart leapt. Somewhere nearby Salty still lingered, perhaps greedy to look into women's files, unaware of the head walker stalking him. "Locate."

"Searching."

"Echo," Ib said. CloudMaster, linked to the scenario in Ib's goggles, churned through Metro's history buffers, looking for the moment when Salty had showed himself just long enough to instruct Metro's system to display the warship. "Echo successful."

"Trace," Ib said.

"Please wait," CloudMaster said. "Trace successful."

There Salty was, the trace a tiny moving dot like a pinprick. "Follow," Ib said. As long as Ib followed his prey unnoticed, CloudMaster could slam data files back and forth from anywhere in the world to find, and deliver Salty's name, address, phone number, gender, birth weight, and so on to Amsterdam's computer crime detectives. As he pursued Salty, Ib found himself traveling along a kind of highway tunnel. Where was this bird headed? They entered a cartoon landscape owned by Columbia Net, the Washington network authority. Here, cutesy animal figures chased each other under pastel skies, with old-style cartoon music. Ib streaked on behind his nearly invisible quarry. Beneath them raged the data stream, giving an illusion of danger, for the icon people were no more than ghosts. One could pass through the stream and, at worst, have to do a reconnect. Cartoon cop cars drove by with pigs shooting rubbery guns. Ib entered a very utilitarian, cold environment. CloudMaster announced: "Metro Emergency Archive."

Ib found himself in a rotunda modeled on the Old Post Office, its huge lobby filled with conceptual chip carousels. The real thing, he knew, was a freezing warehouse full of nitrogen, its storage pagodas tended by figures in space garb carrying oxygen bottles. Here in the cyber-fantasy rendition, a dot that represented Salty drifted among the carousels, poking his nose here and there. The dot entered one labeled Carousel 49, Directory Z. Ib hovered carefully. If he went in, the system might send a message—that it was read-only, or access denied multiple users. With a single keystroke in the Netherlands, Salty could log off and thus escape capture. The trick was to keep him here long enough to make him. Cloudmaster whispered: "Compiling street address. Amsterdam police alerted."

Ib grinned and made fists. He forgot to light a new cigarette. "Yes!" Seconds more, and police cars would be cruising Salty's neighborhood.

"Subject logging off."

"What?" Ib's joy vanished, and he surged forward. Frantically, he entered Directory Z. There he saw Salty's dot. As if he'd turned and seen Ib, he vanished. Logged off.

Lost.

Gone.

But a new voice, a man's filtered through an electrical storm over the North Atlantic and pleasantly accented, said: "Amsterdam police intervening." CloudMaster added: "Escape not over 80% likely."

Heart pounding, Ib drifted closer to Salty's last location. The walls were shoeboxed with hundreds of long subdirectory codes. He recognized a number of files with encrypt keys only someone with high level permissions could access. Touching one brought the words White House into Ib's lenses. Touching the next one brought up Admiral's House.

"Escape not more than 33% likely," CloudMaster said.

Ib's mind wandered toward the words Admiral's House. Wasn't that the old name of what was now called The Vice President's House? The Vice President's residence; afterthought: empty nearly a year now.Vice President Cardoza had been assassinated last December. A search in the Cascades Mountains had turned up some mountain men, but none who could be linked with Cardoza's death. The nation had been without a vice president since last year because of wrangling between OCP and MCP Congress members over the next vice president—each party wanted their own candidate. So what could be going on here in Washington Metro? Idling now because he'd done his best—"Escape not more than 10% likely," CloudMaster said—Ib loitered in the Admiral's House files a moment. His heart flip-flopped and his stomach lurched. Could this be an evil trick by Salty? Ib backed out and checked the entry log file. His own had been the last access to this file since an emergency browndown procedure on—he checked the internet—God, on the hour—of Cardoza's death!

"Escape not more than 0% likely," CloudMaster

said, but Ib ignored the machine. Sweat dribbled down his face as he read the Vice President's resignation, his confession, a warning about CON2 which was about to begin, some hand-written documents scanned and saved as bitmapped files, and a list of names some of whom Ib recognized: General Robert Montclair, General Felix Mason, billionaire Robert Lee Hamilton, some congressmen....

"Congratulations and thank you!" CloudMaster relayed the Dutch voice to Ib. "Hallo? This is Amsterdam calling, ja? Nice cross and Thanks-You. What means R.I.P please?"

"Yes, yes," Ib said impatiently. "Phone off. Lock Admiral's House subdirectory. Copy files NSSO-dot-Ib." That would put the memo into his working directory here. He changed his mind. "Uncopy." Then he amended to copy the files to a directory shared by himself and several colleagues, so he could not be pinpointed by some rival head walker in league with these devils.

Slipping the virtual goggles off, Ib sagged in his seat. Sweat beaded his forehead, and he ran a hand idly across, trailing goggles and wires. This was no joke. Directory Z had not been overwritten since Cardoza's death. Cardoza had sent that message less than an hour before the rocket attack, and Ib realized lives were in danger. Most of all, his own. He thought of his family. Then he thought of his duty. Apparently nobody knew this message had been auto-captured, probably during a browndown. And if he walked away from this, maybe nobody would ever know. But that wasn't Ib's style. He mopped his brow with a towel. Once he opened his mouth, no telling what kind of hell would break loose. His first step, according to military procedure, had to be to notify his immediate superior. That would be the XO, Lt. Victoria Breen. A nice girl, he thought with pity; would it really serve a purpose to put this target on her back? But she was a soldier, he considered, and she had accepted her commission knowing there were risks.

ANN Breaking News with Allison Miranda

HARVEY: Tonight's guest is Jake Forst of America Armed & Free (AAF), an Ohio Delegate to CON2. Mr. Forst, yesterday you and Delegate Lily Denzenhall of the Liberal Caucus, a delegate from Arizona, had a lively debate, a shouting match one might say, about gun control. Can you briefly tell the story for our viewers?

FORST: Glad to, Harvey. Nobody wants to break the limit of ten amendments that we agreed on for CON2, but the liberals are pushing their luck too far as usual. As you know, the Procedures Committee right now is trying to decide whether to open the floor to an unlimited number of amendments. Misguided souls like Ms. Denzenhall want to cripple the Second Amendment right of every citizen to bear arms. I promise you this— if the committee deadlocks; if the floor goes wide open, and she wants to nullify the Second Amendment; then I have the votes for an amendment copied from Switzerland, where every man between 21 and 59 is required by law to keep a military assault rifle in his closet at home. I'd be interested to see if Mrs.

Denzenhall's husband violates that law and winds up in jail. That would severely ruin the day for these whining liberals.

CHAPTER 14

David Gordon was just starting his second week at the 915th Inspector General Detachment, whose commander, Colonel Lionel Jankowsky, answered to the Inspector General of Composite Force, a Major General. The 915th occupied the long, narrow second floor in a brownstone building in Georgetown.

Life was getting a little better every day, David thought as he drove to work with the top down. He was a free man, hopefully a little wiser, he thought. He had just finished Inspector General Officers' School and felt enthusiastic about righting wrongs and maybe uncovering shady dealings.

He lived four blocks from Maxie in Alexandria, and he was sure he'd make more friends. In fact, he had Maxie's number on his fridge, and intended to call Tory Breen soon. It was just a matter of figuring out what she'd like to do together—maybe jog around the Smithsonian?

It was a straight shot in to work, beating traffic if you left before six a.m. Thank God he wasn't in the Atlantic Hotel & Convention Center, where CON2 was in progress. There were 20,000 troops in the city—regulars in the hotel's three towers; National Guard troops in the streets outside the hotel; reservists and regulars camped in Rock Creek Park. By contrast, the 915th I.G. Detachment's leased offices were on a quiet side street with just the right mixed zoning to have small, quaint shops on the first floor and office space on the upper floors of the buildings. Several officers, ten enlisted persons, and two civilian secretaries worked for the I.G., Colonel Jankowsky. Actually, David was a bit puzzled by the nature of this unit, since the Composite had its own large I.G. staff, and the units in the Atlantic Hotel & Convention Center undoubtedly had theirs. Jankowsky ostensibly worked for the general staff of the Composite. Maybe it was detachment they were after, in the true sense of the word, David wondered as he drove slowly down the graveled alley behind the 915th's offices. Objectivity, he thought, looking for a parking space, physical separation from the objects of inspection. To his right was a long wooden fence with tree crowns overhanging. To his left were the backs of shops fronting Ann Street, and on the second floor was a really pretty row of stained glass windows. He wondered what was in there. Looked like a Shakespearean tavern, almost, with dark cross beams over tan stucco. David parked in a large parking lot at the end of the block, opposite the buildings housing shops and the 915th. The parking lot had belonged to a supermarket that was boarded up and looked as if nobody had used it in several years. Blue peeled from the stucco walls along the bottom, with large gray gashes of exposed concrete blocks higher up. The good part, he thought guiltily, was that nobody would ticket him for illegal parking. He walked the 200 feet diagonally across the gravel drive to the back entrance of the 915th's rented store frontage.

On the first floor were a florist shop and a hat maker's shop. David climbed the back stairs. His office was last in the back. The uniform of the day for everyone was fatigues and combat boots. For officers, it included a pistol belt and holstered sidearm. David hung up his cap and field jacket, but kept the sidearm on. He walked down a narrow, carpeted corridor toward the front. He passed several open doors, and exchanged greetings with uniformed enlisted persons. It was a fairly spacious property, and even the privates were not doubled more than two desks to an office. The atmosphere was relaxed and friendly by military standards. Every person here was happy to be here rather than in a tent or crowded into hotel rooms at the Atlantic.

David poured himself a cup of coffee and poked his head into Colonel Jankowsky's office. Whenever a complaint came in that was judged worthy of further attention by the senior NCO, a junior enlisted person prepared a formal folder that would be saved for two years after resolution. Because David was new, Jankowsky personally reviewed his cases before assigning them. David would find the assigned cases in his in-box, study the pertinent Army Regulations, make calls, and report on the issues. Pretty soon, he expected to have cases requiring him to make field investigations, to see the involved parties. He looked forward to being able to travel around the city. CON2 was making history, and he was curious for an overview of how the spectacle was unfolding.

Colonel Jankowsky was a quiet, thoughtful man, tall and graying with a youthful face. Like all the officers in the Composite, Jankowsky wore fatigues and carried a sidearm. "Hey there! How's it going?"

"Fine, Sir. Just came by to say good morning."

"Good morning. Hey, close the door and sit down."

David closed the door and pulled up a chair.

Jankowsky held two file folders. "Got your coffee? Good. David, I've got two new ones for you today. One's a grim one. The other seems just plain whacky." He showed David the two file folders. David caught the jacket names: Corcoran, Mary; Shoob, Ibrahim.

"These two cases are important to me, and I know you'll handle them right. I want to get a feeling for how you work in the field, as I start slipping you more and more important cases." Jankowsky looked up and boomed. "You ready to go to work?"

David grinned back. "Ready and rarin'."

"Good." Jankowsky opened the Corcoran folder and skimmed aloud: "This woman is a 38 year old U.S. Army staff sergeant, E-6, assigned to the Composite, with duty in the enlisted mess in Tower 2. That's the middle tower at the Atlantic, and they're using it to house and feed military support personnel. She's a chief cook slash dietary supervisor, in other words. Plans the day's meals, supervises the cooks, sticks the thermometer in the turkey, that kind of thing." David noted a photo of a heavyset woman with dark skin and oriental eyes, a patient face with a slight smile. In another photo, she sat with a tired looking man with kind eyes. They looked like hard-working people who got few breaks in life. In a third photo, three beautiful young children sat smiling confidently on a couch—eloquent tribute to that hard work, David thought. Jankowsky continued: "Two days ago she approached the chaplain and said one of the enlisted men had been bothering her. The chaplain referred her to Colonel Bellamy, the Provost

Marshal at the Atlantic, but she preferred to turn to us. That was yesterday, and our duty sergeant spoke with her over the phone. Made an appointment, but she never showed up. This morning, one of our clerks called her commanding officer who told her Mary Corcoran was raped by that enlisted man last night. He's in custody and she's in the hospital for observation. It's become a police matter, but I need you to follow through, see the people." He enumerated, pressing the thick fingers of one hand against those of the other. "See Corcoran. See her commanding officer. See the Provost Marshal. See the suspect's commanding officer. See the suspect. Get a copy of the MP report. Get copies of any medical records, at least a summary. Write a memo, wrap it up, and we're done. We've followed through, and it goes to the JAG Office."

"Yessir."

"Oh, and then there's this." Jankowsky flipped open the Shoob file. David glanced through the folder, noting the contactee was a senior Coast Guard enlisted man. "Sounds like a flyin' saucer case. But this guy Shoob's got 25 years in, so let's listen. He's one of the computer jockeys from the Naval Observatory. They're a hotshot systems security outfit in the basement there, called NSSO. National Systems Security Office, falls under D.o.D. Shoob said he would only speak with me, in person. Kept refusing to say what it's about over the phone, but extremely important, something about a file he found. Let's humor him until there's a punch line, then let's hit the gong, flush the guy, and get on with serious work."

A while later, David sat in a private room with Master Chief Ibrahim "Ib" Shoob, a middle-aged, overweight computer specialist. Shoob looked as if he hadn't passed a physical in ten years. Shoob had brought a cup of coffee, in which he stirred several sugars. He smelled of cigarette smoke, and had grayish skin and poochy eyes.

"Chief, what's troubling you that you called us?"

"When is Colonel Jankowsky coming in?"

"He's tied up, I'm afraid."

"I don't want to speak with anyone else."

"I'm sorry, Chief. I'll have to do for now. But I work for Colonel—"

Shoob looked as though he'd been kicked in the gut. Within the sickened, angry look, David read the lightning-quick calculations of a chess player; brilliant, if eccentric. Laser-sharp eyes raked David with irony as he conceded. "You'll wish you hadn't heard my story, Captain."

"I'll take my chances." David looked at his watch. He had to be at Walter Reed by noon to interview Mary Corcoran, then go to the convention center to request an interview with the rape victim's company commander.

"Well Sir," the NCO began in a slow, burry voice, "you might have noticed in that folder there that I work at NSSO."

David nodded. "Yes, I looked through the file. Over in the Naval Observatory complex."

"That's right. The Government builds computer systems, data bases, logic engines. Our job is to break into them before the bad guys do so we can really make them secure. I'm what they call a head walker. Know what that is?"

David nodded. He had a kind of eerie picture of head walkers, wearing thick lenses like ski goggles that offered complete visual virtual reality, as though they were in another world. Headphones and a mike let them talk with the core brain. This, in state of the art systems—no keyboards, glorified TV monitors, tape heads, none of that early DP hardware borrowed from typing and entertainment media.

"That's right, Captain. I'm a Clearance One, which means I can go anywhere, any time, of course on a Need-to-Know basis. Sometimes I have to make a decision about that. All my moves are stored in memory, so I can't fool anyone. My decisions can be reviewed afterwards, so I think twice."

"Let me guess. You stumbled on something big."

"Yessir, I did. I would rather forget all about it, but I'm afraid it's my duty to inform somebody."

"Did you inform your superior officer, Chief?" David held a pencil poised over a sheet of loose canary note paper in the file.

"I did, Sir, and she referred me here."

"She?" David glanced into the file. The name floated up at him: Victoria Breen, 1LT, MPC. Maxie's roommate? David swallowed hard, and his mouth was suddenly dry. "Lieutenant Breen is your superior officer?"

"She's the XO. We're an oddball unit, sort of a composite in our own right, been over in the Observatory for years before this CON2 circus started. General Montclair wanted every uniformed person in Washington under his control, so they assigned us to his chain of command along with various other cats 'n dogs units."

David hadn't really caught what it was Tory Breen

did for Uncle Sam, just something top secret involving computers. "This woman is an MP officer?"

"Yessir. Nice gal, between you and me. She's pretty brainy." (And attractive, David thought, looking at this fat NCO who couldn't lift six french fries at once). "She referred me to Colonel Bentyne—the field-grade over in the Atlantic Hotel who's temporarily in charge of us—and Bentyne got cold feet the minute I started talking."

"I'll get my foot warmer out," David said. At least now he'd have an excuse to call Tory. Maybe to chew her out for throwing this curve ball.

"Sir, you remember the Vice President was murdered last year?"

"Yes?"

Shoob's big yellow teeth looked cadaverous. "Sir, he wrote a memo to his boss before he died, and I found it."

"His boss?"

"The President."

"And you found it." David stared at Shoob and felt like asking if he'd had his head examined recently. "Oh really?"

"Colonel Bentyne said the same thing. I've got 25 years of excellent service, and I'm risking my good name sitting here, Captain."

David softened. "I'll hear you out."

"Thank you. It's all I ask. Then my duty will be done and I can go back to my obscure safe little life." Shoob faltered. "Can I smoke?"

"Sure." David had him move by an open window, and a fan took the acrid blue-gray smoke outside. Shoob trembled as he spoke, and the cigarette shook in his mouth. David had his first tremor of uncertainty. Either this man was a good actor, or he was really scared. "I was chasing an international hacker, and I cornered him. I'm a pro. I don't use an icon or a logo. I try to stay invisible, especially when I'm tailing someone like that. It's just like a city inside the net, only it might be cartoon-like in one area, or Picasso somewhere else; maybe the sponsor likes Breughel or Goya or Tissot; whatever it is, you move through dream worlds like that."

"Sounds enjoyable."

"I used to think so, but it's a job now." He grinned with those spade-shaped caramel-colored teeth and his voice rasped on. "They even got a Pigalle inside, Sir, you know, Pig Alley? These ladies wag a leg at you from a doorway, try to lure you inside to show you more, and it's amazing how many people get suckered. They roll you, literally—it's a hundred bucks a minute in one of those—" His grin faded as he remembered what the conversation was about and why his job was no longer fun. The cigarette started waving up and down again. "I chased the sombitch and he went underground on me, but I stayed on his tail."

"—And he led you—where—?"

"I can't tell you that, Sir."

David dropped the pencil. "Great."

"The strategy was to keep him in the net long enough for the cops in Holland to arrest him. He was in there, and I guess he got greedy looking through all those files. All that personal stuff about people's lives. To a real hacker, the ultimate thrill—to wipe out a murder rap on a prison conviction, or to eliminate an old lady's pension—hackers are evil little losers who can't make it in real life, and this is their way of getting even. So there we were. We were in an emergency backup area of the Washington Metro Grid. I got a glimpse of some files, and it was the date on one that got me. December 14, almost two years ago. Brought me to a screeching stop. Almost forgot Salty for a second, but the cops in Amsterdam were beating his door down by then and I wasn't needed. I made one of those field decisions just then. I knew I could cover; I'd just say I was looking for Salty inside this place. I started reading and here I am."

David held up the pencil. "The Vice President was murdered by private militia types."

"That's what I thought until this."

"You make it sound like he had something to hide."

Shoob took a folded sheet of paper from his inner coat pocket. "The Vice President dictated this. He must have e-mailed it to himself, but there was a transmission outage of some kind, and the local net automatically made a backup copy as the net went down. Nobody knew this, and the copy has sat there for 9 months, waiting to be overwritten by the next blackout or browndown. I made a hard copy." He pushed the paper across the table. "Please read that."

David leaned forward and read the document, looking for the giveaway that would tell him this was some sort of joke. It looked authentic enough, had a transmission slug with Cardoza's name from somewhere in Washington—wasn't that where the Vice President had been killed?—and the date seemed right. David skimmed through the text. Supposedly, Cardoza was going to leave for Washington D.C. that night to see Bradley about an emergency involving stopping CON2, and some ringleaders, something about a plot and a list of names of men who must be watched—

David looked at the back of the paper. "Is that it?"

"Isn't that enough, Captain?"

David's heart beat harder and his skin crawled a little. "He mentions a list of names. Where is it?"

"I have it. Not here though."

"We'd have to get our hands on that list." David hesitated. "Shoob, do your fellow system jockeys ever play tricks on you?"

Shoob shook his head. "I thought about that. No, it would end up costing someone their job. I don't work with anyone that dumb."

"This isn't really proof of anything. I need the list of names. I need everything you've got, Shoob, and A.S.A.P."

"I know that, Sir. I keep looking over my shoulder ever since I found that, and I guess from now on you will too."

"I'm not the paranoid type." Something tingled at his spine. There had been a lot of hysterical press about CON2, about the rewriting of the Constitution. David personally felt the Constitution should be left alone. Could there really be people—influential people—who thought they could do better than those guys back in 1787? "Naw," he said, "this has to be a joke."

"Wait until you've had time to think about this, Sir. Here is a man, the Vice President of the United States, involved with a bunch of military, business, elected, and religious leaders—a whole lot of power there—and one day he wakes up and realizes he's square in the middle of a conspiracy to help us more than we feel we need to be helped. They think they have a patent on morality and values, and they're going to make us eat their brand of baloney. I figured from the moment I touched that file, I have my neck out about one mile." He stabbed a finger in David's direction, and his voice took on a low, shaking enraged frustration. "I have a wife and kids, I'm working on my Ph.D. in Computer Science, and I'm about to retire. I've spent a lifetime setting up my ducks, and here I am caught up in this chicken shit. You think I made this all up?"

David stared at him. "I wish you had." He swallowed hard.

"So do I. Now you do your part, Sir. You wanted to hear my story—" Shoob calmed himself a bit and toyed with his cup. "I was afraid to bring the list, in case—"

"—Someone stopped you on the way?"

"Frankly, yes. I have an idea, though. Will you meet me this evening, say at nine? At the Naval Observatory? I'll take you inside, give you the tour, give you the list, and say goodbye to this whole thing. Let you handle it."

"Deal."

CHAPTER 15

Tory Breen, 28, wearing a sparklingly perfect and creased dark-green Class A uniform, drove her moss-colored Jaguar to the Pentagon. She'd been invited to meet a certain special general. Her black regulation purse and a pair of white gloves lay on the passenger seat. She wore a 9 mm. automatic in a polished holster, with a crisp white lanyard running up under her right epaulet which bore her unit insignium and a lone silver first lieutenant's bar. She wore her trousers bloused into black polished combat boots. Her brass gleamed, including crossed muzzle-loader pistol MP motifs on each lapel. She'd had her hair done and spent hours preparing for this meeting.

Driving on this radiant Autumn day, she decided her grandmother must have had a hand in this, for why else would the general's office contact her? Tory hadn't really thought about asking to arrange a meeting—it embarrassed her that she might seem like a junior officer unfairly currying favor. Loosen up, she told herself, anyone else would at least contact the man.

She parked and then walked, miles it seemed, through parking lots and long corridors in the aging building, until she found his office. She stopped in a ladies' room, nervously straightened her lapels, and looked herself up and down for the nth time. Then she found her way down the carpeted, hushed corridor in a tomb-like section of the Pentagon's E-ring. Here, retired reserve generals recalled for temporary duty had especially large offices.

She knocked hesitantly but firmly with a white-gloved fist on the office door of General Rocky Devereaux, U.S. Army (Retired).

The odor of old cigar smoke permeated the area, one of the few where smoking privileges had not been entirely extinguished. From the silence, she thought there might not be a soul alive in there. On the door was a wooden sign with carved letters, "Rocky Devereaux, U.S. Army," and beside that a chipped, faded wooden rooster. The rooster had a cigar in his mouth, cocked up at a defiant angle like his raised boxing gloves; on his past-century steel pot helmet were four stars. She held her ear to the door and knocked again, louder. A voice slashed through the air like scissors ripping paper: "I said come in, for chrissake! Is everyone deaf in this goddam place?"

She turned the handle and stepped inside. In this ancient room that dated back to World War II stood a slim white-haired man surrounded by an atoll of cigar smoke. He wore simple fatigues and a black leather belt with a holstered .38 caliber revolver. He stood framed by a window with a crack in the glass, and turned as she entered. His back was straight, and he had his hands folded behind him. His white hair had stubborn peaks in it, and his eyes an impatient fire. He looked ready to bark at her, and she stiffened in anticipation, but when he saw her his eyes softened and his mouth opened helplessly. "My God," he whispered, so she barely heard him.

She came to attention and saluted. "Lieutenant Victoria Breen reporting, Sir."

"My God," he repeated. He returned her salute with a careless flick of the hand and stepped closer as if to take hold of a ghost. "You look like him."

"I hope not, Sir." She knew from photographs she had something of Granddad that gave her soft face firm edges. He took the cigar from the corner of his mouth, and stared at her. Then he laughed. "Of course not, you look a lot prettier. Sense of humor, too. Welcome aboard, Breen." He stuck out his hand. "Last time I saw you, you were about this tall." As they shook hands, he held his other hand by his knee.

"Thank you, Sir. I was five. Thanks for receiving me today."

He offered coffee, and she accepted. "My pleasure. Your granddad was a great soldier, Lieutenant Breen, what's your—?" He poured.

"Tory, Sir."

"Your grandma wrote to me."

"So I heard, Sir. I appreciate your interest, and it's really nice to meet you once more." Actually, she'd been mortified at her grandmother's meddling.

"I admired your grandfather, one of the best friends I ever had. When Eleanor called me, said you had some rough times…"

Maybe he knows, she thought.

"…and you were thinking of switching from the M.P. Corps to something else, maybe Data Services Command, I said of course I'd take a look at your file. When I saw all those awards and all that effort, I agreed to write a letter for your file, detailing the solid Army background in your family and so forth. Sometimes it isn't what's said, but who says it, or how it's said. Couldn't hurt you." He held his coffee cup in one hand, the cigar in the other, and sat against the morning light in the window. He had a bit of paunch, she saw, and white hair stuck out of the V of his shirt lapels; the curtain folds in his neck quivered as he spoke in quick, energetic bursts; a few veins showed on his cheekbones; the bridge of his nose had a scar, and the jutting jaw spoke of pride and toughness. A tear twinkled in each of his cloudy-gray eyes. "Victor Breen used to go into Saigon every second weekend and bring me back a box of good Virginia cigars. Should have killed me by now. By rights he'd be sitting here instead of me. Guess you were named after him, huh?"

"Yessir."

He set the cup down and turned away to wipe his eyes. They talked some more, and as he reminisced, he seemed to look directly into the past, as if it were a diorama. Sometimes he smiled at how it had been. "I can still see me as I got off the plane near Saigon, a green butterbar. A couple of weeks later upcountry your granddad walked into a burning plane and pulled guys out. But you know what? He was the kind of soldier that people just follow." He swept his cigar in an arc. "Follow! He had charisma. Couple of fellas walked right in there behind him and pulled more guys out. All the while he kept shooting VC that kept popping out of the elephant grass. Took some bullets, but he saved a bunch of lives. A year later—" She thought he was going to choke up again, but he didn't. She knew—Granddad had been hit in the head by a stray bullet during a firefight on some brown river where the sun kept twinkling and the water lilies kept rocking and the bugs just kept walking on the water that was briefly stained with a swirl of red. It was Tory's turn to feel a deep welling up, but she postponed it. He looked at her. "You a Pointer?"

"Nossir. Iowa State, Sir, double-oh-nine."

"I see. That's okay. I've seen fine officers come out of ROTC." He considered. "The first ten years is hard work. After that it's politics. But you need to start meeting people. Let's go see who I can introduce you to."

"Yessir. Thank you, Sir."

"Another thing. Keep your nose out of trouble, hear? It's gonna get awful nasty over there in that convention center before they're done screwing up our Constitution." He rummaged for his camouflage cap. He muttered: "Victor Breen, my God! He'll throw lightning bolts after me if I don't treat you like my own granddaughter. You come see me on and off, okay? I'll be camped in Rock Creek Park with the Composite. The wife and I enjoyed some dandy Bull Moose conventions at the Atlantic. I hope we get this crap done so I can get back to my real estate and my fishing hole."

Rather than walk through the huge building, General Devereaux chose to take a long, brisk walk in the open to reach the mess hall. His chief of staff and assistants trailed, Tory at the rear with a command sergeant major who looked gentle enough to be a tailor or piano tuner. The open air between buildings was bracing. Gray, sweltering summer had changed to cool, bright autumn. Leaves had turned from green to wine red and siena and banana yellow. Evenings were clear-skied and had snap—sweater weather, football time, Tory thought.

The flag officers' mess, located on the second floor of the A-ring, was a cavernous hall partitioned with oak paneling into separate dining areas. General Devereaux met three other retired reserve generals. He introduced her to his friends in turn: "Mark Nash, 699th Maine, drives tanks around. Ernie Thompson, 919th Virginia, artillery. And Conrad MacIntosh, 888th Colorado, transportation, trucks." They were all very nice and shook her hand. Tory was so overwhelmed she hardly tasted her lunch. Afterward, free of generals and decorum, she stopped by a big old tree, leaned against its shedding white side, and wept.

CHAPTER 16

After the strange, haunting, maybe crazy interview with Ibrahim Shoob, David prepared to leave Walter Reed Army Medical Center to interview Mary Corcoran. First, though, he 'commed Tory to ask about Shoob. A clerk answered: "No, Sir. I'm sorry, Lieutenant Breen isn't here this morning."

"Are you expecting her back?" David glanced at the clock. It was noon.

"Hmm... She's at the Pentagon—oh, here she comes now." The clerk took a moment to transfer the call from her com button to Tory's. "Hello?" Tory said.

"I hear you were at the Pentagon," David said. "About our man Shoob and his flying saucer story?"

She laughed. "No, it was a personal matter. You think Ib is full of beans?"

"He's full of something, and I only hope it's not really what he says."

"I know," she said darkly.

"Hell of a greeting card to send me. Why me?"

"You said people bring you problems. Okay, there's a problem." She paused. "All right, so I also wondered if we could have lunch sometime."

"I was trying to figure out a way to ask you that," he said.

"See, so that's solved. Can you help Ib?"

"I don't know. Is he—I mean, he's not nuts or anything? Drink? Take drugs?"

"He's as straight as arrows get, Captain."

"Say, if we're going to lunch, can you just call me Dave and I'll call you Tory?"

"Hmmm. I'll call you David. You're more of a David than a Dave."

"Though you're more of a Tory than a Victoria."

"Yes, please call me Tory. Sort of breaks the ice a little better."

"Tomorrow? Noon?"

With her *byyye!* echoing in his ears, David left for Walter Reed carrying his briefcase. Rather than drive through the insane traffic, he took a shuttle bus on Jankowsky's advice. He wore his regulation raincoat over his fatigues, for the crisp autumn sky was clouding up and the first few droplets feathered the windshield of the shuttle van. The 9 mm. NATO standard rode high and awkwardly inside the coat.

It was lunch time, and he was hungry. He checked his watch. He had time before his scheduled interview, so he found his way to the cafeteria. He crossed the threshold into a clamor of people and dinnerware. The huge room was filled with the aromas of beef, bread, and coffee. David joined a long line and shuffled along inches at a time, holding his tray.

He'd noticed a cloverleaf of helicopter pads near the building. A group of flight-suited pilots and nurses sat at a table in the bustling cafeteria. He noticed a hand waving, then a certain ash-blond head—Maxie! He waved back, and she lit up with a grin of delight and waved again.

He bought his lunch and, awkwardly holding the

tray and briefcase, made his way to a free table near her. She joined him, looking dashing in her olive green flight suit, pockets brimming with gear, stethoscope draped around her neck, camo fatigues bloused into jump boots. She had evidently finished lunch and brought along her cup of steaming coffee.

"Hey you!" he said. She slid in opposite him in the booth. He added: "Been a medevac pilot long?"

"Combat flight nurse." She whacked his arm. "Silly."

"You look incredibly cool in your flight suit—say, your roommate sent me a zinger."

"I was kinda hoping she would." Maxie radiated conspiracy.

"This is a real zinger, Maxie."

"Is that good or bad? I mean, is a zinger like a kiss, or is it—?"

"Either the guy she sent is ready for St. Elizabeth's, or we're all in big trouble."

"Oh that. Tory mentioned it and I don't buy it either. There's an explanation for everything," Maxie said. "You watch and see. Meanwhile, you ought to call Tory and thank her for sending you business."

"I already did. We're having lunch tomorrow."

"*Ooo.* You work fast."

"You're pretty fast yourself," he said, adding: "Thanks."

The MAES detachment cleared out in a body, carrying trays and mugs, and she excused herself to tag along. He got a kiss goodbye on one cheek. As she dashed off, David looked around to see if anyone had noticed the kiss—a no-no for people in uniform. But that was Maxie. He chuckled to himself as he speared a chunk of beef dripping with gravy. If Maxie got to be a general, people would probably have to kiss each other rather than salute...

A quarter hour later, David found himself in a completely different space, waiting in a floor polish-smelling corridor while a nurse stepped into a room to announce his arrival. The nurse whispered: "She's just been sedated, so she'll be out again. You could talk with her for a minute." The nurse motioned for him to step inside, then positioned the door halfway open behind him. Twilight filled a four-bed room that smelled of fruit or soap or something. Shafts of sunlight angled in through venetian blinded windows. As David's eyes adjusted to the gloom, the curtains and the draped beds looked shroud-like. On a night table, David saw the source of the smell: a large basket of flowers, and a love letter; the husband, poor guy. "Mary?"

"Yes." The voice was a whisper, a moan. He followed its faint echo to a corner bed. And stopped at a grotesque sight. Blinking, he saw what looked like a Hallow E'en pumpkin wrapped in a sheet, grinning at him. As his eyes dilated further in the underwater light, he made sense of what he saw. A woman of nondescript age was sitting, propped up with pillows in a hospital bed, a poignant reminder that rape was a crime of violence, not sexuality. She was draped in sheets except for her head. Her eyes were swollen like plums. Her upper lip had been split, revealing her teeth, and was scabbing over. She raised a hand, and David took it. It felt dry, and warm, and firm. She whispered: "I look worse than I feel. It hurts to smile, hon."

"I'm glad you have your sense of humor, Mary." David pulled up a chair. He introduced himself. "I wish we'd known more about this sooner."

"That's my fault, Captain. I didn't want to make waves."

"Nothing is your fault about this, Mary, nothing. You're the victim of a bad guy and the Army hasn't been so swift taking care of you either."

"They are taking good care of me, Sir."

"You're a good soldier." David sighed in frustration. "Mary—?"

"Yes, hon?"

"Maybe we can piece together your story and figure out some way to help other women a little sooner, maybe prevent things like this happening."

"Yes." Her plum lids appeared to be narrowing.

"Mary, you went to see the Chaplain. Did someone in that office meet with you?"

"Yes."

"How did you present your story?"

She licked her lips and spoke slowly. "I was crying a lot. The sergeant was very nice."

"Which sergeant?"

"Composite Force ... Chaplain's ... Office." It was a whisper.

"Did he write everything down?"

She whispered something, and David asked her to repeat. "Tape," she said.

"Did they promise they would talk with the man?"

"Yes. But ... couldn't."

David frowned. "Why not?"

"Top Five."

"Pardon me?"

Mary's eyes were shut, and her breathing was

becoming regular. As he watched her sleep, her hands gripped the edge of the sheet. Her head tilted back, her face assumed a look of fright. She shook her fists ineffectually and moaned at some awful dream. He tried to comfort her, squeezing her hands gently until they relaxed onto her stomach and he covered them with a sheet. He wanted badly to see the guy who'd done this put away. And he was puzzled by her last statement. What was Top Five? And why couldn't the chaplain's assistant talk with her assailant?

A shuttle bus took David south on 16th Street. At Dupont Circle he changed shuttles west into the armed camp surrounding the Atlantic Hotel and Convention Center, near the Islamic Mosque and Cultural Center adjacent to Rock Creek Park. There were small demonstrations going on outside the barbed wire barriers, but police were out in force, at least equal in number to the demonstrators. Through a thin drizzle, the sky glowed with bright opal light lacking penetrating power. Thick shadows brimmed behind every shiny surface.

David left the shuttle and walked toward the hotel. National Guard troops in fatigues and MP insignia were massed behind plywood blinds just inside the barbed wire. David was stopped at several checkpoints by National Guard soldiers in fatigues, helmets, and field gear, carrying rifles. The ring of barbed wire around the Atlantic stretched four city blocks. Engineer troops were dividing the streets around the hotel using tank traps. Flatbed trucks hauled in the man-size concrete pyramids, and cranes lifted them into place every few feet, three rows deep, to stop any bomb-carrying vehicle. David walked through a zigzag lane in the tank traps, past soldiers in sandbagged machine-gun nests. The hotel had a huge underground parking garage three floors deep. David boarded another shuttle that detoured through underground caverns filled with olive-drab military vehicles. He glimpsed shaven-headed soldiers carrying heavy ammunition boxes, cleaning rifles, repairing equipment. For a moment he thought they were either Marines or Army Airborne, but the uniforms were different—their fatigue mottling was a subdued blue and yellow he'd never seen before. The shuttle let its passengers disembark in front of the main hotel entrance of Tower 1.

The Atlantic had a vast, domed meeting hall off to one side, similar to the U.N. building in New York, but with three towers instead of one. The towers and the hall shared access through a magnificent five-story lobby and greenhouse containing a living rain forest. David enjoyed his walk through the miniature jungle and took an elevator up into Tower 3. The Atlantic was a line of three 35-story towers, joined in the first five floors by a magnificent lobby. Tower 1, in which currently the CON2 delegates stayed, also boasted the main entrance to the entire complex. Tower 2 served as barracks for several thousand lower-ranking enlisted personnel. Tower 3 served as an office building, headquarters, and military command post.

First, David visited the Chaplain's office. He got to speak with a staff sergeant William Duester, who had been Mary Corcoran's contact. Duester was a small, trim man with light-brown hair and a thick maple-colored mustache. His quick gray eyes were at once sympathetic and hard. He rose and offered David a seat. "What can I do for you, Captain?"

"I understand you taped a conversation with a Sergeant Mary Corcoran, who was raped and beaten a few days later. She also contacted our office, and I'm just sorry that we didn't act sooner."

Duester nodded. "I agree with you there, Sir. I feel the same way." His eyes had a troubled glitter. "Trouble is, Top Five has confiscated both our copies."

"Top Five?"

"General Montclair's headquarters, Sir. They're strictly off-limits to us, but they can nose around here all they want. The Chaplain objected, but Colonel Bronf insisted. That's the story I got. Anyway, I don't have the recording to give you. It's gone. Unless you can find a way to get up to Top Five and get it back." He laughed. "I'm joking. Nobody goes up there."

Lieutenant Colonel Rick Bellamy's office was on the 12th floor of Tower 3. Bellamy, the Provost Marshal on location, was an amiable man of 40, tall and sandy-haired. "Come on in, Captain," he said. "Pour yourself a cup of coffee. Have you seen the view from here?"

Bellamy's corner office had two large windows, one overlooking the lobby and looking toward the middle tower, the other window overlooking the domed meeting hall and, beyond that, a southeasterly view toward the centers of government. "There's the White House," he said. David noted the Washington Monument obelisk, the Capitol dome, the museums on the Mall, and other magnificent structures lost in haze beyond.

"Sir, can we get into Top Five?"

Bellamy frowned. "That would be the top five floors of this building. General Montclair's headquarters. Off-limits to everyone but General Montclair and his crackerjack troops. I was there a few days ago and got thrown out. My first and only time. Why?"

David sipped his coffee. "I need the recordings of Mary Corcoran's conversation with Chaplain's Assistant Duester. Top Five came and took them."

"I know. It's a tough situation. I'm supposed to be the top cop here, and they bypassed me completely."

"Too bad Corcoran didn't contact you, Sir."

"Agreed. I would have forwarded the recordings to Composite HQ before these turkeys could grab them."

"Any idea why they'd grab them?"

"Publicity. Can you imagine the media interest in something like this? Any news out of this building is hot news right now. I think General Montclair would not appreciate the attention."

"I understand, but I have a job to do." He remembered Jankowsky's admonition to handle these cases to the best of his ability. "I need the recordings to complete my file."

"You could close out your report by saying Top Five confiscated them."

"I have to go up there and try. Who is Colonel Bronf?"

"He's Montclair's assistant chief of staff for security."

"And I'll need whatever you have regarding the criminal investigation."

Bellamy held his coffee mug in one hand as he stood relaxed. The other hand was tucked into a trouser pocket, non-regulation. "I can give you my patrol MP's crime report on Corcoran's rape. It was our case, until Top Five threw us off the case. My investigation is incomplete."

"I don't understand the setup here, Sir."

"The Pentagon runs Composite Force directly, through the operational units stationed here and at Rock Creek Park. Everyone has to have their finger in the pie, in the name of checks and balances. You've got the reservists in Rock Creek Park. Then you've got the National Guard from Virginia, Maryland, and Delaware camped out in the streets around the hotel with their barbed wire and tank traps. Then you've got my Regular Army MP battalion guarding the inside of the hotel except the assembly hall, which has private civilian security guards. The delegates have immunity from arrest or prosecution, so they can do whatever they want and get away with it; the guards are just window dressing. Where it gets dicey is this. The top five floors of Tower 3 are General Montclair's operational headquarters, a totally separate command that answers separately to the Pentagon, and Montclair seems to have brought in troops of his own—"

"Those shaven-headed types? "

"Yes, commandos specially trained for this duty. I asked Colonel Bronf about those guys, and he told me I didn't have a need to know. Trust us, he said. Okay, I won't argue. I'm the Provost Marshal here, the police chief, but they won't allow me or my people above the 30th floor of Tower 3, nor are we terribly welcome down in the lower garage, where they have their armory. And what an arsenal. I guess they're prepared to repel an invasion force if need be."

David changed tack. "I'm going to see Colonel Bronf, and I want to also see the alleged rapist."

"So," Bellamy said sighing and sitting down, putting his feet up, "you want to try your luck upstairs."

"I've got to try, Colonel. Besides, I can get a warrant from my boss, or his boss, or whatever it takes. I mean, we're all part of the same armed forces, aren't we?"

"You've got spirit." Bellamy dictated the number, and David entered it into his lapel com. After about ten minutes of bouncing from one enlisted clerk to another, David spoke with Colonel Bronf. David explained his mission. The colonel said: "Take the elevator up to the 31st floor of Tower 3. Step outside and wait. Someone will escort you to my office. Under no circumstances are you to wander around. Got that?"

"Yessir. Thank you." The line went dead, and David gingerly rang off.

"I give you credit," Bellamy said. "You got invited up. Then again, I made the trip a few days ago, on an unrelated matter. Maybe it's beginner's luck. Your charm will wear off." He rose to walk David into the 12th floor lobby to the elevator.

When David stepped off the elevator on the 31st floor, an officer and two enlisted men were waiting for him. Two were privates wearing MP bands and sidearms; the third introduced himself as Major Lee, probably a Korean-American. Lee had a handshake like a steel trap, and a smile just as chilly. "We appreciate your coming," Lee said, "because we want to cooperate with our neighboring command to the fullest."

"Separate command, I heard," David said as they trooped down a long corridor. Everywhere, in the periphery of his vision, he spotted men busy loading, piling up supplies, moving ammo. It was dusty dirty work, but the men seemed in good spirits. There was a silent intensity of purpose. "A healthy thing," Lee replied to David's question as they stopped outside a door whose plaque told David he was about to see General Montclair's Deputy Chief of Staff for Security. "This is a completely separate command. We are the real protection for CON2. The Composite is essentially our support and backup. We've got our own everything—Quartermaster, Field Hospital, MP Battalion, G-1, G-2, you name it. We don't even shop in the same exchange. It's a matter of checks and balances. It's been well thought out at the highest levels." Lee led David into a large office and introduced him to a bald, sweaty man who smelled of cigarette smoke and looked like he could stand a shave and a diet. Colonel Bronf excused himself from a conference with a lizard-faced major and turned his attention to David. The lizard-like man had remarkable mud-colored eyes, angular cheekbones in a forward-thrust face, and a small, dry-looking mouth. For a second, David thought the man's tongue slithered, forked, over his lips as he stared at David; then he left the room. Nah, David thought, this place just spooks me.

"What can I help you with?" Colonel Bronf boomed.

David explained his purpose, concluding: "Sir, I need to interview both the accused private and his unit commander. And I need the Chaplain's Office recordings."

Bronf had black brows and a dramatic face. "Well now, Captain, that's not likely, unless you get travel orders, because the private has already been transported to await trial at his parent unit in Oklahoma. The recordings have gone there also."

David felt shocked. "Sir, with all due respect, I believe the accused was supposed to remain in this military jurisdiction."

"Well now Captain, that's where you're wrong. Not a lawyer, are you?" Bronf glanced at David's lapel insignia. "Infantry. Well, that's nice. I've had this conversation already with Bellamy and one or two other people in his chain of command, and I'm getting tired of repeating myself. Our private is a stupid son of a bitch who raped a woman and cast the U.S. Army in a bad light, just when national media attention is focused our way. I don't appreciate that and I assure you that General Montclair takes a dim view. So, the private can't get a fair trial here." He extended his hand. "Goodbye, Captain. Tell your boss we'll be happy to cooperate in any way we can, but we shipped the private as far away as we could, and nobody is bringing him back here. Have a nice day."

For a moment, David boiled. He wanted to take this smelly, fat officer, slam him against the wall, and choke him until he lost the attitude. At the same time, he remembered that he must check his temper. He must not let this guy win the day. He felt the M.P.'s and Lee rustling by his side in case he made a move, and he relaxed abruptly. "If you say so, Colonel. I'll note your comments in my report. Thank you."

"Back so soon?" said Bellamy when David rejoined him downstairs. "I told you. They keep to themselves and, since they get away with everything, they must be under orders from way up."

David was still angry. He suddenly hated politics and couldn't wait to get back to the real Army. Outside, gray storm clouds moved across the city. Only the needle of Washington's Monument protruded clearly. Its red aircraft warning lights winked in slow and painful rhythm against the shrouded dome of the Capitol.

They spoke a few minutes more, and David was glad to be back in the free, fresh air away from the hotel. As he looked back on it, its white walls gleamed, but its windows were like eyes following him with their dour gaze.

CHAPTER 17

Just before dusk, David drove toward Observatory Circle. He was in his own car, heading home to Alexandria, and the promised rendezvous with Coast Guard Chief Petty Officer Ibrahim Shoob was on his way. After six p.m., there was a faint sunshine in the air, like a giant lie—as if it had been a sunny day. By the time David arrived at the intersection of Massachusetts Avenue and 34th Street, it was getting dark.

No sign of Shoob.

David sat in the car, parked at the south-bound curb on 34th Street, with the window half rolled down, and listened to soft music on the radio. He finished a sandwich and a carton of milk and wished he had coffee. Atop several buildings in the island of grass and trees were small domes housing telescopes. The empty vice presidential mansion loomed darkly.

Massive tree crowns all around floated silently, and David wished he had not agreed to meet the old NCO here at this hour. In the darkness, fog rolled like a wall across the road, under the trees, up the lawns at Observatory Circle. It thickened as it went, and cars crawled past blinded by their own headlights. David found himself being studied for a minute by a prowling police car. Of all the dumb places to arrange a secret meeting, he thought. Where was Shoob?

After a half hour, David was ready to drive home. Thinking better of it, he got out of the car to stretch his legs. Traffic had died down, with only an occasional car passing. The street glistened wetly in the fog under street lights peering through leaves. David decided to give Shoob one more chance. He'd walk up to the NSSO building, look for him, and then return to his car. If Shoob hadn't shown up by then, David would drive home. He crossed the street and walked up the central drive. A black car crept out of nowhere and rustled at his side. "How's it going, Captain?" called a man's voice. "Got a minute?"

David stopped, resisting the urge to loosen the holster of his service revolver. He saw two men in suits and raincoats eyeing him. One flashed a badge. "Secret Service. How are you tonight?" The speaker was a young looking man with steel rimmed glasses, prematurely balding, very pleasant. Preppy type. But there was an unmistakeable tension in the air all around.

"Fine. Looking for someone." David stepped close and, unbidden, opened his wallet to show his military I.D. card. The Secret Service man nodded, barely glanced at it. "A kind of heavy set Coast Guard NCO," David said.

"Sorry," the blond man said languidly. David heard a click as an assault rifle went back on safety inside the car. "Hope he shows up soon. Good luck."

"Thanks." David watched as the long black car rolled away toward Admiral's House, and fog closed behind it. With it went the immediate tension, but David realized that his knees had been shaking, and they weren't still yet. In five minutes he reached the center of the circle, passed around the main Observatory building, and approached the NSSO building completed after 2000. NSSO had most of its offices in three underground stories; the one above ground story blended innocuously with its antique surroundings.

David found the front door locked. A dim bulb gleamed along a deserted corridor inside. "Chief!" David rapped on the door. "Chief!" He walked around the building, pausing under a light globe. "Chief?"

Nothing.

He started for his car, picking up stride. This place was spooking him, and he'd be glad to be home. Time for a hot bath, a drink, a good night's sleep. Fog rolled thickly, and a chill moisture beaded on glass surfaces all around. In this pea-soup moisture, sounds carried well—too well; he heard a mix of muffled sounds, some of them nothing more than a volume of air blowing against a wall or swishing through trees. The fog itself seemed to stalk silently all around him, circling him like dim shark shapes.

He heard a man's voice—or was it the cough of a starter turning in a car?—and whirled.

Was that a bulky form lumbering down the path 100 yards away, or a glimpse of a moving pine bough, a wall of fog behind another wall of fog?

"Shoob!" David cried out. "Shoob?" He peered into the mist, which alternately closed and opened, and David squinted desperately, wiping his eyes with his hands, to stare more intently. He drew his gun.

Wiping water out of his blinking eyes as he took one step closer, then another, he sensed that something was wrong.

He heard a muffled shout and started jogging. "Shoob!"

He inserted a clip from his web belt, and unlocked the safety. This sent a metallic clatter echoing through the damp complex, bounding off walls and returning to its source.

David called out: "Shoob? Are you okay?"

The fog closed in thickly, swirling.

There was a dragging sound, like heels in gravel.

David heard a sound of struggle—

—a fist whacking flesh—

—the sound of a door slamming.

David ran toward the sounds. His path took him around the central garden with its greenhouses, and back onto the main drive that led to where his car was parked.

David heard a car start up, saw twin red taillights...a van.

"Hey," he called out, "wait! Stop!" He wanted to check the inside, prepared to be embarrassed if this were a mistake. Shoob's paranoia seemed to be rubbing off on him and he must get control of himself.

Red taillights swam away toward the street. David put on one desperate sprint, but he was too late. The van pulled out, turning smoothly, changing gears, and tooled away, its engine becoming fainter in the mist.

David ran toward his car, holstering the gun and thinking—should he try to chase them? Would he miss Shoob if Shoob showed up here after all? Or had Shoob been nabbed? Dammit! As he jogged puffing toward his car, he knew the answer—he'd never find them in this fog. He wouldn't recognize the van if he saw it.

He drove to the Vice President's House, hoping to alert the two Secret Service men, but, bafflingly, the house was dead still and David could not find a soul as he drove crawling around the house.

What am I doing? He asked himself as he waited in the main drive once more. He turned the engine off and waited, listening to the sound of his heartbeat, the whisper of an occasional car innocently and slowly crawling past on Observatory Circle.

He called the local police and spoke with a dispatcher, but felt awkward. What could he tell them? To check every van within a five state radius?

He called Jankowsky at home. "I'm sorry to bother you, Sir, but I think Shoob may have been abducted from under my nose.

"You think? Did you see it or not?"

"Not exactly, Sir. It's very foggy, and he wasn't where he was supposed to be. I heard noises, and a van drove off."

Jankowski processed for a moment. "Go home."

"Sir, I have to wait for the police."

"Oh shit, you called the police?"

"Yessir, under the circumstances…" An alarm bell went off. Something wasn't quite right about this conversation.

"Okay… okay…I understand. You did the right thing. Just go home, okay? We'll handle it from here."

"We, Sir?"

"Go home."

"Yessir."

At that moment, a police car with flashing lights slowed on 34th, started to turn into the driveway, and stopped. The lights stopped flashing. There was a brief pause, the twirling lights went dark, and the police car drove slowly away. Called off? By whom? Why?

As David drove home through the fog, he called Tory.

She sounded concerned, thoughtful, cautious. "Everything is so strange these days. Poor Ib—I'm worried. I could call his wife, see if he's home."

"Why don't you do that and call me back?"

He felt thrilled to hear her voice. It was chilly and he turned the heater in the car on.

Minutes later, as he rolled by her house, she called. "David?"

"Hey, look out the window." He slowed.

A figure appeared in a first floor window. A woman. She waved. "Is that you?"

"Do you always wave at strange cars?"

"Just certain strange cars."

"How's Ib?"

"Not home. I didn't want to scare his wife, Hala, so I said it was something about work that could wait until tomorrow. She didn't seem worried—said this is his night to meet with his book club; they sometimes meet until ten or eleven."

David tooted twice.

"Want to stop by?"

"Wish I could. I've had a big day, and tomorrow will be more of the same. Tell me again that you'll have lunch with me. It's all I ask." He glanced back and saw her still leaning out the window before her house receded among the trees.

"I give you my word, mon capitaine."

"Ah oui, cette joie—je suis—how do you say happy in French?"

"—Uppee."

"Thank you. I am very uppee to be your friend, mademoiselle."

🌐 ANN Breaking News with Allison Miranda ⚡

ALLISON: We recently asked Chairman Carberry how he feels about the strength of the Ten Amendment Limit.

CARBERRY: I've heard all the scare stories, and I'm here to tell you that I am still in control, and that limit of ten amendments is not going away.

ALLISON: What about the possibility that the delegates might revolt and have a floor decision, which would ignore the Procedures Committee entirely?

CARBERRY: It's not going to happen. We're going to get things ironed out in the next few days. As I said, I'm still in control. Then we'll all go home. Let's not worry prematurely about problems that may never arise.

CHAPTER 18

Tory felt thrilled about this interesting new man as she sat in the plush chair by the window. The wall tv flickered with news, a talking head speaking softly, but her thoughts were in outer space. David Gordon. She couldn't help saying his name quietly to herself every few minutes. She was finding it hard to concentrate on the novel she was reading, and yet she wasn't interested in the news either. She hoped she wouldn't make a fool out of herself at lunch tomorrow—but he seemed such a fun person, so really serious and quiet yet lively and certainly decent. And yet, she already felt the pain beginning, the fear of disappointment, that dark wall she would never be able to get past, had never been able to get through with any of the men who'd taken an interest in her and then—

Her reverie was interrupted by Maxie, who stormed out of the bedroom dressed to go out. "Tory, ya gotta go with me. I'm not going alone, and I'm not staying here."

"Maxie..."

All her protests were in vain. Maxie's beau had been mean to her, and she wanted to go out man-hunting. Tory was tired. She was a little worried about Ib, although surely he was at his book club and he'd contact David with his morbid fears and conspiracy papers tomorrow. She wanted to climb into the feathers and fall asleep daydreaming about David Gordon. Maxie, more hyper than usual, begged, pleaded, and cajoled with Tory to accompany her on a wild night out this evening. Tory didn't drink much—two glasses of wine and she had a headache. She worried that if Maxie went alone, she'd wreck her car driving home drunk, so she agreed to go along.

As Tory finished dressing and stepped to the curb, Maxie was already in the gray Porsche. Tory walked through the fog and got in. Maxie looked crisp in sweater and denim skirt. The usual blonde whisp floated over her forehead.

"Why don't you give Van Meeuwen the shoe?"

"I don't want to talk about it."

"Okay." Tory couldn't stand Van Meeuwen.

Maxie rummaged in her glove compartment. Out fell expensive lipstick, perfume, a mechanical pencil, a USO New Testament, cigarettes, surgical gloves, a stethoscope, a. field NBC (nuclear, biological, chemical) kit. Even so, Maxie was class, like her blondness, which wasn't overly gold or loud, but soft and bright as a sunbeam as it whipped energetically around her temples. She had a handsome wide face, with crinkly eyes, a model's streamlined nose, a few freckles, and a sensuous mouth. Tory had once thought, if someone wanted to have lots of plastic surgery, they'd want everything to end up like what Maxie had naturally. In fact, though her white uniform looked tailor-made, it was bought off the quartermaster shelf; she was just that thin and shapely. She looked ravishing in her Army officer's nursing whites, and she'd look just as ravishing in her flight suit. Then again she smoked, occasionally drank too much, and regularly received speeding tickets. "That's our Maxie," people said.

Maxie tore down the city streets. Tory closed her eyes. "Gotta give you driving lessons."

"It's been tried." Maxie laughed and lit an imported oval with gold imprinted paper. Tory rolled her window down. Maxie drove around the Beltway and then westward out of town. Soon they cruised along tree-lined country roads.

Maxie said tipping her soda can up but keeping her eyes on the road: "I hear you and David Gordon are having lunch tomorrow."

"He seems to be a nice guy," Tory said guardedly. The last man in her life was an Air Force officer transferred to Alaska a year ago, from whom she'd never heard again, after a hot and steamy romance of (she'd counted, fool) 117 days. Tory had forced herself to forget his name, his rank, his serial number, and his state of origin. She couldn't really remember at this point what he'd looked like. Didn't want to.

"Whoo-hoo!" Maxie whooped, pulling an imaginary train-whistle. Tory was puzzled. Maxie could have had David, at least as a fling, certainly as a friend, and yet she always seemed to fall for guys who hurt her. Paul Van Meeuwen, Maxie's current squeeze, a handsome doctor in his mid-30's, performed buttpucker surgeries at Walter Reed, played 18 rounds of golf on Saturday, owned two houses and part of the family tire fortune, sponsored Formula 1 races at Watkins Glen, and loved Maxie—in that order. Tory wasn't convinced but didn't want to say so for fear of seeming jealous.

They drove through a guard gate onto the small

Virginia military reservation. The Porsche stopped in a cloud of dust outside the Officers' Club. Maxie turned her huge keyring and the motor went from hum to silence. Tory had once asked why she had so many keys. They were for half of Washington, Maxie said; and she kept them all with her to remember the people she loved.

Tory got out and zipped up her jacket. Her breath steamed as she stared at a dilapidated building. "Yu-uk. Want to leave?"

"It'll be an adventure!" Maxie protested. Tory went along, though she'd always hated these places. They stopped at the ladies' room to touch up their makeup. Then they walked through the swinging doors into that redly glowing, music-pulsating world of clinking glasses and laughing voices. They found a table. A waiter took their orders—Campari and soda for Tory, martini with a twist, up, for Maxie. Tory leaned forward under the waiter's tray. "You change that to white wine, you hear?"

"You're right," Maxie said. Tory thought Maxie seemed a little off tonight.

"Hello," said several men all at once, holding drinks and looking charming.

"Are you one guy with five heads?" Maxie said.

The men separated and babbled: "I'm Bill. I'm Bob. I'm drunk. Ha ha ha. No really, we saw you here and. Two beautiful women. Bookends, a dark sultry one and a light happy one. The blonde, now you must be a nurse."

"That's a rodge," Maxie said.

"And you," Jeff said, kneeling by Tory so his head was level with hers. "You are a chopper pilot. You have that glint in your eye."

"I've got the glint," Tory said, "but not the chopper. To chop onions, maybe."

Jeff had hair on nine of his fingers. Tory exchanged glances with Maxie. "This is an infantry post," Jeff said. "Ahah! You run a tight ship in the AG's office." He snapped his finger. "No, you are the AG." AG was the Adjutant General, responsible for personnel and administrative matters. She leaned forward and patted the hand with the missing ring. "I'm a truck driver."

Jeff grinned coldly. "A truck driver."

"Honest. Big rig." She extended her arms out as far as she could. "Big, big truck. Full of frozen chickens."

"That's right," Maxie said. "And we have to hurry up and drink, or the chickens will thaw. Then we'll have to drive extra fast to make it to California before they spoil."

"But you're a nurse," reminded Bill or John or Bob or Stu.

"That's why I have to ride along, to take care of all those chickens."

"Civilians," said one of them with a wave-off as they left for easier game.

"Thank you," Tory said.

The men drifted off and had a fist fight and the MP's came. At peace for a while, Maxie and Tory chatted. Then a young blond guy who'd been hanging back shyly came over and offered to buy Maxie a drink, roses, anything. Maxie laughed at the inventiveness and bantered with him a while. Tory's mind drifted to other things. One Campari, and it went to her head a little. Now what about Ib and his strange file? His strange behavior in general. Men and their strange—

"Tory!" Maxie shouted, shoving her, and Tory

realized she was leaning tiredly in her seat. "Hey, come on!" Maxie said. Jeff and Bob and whoever were back. Two cold beers slid across the table in a wake of suds and shaved ice. "Lady," Jeff said, "you have some serious laughing to do."

Tory laughed. "Probably another true statement."

A Major Krest or Krist, biggest guy of the lot, who spoke with a beer in his fist and a pointing finger big as a salami, shouted hoarsely: "I don't know about you guys but I'm going overseas to police dick heads, pardon my french, a single man, unlike some of you gentlemen—" Everything Major Kryst said came out in a hoarse blare.

"—Everyone here is single—" interjected someone.

"—And I," continued Major Krust or Krost, "for one, would like to spend my last evening in the civilized world, if you can call this armpit of Gehenna such, with two of the most beautiful women I have ever seen. Gentlemen, I give you"—he pointed finger and beer bottle at Maxie—"the golden glow of sunshine peering through mother's grape bower on the morning of perfect civilization. Am I right, gentlemen?"

They all clapped.

Major Krast continued: "Gentlemen, I give you for your astonishment and breathless introspection"—pointing at Tory, who found herself genuinely gasping at the flattery—"this violet-eyed Mona Lisa whose memory shall haunt me across the wine-dark sea, this siren whose song draws bolder sailors, soldiers, and merchant marines than I onto the pounding shoals of divorce, dementia, and other self destruction. Am I once again right, Gentlemen?"

They clapped and whistled and cheered.

"Barkeep! Barkeep!" the major bellowed, mangling Homer: "Line 'em up! I want to go down to the she in sips! Ladies," he said turning, "will you grace us by telling us your names, nicknames, aliases, any old monicker will do for a love-starved old pirate crew like us."

"Maxie." "Tory."

"Ahah!" he bellowed. "Max 'n Vic. A shopping center for our hearts. Gentlemen, we take our hearts in hand like shopping carts and wheel them hungrily from the rutabagas to the antofagasta oysters, hoping for a dram of such sweet liquore as resides in these noble vessels, these falernian bottles, these amontilladan casks!"

Tory estimated later that she laughed nonstop for two hours. Or was it three? She didn't drink much, but it didn't take much. Maxie got pretty looped, but she always had a hard inner core of self-control. Singing loudly a number of marching songs, from "Far Away" to "See the lady in red, she makes a living in her bed," the men carried Max 'n Vic on their shoulders. "Home, home, sweet soldiers, 'tis the dawn light calls to mine forsaken heart!" bellowed Major Karst or was it Kurst.

"Let us cast lots for their delicate hands," ventured an understudy thespian.

"No, no," shouted Tory, still laughing, "our car will do nicely." Her anxiety was moot, however, for at that moment up pulled the long prisoner van of Company A, 194th MP Battalion. Six armed men in olive green, with white hats and night sticks, stepped out. A sergeant said: "Gentlemen, you have just awakened the wives of all senior officers on post."

Tory covered her face with her scarf.

"My good man," Major Kirst said.

The NCO held up a hand. "Gentlemen, I can offer you choice—a ride home, or a ride to the station. Anyone who wants to go home, please board now."

"Ah, 'tis a ruin upon fair Ithaca's face," grumbled Major Kerst, but he meekly joined his fellows in climbing in. Max 'n Vic waved goodbye as the van tooled away.

Tory drove. She and Maxie grew increasingly quiet on the way back to Washington. The car's powerful engine purred hypnotically, and Tory cracked a window to get the cool night air. She didn't look at Maxie much. Smelling cigarette smoke, she assumed that Maxie was quietly indulging in her nasty habit. "I did have a great time after all," Tory said after a while. Then she looked over and saw that Maxie's face was covered with tears. "Maxie! What on earth!"

"Oh Tory," Maxie said, "I feel terrible."

"What? You gotta throw up?"

"I'm such a total failure."

"No you're not."

"I am, I am, I am. Oh!" She bawled loudly for a minute or two. Then she spoke lucidly, with only an occasional sob. "I don't have a decent man in my life, and I never will. You'll fall in love with David Gordon, I know you will. He's such a nice man, he'll love you madly. I'll never have anything like that. Just stupid guys who drink and tell jokes and wind up in the pokey, like that dumb major back there. Or Van Meeuwen, that bastard—don't think I'm kidding myself for a minute."

"Then why do you waste time with guys like Van Meeuwen?"

"I dunno. I have to, I guess. I'm an only child and

my parents' only hope in life. I'm a rich girl and I hate it, Tory. They trained me so well, sent me to all those stupid schools, and I can charm Lincoln off a penny, but what good is it, I'm so empty inside!"

"Maxie, where is this all coming from? You're a wonderful nurse. You help people and save lives every day. Look at how David brought you flowers and all. People really do love you, Maxie, not your money or your smile. You are a great person."

"Thank you." Maxie was silent for a while. She lit another cigarette and stared out the window at the passing night lights with tear-stained face. "I'm sorry, Tory. Don't mean to spoil your night." She blew her nose. "Actually, sometimes I don't want to be a nice person or a great person. I just want to be me, but I don't know who that is underneath the charming hostess and all. I could have had a thing with David, maybe, but I couldn't let myself. I'm ashamed to say. It's got to be a doctor or a judge or a senator. Lotta money. That's what my folks beat and pressed and nagged into me. Try growing up with my mother! Not to mention my father." She blew her nose again. "That's why I'm going airborne. I'm going to show them." She put out her cigarette.

Tory said gently: "You're going to show yourself. That's all that counts." It became quiet in the car. The long monotonous miles ticked away and Maxie slept soundly, slumped against the window.

CHAPTER 19

As David drove to work in the morning, he listened to radio news. CON2 was dominating the news as always these days. What did the Procedures people think they were doing? He hoped they would not cave in to extremists. He parked in the I.G. office's quiet neighborhood and walked along the narrow, tree-shaded street of redstone houses. Puddles littered the sidewalk, but the sun was out.

Colonel Jankowsky called David into his office and shut the door. "Wow," Jankowsky said, "both these cases have blown up on you, huh?"

"I didn't know being an I.G. officer would be this hard."

"I just wanted you to know that we believe Shoob was in fact abducted. I want you not to discuss the case with anyone, even our chain of command, unless I know about it first, okay?"

"Yessir. What about his XO?"

"The officer who referred him?"

"She's concerned about him."

"Keep in touch with her. She knows he's been abducted?"

"I called her last night."

"Damn. Okay, I probably would have done the

same. Tell her to keep her mouth shut too, okay? Our office will investigate, along with the Provost Marshal and C.I.C."

David walked down the hall to his small corner office.

His lapel com buzzed, and he answered. It was Tory. "David, Ib never came home last night. His wife is frantic."

"Oh Jeez. I'm sorry. I should have gone to the police."

"You didn't have enough to go on. I just called the civilian police, and they'll work with the JAG office at the Composite to look for him."

"So are we optimistic?"

She paused. "At this point—it's anybody's guess. A little part of me still wonders if he was losing his mind and maybe he's just wandering around in a daze somewhere."

"That would be the easy way for this to be resolved. Will you still be free for lunch?"

"I'll call you around eleven."

David went down the hall to speak with Colonel Jankowsky.

Jankowsky looked anxious, rubbing himself on the head. "Sit down. Close the door. I want you to write up a report and submit it to me, recommending a hold on our case until the police investigation is resolved. Meaning, until Shoob shows up, one way or the other, and C.I.D. finishes their investigation. There is really nothing we can do while it's a police investigation."

"Okay."

"Now, the Corcoran matter. I just found out that the local authorities here in Washington have declined to indict Corcoran's assailant. Also, JAG has waived the right to extradite. The case is changing jurisdiction to Fort Hood, Texas, where the accused is being held."

"That's odd, Sir. I thought we were going to press them."

"Nobody is pressing anyone. Everything here is strange. I'd have thought Composite Force would throw the book at this guy—either from Bellamy over at the Atlantic, or someone on the Rock Creek side. It's politics all the way. There's been no push on from General Norcross at the Pentagon. General Montclair at the Atlantic evidently wants this blemish out of town, and I can't argue with his logic. They'll try this goon at Fort Hood. So wrap up your report, let me have it so I can sign it, I'll forward it on to Fort Hood, and we move on to other things. It just shows how fouled up the whole chain of command is these days."

"Yessir. I'll have that report on your desk this morning."

David hurried to finish draft reports on both the Shoob and Corcoran cases. Tory called at 11. There was no change—no sign of Shoob. After dropping the folders in Jankowsky's in-box, he stepped out of the brownstone, onto the sidewalk, and waited for Tory.

It was a bright, sunny day, almost a false Spring. People scurried here and there with a lightness of step, and the tree crowns were bright. Right on schedule, a lovely, sleek dark green Jaguar purred to a halt. A slender hand pushed the door open, and he heard her voice sing: "Hi! Hop in!"

David eased himself in and pulled the door shut.

Tory said: "Were you scared last night?"

He remembered the fog. "Maybe not scared. It was weired. I was spooked."

Someone honked behind them, and she shifted gears. "I think we'll grab soup and sandwiches. That okay with you?" She was a quick, sure driver. The car exuded an atmosphere of her: clean, smelling of buffed leather and some cleaning agent that had a faint bouquet not unlike bubble gum. David enjoyed her ambiance around him. In various nooks sat a racquet, two paperbacks, a folded blanket; a chocolate colored stuffed female teddy bear with a red bow in her hair and a blue-and-white checked dress; a police whistle on a white lanyard whose loose end seemed to be looking for a holster.

"I'm sorry I got you into this," Tory said.

"Well, I guess here's where I say it's all part of my job."

"I'm buying you lunch."

"Not necessary. But I see I'm scoring points."

"You certainly do keep your sense of humor."

"And you?"

"I try, but I'm too worried about Ib. Tell me everything that happened." He told her. She drew a deep breath. "I hope he'll give them what they want."

"The list?"

"The damned list. The documents, whatever they are. Yes."

David didn't answer. He had a feeling Ibrahim Shoob wouldn't give them a thing. And he was afraid to think what they would do to Ib. "Tory." How nice that name sounded. "There are a lot of people working hard to get him back in one piece."

"You're right. C'mon, I'm starved." They drove past

Composite Force's encampment in Rock Creek Park near 16th St. and Arkansas Ave. On what was normally a picnic lawn were several large, sprawling tents in a mix of camouflage styles from earth tone desert to mossy green forest colors. Arrayed in hypnotic multitude beyond were countless smaller tents. David imagined probably Civil War troops had bivouacked there about 150 years earlier. Tired looking Army Reserve MP's directed traffic. "Poor guys," Tory said, "I wonder if they're getting their baths and laundry services."

He nodded. "Somehow, the Army always manages to come through. It's not pleasant, nor unpleasant, it's just the Army way. You're a nurturer like Maxie."

"Just a well-trained X.O." She parked near Sheridan Circle and they walked to a fancy diner on 22nd Street. He and Tory Breen were just two of thousands in uniform in Washington these days. She looked slender and efficient in her fatigue uniform with jump boots and women's cloth garrison cap. David continued to notice new things about her—the copper glow in dark brown hair pinned up under her cap; the tiny space between her upper front teeth; the dark, serious something in her eyes that could change to a sparkle of laughter. As they sat at the busy lunch counter, she eating a salad, he soup and half a sandwich, he noticed the peach fuzz on her beautifully shaped cheekbones, the way she had of crinkling her lips in a wry smile.

"I wish I'd taken Ib a bit more seriously," David said.

"Maybe he's back already," Tory said with a bright look of hope beyond hope. She commed her office. "Jet? This is Lieutenant Breen. Any sign of Ib?" Her

JOHN T. CULLEN

face fell as she listened to the other person's reply.
"Nothing yet," Tory said. "David, it's fine to wait for
the cops and all. I feel frustrated and helpless. Maybe
it's the M.P. officer in me. I want to do something."

"Tory, if you'd like, I'll help you look for Shoob."

"That's good of you." She sniffled, wiped her nose
with a paper napkin. "Would you do something for
me? Meet me outside my office after work? Please?"

"Sure."

"We've hardly met, and already I'm asking you
for—"

"It's okay, honest."

"—you won't like me when you find out—"

"Huh?"

"Never mind." She picked up her car keys and rose.
"Come on, I have to drive you back to work." She
gave him that hurt, haunted look that he'd seen once
before. What was it with this woman? And why did
he find himself drawn to her? There was definitely
some emotional cauldron under that beautiful face.
Could there be two Kristys in the world, and could
he have met both of them?

She dabbed her eyes when they were in the car,
and she was in charge and driving. "Sorry, David."

"It's okay. Listen, here's what I suggest. After work,
we'll hit a few spots. It may not accomplish much,
but it'll make you feel better."

"Good idea. I'll call Hala and ask where his haunts
are. Who knows, we might hit it just right and learn
something helpful."

"I'll make dinner this evening, and I'd like you to
come."

She smiled at him gratefully and sadly.

"I'm serious. Just a simple pasta dish. You'll see. I

make a pretty good chicken cacciatore. Makes me feel better when I'm down."

They drove in silence, and he wondered if he'd said too much. He didn't want to push things, though he was cautiously interested in her.

She pulled up in the alley behind the 915th, looked around to see if anyone was watching, and planted a dry, warm kiss on his cheek.

He sat in stunned silence. His anxiety disappeared, replaced by the balmy knowledge that she liked him.

She pushed his shoulder gently. "Go on. I'll see you this evening."

He stepped out, walking on air, remembering for the first time since the early days with Kristy what this feeling was like. Scary, intoxicating... oh come on, he told himself, I've just been high and dry for too long. The glow in her eyes, during just a briefly flickering glance, and her faint mysterious smile, told him she really liked him. Then she gave him another brief glance, and it was that haunted look again.

He watched her drive away. The Jaguar slid away in sure, quick strokes amid the confused traffic of a capital in the throes of a revolution. David also felt a little disturbance going on in his heart. Nothing revolutionary just yet. Just a little corner riot or two. One or two squad cars from the Emotion Patrol. Nothing to lose sleep over. Yet.

🌐 **ANN Breaking News with Allison Miranda** ⚡

ALLISON: We're speaking with Delegate Joe Reynolds, MCP—Ohio. Mr. Reynolds, as a member of the Middle Class Party, you promised to abide by the agenda of ten amendments. Today you swore to add an eleventh if the amendment limit goes away, either by Procedures Committee or by all-out floor rebellion. Why?

REYNOLDS: I was appalled this week reading a leftist position paper suggesting that "under God" in the Pledge of Allegiance should be changed to "under gods" or else deleted so atheists and other kooks won't be offended. Over my dead body, pal. It's one God, not two, not fifty, not zero, and He belongs in our Constitution. My amendment will enshrine the present wording in the Constitution, and drive home the point that this is a Christian nation, not an atheist one. It will eliminate any separation of church and state.

CHAPTER 20

Colonel Jankowsky was waiting when David returned from lunch. As David shut the ornate wooden building door, Jankowsky stepped into the hall and said: "You remember our friend the violent private? IQ of 70, emotional age in the Terrible Twos, long rap sheet before he decided to join the Army?"

"Sir, you're a little bit ahead of me." They walked together to David's office.

"They found him dangling from his belt in the stockade in Oklahoma. The son of a bitch committed suicide."

"Pardon me?" The picture did not make any sense. David knew the suspect's kind were generally self-loving, emotionally shallow individuals who always blamed their crimes on other people.

Jankowsky slapped faxes down on David's desk. "Charges were never actually filed. Mary Corcoran has had an emotional breakdown. She'll be discharged from the Service, 100% disabled."

"A damn shame, Sir."

"He'll never bother her again."

"Just in a thousand nightmares."

"The case is a wrap, David. I have your report, and we've got to put it behind us."

"Sorry, Sir. It just seems so pat. And it's odd, this guy wasting himself."

"I was thinking that too."

"No word on Shoob, Sir?"

"Nothing." Jankowsky paused. "We need to talk." He closed the door. David, feeling alarmed, sat down at his desk. Jankowsky leaned against the wall by the window. Oddly, he lowered the venetian blinds, and stood toying with the cords. "I'm going to level with you, David."

"Okay, Sir." Good God, what have I done? What is he going to say?

"David, we were talking earlier, and we've said several times that nothing here is what it seems."

"Yes?"

"I ran a security check on you. Pushed it through, top priority."

"Yes?"

"You now have a Maximum Secret clearance. Do you know what that means?"

"No."

"It means you could, if necessary, start working for the Secret Service this afternoon. It's the same as a Presidential clearance."

David was relieved and stunned.

"This means, David, that if you violate the terms of your clearance, it's not just a misdemeanor or a federal crime. If you accept this clearance, and if you betray our trust, you will be guilty of high treason. That still carries the death penalty under some circumstances. So I'm giving you a chance to back out now. Go to some other unit where you can push paperwork around and go home at 4:15 and be a sorry ass."

David sat gaping.

"If you want to be part of this team, and I think you do, now is the time to say so."

"I don't know, Sir. Sight unseen—I have no idea what you are talking about."

"I understand. I don't blame you." He paused. "If it's any help, I've reviewed your records. You have a brilliant war record. I've watched you in action. You're a heroic man. You have a sense of honor, and common sense to boot. I think you'd welcome a chance to serve your country."

David nodded. "Okay. If I can serve. I'm in."

"Thanks." Jankowsky shook David's hand. "See, not everything is what it seems. Like my little unit here. We don't really need to have a separate I.G. detachment here."

"I wondered about that, Sir."

"The truth is, while I am an I.G. officer, and this is my I.G. detachment, we are a cover for a Federal investigation. A civilian investigation involving several agencies—the FBI, the IRS, Treasury, and various state police forces."

"Geez, who are you after?"

"Robert Lee Hamilton."

David whistled.

"I should properly not say we are after Mr. Hamilton. When I say we, I mean these agencies. I am a facilitator, if you will. This is on orders from the White House. Need to know is Maximum Presidential. We believe Shoob really did stumble onto something. You didn't tell me you were meeting him at the observatory."

"I'm sorry—"

"Don't be. You weren't prepped. You were acting expediently, trying to get to the Corcoran matter, which is stirring up some other issues. But more of that another time. We need to find Shoob because we need the list. We know there is a conspiracy involving CON2, but we don't know who or why. If we had the list, we'd know whom to investigate. The President believes insiders in the White House and the Government conspired to kill Vice President Cardoza and pin it on militia groups. The President has ordered us to monitor—not Hamilton, which would be illegal—but certain individuals who might reasonably be expected to be contacted by Hamilton—if indeed Mr. Hamilton is guilty of anything, this is all if's—and offered any bribes to throw the convention one way or the other. We have wiretap authority under a sealed memorandum from a federal district magistrate. The reason I'm telling you all this is because it's important that you know what really is going on so you don't fall on your face. Shoob might try to contact you, or he might have left the list with someone else. Right now, you are a magnet of sorts. You will continue your activities as I assign cases to you, but everything will be secondary to finding Shoob."

"As a matter of fact, Sir, I'm going to be looking for him this evening. With Lieutenant Breen, his unit X.O."

"The gorgeous woman who dropped you off?" Jankowsky's eyes twinkled.

"I didn't think anyone saw, Sir."

"You've been tailed every minute since you arrived in Washington."

"No kidding."

"All part of the spook game. You'll get used to it. We had your clearance under investigation while you were in I.G. school. Remember Colonel Rick Sutcliff at Ft. Bragg?"

David nodded, stunned. He clearly recalled the Afro-American officer, a West Pointer, who'd made such a big deal of reviewing the A.R.'s and moving David safely to this command to preserve his best interests and those of the Army.

"Sutcliff was scouring the Army for a guy just like you. It was fate that you showed up on his doorstep with the broken legs and the career problem." Jankowsky rose. "Come on, David. It's time for you to see your other office. You have two places to hang your hat."

Jankowsky slipped on his saucer cap and raincoat. David did the same and followed Jankowsky down the stairs and into the back alley. Their booted feet crackled on gravel. They walked along the building, passing several rear service doors. David noticed again the dim outline of stained glass windows behind protective wire mesh. Jankowsky knocked on a door, and they were admitted by a trim, husky buck sergeant in fatigue uniform and side arm.

Jankowsky led the way up a narrow, dimly lit flight of wooden stairs. At the top he knocked on another door. As they waited, David noticed a surveillance camera turning to look at them. A buzzer sounded, and the door slid open.

Jankowsky and David entered a rich looking, though subdued, tiled foyer. It was round, with a domed ceiling, and a curving stairwell running to a higher story. David heard a hum of activity, a chatter of voices in small offices along thickly carpeted hallways. A short, lively man, brawny and dark-haired, stepped out to shake their hands. Introducing himself to David as Special Agent Tony Tomasik, FBI, he led them into a small office whose walls were lined with books. It was a small but cozy work space, with a stained glass window. Tomasik noticed David staring at the scalloped and ogived concrete window triplet that contained glowing red and blue stained glass. The theme was abstract and hard to make out. "This was a chapel at the turn of the century. Belonged to an order of religious educators. They sold to a university, which made it a drama playhouse. Finally it was partitioned into offices, and here we are."

Jankowsky said: "My I.G. detachment is kind of a Trojan Horse. I'm a reserve Army general, and I was indeed an I.G. officer. "The President realized that it would be insensitive to assign Military Intelligence directly to snoop on CON2, so we're playing this shell game, with civilians investigating civilians under civilian court order."

Tomasik said: "Welcome to U.S. Federal Task Force 20XX Dash 97A. You're still working directly for Colonel Jankowsky, but I'm in your matrix of operations. We'll work very closely together when the time comes."

CHAPTER 21

That evening, David drove to the Naval Observatory, where Tory met him outside. It was dark already, and most of the employees had gone home. Under the trees, with the fog creeping between his ankles just like the other night, he nearly hugged her as she came out to meet him, but remembered they were in uniform and it was against regulations. Tory seemed to have the same impulse, for she brushed dangerously close to him, bundled in her long coat and scarf, purse strap over one shoulder and garrison cap rakishly down over her forehead. She looked darkly around. "You came."

"You're surprised."

"I'm—grateful."

"It was like this last night."

"Spooky." She shivered. "Poor Ib."

"Where do you want to start?"

"I called his wife, Hala, and got a list of places Ib liked to hang out. She was so grateful that I called."

He regarded the skyline that burned like a million candles on a funeral mound. He scratched his head. "Tory, that's a huge haystack. And one NCO is a small needle."

"We'll just check a few places, okay?"

"Let's go," David said. "I'll drive, you look."

"I'll buy you gas."

"Don't be silly."

David drove through the sparse evening traffic. Heavy police patrols were everywhere, and pedestrians few. The emptiness of the streets added an eerie quality. CON2 was in session, and the city blocks at and around the Atlantic Hotel and Convention Center looked like fortresses of light, burning at all hours in the meeting rooms visible from far away. The three towers looked as if they were on fire inside. From road block to road block, David drove as Tory directed him from one Ib-hangout to the next—a computer store on K Street. A bookstore on Vermont Avenue. A library branch always open late, over in Foggy Bottom. A Palestinian market in Alexandria. He'd wait at the curb while she ran inside to speak with the management. He'd watch her animated conversation as she described Ib—the manager would nod yes—and then she'd spread her arms asking where Ib was and the manager would head-shake. Tory would run back to the car ready for the next place.

After two hours of this they came to a street that looked as though, if there were a literal end of the earth beyond which you could fall off, it would be within walking distance. They sat under a street lamp while he watched her think hard and dab a few tears. He waited for her to give up. The trees on either side of the street looked dark and ominous, despite streetlights reflecting in puddles. The jagged brick walls of a ruined building nearby looked threatening. Its sagging doorway offered a trip to nowhere, maybe off the edge of the world into some black abyss in which a few stars suffocated. A light wind stirred in the autumn leaves, and the air smelled faintly smoky.

"Well," she said.

"Well," he echoed.

"We can't sit here all night or we'll get mugged."

"I'm starting to worry a little bit about that," he said. "Even though we are both armed and dangerous."

"All right," she said sighing. "I had to try. Obviously the civilian police have the manpower and the resources—"

"Don't berate yourself." He started the car. "Why don't you go home and change and then meet me at my place. I'll have some dinner ready."

"That's the best idea yet. Are you sure you're up to it?"

"I'm sure." He drove back to the observatory so she could get her car.

Later that evening at his apartment, David showed Tory to the reclining chair surrounded by his shelved books, while he finished dinner. She wore a dark-blue sweatsuit with 'U.S. Army Olympics' in white letters along one leg.

He had the french door open, leading to the patio. A cool, damp wind blew in, smelling of hedges and late flowers. The kitchen windows dripped with perspiration from pasta water bubbling in a pot, not to mention chicken cacciatore simmering in a piquant sauce, and garlic bread baking in the hot oven. "Dinner in five minutes," he said.

"Smells wonderful."

"Didn't realize you were in the Olympics."

"I wasn't. Well, I almost was. I didn't quite make the team back at Fort Jackson. That's where Maxie and I met."

"What event?" He peered into the livingroom.

"Track. Cross-country."

She looked tired, her head back, eyes closed and shadowed; her stocking feet elevated on cushions. "I may have a lead. Or another problem, depending on one's viewpoint."

David set the steaming dishes on the table, then returned to the living room, dabbing his forehead with a cloth. "Talking in your sleep?"

"I'm wide awake." Her eyes opened and she sat upright. "It occurred to me in the shower at home. Ib Shoob and Tabitha Summers were pretty good friends. She was this very senior GS-17 civilian computer expert. They'd bicker, because they are both brilliant. Tabitha suddenly retired about two months ago. I was new then, and didn't know, but everyone else thought it odd. She really liked her work."

"Coincidence," David suggested. "He wasn't sitting on this for two months."

"What if he was?"

"We could call her right now."

"That's an idea." She fumbled with her com, and David waited. Her face brightened. "Tabitha? Tory Breen. How are you doing?" Tory listened. "Yes, right. Actually, I wondered if you knew that Ib was kidnapped the other night. I've been out of my mind with worry. Have you heard from him?" Her face betrayed disappointment as she listened. "If he tries to contact you, will you let me know?—yes, that's right—same office—yes, I'll let you know the minute I hear anything—what's that?—no, I tried looking, and you get frantic and all, but once you're out there looking, you realize it's hopeless; you just have to rely on the authorities because they have all the resources —yes, okay, keep in touch, bye!"

Tory rang off and shook her head bleakly.

"I'm sure the police are doing all they can." David reached out. She accepted his hand and he pulled her upright. She had a firm, dry grip, the back of her hand warm and smooth. She walked in long and graceful strides.

He pulled a chair back and she sat at the kitchen table, visibly pleased at his gentlemanly gesture. "It's so cozy here," she said with a genuine lilt of surprise as she eyed the wine rack, the shelf of cookbooks, the pots hanging from the ceiling to save space. He said: "I've been batching it for over a year now. I may have been a fast food, socks all over the floor guy once, but a good man learns well."

"Been married?"

"Afraid so. You?"

The haunted look fled past. "Ah—yes and no." She grinned and raised her glass. "Here's to a good man."

He touched his glass to hers. "To a good woman."

"Sometimes."

"You seem pretty good to me."

Soft pop dinner music blended with the steady hum of the oven exhaust fan under its enamel hood and made a self-contained world, almost as in a submarine. The ceiling lamp hung low over the heavy oak dining furniture, casting an island glow. A few sips of blood-red Italian wine, and David saw color in her cheeks, a glow in her eyes. The specter of Ib Shoob's disappearance hung somewhere beyond the lamplight, in the shadows, part of a world they were trying to forget for an hour or two. After dinner they sat in the living room on the shag rug. David set out a pitcher in which he diluted the red wine with sparkling water, throwing in a lemon slice. He cut up a few oranges and joined her before a small, crackling fire. She cried a little bit and David gently stroked her hair. It felt thick and warm to the touch; and smelled faintly of chestnuts or sandalwood.

Tory used her napkin to wipe tears away. "I'm sorry. Yes, I know that." Her face seemed to linger in the atmosphere when all else had gone hazy. He found himself being drawn in by her hungry eyes, her lightly parted lips. He slowly embraced her and kissed her on the cheeks. Holding her firmly, feeling her hands on his shoulder blades pulling him toward her, he sought her tongue with his. For an instant, their eyes fluttered open in mutual surprise. Then he saw her eyes close in dreamy acceptance. He asked the question he'd been wondering how to ask: "Is there anyone in your life?"

She shook her head and murmured "nuh-uh," with her eyes still closed. He lowered her gently on her back and lay beside her. She felt good against his limbs, against his side, her cheek against his cheek. A soft rain pattered outside, competing with the crackling in the fireplace. He felt her hand exploring his back, his neck, her feminine fingertips ruffling the hair and skin at the base of his skull giving him goosebumps.

She stopped suddenly, stiffened with some realization, paused—and then continued again, relenting in some battle within herself.

"What's the matter?"

She was silent.

"Dinner okay?"

"Everything is perfect. You are perfect."

He enjoyed feeling her curves through her clothes without touching anywhere tabu on a first date. He tugged her gently with one hand, and she resisted. Then she rolled closer to him, laid her head on his chest, and placed one hand, palm down, where she could feel his heart beating. He heard the pace of her breath quicken gradually as their body heat mingled and their closeness aroused her.

Gradually, comfort overcame arousal, and they fell asleep holding each other.

The living room clock struck eleven when he suddenly awoke to find her sitting up beside him. She looked surprised and sleepy. Her arms were raised, hands lifting thick garlands of dark amber hair, hairpin pinched between her lips. "I have to go."

"I'll walk you."

"That's sweet of you."

"Dangerous out there."

"You'll protect me." It was a tease, but she ran her fingernails fondly around his ear. He got goosebumps again.

After they bundled up, and he locked the door, they walked the four blocks between his place and hers. They held hands on and off, but both were independent spirits comfortable to orbit near each other without crashing into one another's affairs. Still, David felt himself remembering the wonderful pleasures—so unexpected in their timing—of falling in love. She was subdued and elegant—while Maxie was the blonde version, the light wine, a spumante, Tory was the dark version, the cabernet sauvignon. He kept glancing at her, and liking what he saw: dark sensuous eyes, slight smile, quirky poise when she said something witty or sarcastic or teasing or sad. Droplets pattered from trees on lawns, but the rain had stopped. A light fog stalked their heels. She slipped her arm through his. They arrived at her condo entrance and stopped. For a moment they were both awkward, away from the earlier spell, still strangers to one another. The disappearance of Ib Shoob, and his ominous discovery, hung in the atmosphere around them. He knew she would lie awake late tonight, worrying about Ib. She looked intently into his eyes with that dark, haunted look again. She placed her fists against his chest in frozen pummeling. "So much to sort out, David. So much that can't be said. I wish it were easier."

"What are you talking about?"

"Let's just say that I have a phobia about trusting. In time, when you—" She fell silent.

"When I what?" She was doing it again—pushing him away while she pulled him close. After the madness of being married to Kristy, this woman wasn't even a contender for getting his frustrations up. He couldn't think of anything to say.

"I'm not perfect. Almost definitely not right for you. You'll make up your mind soon enough."

"Okay. One question. You haven't had a sex change or anything?"

She burst out in laughter. "Oh God no, nothing like that." Her laughter turned wistful. "It's nothing like that, sweetheart. There, see? I called you that. At least I'm full of affection." She took his cheeks in both hands and leaned close to kiss him—briefly, just a brush of their lips—and let go.

Before he could protest, she lightly placed her fingertip on his lips to silence him. Her eyes looked large and dark. "Let's enjoy this for a while without asking too many questions. Then, in time, we'll ask the questions and think about the answers. Okay? Keep it light? Worry about Ib for now?" She gave him a quick kiss, no more than a flutter of lips against his, and, a minute later, a wave of the hand from the other side of the pool on the other side of the steel bars separating them as she strode upstairs and he turned to go home, alone in the night.

CHAPTER 22

In the morning, as David picked up his mail in the foyer—a letter from his sister Dora, which he sliced open with his finger—Colonel Jankowsky signaled for him to step in and close the door. "Find anything last night?"

Love, David thought, maybe. "No sign of Shoob, Sir." Love, if that's it again, that crazy, mysterious, upsetting, dark force...

"Stick with this lieutenant and help her try to find Shoob. Keep a tight lip about this place, and watch your back. I'll fill you in a little more as warranted."

"Yessir." He felt a little prickle of sweat under his collar—did sticking around include lying on the rug with her? Would Jankowsky nail him if he found out...? Something was going on here, maybe lots of somethings.

David met Tory for lunch, and afterwards, she drove them to her office at Observatory Circle. "There is someone I want you to meet," she said, "a young Marine Corps staff sergeant, Jet Steffey. She's a head walker, like Ib. I'll let her give you a tour of Ib's world

278

so you have a better idea what we're up against trying to locate his files."

As they approached the Naval Observatory along the tree lined street, David said: "Looks different in the daytime." On their left was the Vice Presidential mansion, still shuttered but not ominous. All around were buildings of the Naval Observatory complex, many with small observatory domes on their roofs, others with antennas and microwave dishes. Tory pulled into a parking spot marked XO. Tory shook her head: "I always think about you getting shot, and Ib getting abducted. Night or day, this place is starting to give me the creeps."

She gave him a brief tour inside the National Systems Security Office (NSSO) building. He had an impression of windowless offices, of short corridors angling into other short corridors; and of military personnel with close mouths, guarded looks, and multiple security badges. She showed him her office. Unlike the others, it had a nice big view window overlooking green lawns, big old trees, and the red brick walls of 1890's naval architecture.

Her office gave an impression of neatness, yet warmth and personableness. On her desk sat a photo cube showing off family. In one corner was a bag overflowing with exercise clothing. He nudged her. "You jog wearing pink socks?"

They both stared at the wool crew socks peeking from the unzipped bag. She nudged back. "That was a laundry accident. I was going to ask if you'd like to go jogging with me, but if you feel that way about my socks, imagine how you feel about me."

He whispered "I will wear baby blue socks, okay?"

"I might give you another chance," she said rolling

her eyes in mock sternness as she turned to leave the room. He followed her past a row of small offices, each occupied by a warm body and crammed with equipment. A door with a sign M/CPO Shoob remained conspicuously shut. Tory introduced David to a pert young Marine Corps staff sergeant named Marguerite "Jet" Steffey. Steffey had a dimpled chin, mischievous eyes, and a pixie face. She seemed of exotic extraction, with cafe-au-lait skin and a Hispanic accent. "Nice to meet you, Sir," Jet said.

"Captain Gordon was one of the last people to see Ib," Tory said.

Jet said: "We're all so worried about him."

David felt awkward at her hopefulness. "Let's hope for the best." If only I'd believed him—or gotten to Observatory Circle sooner!

"Captain Gordon's with the I.G.," Tory reminded Jet.

"Chief Shoob is my client. I'd like to learn more about his work," David said as he sat down in a special chair, like a cockpit seat.

Jet started to put a headset on it, then wrinkled her nose. "Ib's old head set smells of sweat and tobacco."

"I'll let you borrow my goggles," Tory said. She left the room and came back in a moment. Instead of a clumsy head set, these were more like eyeglasses.

With delicate fingers, she put them on David. "That feel okay?"

He swallowed the temptation to tell her how wonderful her fingertips felt. Instead of a lens, each eye was covered by a black hemisphere, a 180 x 180 degree theater. Things wanted to look three-dimensional inside them. The goggles were very light, with peripheral vision.

"Tell me if you get any VR effects," Jet said.

"I'm already a little leery," David said. "Seriously, I'm okay."

"It is a little strange at first," Jet said.

Virtual Reality made some people feel ill, or panicky. It was a radical transition, an immersion, like the dive of a submarine. David's V.R. persona stood looking along the sidewalk on an avenue in a big city. The whole scene was an ink sketch as if from a fashion artist. The picture was frozen, without motion, but with depth all around. The figures were lean and had poise. He had a feeling of vertigo, as if in a rocking boat. Jet's hand guided his grip to a metal hand rail in the real world.

He heard Tory: "I've tried it. You almost have to learn to walk again."

Jet made some adjustments and talked: "Some people have to bail out right away. How are you feeling?"

"A little funny," David said carefully. "But I think I'll manage."

"You can bail anytime," Jet said.

"We won't tell anyone," Tory jibed, poking his ribs.

"Ouch." He reached out blindly to his left and poked something soft that retreated; Tory.

"Here we go, Sir," Jet said.

He felt Tory behind him. She had her hands on his shoulders, rubbing his muscles, fingering his neck, and he felt a delicious thrill at her touch. He patted her hand, and she secretly squeezed his hand with hers.

"Are you ready, Sir?" Jet asked.

David stared at the frozen tableau of sketch figures. "Yes."

"I'm taking us in." Suddenly, there was movement. A blur of it. David sat back involuntarily. All around him, the pencil sketches were moving. Clouds raced across the sky. Cars roared past.

"Remember, Sir, it's all a metaphor."

"Can I see you?"

"Negative. Ib and I don't use icons of ourselves. Especially when we chase a hacker, it's stealth all the way."

The sketch people were becoming clearer. Shaded cheeks became flesh and on occasion blushed. Eyes glanced through him with airbrushed insouciance. Couples rushed by in the growing dusk, dressed for the opera or the theater, maybe late from dinner and searching for tickets in a wallet or purse. The metaphor was filled with charming detail like that. But David knew it was all wallpaper, as the trade called it. The real meat of the matter was the niagara of information flowing in a powerful data stream behind the scenes. Picture a vast water pipe. An underground river. Nothing looked quite real. You always knew it was a picture or a painting or a video clip. "We're in the Washington Muni stream," Jet explained. "The city did a nice job, don't you think?"

"It's overwhelming," David said sincerely, holding the metal bar with both hands as they flew along the sidewalk at a dizzying pace as though jogging, but without the bouncing. Sometimes they went around people, other times through them.

"This is mainly transit," Jet said. "Public domain. We're in the system and we can go look at available files. Want to go to the bank? Look up the current interest rates?" David found himself -turning tight and entering a heavy door among Grecian pillars. They entered a lobby, and the whole tone changed. The sketch people were gone, replaced by wholesome cartoon people in solid colors. The entire bank was a realistic cartoon in cheerful, toned-down hues. "World InterBank does it their own way," Jet said. "Everyone does. Some places are like being inside a DaVinci or a VanGogh or a Rembrandt painting. Other places are wild like Zap Comics." They stood before a huge book of sorts, with marbled covers, gilded edges, and a fancy satin bookmark. The ledger pages turned slowly, revealing banking information. Real estate loans were at a 26% nominal rate for A minus paper, reflecting the times that had brought about CON2.

"I believe you," David said, trying to decide if a brief queasy feeling was lunch trying to come up his gullet like a message up a pneumatic tube. The VR Effect had been documented over twenty years now. Many people had violent reactions of vertigo and nausea; the younger, the worse the effects. The longer they stayed in virtual reality, the longer it took to recover. In an early documented episode, a worker who had been in VR for several hours went to get a cola—and when she tried to drink it, poured it in her eyes.

"I'm sorry, Sir," Jet said, "I'll try to slow down. I'm so used to zipping around here. Sometimes I feel like a jet pilot," Jet said. "That's not how I got the nick-name—"

"—But it fits," Tory said somewhere and they all laughed.

"We are riding the most powerful computer in the world, " Jet said.

David snapped his fingers. "Oh yes, yes, what is

it—CloudMaster. Wow." There were only a few of these machines in the world, he remembered reading.

"We have one here in the building," Tory said. "I'll show you afterward."

"Somewhere in here," Jet said, "Ib said he discovered something so important he couldn't sleep nights."

"How much did he tell you?" David asked.

Jet seemed to hesitate, driving along a virtual boulevard in a cartoon land created by the metropolitan water department. They were cut off by a Ford Model T full of dogs in suits with violin cases. The Ford was being chased by a similar car full of dogs in police uniforms who waved tommy guns. Pretty soon there was a racket as cops and gangsters fired machine guns at each other. Then Jet cruised into a Pentagon data suburb, and it was no-nonsense straight lines and pencil people again; no sound of any kind. David felt as though he were floating rather than being driven.

"Go ahead," Tory urged Jet.

Jet said: "He found a message from Vice President Cardoza just before he was killed. Ib never told me what was in the note, but it must have been important stuff. Now you're here and he's missing. That's all I know. Oh and one other thing."

"What's that?" David coaxed.

"He told me he was thinking of asking for a transfer. He said sometimes he envied the civilians, like Tabitha. She resigned and I think it had something to do with—"

"Who's Tabitha again?"

Tory cut in: "Tabitha Summers, the woman I mentioned the other day. She was a systems security analyst, GS-18. Twenty six years' service last January, planned to go for thirty. Suddenly changed her mind and retired."

"She and lb were pretty good friends," Jet said. "All three of us were. They were a lot older, and I got the feeling they were trying to shield me from whatever they thought was going on. They seemed paranoid. Until—"

"Until lb disappeared," Tory said.

"That's right," Jet said.

"If you find out anything more, please tell Lieutenant Breen right away."

"Sure," Jet said. "That's the tour. Unless you want to visit anywhere else."

The scene shifted high up over the virtual city, toward a sun logo containing the words SPUS EXIT and circumscribed with the words Shanghai Portland Utility Software in English on top and Chinese characters on the bottom. As pixel sunlight rastered the rooftops, they rose up into the sun, which flared briefly, then closed like a camera shutter, leaving blank screens. David took the glasses off. He rubbed his eyes, shaking his head. For a moment the regular daylight hurt his eyes. Then they readjusted. His stomach still felt a bit queasy. "I wouldn't want to do that for a living."

"Thanks, Jet. That was really impressive."

"Any time, Sir." She shook his hand and beamed rather proudly.

As David and Tory headed for Tory's office, he glimpsed CloudMaster through a slightly ajar door in a plain room with painted-over windows: a huge egg shape that glistened ominously amid grappling shadows. Tungsten steel bolts big as fists anchored it to the yard-deep concrete floor.

Tory stopped David from peering within in fascination. "No time to sight-see. I'll give you a tour when we have time."

In Tory's office, David pushed the door shut and sat on the windowsill. She plopped in her chair by the window. "I have an idea." She spoke to her com button: "Call Tabitha Summers in Falls Church." Routing the call took seconds. Tory plugged her com into the desk phone in Conference mode.

"Yes," said a middle-aged woman flatly.

"Tabitha, it's Tory Breen."

"Lieutenant Breen. How are you?"

"I'm fine. We still don't have any sign of Ib. I was wondering if I could bring Captain Gordon from I.G. out there and if we could talk with you."

"I'm out of the business."

"I know you are. I was hoping—"

Tabitha Summers said something curt and indistinct and rang off. As the line went dead, David looked at Tory. "What was that last thing she said?" They listened to the recording again. Tory guessed: "'Ib should have kept his nose out of it.'"

"That's great," David said. "Will you try to call her again?"

Tory frowned. "Maybe Jet can talk with her. That's it! They were friends." She pressed the intercom. "Jet, would you come in here a moment?"

A little while later, David, Tory, and Jet rode toward Falls Church, Virginia. David drove, threading his way through the first hints of rush hour traffic leaving the nation's capital. It was windy and clear. Flags snapped on their poles. Tory and Jet spoke a mix of shop talk and concern over Shoob. At the last moment, Tabitha Summers had agreed to see them—only because of Jet's pleading. Tabitha lived in a farmhouse outside of Falls Church, inside the Beltway. The leaves were just beginning to turn, and already a magnificent Fall was in the air, like a joyous hymn in a cathedral. Trees surrounded Tabitha's ranch style home on all sides. Tabitha met them on the front porch as they trod crunching on gravel across her driveway. She was a tallish, trim blonde in her late 40's, wrapped in a purple woolen shawl as if freezing. There was fear or anger or both in her blue eyes. She nodded as Jet waved. Jet rushed up the stairs and hugged her friend. The hardness melted in Tabitha's face and she said: "It's good to see you. I just wish Ib were with you."

Tory stepped up and shook Tabitha's hand. David rested a foot on the wood stairs and looked around, trying to be disarming. "Beautiful place you have out here."

"I like it well enough. I don't see many people from out of town, so let's get this over with."

Tabitha led them into a gloomy parlor filled with old furniture. Leaded cabinet windows gleamed between ornate scrolls and little corner pillars. Wood cherubs sang silent, eerie songs. What was written on their scrolls in this half-light? David wondered.

"I made tea," Tabitha said.

Tory rubbed her hands as if starting a fire. "Sounds great."

After a brief exchange about the relative merits of Darjeeling and Green Tea, after they were all seated, Tory drew Tabitha out. "We're very worried about Ib. I was wondering if he said anything to you—?"

"He didn't tell me much that could help you," Tabitha said.

"You were his best friend at work, Tabitha. If you will just tell us everything you can, maybe something will set off a spark."

Tabitha looked into the past. "He always had that paranoid streak, so I never really knew when to take him seriously. At one point he said that, when they took CloudMaster from us, it was like stealing the atomic bomb. All the civilians in our branch at NSSO were moved off the system about two months ago when CloudMaster was moved from Navy control to the Composite."

Jet said: "We were all pretty bummed when Tabitha left."

Tabitha picked up: "That's when I decided to retire. I had turned down top billets in either California or Arizona because they promised me a two year contract here using CloudMaster. Then they threw me off CloudMaster, and that did it." She half reminisced, half explained: "My resigning didn't have anything to do with Ib. He was always grumbling around like an old walrus. CloudMaster is a wonderful machine. It's a massively parallel processor capable of handling up to a million variables. It doesn't use any specific data addresses for processing, just temporary swarms of subatomic particles in a cloud chamber shot through with laser beams. Maybe you saw the machine. Looks like a giant steel egg the size of a locomotive. It was designed for weather forecasting. Using CloudMaster, you can model the weather around an aircraft carrier in a hundred square mile footprint ten miles high, down to the cubic yard. You could tell from the other side of the world how many raindrops will fall on a given square yard of carrier deck. You can tell how much icing a plane will get as it takes off and climbs to altitude. Very powerful. Beautiful thing to work with. My job was to provide network security. Imagine if someone could hack their way in and make you think it was too hazardous to fly, even though it wasn't—long enough to suspend flight operations so enemy strategies could be carried out against us without air defense by us. It was the most fun and challenging assignment I ever had."

"Did Ib ever mention a file he found? Something to do with national security?"

"What kind of file?"

"I can't go into detail." He felt somewhat foolish. If she didn't know, he couldn't tell her. What if she knew, and wasn't talking? If so, why?

"This country is falling apart," Tabitha said ironically. "The Constitution is being trashed by morons who think they are great intellects, my career is washed up, and you can't tell me about some piece of paranoia of Ib Shoob's."

David asked, "Do you think Ib's disappearance has anything to do with CON2?"

Tabitha glowered at him some more. Then she rose and said: "I have nothing more to tell you. If I hear from Ib, I'll tell him to call you. I'd appreciate that you never come here again. Jet, call me anytime, long as it has nothing to do with this. Tell Ib to give me a call when he gets back. I'll ring you next time I'm in town. Let's have coffee."

On the way back through the gorgeous countryside, Jet said: "That wasn't Tabitha. I mean, it was her, but I've never seen her like this. She was like a total stranger. I don't think she'll ever call me."

David called Colonel Jankowsky to report on his afternoon. Jankowsky said: "Nothing more, David. We're having a hell of a time with General Montclair's headquarters, trying to extricate the medical file on the suicide in Texas, as well as their MP file on him, just to close our own paperwork." He added: "You'd almost think they're running their own army over there." As if realizing he had breached etiquette by being critical of a general officer, he changed tone again. "By the way, Colonel Bellamy called.—Rick Bellamy, the Provost Marshal for the military people at the hotel? He wants you to call him. Says it's important."

David immediately called, but Bellamy's com button was only taking messages, so he left a message. "Sir, it's David Gordon. Got your message. Let's touch base in the morning, or call me this evening if you wish."

David took Tory to a small restaurant that evening. There was something sweet and smooth and agreeable about being with her. As they sat under the yellow light of a booth in a family restaurant, he knew she might be feeling something for him too. But she was very cool, and didn't show it. They sat in a cozy corner and ordered matching baskets of chicken stix and fries, and milk shakes. In the middle of dinner, on impulse, he raised a chicken stick toward her mouth. She looked up, crinkled a smile at him, and accepted it in her mouth with a wink of indulgence. "That's wonderful," she said with a luxuriant, sensual groan. She raised a chicken stick to his mouth, and he imitated her.

"David, I'm feeling this overwhelming urge to take you home with me."

"Oh no."

"I'm not joking. David—"

"Yes?"

"It's just—I'm not ready for anything, you know, complicated."

"I'm not either." He wasn't. Yet, he heard a distant chord from his heart strings.

"You make me feel rather odd inside," she said holding his hand.

"Like how?"

"I'm not telling." For a moment, with her mysterious smile, she resembled the Mona Lisa.

CHAPTER 23

In the morning, David met Colonel Bellamy by the Reflecting Pool. Bellamy had commed and requested the meeting and the place.

This was the Mall, the heart of Washington, under the magnificent plan laid out by Pierre L'Enfant and fulfilled by the African-American architect Benjamin Bannecker. The area was laid out like a cross. At the south end was the tallest structure (by law) in the city, the 555-foot needle of Washington's Monument, looking off to the Potomac. From the monument to the center of the cross, where David sat, was the long, narrow Reflecting Pool. To the east, across a meander in the Potomac, was the rounded roof of the Jefferson Memorial. To the west, across some park land and the ubiquitous monuments, sprawled the White House. The north leg of the cross was the Mall. Along its sides were various cultural institutions, including the Smithsonian and the Hartshorn. At the far end of the Mall was the Capitol, housing Congress. Just behind the Capitol to the left was the Library of Congress. To the right was the Supreme Court. David had come here more than once already, enjoying the view. It was one thing to see the various views in a book; it was another to stand in the middle and scan them all with a turn of the head.

Bellamy approached, a robust figure in a long Army raincoat despite the sunny weather. People milled here and there, some hurrying from one building to another, as if there were no CON2 stirring up chaos, as if everything were normal. David looked past Bellamy to see if there was a tail. At that, he shook his head and wondered if the conspiracy atmosphere in the capital, tinged with Autumn sadness, were getting to him. Free of the oppressive hotel, Bellamy seemed a big man with a hard smile. And a rough handshake. "David, walk with me. Don't look behind, because we have to assume we're being followed."

"I thought it was just me being paranoid," David said.

"Far as anyone knows, we're here to rehash the Mary Corcoran thing," Bellamy said. He looked at the sky. "Hell of a town. Have you and your boss realized you're never going to get any information out of those people in the Top Five in the hotel?"

"Corcoran's a dead issue unless the Pentagon wants to stir it up again. The suspect killed himself."

Bellamy uttered a short, harsh laugh. "Am I surprised? Sure, call me nuts, like Shoob. But I sit there every day and watch those skinheads going up and down in the elevator carrying boxes of ammo. Even a fool would wonder what is going on."

"Sounds like General Montclair is taking no chances."

"That's becoming apparent to me."

"I hear that some delegates are talking about proposing more amendments."

"Yes, CON2 is about to fall apart. Almost like

Murphy's Law, isn't it? Plan for the worst. By now, most people with any sense are scared to death and wish they'd never been lulled into voting for it. Beyond that, sure, I lie awake nights worrying. Sometimes, I wake up at three or four in a cold sweat, afraid the loonies'll hit the hotel with one of those fertilizer bombs they like because they're so full of crap. I wake up strangling a yell because I think we're going up and it's my last two seconds on earth."

"I don't envy you being billeted in the hotel, Sir. You and the others."

"I have a question, David, and I need you to check it out for me. I know you don't work for me, and I don't want to cross your chain of command, but—"

"Sure, I'll do whatever I can for you. But why me?"

"Because I have nobody else I can go to. I don't know whom to trust among the senior people. Even from the simple standpoint of not looking like a fool. You're young, you're eager, you can't possibly be in cahoots with anyone, and besides, if you can't keep a secret, I'll deny we ever had this conversation."

"I can keep a secret."

"Very well, then. I've been mightily p.o.ed, in my own quiet way, about these skinheads crawling all over the place, raping the rest of the army. They hardly even salute officers except their own. It's scary, David. As if the SEALS or Green Berets had gone mad. Only they're not part of any bona fide special forces I know of. I've checked."

"You're talking about those commandos with no hair and wild eyes."

"Yes. Nominally, they're part of Montclair's headquarters. There must be a couple of thousand. They keep coming and going, day and night, lugging ammo boxes, machine guns. The bottom floor of the parking garage is end to end with LXs and deuce and a halfs." LXs were lightly armored infantry vehicles, shaped like a steel cigar tube on ten big wheels, each carrying a dozen soldiers. Deuce and a halfs were the venerable two-and-a-half-ton trucks used for generations by all U.S. services. Bellamy continued: "Normally, soldiers report to a new command from all over the world, men and women, except in combat arms, from every possible unit. These are all men, all white, and most came here under orders from the same duty station in Texas where our friend was killed."

David felt a rip of fear across his gut. "I had wondered if our nasty private was murdered rather than a suicide."

"He didn't hang himself. David, do me a favor. Do me, do us all, a favor—see what you can dig up on a unit called the 3045th Military Intelligence Detachment (Reserve). Go back as far as you can. The skinheads all seem to belong to that unit."

"How did you find that out?"

"Never mind. The clerk who stumbled on it would be dead if anyone knew. The problem is, I can't do the research because they're watching me over there. I know that sounds paranoid—"

"I have a question for you, Colonel Bellamy. Do you know anything about a super computer called CloudMaster?"

Bellamy shrugged. "Not much. Big Navy weather modeling jobbie. The U.S. plans to market them around the world. There's one in the hotel, another in the White House."

"That's odd, Sir. There's at least one other one in

town requisitioned by the Army to support CON2. What I'd like to know is why they need all that computing power. You can tally a thousand votes with a pocket calculator."

Bellamy frowned. "I kind of wondered, myself; I sorta thought they were keeping track of all the logistics—20,000 troops in the Composite Force, plus whatever Montclair is fielding, not to mention the civilian police services. You're right. It doesn't add up."

They shook hands and parted company.

David walked the length of the Mall, around Capitol Hill, and into the Library of Congress. There, in a recently established National Military Archive, he sat in a small, too-cold air conditioned room at a table while a departmental assistant brought him permadisks recorded from old microfiche records. "There you are, Captain," she said, "unit histories since 1945." She was a 30ish woman, not bad looking, but stern and as frigid as her domain. David wondered if the air conditioning was designed to prevent people from staying too long, or to keep her from melting. "You can have another stack going further back, once you're done with those."

"Thank you," David said, slipping a disk into the reader. No head goggles here. The image showed on a flat-screen that hung like a picture on the wall. It was slow, monotonous reading. The only splashes of color were the various unit emblems—shoulder patches, guidons, flags, decorations. He started with the numbers and ran a sort check. Should have known; there was no 3045th. He went to the Regular

Army and stepped through the various Military Intelligence agencies and commands. Should have been easy, he thought. The field was narrow enough. The problem was that some units overlapped and others were blanked out for security reasons. Even though the Cold War had been over for 20 years. Having scanned the active Army, he switched to the Reserves. It got tougher. The MI units sprawled over 48 states. Some outfits overlapped with National Guard units, others with Regular Army units. He traveled up and down alphabetic and numerical listings. Nothing resembling the mythological unit Bellamy had asked him to search for.

Could the 3045th be a fraud? It hardly seemed possible. David rose to stretch his legs. He stepped into a lounge for coffee. As he sipped his coffee, he looked through a window that opened on a large bay office. He spotted the librarian's unsmiling face several dividers away. She was speaking with two military officers. All three were nodding. He didn't recognize either of the two joes. Could be public relations officers, maybe historians; anything was possible. Then again, could they be following him, checking on what he was doing? Ridiculous; you'd send plainclothes guys to do that, not guys in uniform visible from a mile away. Unless—in today's Washington, maybe a military uniform was a good disguise. David finished his coffee, crumpled the paper cup, and threw the cup into the empty steel waste basket with a slam. He wasn't going to start looking over his shoulders every five seconds.

Returning to the reader in the small office, he went back over the disks he'd looked at. There were active, reserve, active reserve, inactive reserve—wait a minute.

As he searched, he discovered more categories. Under Reserve, Temporary Status, Budget Review for 1956, he found the 3045th Military Intelligence Detachment (Reserve) (Military Government). The 3045th was one of several reserve components, most associated with one or another major American university, whose mission was to train U.S. Army officers to take over governments in conquered countries. The supreme models were, of course, Germany and Japan, defeated in World War II, and governed directly by the Allied military forces for several years. Officers and men of the 3045th had served with distinction during the period 1946—1949 in West Germany. Some of the members had served with OSS during World War II, recruited from Yale, Harvard, and the like. The unit was disbanded in 1957. Some members moved on to MI units in related missions, but access to names and units was classified top secret with Joint Chiefs of Staff-level Need-to-Know. David was excited and frightened. And frustrated at the lack of further leads.

CHAPTER 24

David had just finished briefing Jankowsky on his meeting with Bellamy, when Tory rang him on the collar com. "David, can you talk?"

"Something about Ib?" A fist seemed to tighten in his abdomen.

"Nothing yet."

"Where are you? Is everything okay?"

"I'm at the Atlantic Hotel, David," she said with a sigh; "my unit is being moved here!"

David frowned. So the military team using Cloud-Master at NSSO was being transferred from the Observatory to the computer center at the Atlantic Hotel & Convention Center. Colonel Bentyne, her commanding officer, was directly under General Montclair's command.

"I'll be coming to this horrible place every day."

"I'm sorry to hear that. Look on the bright side, Tory. There is a shuttle to the hotel. You can ride to work with me in the morning and then shuttle on."

"That would certainly be a bright spot. I don't like this at all, David. Jet's pretty gloomy about it too. There's fourteen of us, and nobody's happy about it. Aw hell, it's the Army. What did I expect?"

Somebody was tightening control, David thought.

Somebody was bringing all the toy soldiers together where they could be better watched. "There's an upbeat soul. Want to meet me for lunch?"

"Yes."

"You sound like you need cheering up. I'll meet you at the Atlantic and we'll find a little place."

Wearing civvies, David met Tory in the main lobby of the hotel. She was dressed much like he was—jeans, plaid shirt, sweater, light jacket—because her crew were packing up the office records and supplies. "I'm taking the rest of the day off," he told her as they walked toward the elevators. "What a magnificent lobby," David said as his eyes raked across an acre of hillocks, waterfalls, palm trees, and more greenery. Massive marbled columns in soft honey tones swirling among soft cacaos, loomed into the ceiling. In the cavernous lobby, David turned his gaze upward through the hazy emptiness. Way up, shafts of sunshine cut through small high windows and even higher skylights and leaned through the atmosphere fading intofragments filled with lazily whirling dust motes like lightning bugs.

She whispered: "Isn't it wonderful? I still hate the idea of working here." She pushed a button. "My car is in the basement garage. I'm done packing my desk, and I don't need to hang around." They stepped inside, the door closed, and the elevator descended.

"Want to spend a few hours with me?" she asked.

"I can't think of a better way to pass the afternoon."

The door opened upon a dark vista of concrete and weak lights. The place was packed with light armored infantry vehicles painted with blue and yellow camouflage blobs. Fifty caliber machine gun barrels bristled ominously from ball turrets. A squad of commandos looked up in surprise while unloading ammo boxes from a pallet. Their sergeant frowned as he stepped toward the elevator. "What are—?" he started to say but the door closed.

"Next floor up. Who are they?" Tory asked as the elevator rose.

"You sorta get used to them, and sorta not," he said echoing what Bellamy had said. They found her car and drove out of the garage, into a welcome gust of wind and daylight. "What a relief to be out of there," she said.

"It'll be over in a few months," he suggested, wondering inwardly, how long did a bunch of idiots need to completely screw up the Constitution? If the Constitution radically changed, the Supreme Court would be almost meaningless until a new body of interpretive law had been built from the ground up.

They passed a cordon of trucks outside, drove past the checkpoints, and into the heart of the city. Despite CON2, the machinery of government was in full motion, and the sidewalks were jammed with pedestrians dressed for office work.

"There is one place I'd really like to go," Tory said.

"You name it."

"You can say no."

"I won't."

And she explained as they walked slowly along the paths and lawns, her arm slung through his, their bodies close together. Victor Breen had been a hero of the Vietnam War, a Medal of Honor winner, killed in battle. That was 1972, eleven years before Tory's birth. She had a much older brother named Vic who'd been five when her grandfather's coffin came back from the Orient and who'd told her in loving detail about the funeral. The Army had buried Victor Breen at Arlington in a light drizzle while a few scattered flowers came into a late bloom along the endless somber green. Vic told of a U.S. flag draping the coffin. Men in uniform with lots of stripes and braids had attended. Soldiers had fired guns. Taps had quavered hauntingly where Tory and David walked today; Vic retold the story about once a year when the family reunited for Christmas at the house in Davenport.

Today, Tory carried a bouquet of flowers.

"Nice place for a stroll," David said, holding her lightly, appreciating the specialness of the place.

"It's gorgeous," she said. She seemed to be growing distant, he thought.

She folded her arms upon herself against the brisk wind, and pressed against him. He liked the feel of her shoulder, then an arm, an elbow, a hand, against his side. They came to the weathered stone. She knelt and laid the flowers lovingly on the grass beside the simple white headstone that read Victor Breen, Col., USA. Moss grew on the stone, filigreed with hairline cracks by many winters and summers. He noticed her eyes brimmed and then tears twirled through the air and spangled the young green grass. Somewhere over a hill covered with brittle orange leaves, at some new gravesite, a volley of shots rang out. Thin, distant strains of Taps floated through the air.

David gave her a paper napkin, and she blew her nose. "Sorry."

"It's okay." He held her, feeling the delicacy of her long body, the wiry strength in her arms, yet the softness of her body. He felt the liquid pressure of her firm breasts against his belly as he held her. They stood silently for a long time, entwined, inhaling one another's scents, breathing together, stroking, cuddling, holding.

They held hands walking along the paths. The trees were dense, and the sunlight dripped through like a silvery wine full of bird twitter. She held his hand but pulled away a little bit. "David, I guess you like me."

"I like you a lot."

"I like you very much, David."

She pulled her hand away and sat on a boulder. He sat on a boulder near her. She had that cloudy, haunted look again. He watched her hands—strong, feminine, with long fingers—as she picked a leaf apart. She was silent, tearing leaves apart in an intensity that told him to be quiet while she gathered her thoughts. Finally, she wrapped her arms around her knees and looked away. "I wish that we lived in another world where things were easier."

He waited.

"I wish—you would—love me."

He said nothing. He loved her already.

"I wish—I could be more woman to you."

He listened intently.

"My granddad may have been a war hero, but his son—my dad—was bad news. My dad was a hippie and he ran off to Canada. He did drugs. He married my mom, who was a dropout and a hippie. They got into drug dealing, some of it involving a lot of money. They weren't nice people. My dad went to prison when I was 12. My mom left us a year later, me and my brother Jeremy. The only other person was my grandma, but I was 14 going on 40 when this thing happened to me, and until then we just hoped she wouldn't come to take me away."

"We?"

"Jeremy and I. I was full of anger and I was wild. I was running around with boys when I was 12. And then, when I was 14—" She paused, choking back a sob. Tear drops fell down. "When I was 14, I was sleeping with all of Jeremy's friends, one by one. They were older boys. Teenagers. I got tattoos."

She rose and opened her shirt and pulled up her undershirt. There was a peach on her belly. She pulled up her trouser leg, and there on one ankle was a grinning death head smoking a joint.

She sat down. "I had my lips and my tongue pierced. I wore my hair green and purple and blue. I slept with every one of those guys. I wanted so badly to belong, to be accepted." She paused. "And then I got pregnant. But I had like several venereal diseases at the same time. And I had no idea who the father was, and I—got an illegal abortion. The only lucky thing is that, by some miracle, I didn't get HIV. I couldn't afford a safe medical abortion, so I paid a woman who worked for county animal control. Then I got a really bad infection and had to have my plumbing removed." She wiped her hand over her eyes as tears flew from her wrist. "The same week, my brother was murdered in a drug deal. Then grandma showed up. She took me to Iowa to live with her in Davenport. I almost died, and that set me straight. I caught up on my schooling, I went to high school, I got good grades, and whenever they talked about birds and bees, you know, Sex-Ed, you know, or some girls talked about their periods or taking precautions, I just cried and cried, because I would never grow up to be a woman. I went to college and I made it through ROTC and got my commission. I was a pretty good athlete and I won my self-respect. I wanted to be an MP officer so I could right wrongs. My grandma is still alive. I haven't heard from my mom in years, and my dad never answered my letters so I stopped writing him. He got out of jail a couple of years ago, and I think he lives up in Canada somewhere."

Tory paused. "I'm comfortable with who I am, but you know, I get tired of having this conversation with guys." She looked at him regretfully.

David took a deep breath. "I'm sorry to hear all that."

She said: "I've given up on men—for serious relations anyway. Last time I got this far with a guy was probably three years ago. Last two guys ran off on me when I told them. The last guy said he just couldn't even be aroused by me anymore when he found out."

"I'm not going to say I love you, because it's too early. I can tell you that I think about you all the time, and that I think you're wonderful."

"Give it time, David. You'll decide you really want to have children, and I can't help you there. I'm not really a woman, in that sense."

"Oh stop it." His heart ached for her, for himself, for both of them. His mind whirled as a waterfall of emotions tumbled through his thoughts.

"I have to take estrogen all my life. You'll want a woman, not an android."

"I think you are a wonderful woman. Why are you so hard on yourself?"

"Because it hurts, David. It hurts, way down, all

over. I have to do this so you'll go away before I start trusting you and then I'll really get hurt."

"I can go away if you want me to, but I sure don't want to."

"Kids, David. Have a brain. Think about it."

He thought about it. "Well, in a sense, you're right. I'd love to have kids. My sisters keep having them all the time. Maybe that's enough for one family, huh?" He thought another minute. "I want to keep seeing you. We can take it slow, can't we? Let's just enjoy being together and see where it leads? I think those guys you mentioned were pretty selfish."

She shook her head wistfully. "You are such a nice guy. You have great genes What the world needs is babies from guys like you." She rose. "You have a great future in front of you. I lost my future before I knew what I was doing." She dusted her rear off.

"Not your entire future!"

"My eggs are gone, David, forgive me for sounding dramatic. I have no genes to pass on. No, you and I aren't for each other. I can see that. When you've had a chance to think about it, you'll decide to go off and find someone who can be a real wife to you and give you kids."

He felt it was his turn. "I was married three years and didn't have any children. The way Kristy—my wife—well, I thought I was going to die when I lost her."

"Been long?"

"Almost two years, really. It seems like yesterday, but when I think about it, it seems a long time ago."

"Maxie told me a little about you."

"She is such a little conniver."

Tory laughed. "Yes, but aren't you glad?"

David caught her to him, pulled him against her. He lifted her chin and looked into her eyes. "I don't know if we are going to fall in love, but if we do fall in love, I will love you as you are. I guess I never thought about it until now, but I suppose people who can't have kids can go adopt one."

She shook her head. "You'll want children of your own. You'll move on, and I won't blame you."

He did not know what to answer. Her negativity shocked him. He reminded himself that she'd been in this place before, had had time to think it through, and her attitude was deeply reinforced. What if he fell out of love—no, he wasn't in love yet, how could he fall out of love then? He felt confused and pressured.

She embraced him lightly, pulling him toward the warmth of her sweatered bosom. "You're not sure, and I don't blame you. Look, I care a lot about you, and I'd like to enjoy you while you last. Want to do that?"

"A day at a time."

She traced her fingertip along his eyebrow, down over his cheek, to touch his lips. "I think that's a wise policy." She embraced him, brushing his buttock with her palm. "Let's just enjoy each other for all it's worth. Don't let me get uptight about trust again, please?"

"Oops. I don't do other people's emotions. You're responsible for those."

"Right. Well said. It's just that I get all uptight because I expect the worst. I'll try to stay on the light side. Just don't make me any promises, okay? You can lie to me, cheat on me, do anything you want. Just don't promise me anything."

"Well," he suggested, "why don't we lighten up and go have a little fun."

She murmured: "I will be good to you while it lasts."

They walked to his car, arms linked, and kissed long and ardently. Then she pushed away. "Come on, let's go see some museums."

They heard another volley of shots and the melancholy hum of "Taps."

Shortly, as he drove her car across the Memorial Bridge over the Potomac River and into the city, she sniffled quietly into her hankie and he thought he could still hear the echoes of that grieving bugle flowing like wine among the hills. He wasn't sure if she was crying more about the loss of her grandfather or the loss of her future.

Luckily, the city had jazz and noise and speed to wipe away tears and sadness. Famished, Tory and David had burgers at a little restaurant, then walked along the Mall. They studied fossils and airplanes and colorful gems at the Smithsonian. They walked and talked and laughed and fed ducks and clowned around.

When the sun glittered low among rusty colored leaves, and shadows grew long, she slipped her arm through his. They walked along an endless park, under streetlights, under the watchful gaze of dozens of hungry-eyed young soldiers.

"I had you figured for a rich boy."

"Sorry. That's Maxie's game."

"I know. Isn't it disgusting?"

"Yes, poor thing. I almost had the hots for her, but I was so broken up it was all I could do to go to dinner or a movie. My wife had me so spooked."

She crinkled in a truthful smile. Her voice was silky. "Maxie told me all about you. I thought when she introduced me to you that you seemed so sweet and handsome, I might just let go a little."

"She pushes people, doesn't she?"

"Yes." She burst out in a single giggle of admission. "I thought you were so perfect and I was amazed you weren't—what's the word—haughty."

"I'm not perfect at all, as you can see."

"Stop berating yourself. I think you are wonderful."

She made a wistful face. Her eyes radiated vulnerable belief.

He wanted to do hand-stands to convince her. He gesticulated. "Look at me. I am nothing. I did not know how nothing I am until you came along. You are a goddess. I never figured for a moment that you—well, and I—" He looked around, seeking a metaphor.

After a pause he said simply: "You have made me into a god. I feel like a god when I am with you."

She sniffed once, almost amused, and put her arm through his. They strolled on, wrapped in a silent coccoon in which they both felt that their personalities had melted and were flowing together like two shades of hot pudding.

They spent the afternoon wandering through museums on the Mall. They gaped here and gawked there, they snacked and played and laughed and clowned around the fountains. They kissed often. She felt light and yielding in his arms. The tip of her tongue made little darting motions between his lips and her breath came in quick gasps as she held his face between the flats of her chilly fingertips. He took her hands and kissed her fingers, smelling bath soap and leather and a light perfume. Too quickly, afternoon wore into dusk and then night fell.

Tired but happy, they walked along city sidewalks toward his car. Just then, he felt a vibration in the sidewalk. She frowned and mouthed: "What's that?"

The vibration became stronger, with a growing roar of noise. David and Tory and other pedestrians froze at the spectacle of a long column of huge, dark vehicles speeding down the street. They were a battalion or more of combat support vehicles, headed by several humvees, followed by a mobile command post, a communications truck, and an endless stream of flatbed trucks carrying massive shapes whose passage made the streets shake in rhythm with their continuous loud rattling and rolling sounds. Pennants fluttered on antennas as the dark convoy streaked past.

"What are those, tanks?" Tory said, as her body soaked in the vibrations.

David felt troubled as he glimpsed the hulking objects atop the flatbeds. They were partially covered by canvas, but she could see their ugly sides painted in blue and tan camouflage colors. The primary gun barrels protruding from the canvas covers were longer than those on any main battle tank he'd seen, and thicker. His combat arms background came in handy, but his knowledge gave him no joy. "Strange. Those aren't tanks. They are—" He had to think back. "They are SPH-2010s. Long Toms. They are 200-millimeter self-propelled howitzers. They're big mobile guns. You drive them someplace and then you besiege your enemy, kind of. Like if he's inside a mountain, those guns will reduce the mountain to rubble. If he owns an airstrip, up to so many miles away, he'll soon have just a big hole full of water."

Tory laughed, looking a little scared. "Siege guns? They need siege guns, here in Washington, to protect a hotel?"

David shook his head, made a sour face. "I dunno. Not my area of expertise. If you pointed one of those at a building, it would be like dropping a 500 pound bomb. One round could probably take out a good chunk of a city block."

The procession was gone in five minutes, dark as the night from which it had come and into which it went. The ground stopped shaking, the air smelled sweeter, and people resumed their light-hearted chatter in the shadows on the streets.

"I guess the bigwigs are taking no chances," David said. Somewhere inside of him, a nagging question mark would not go away. Then she diverted his attention. She pulled her arm away and pointed. "Look, a deli. I'm getting tired and hungry. I'll buy dinner."

"I'll go for that," he said as they walked toward the lights and the food aromas. She seemed suddenly shy and awkward and he couldn't think of anything to say. The deli was an afterthought in a food wholesaler's rambling brick warehouse. It was a drafty barn but they found a cozy wood-paneled corner with three shaky little tables. A hooded gas pylon glowing and sputtering in the corner levitated a sphere of warmth. The deli itself was a busy place, fun to watch. Noise echoed into the high ceilings. Delivery people came and went with cheese wheels, beer barrels, baskets of fresh bread, even flowers. The steady line was five or six customers deep, and the counter staff in white coats and red hats were a blur of motion.

Afterward, outside, she slipped her arm through his. "This has been a remarkable day, Mr. Gordon."

"I think so too." They sauntered from street light to streetlight bumping hips and feeling alive. "If we weren't in this crazy situation," he said, "and if we had this sidewalk and these lights and that good camembert back there, we could probably—" He stopped, turned, and looked into her face. He felt her body against his, as he embraced her. As in a slow dance, maybe to regain some psychic balance, she embraced him. He cupped her shoulder blades, remembering that evening on the rug. She closed her eyes and tilted her face back as he kissed her. Their lips met in a mutual groan of pleasure. Her fingertips played in the gulley of his spine and sent electric tingles through his frame.

Moments later, on the way to the car, she slipped her arm back through his, and pressed against him. "How long do these constitutional conventions last?" she murmured with a wink.

"Well," he murmured back, "I think the last one was in 1787 and went all summer."

"Oh good, we'll have time for more of this camembert."

CHAPTER 25

There was no sign of Shoob the next day. David and Tory had lunch and agreed not to fall in love, but in like.

Late in the day, Maxie phoned. "How would you like to start meeting some Washington people tonight?" It was her euphemism for the swirling social set that made the capital a modern, urban Versailles. Social events bored David, but Maxie persisted in trying to talk him into going.

"No."

"Do it for Tory, David. She's been moping around, worrying about her friend the NCO."

"Maxine, there is something more to this."

"Oh all right, you stubborn elk. Someone very important wants to speak with you."

David felt a tingle up his spine. "Does this have something to do with—?" He stopped. The phone might not be secure.

"Not directly," she said. He heard in her tone that she knew he'd been about to say Ib. "It's someone who has to be very discreet."

"What are you getting mixed up in, Maxie?"

"Nothing. I just know people. People know me. Don't forget, my little ol' family has been active in

313

this town for over 200 years. When people want something indirectly, they start thinking about who they can go through." She added: "I'm going to coax your girlfriend into going, so that ought to give you motivation."

"Now, Maxie—"

She laughed brightly. "I just thought you'd like to hear those words. Been a long time for ya."

David wore a dark suit, Tory a long black gown that made her look definitively graceful. "It's a real Capital ball, David," Tory said as they walked to his car. "This may be the only chance in our lives to attend one." The affair was at the Russian Embassy in honor of a newly arrived ambassador. Maxie looked like a doll, in a royal blue crushed velvet dress, her smile like a light as she moved easily from one group to another. Yet, her proctologist had not come and at the last minute she'd snagged up one of the single officers in her condo unit, a Marine Corps captain named Jack Standish from Chicago. He was a tough, funny guy with a pink face and a negative streak, talking from the side of his mouth, but he possessed a rock-like dignity that passed well in a crowd. Maxie was driving, but Jack had already had a few beers by the time she tapped him for duty.

A six piece orchestra played jazz and chamber music in one corner of the ballroom, and ten or twenty couples danced. David danced by turns with Maxie and Tory, as did Jack Standish. "Some crowd, huh?" Maxie whispered in his ear. "There must be five or ten thousand people dancing. Oh not all here; they drift from one party to another all evening long. I couldn't do it all the time, could you? But business gets done. Lobbyists show up at these things if their senator does."

At one point David, on his way to the men's room, heard Standish declaiming amid a knot of smokers on a side patio, from the side of his mouth: "...It's the next war, folks, seriously, this country's got to take back what it gave up. That's why we're in the shape we're in. No twenty cent camel jockey gas, no cheap gold from South Africa. This President doesn't know up from down. Gotta go in there, team up with the Russkis, contain Germany, contain Europe. Then ya gotta pit the Japs against the Chinese, break up the Orient. That's the only way."

Back in the ball room, David was offering Tory ice cream and finger wafers, when Maxie returned from a brief, mysterious excursion, and nudged him: "There is someone who wants to meet you."

"Oh?" His mind raced in overdrive, searching for that address.

Maxie dazzled and disarmed with her crinkly smile. "Hey, it's what I do best, maybe the only thing, connect people with each other."

"You're also one hell of a nurse," David reminded her.

"Ha," she said, "I always forget that part. Come on." Signaling Tory to stay, she led David across the ballroom. Women all around were perfumed and tanned and white-toothed, their smiles and eyes and their very posture languid with the insouciance of having. The men were charming, tough, with darting predatory eyes, fighters, top of the heap. Like their golf or their drinking, this was part of their job and they were the best there was.

Out on another side patio, Maxie introduced him

to someone he thought he knew from somewhere, but didn't quite recognize. It was a strange man, an emotional effusion, wringing his hands, then David's. Not a bad looking guy, white, late 30's, David's height, with wavy black hair. Wearing a gray suit, black shoes, could be a banker. "Meet Vern Consiglio. You've seen him in the news."

"Pleased to meet you, Captain Gordon. Thanks for coming."

David shook his head. "I'm sorry, I don't—"

"Vern Consiglio," the man said pumping David's hands some more. "Assistant Chairman of CON2."

"Oh!" David said. "Now I remember. Yes." Maxie excused herself, having provided the social glue. "Why of all people did you want to speak with me? And here?"

"That's just the point. May I call you David? Call me Vern. The point is, nowadays you don't know whom to trust. Clandestine meetings are always safer, unless the parties are wired. Are you empty?"

"I've seen enough spy flicks to know what you mean. Yes."

"Unfortunately it's no longer a spy movie, David. It's real. I was speaking with a mutual friend of ours and he said you're doing an investigation—"

"Whoa," David said backing away. "You have the wrong guy. I'm just a little infantry guy with two broken feet, trying to hang on to his three hots and a cot."

"No, no," Vern said, "it's your show just as much as mine. David, don't you see what's going on here? I can't reason with Stan Carberry." Carberry was the Chairman of CON2, a retired U.S. senator from California, and a lifelong advocate of modernizing the Constitution. Consiglio was a little-known conservative lawyer from upstate New York. As one columnist had written, if this were a generation ago, Carberry would be a Democrat, and Consiglio a Republican. Both those parties were in the trash heap of history. Today's Middle Class Party, the only remaining super-party in a sea of splinter parties, was an alliance of desperation.

Consiglio said: "Carberry is so intent on guiding this convention down a middle path that he doesn't want to hear that more and more voters are becoming opposed to it, there are more threats to it, and dammit, I'm willing to think there may be people waiting in the wings to do something desperate if Carberry can't manage the convention."

"I understand what you mean, but I don't have what you want."

"A list, our mutual friend said."

"Already been gotten to."

"By whom?" Consiglio mirrored shock.

"I wish I knew."

"Is that being looked into?"

"Of course."

"Bellamy didn't know that."

"There is a breakdown in communication on every front."

"You can say that again." Consiglio slapped himself on the forehead. "Aw for God's sake. This gets worse by the minute." He pulled out his business card. "I've already decided we should have never had this convention. I can't convince Chairman Carberry of that. He's the only person who could get it called off; start a recall landslide from the states. Only one state—Vermont—has actually recalled its two delegates. If you learn any more on your end, will you call me immediately?" He offered the card. "Call me day or night. Give me some ammunition so I can go to Stan Carberry and prove to him that he's got to call off CON2."

David reluctantly accepted the card. "I'll see what I can do."

"When you accepted your commission," Consiglio said hotly, "you swore to uphold the Constitution—" Then he backed off. "I'm sorry, I don't mean to lecture." They shook hands, and Consiglio added: "Whatever you do, keep a tight lip. We never met, okay?"

David was glad to get back to the table where Maxie and Tory sat. Jack Standish was just having another double scotch. His collar was open, and his tie loose. "Yes, gotta outflank, outfox, and outfart the whole stinkum rabble," Jack was just declaiming.

"Jack," Maxie said through gritted teeth.

Jack waved to some Russians. "Da! Nyet! Spasibo! Your Aunt Tillie!"

"Time to get out of here," Tory suggested.

"Jack," Maxie ground again.

"Aw yer Aunt Tillie."

"David," Tory said nudging.

"A man's duty," he sighed. "Jack, I'm takin' you in, pardner. You gonna come peaceful-like, or do I have to shoot you off yore hoss?" He whispered in Maxie's ear: "Where do you find these guys?"

After a brief protest, it was ordained that David would take Jack home, while Tory would take Maxie out for a drink someplace, just the girls.

CHAPTER 26

Fifteen minutes later, the two women were headed away, Maxie driving the growling Porsche. Tory couldn't help but admire again the beauty of her friend as the city's night lights played over her features. Maxie was every man's desire, every women's envy: by turns elegant, subdued, lively, poised. Inside, Tory sensed, was a more frail creature, not so self-confident. "Maxie, what was that all about?"

"What, dear?"

"You took David someplace."

"Oh, that."

"Is it a national secret?"

"Yes."

"Aw come on."

"Does he know yet?"

"Yes."

"Was he shocked?"

"Well of course, Maxie. Who wouldn't be?"

"Is he taking it in stride?"

"He's a sweet man. Very sincere. Very brave. He's got guts. I don't dare hope, but a man with that much character might be big enough to stay with me."

Maxie reasoned: "You're beautiful, you're passionate, you have a lot to offer. I keep telling you, sooner or later it'll happen for you. David was so badly hurt, the poor thing. And you're right, he's really a straight shooter. He won't hurt ya, Tory."

"Oh, it'll be okay if he just lets me down easy."

"Give him a chance."

"I will." She gripped Maxie's hands, and Maxie gripped back. "I will!" They rocked from side to side snapping their fingers.

A while later Maxie said, as she puffed on her cigarette: "Listen, kiddo. You've heard of Robert Lee Hamilton?"

"Yes. Don't tell me he's a relative of yours."

"Yes, as a matter of fact."

"Max."

"I am serious here, Tory. You know we always have colonels on both sides of everything. Well, old Robert Lee Hamilton—I only met him once or twice when I was a teenager—he's got Bodley relatives. All related to Robert E. Lee, of course. Of course, now maybe it'll be generals on both sides. You see, there's an Admiral Lee and a General Bodley, both on active duty. One is in California, the other is in Oregon."

"You're chattering, Maxie."

"Yes, and I love it."

"So what's the upshot?"

"The upshot is that this country is in a hell of a lot of trouble, and I hope I didn't make a mistake tonight."

"A mistake?"

"I don't want David to get hurt."

Tory held on as Maxie drove. She had a blurry glimpse of neon signs promising shopping and night life. The car shot down a ramp, bounced into an underground garage, and slowed behind a long limousine. Tory read signs: 'The Riverside. Valet Parking. Formal Evening Dress Only.' "Where are we going, Maxie?"

"Someplace quiet. I want to eat, and I want to chatter mindlessly with you, and then I want to go disco dancing until our brains turn to gelatin. And I want to forget CON2." Maxie grabbed her purse and wrap. "It's on me."

"I brought my checkbook and credit cards just in case."

A young man in valet uniform drove the car off. Maxie and Tory followed a Persian carpet down marble hallways, with a potted palm in every corner, to a dusky vestibule. Waiting in the shadows were the Maitre d' Hotel and his staff. "Bodley," Maxie said.

"Of course," said the Maitre d', a handsome darkskinned man in his fifties, with gray hair on the sides, as he checked a clothbound register, "party of two, smoking?"

"Maxie."

"I'm sorry."

"This way, ladies."

"And you a nurse."

They followed him through a dining room of about twenty round tables. Lots of white hair; red faces with bulging eyes; paler faces jealous. Wrinkles. Money. An Afro-American woman played piano with soul and subtlety. A big woman, black as ebony, she sang in a bluesy voice rich as an instrument of many fine woods. Even when her fingers crashed down on two octaves' worth of keys at once, and her song became robust as a shout, her voice still carried languor and smoothness. And each time she backed off quickly, into a lovely reverie. "Martini," Maxie said when the waiter came. "You hungry, Tory?"

"Starved."

"The evening wasn't so bad until Jack got polluted."

"Maxie, the guys you—"

They ordered finger food to fill the empty spot. Tory ordered a Campari and soda on the rocks. It was light, it was dry, and it promised she wouldn't wake up with a hangover. "Don't overdo the martinis, Maxie."

"Okay!" Maxie put a long cigarette in her mouth. Then she emptied part of her purse on the white linen, until she found her gold-plated lighter. "Seriously, you're so rock-stable for me. Other women I've known, that are rich, I can't go anywhere with because they put on airs." Cigarette smoke drifted around them. Maxie certainly did not put on airs. Didn't need to. At another table, a man with red cheeks and violent eyes stared hungrily at Maxie. His heavy, pretty wife with gray grandma bun looked pained. Tory whispered through her fingers: "I think that guy over there is wondering why he didn't see you on the menu."

Maxie twisted her neck, blew smoke, and scoped the guy in one glance. "He's making you, Tory, not me."

"No way." Tory said. She was not a butterfly, like Maxie. She frequently found herself stared after, but from a distance; men seemed threatened by her seriousness. Except David.

"Ignore him," Maxie said. "We won't make a scene." She laughed quietly. "We could turn and stare at him. Make comments. Throw grapes."

Their drinks came. "Sure. And get carried home on

the shoulders of—well, no officers around, but hopefully some gentlemen."

"—By an act of Congress. Cheers." Maxie lifted her glass. Tory clinked with her. The waiter came with more drinks. "I envy you, Tory. How's you and David?"

"Me and David is 220."

"High voltage."

Tory squirmed in embarrassment. "Probably just a crush."

"—Awww—"

"—I know, bummer, huh? But he's sooo cute. Tall, dark-haired—"

"—And handsome—" Maxie teased. "I don't know about crush. He's kinda like you. Very determined. Maybe I should have—"

Tory flicked glances right and left. "Maxie, change the subject, dammit. Maybe the date of your life is right here someplace, waiting to take you in his arms."

The singer bellowed and smashed the piano, then uttered a long wail, and finger foods arrived. Maxie ordered another martini and lit up again. The singer went on break and a nervous sixtyish white man came out and played Chopin and Liszt. "Maxie," Tory said, "I wish you'd at least date other men while this guy jerks you around."

"Maybe you're right, Tory."

Tory was cautious; didn't want Maxie to drink too much and get bummed and start crying. "You're great people, Max. Give yourself a chance with decent guys."

"You know I have a few drinks and I agree sincerely that men like Van Meeuwen were no good for me.

And I don't believe a word of it the next day. Can't help it."

"In vino veritas."

"In vino wino. I'm going to quit smoking and drinking as soon as I'm fully air qualified. Then I'm going to meet Mr. Right."

"And dump Van Meeuwen? Does it have to be a doctor or a senator, Maxie, for crying out loud!"

"Tell you what, Tory. I'll get my parents to fork over another half million bucks for therapy and then maybe I'll run away with a starving musician." She stubbed her cigarette out. "Aw hell, let's stop talking about me for a while. I sure like David Gordon. Take good care of him, Tory."

"You think he's getting into dangerous waters."

"I hear rumors."

"Like?"

Maxie shrugged her little freckled shoulders. "There are always rumors. It's just—well, right now, there are a lot of angry people."

"People have been angry for years."

"Yes, but some people I know are sending their families out of town. We're talking, like, pulling kids out of school suddenly. Wives taking unpaid vacation. People going far west to be away from here while CON2 goes on."

Dinner arrived, and their conversation turned light. A glass of wine for Tory, three for Maxie, and they found themselves laughing and forgetting their surroundings. The pianist left, and soft music trickled in through a p.a. system.

Tory said: "Hey, check out the guys." She'd spotted a noisy throng of six or seven burly young men in tuxedos, waving champagne bottles. They were accompanied by an equal number of gorgeous, petite oriental women in pastel silk gowns.

"Oh fuck."

"Max?"

Maxie, her face contorted in pain and fury, stubbed out another cigarette. "The gorgeous one is Van Meeuwen."

"Aw geez," Tory said.

"Just sit tight," Maxie said. Her face was a white mask of fury. "That's him, third from the right." She pointed to a handsome, scoffing young man with arrogant eyes, who looked very self-assured as he helped his date into her seat. That kiss on the mouth as he leaned over her ruled out any reasonable explanations, Tory thought. The men couldn't see Maxie from their angle. In any case, Maxie's slight figure was barely visible behind a large plant. Luckily, Tory was looking toward Maxie, so Maxie was looking away from Dr. Schmuck and Friends. Tory not only watched him frenching the girl, but actually checking out Tory as he did so. "Let's split," Tory suggested.

"Just a minute," Maxie said, downing her wine.

"No." "Yes." Maxie picked up the pitcher of ice water.

"Maxie."

"Okay." Maxie put the pitcher down.

"Let's just—"

"Follow me." Maxie picked up her purse and gloves. Tory followed her to the boisterous table.

"Good evening, Dr. Van Meeuwen," Maxie said. Tory heard a plunk as Maxie dropped her engagement ring into his drink.

The young doctor looked surly, as though he wasn't

sure how much energy he should expend, having been caught. "Maxie, I can explain."

"You don't need to, Paul. You're an asshole, and I never want to see you again." Maxie strode off. As she turned to follow, Tory noticed the scoffing look as Van Meeuwen rolled up his eyes, and his friends tittered. As she left, she added: "Well said, Maxie."

Out in the garage, Maxie bawled her eyes out while Tory waited for the car. By the time the valet brought the car around, Maxie was wiping her swollen face with a hankie and appeared to be regaining control. She asked Tory: "Would you please drive? I think I may have to cry some more on the way home."

As they crossed town, Maxie said, "Thanks for being my friend."

"Lots of people love you."

"I am so grateful you were there with me."

"You were incredible, kid."

"I feel like he stuck a knife in me."

"It hurts," Tory agreed. "I hope, Max, that you're finally done with this eraser head. Or are you going back for more?"

"You drive like I do," Maxie said.

"Dammit!"

After a long silence, Maxie said: "I'm sorry."

Tory found herself yelling: "You should be sorry. What is it with broads like you? You pick these dingdongs, these nobodies, and you let them walk all over you, and then you keep going back for more. All because you're scared. Or you're lonely. Or you feel sorry for yourself. Especially after 600 martinis." Tory was almost out of breath, but she still had a little yelling in her. "And so in the meantime, everyone around you has to feel sorry for you, and I'm sick and tired of it. Wake up! Get a life! Get a brain!" They sat in stunned silence all the way home. Tory cringed in her seat, wishing she could suck every word back into her mouth. Her ears hurt from the echoes of her sharp words. She cried a little herself.

Maxie said as they arrived at the condo and got out: "You know what? I needed that. Next time I meet one of these dingdongs, I'll picture you yelling at me and it'll make me think twice. Look, I'm really sorry I made you sore."

Tory felt a gush of relief and embraced her. Maxie hugged back, small but made of steel cable. Tory made sure Maxie got to her bedroom all right. Maxie passed out on the bed fully dressed and Tory covered her up before closing the door. Minutes later in the peace and quiet of her bedroom, Tory fell into bed and drifted off to sleep. Somewhere in a dream, she stood on a river bank and yelled over the water. She kept reaching out to two men in a canoe, trying to warn them that they were paddling too close to the deadly falls, but they only smiled and waved back, unaware of the great danger. One was Ib Shoob. The other was David.

CHAPTER 27

In the morning, David told Colonel Jankowsky about his meeting with Vern Consiglio. He concluded with "... Obviously I had to tell you, Sir."

"You did the right thing, David. In the military we have a chain of command. We don't go working on the outside for civilians, no matter how much we believe in their cause. You proceed as normal. I'll feed you some more case files, hopefully easier ones than you've had so far, and you just do your job. I'll have to kick your information upstairs, of course." He paused, apparently noting the worry in David's mind. He added: "That's the chance the Vern Consiglios take when they try to outsmart the system and use junior officers. I understand it's very sensitive information and it will stay in Tony Tomasik's chain of command."

David opened a stack of five case files. A mess unit at the Composite required a certification inspection, and he'd have to locate the military health inspector to get him in on it. A senior NCO at a motor pool had phoned in a tip that his company XO and two fellow NCO's were stealing expensive tools; David kicked that one over to CID. And so it went, until the desk phone rang. It was Tory. "David, can you come over here, like right away? I'm at my old office at Observatory Circle."

"What is it?" Her hushed, explosive whisper gave him a chill.

"Jet's found something."

"I'll call you from the car." Leaving word with a secretary, he hurried outside, pulled his car out with screeching tires, and drove toward the Naval Observatory. The sky was a mix of sunshine and gray cotton clouds. He had to turn on the windshield wipers two or three times to clear away accumulating drops from a rain he couldn't see falling. The tires sang on wet asphalt as he pulled up the observatory drive and parked under a big tree. His feet crunched on the road surface as he walked toward the NSSO building. Tory and Jet hurried to meet him, both wearing raincoats. Tory's dark hair bunched up in the wind, and Jet's lank hair flew. Tory said: "We were just checking to see everything got moved to the Atlantic Hotel. Jet was poking around in the net—"

He followed them back into the building, left and right through the short zig zag hallways designed to make life harder for anyone not familiar with the layout, like a spy or an intruder. "In here," Tory said opening a door, "it's soundproof. There are cameras in the ceiling, so turn away from them and nobody can read your lips later on film." She laughed nervously. "Aren't we getting paranoid?"

They were in the Secure Room. "Ib loved this place," Jet said.

"Wow," David said, getting his first close look at the behemoth he'd only glimpsed during his earlier visit. He stared with greedy curiosity at the fifty-ton diving helmet or egg or whatever, made of burnished steel, with chrome-plated rivets, mounted in a heavy concrete base painted red, that was CloudMaster. But no time to ogle now. "Go on," David encouraged.

Jet handed him goggles like he'd worn the other day. "We're going to play back tape. Ib covered his tracks very well. He could have fooled a lay person or even another head walker, but I know some of his tricks. Here we go, Sir. This is recorded, so don't try to do anything. No turns, no walking. Just hang on tight." David held a sissy bar as they followed Ib's tracks on the spoor of a European hacker. "Ib destroyed the paperwork, and he hid the work disk in a common area so it could have been the work of any of us at NSSO. I finally figured out where Ib stashed his records." Jet had turned on her seldom-used icon, a slender waif in a dark jump suit, right out of the 25th Century or someplace. David's path of vision followed the icon's appealing figure into a tall wire-frame meant to look like a high-rise. They descended staircases into the earth, all gray except for the red railing that spelled danger. They came to a door, and the waif made a waving motion. The door opened, and they stepped into what looked like a storeroom. A sign on the wall read: "Ib's Klub House. Keep Out." In a fit of humor, the old Coast Guardsman must have pixeled the drawing that occupied one corner—of an easy chair, a table with a beer and a book, and a raccoon-tail hat on a peg. A cigarette smoldered in an ashtray. The waif touched a switch in the wall. Instantly, Ib's likeness appeared in the easy chair. He smiled and waved. The big belly, the swollen ankles, the double chin were well rendered. "He has a good sense of humor," Jet said. "Here is the trip disk." The waif stood prettily on tiptoe before a bookcase. Its finger scanned from left to right, and then pressed a certain book. Instantly the scene changed. "We're following Ib's footsteps now, Sir. Through various net city neighborhoods. That is, data addresses. Archives. The phone company. The power company. Banks. Stores. He was chasing a Dutch hacker named Salty who got into the power company's files, then a bank's."

"That's what he told me when I first met him."

"That's right, Sir. Now we know where he went and what he did. We may be able to dig up that list of names yet."

"Have you been in there, Jet?"

"Nossir, I'm afraid to get too close. Afraid I might destroy evidence."

David watched the icon of an old sailing ship rotate in the air of a huge bank lobby. The ship's cannon boomed. Jet speeded up the record. "Blink your eyes, Sir. We'll be there in a second." David followed a blinding blur of light and motion. Then they were standing still in what looked like a train station. It was Grand Central under the ground, he thought; only from high windows did harsh sunlight stab inside and lose itself into smoky darkness. And in the darkness stood huge drums. Kiosks, he thought. "They're called carousels," Jet said. "This is the city's emergency data recovery archive. The carousels are just representations; the real things are huge wafer disks in a cold room. There must have been a brownout the night the Vice President died."

David was intrigued. "Why do you say that?"

"Watch," Jet said. David felt Tory's fingernails biting into his shoulder as the three of them followed the last steps before Ib's discovery of the secret that would result in his disappearance. Inside one of the shadowy carousels, Ib appeared to be browsing around. The insides were covered with thousands of tiny written labels organized into columns, each column further divided into squares. Ib focused on a column labeled Directory Z. "Carousel 49, Directory Z," Jet said. "Now watch before we go in." A bunch of information displayed—numbers and text, flashing busily. The waif pointed to a date amid the data. "See this? It's the night the Vice President died, a half hour before his death."

"Oh wow," David said as the proof of Ib's discovery began to hit home. Tory's fingers dug into him as she whispered: "David, it's the most important part! The proof! That address hasn't been touched since Cardoza's death. Nobody could fake that."

"I checked," Jet said. "There was a browndown minutes before Cardoza was killed. This message was on its way to the VP mansion, there was a browndown, and it got sucked into here instead. Under normal conditions, as soon as the browndown was over, which might be in a few seconds, the messages get barfed back up into the net, and they go to their destinations like nothing happened. Only nobody bothers to erase the emergency archive. So the data stay there, until months or years later, when there's a future power failure, and it's this carousel's turn in the cycle to be overwritten. Ib made sure he merely copied what's in Directory Z, without a save that would put a more recent date in the processing registers."

"If only I'd believed him sooner," David said. He felt dark piano keys of fear banging in his soul.

CHAPTER 28

Maxie called as David drove home. "Would you like to share dinner with us?"

"Sure. If you don't mind that I'm hungry and tired."

"Hungry we can fix. Tired I'm not sure."

He stopped briefly at home and changed into casual clothes including clean black sweats. When he arrived at their apartment not long after, Tory offered him a glass of wine. They made small talk as she straightened some things and they drifted toward her bedroom. Her bedroom door was open and he waited in the doorway—the room seemed neat, but not too neat. Some books were out of place. Three bears sat on the bed, facing different ways. A hair brush, a cologne spray with the top beside it, a crushed tissue with lipstick on it, lay on the middle of her vanity. The bed was freshly and tightly made. An Army duffel bag peeked from a half-open closet, black padlock anything but feminine. The aquamarine-and-black checkered deck shoes she'd worn to his house sat against the wall, one toe overlapping another as though someone pigeon-toed had worn them. A row of dresses peeked from a closet, conveying dressy but comfortable.

David joined the two women for a light dinner.

From a half-open patio door, the kitchen air cooled sweetly, smelling of leaves and grass. They were all tired and ate quietly. They felt comfortable together, bonded by the Army and a dozen less tangible realities. Maxie played hostess, passing dishes around. She'd made a salad with good things in it, tomatoes, bits of ham, cheeses, chickpeas, a light dressing. He'd kicked off his shoes, following the women's cue, and wiggled stocking feet in the thick carpet.

Maxie broke the relaxed silence. "Must be the night for sweats." She wore sweat pants and a loose white T-shirt that barely hinted at girlish breasts. Tory wore light blue sweats and an olive drab T-shirt; she was nearly as tall as David, and more statuesque than waifish Maxie. "Next time we can coordinate," Tory said stifling a laugh, exchanging a look with Maxie. Then Tory's dark, serious eyes focused on David. There was some electricity in the air that evening, David thought, feeling its subtle and persistent charge invigorate him like a cleansing and exhilarating halo of good ions. If it was a conspiracy, it was a sweet one; if it was dark, it was velvety, meant to envelop in good feelings. He let the two women snare him in their plot. He remembered how at home Tory had felt a few days ago at his place, and returned the compliment. "You have a nice place here. I feel right at home."

"Thanks," Tory said. "Do you like to play Monopoly?"

Maxie rolled her eyes up. "Oh no, that's like when I was a kid."

"It's not so bad. It's cheap, you don't have to go anywhere, and you don't wake up with a hangover."

David grinned. "It's been a while since I played

Monopoly, but I used to really like the game. I used to drive my sisters crazy because I'd put up all these hotels and they'd land on them—"

"That's it," Maxie said, "he feels at home because we're his sisters."

"Believe me," he said, "one lifetime growing up with sisters is plenty. No, I don't think of you that way."

"Friends," Maxie said, extending a hand. He shook her hand, then extended his hand to Tory. She shook, too, with a giggle. "Pals," she said. Then she told Maxie: "Nice dinner."

"Yes, nice dinner," David said, taking his plate to the sink. Tory stretched wide, yawning long. He took that as a hint. "Well, I'd better be moseying along."

"Oh no!" both women said at once. Maxie said: "I've got to run to the store. Won't you stay with her and guard the house just that long?"

"I have enough energy for one game of Monopoly," Tory said.

He shrugged. "Sure." As the Monopoly board appeared on the table, he tried to remember if you had to buy three houses on each square of a color before you could buy a hotel. He wondered if they put $100 in the pot to start out. Maxie had her shoes and coat and was headed for the door, mittens in one hand and pocket book swinging on its long sling. "I'll see you guys later!"

"Bye," Tory chimed, closing the door. She turned to David. "How about a nice glass of wine?"

"Sure, but I'm tired and a glass of wine might just knock me out."

"Why don't you rest? Come in the living room and I'll fix a few cushions for you."

"Shall I bring the game?"

"If you wish."

He didn't hear a great enthusiasm in that reply, but he picked up the game, careful not to spill the pieces through its torn cover. He set the game down on the living room floor. She brought a wine bottle and two crystal glasses. She set a vase of red flowers on an end table and turned the lamp above the vase down low. He wondered how they would play the Monopoly game in fifteen watt light, but then again he still had that sixth sense of a velvet conspiracy. Tory lit a fire in the fireplace, using briquettes and small chunks of hardwood. Instantly the room took on a faint smoky aroma that reminded him of walks in the autumn woods long ago with his mother and father, and nights when the fireflies still glowed but the first hint of freshness was driving the summer laziness out of the early darkening air. He lay propped on a series of cushions facing her. She eased onto one elbow, facing him. Her eyes glittered with messages obscure and urgent. He would take his time, because she was giving him all night. It was a delicious stretching out of something wonderful, like—he smiled inwardly at a funny thought, and she must have seen him light up. "What's so funny?"

"Oh, I was just remembering something, don't know exactly why. When I was a kid, taking a long time to unwrap a candy bar, enjoying the thought of how good that candy bar was going to be, trying to stave off each bite as long as possible. Including the first bite."

"Do you still do that?" She pulled a blanket over her legs.

"Which, the first or the last bite?"

"All of what you said." She pulled another blanket over her back.

"I think so. Only with really good things."

"Really, really good things?"

"Really, really, really good things."

"Maybe you could explain a little more closely."

"Do you mind if I sit close so I can explain better?"

"Oh, please do. I can't wait to learn all about this."

He nudged himself across the two or three feet of shag. "Well," he said, setting his wine glass down on the brick footing of the fire place, "Maybe it would be best if we used a, you know, an example." He took her hand.

"A ferinstance." She held his hand, pulling lightly.

He nudged closer, heart pounding in his collar, mouth dry in sweet anticipation. "Yes, that's it. Well said." He smelled her hair, her faint perfume or soap.

Firelight flickered on her face. "I don't think I've had one of those really, really, really good things in a long time, David, before I met you."

"Here's one now," he said and bent down to kiss her. Her hands rose and he felt the coolness of her fingertips as she guided his cheeks close. Her mouth was ready for him, warm, wet, moving as her hands closed around the back of his head, as her fingertips dug hungrily into his hair. Her breath came in gasps. She half-turned, thrusting her hip against his. He sighed deeply and surrendered with fast-beating heart. "You didn't offer me a blanket," he said. "I was wondering if you wanted me to be cold."

"Oh no," she said sincerely, "I was planning how I could get you over here under the blankets with me." She pushed him aside just an inch or two, enough to pull more blankets over.

"Did you plant those there?" he whispered, raking her cheek with kisses. He could see the pulse beating fast in her neck, and he kissed the throbbing little spot. She lay back. Her eyes glittered in firelight as she stole her free arm around his waist. Her expression was hungry, and she closed her eyes as he leaned forward to kiss her on the mouth again. His fingers stole about, feeling soft spots everywhere, playing up and down her curves. His fingertips found the border of her T-shirt and crawled underneath up the flat of her belly until they reached the firm strap of a sports bra and the sudden curve of one breast, then the other. They were delightful to the touch, firm, each a full handful, the cotton bra a flimsy thing barely in the way. She writhed against him, and her fingertips racing among his vetebrae as if searching for all the switches that would make him tingle.

And tingle he did, as all his cares fell away. He heard a distant car swish by, saw the movement of headlights on the ceiling, painting languid shapes of light that fled like manta rays. In this otherworldly, underwater fantasy of fleeting shapes and stopped time, David felt himself tempted by a rousing passion.

She threw the blankets back. "This candy bar is going to melt."

"I got one that's not melting at all," he said, aware of himself.

"Come with me." She rose and offered a hand.

"What about—"

"I think she went to Florida shopping," Tory said.

He put his arm around her waist, and she put hers around his waist, as they went to her bedroom, each carrying a half empty glass of wine. She put on soft music; something classical, very Debussy, La Mer, its textures gliding over and around and through one another like the surfaces of a shifting sea. As she stepped to the window, tugging at a shade, he stepped behind her and put his hands on her waist. Gently, he turned her, and she turned in his arms. They resumed their kiss in a languid embrace, as if in a dance together. He held the long curves of her torso, felt her flat belly against his. His fingers explored the thick drawstring in her sweatpants. It was elastic, and gave as he tugged. He felt her fingers working on him. In a moment, he felt the cool night breeze on his buttocks. His hands roved down her back, glided around her rear. He groaned, turning up his face as her hands sensuously enveloped his most delicate parts. With a near-awkward dance, she stepped out of her panties, and they sank onto the bed together locked in an embrace.

He kissed her passionately, trying to prolong the suspense. Her tongue worked against his tongue and her ragged gasping began to become a rapid series of soft pleading moans. He reached down and pushed her long legs apart, gently massaging her in urgent circles. He felt warmth, jelly, moisture. The insides of her thighs were damp. She turned her head from side to side, eyes closed. Her hips pressed toward him as he entered. She breathed in rapid gasps as the first of many orgasms arrived. Seeing her at the edge, wanting to be there with her, he slapped rapidly against her soft skin until they both arrived, moaning in unison, and collapsed together exhausted but happy. Thus, they fell asleep.

Later in the night, they stirred in their sleep. David

reached out for her. The bed felt cool, the sheets soft. Still mostly asleep, they rubbed their legs and thighs and bellies together, enjoying the friction of smooth skin on smooth skin under warm blankets. He kissed her nipples, alternating from one to the other. She pulled at him gently, cuddling and caressing him. He kissed her below, smelling the sweet clean fluid like a fog by the sea with just that tang of suggestion. "Hurry," she whispered. With a cry of hunger, he entered. She turned her head sideways and pulled a pillow up to muffle the wail that escaped as he rocked in her. They were perfect for each other, he and she, rising toward the sun together, she sobbing, he thrusting hungrily but with a hand gently under her head lest she hurt herself against the headboard—until all the passion was spent and then they lay together, afraid to say I love you—just yet.

David awoke hearing the sound of a trash truck somewhere. He was naked, and stuck to the sheet. As he peeled the sheet back, he saw Tory's sleeping figure and marveled that she was really as long and beautiful as he had imagined. She stirred, yawning, and touched her fingertips to her eyes. She turned so he was in her peripheral vision, and said "Hi." She turned fully to regard him, as though this were the moment of truth.

"Hi," he said. He lay back and pulled her to him. "You are beautiful."

She crawled on top of him and pulled the blankets up over her back. He felt himself growing erect, straining for her. She received him readily. They lay thus, in that soft gray light, that was timeless and underwater, and rocked unhurriedly in tiny motions, like two vessels drowsing at the docking post. Like a long, slow afternoon—

After making love, they lay looking into one another's eyes. David saw the time and groaned as he sat up. "We can't be late for work."

Tory sat beside him and cupped his face in her hands like something precious. Her eyes gazed fearlessly into his and he read passion and sincerity in them.

"I feel swept away by you, Tory."

"You better not hurt me, David."

"I couldn't."

Her voice was low and fragile and dangerous. "I've been hurt before, as I am sure you have, and I've walked away and picked up the pieces, and in the last year or two I decided why is it worth that kinda hell, I'll never fall in love again, and then I stumble over a guy like you, and maybe here I go again."

He wanted to say I love you but he wasn't ready to do that yet. It was coming, like a train, and the tracks were humming a mile up ahead, but that big old train had to take its time. He knew it and he hoped she knew it.

She continued in the same tone, hardly catching a breath. "I'm a pretty straight shooter and I expect the same of you."

He gazed at the ovals of her cheeks, the seriousness of her lips, the lightning in her eyes, the resolve in her chin, and loved her already. "I'm falling for you, Tory, pretty heavy, and it's a scary ride, but I'll go it if you want."

"I don't want anything from you except you open the door for me and you hold the chair for me when

I sit down and you don't ever, ever yell at me or raise a hand to me, do you hear?"

"Yes."

"What do you want from me?"

He thought for a moment. What could he say? He'd been hurt too, but he wasn't going to make a speech.

She shook his head gently between her palms. Her face came close as if she wanted to kiss him or maybe peer into his skull. "What do you want?"

He held her, one hand on each side of her, his fingers feeling her ribs, as though she were a vase or an amphora or an urn containing all that would ever be his in life, free, just there for the taking, as long as he had the courage and the will just then, for she stared unflinchingly into his eyes. He felt the steady beat of her heart, the pulsing of her blood—or was it his? He felt the generosity in her open palms as she held his cheeks in her palms. She whispered one last time: "What do you want?"

"I—" He wanted to say, yes I'll do those things and not do the other things you said; don't go off with another man; maybe cook dinner once in a while or pat the pillows up or tell me to take my feet off the sofa or praise me if I remember to do the dishes. I want a corner to sit in and read and I don't want you to rearrange my books, or throw out my newspaper, or close the magazine I leave open. All that came out was: "I want you." But there was that little corner of uncertainty, and he heard her make her prophecy again in Arlington: "You'll want children of your own, and then you'll leave me." He resolved to watch that little doubt carefully; if it grew, he would have to bail out, in fairness to her and to himself. Could she be wrong? Could it be doable? His heart raced at the thought.

Her eyes drooped briefly: "I can see the little doubt inside you. It's okay." She brightened, and kissed him a peck on the lips. "You said what I wanted to hear. C'mon, I'll race you to the shower."

A minute later, in the warmth and soapy steamy enclosure that was barely big enough for two people, their moment of gloom disappeared and she said: "Hint, big hint: I like romantic letters and cards. They don't have to ramble on and on, but I like them."

"Duh, where can I find one of them?"

As she shut the water off, she said: "David, this is like wartime. You've seen those old movies. When you've got something, you better reach out, grab it, and hang on. Who knows where this will end."

"Those are the old movies," he agreed. "Do you like to go for long rides in the countryside?"

"I sure do. All the way out to Tabitha Summers's place, I kept looking at you while you were driving. You looked so strong and handsome."

"Gawrsh, Lottie."

She whacked him with the washcloth.

He examined her bottom. "Hey, you get pink all over when you're wet, huh?"

"Just when it's very warm."

Breakfast was a blur of Maxie moving here and there as she made breakfast—hot oatmeal; milk, sugar, coffee, bacon. David and Tory sat contentedly at barstools around the service counter.

David was used to wearing a sidearm while on duty since this CON2 had begun; he thought nothing of seeing Tory armed, since she was an MP officer. But here was Maxie, 100 pounds soaking wet, casually holding a spoon of oatmeal in one hand and a piece of buttered toast in the other, while, over her white T-shirt that hinted of breasts, she wore a shoulder holster, and hanging in this apparatus was a huge 9 millimeter cannon. He was going to ask if it didn't drag her down on one side, but some instinct told him he'd better not poke fun at her. Never poke fun at a person packing a piece, even if it's Maxie, he sniggered inwardly. So he ate quietly, enjoying Tory's nearness.

CHAPTER 29

Ibrahim Shoob's body floated in the C&O Canal like a mass of dissolving bread, long drained of any blood. David got there as fast as he could. Tory had called his office from hers, sobbing, to tell him the news.

David felt a pang of remorse, a sense of failure as he stood staring at Ib's body. Tory gripped his arm with both hands and stared helplessly.

The corpse was the color of dirty canvas and bloated from days in the cool water, jammed in the dark under a bridge until a kayaker had dislodged it this morning. Small fish and maybe a turtle or two had nibbled at it. The eyeballs had probably been a delicacy—if the kidnappers hadn't gotten them first. Tory turned away, retching, and David felt overwhelming pity for the dead NCO. Police divers were searching the area for evidence, a murder weapon, anything that would explain his grisly fate. A stainless steel wrist bracelet gave Ib's name, rank, and blood type. "It's official," Tory said. "He's no longer missing, and I'm sure they'll declare it a homicide. Although" —she gave the dissolving sea cow-shape a last look—"it may be hard to learn much from that. Poor Ib."

That afternoon, David accompanied her and two Coast Guardsmen to the Shoob home. It was a journey he didn't want to make, but he went to help Tory. Hala Shoob let out a wail as she saw the four uniformed persons step out of a U.S. Government vehicle—David, Tory, a Captain, and a Master Chief. A cousin, same age as Hala, appeared and chased a crowd of children out of the living room. Hala was more pitiful this time, anger overwhelmed by grief. A heavy person like Ib, clutching a hankie, she collapsed sideways on the couch and cried loudly and heartbrokenly. After a time, she composed herself and made coffee. The cousin helped, distributing sweet pastries at a living room table. It almost turned into a ceremony of welcome rather than a liturgy of bitter farewell. David supposed keeping busy afforded Hala some relief from her pain. As the many pictures of her and Ib around the room attested, they had had a wealth in family togetherness. There were smiling kids, a smiling Ib proud in his dress uniform, a smiling Hala proud of her husband and children. Tory excused herself after a while. Hala thanked her, wringing Tory's hands and thanking her for having been a good officer. She wrung David's hands also, gazing up at him with fiery Arab eyes: "My husband," she said with a sob, "my husband loved the United States more than most Americans do. He was a fine patriot. You find those men who killed him, you find those men and bring them to justice. Do you promise me that?"

"We'll help the police in every way." Tory and David saw themselves out, while the Coast Guardsmen continued their vigil with the family. David and Tory walked to his car. Because they were in uniform, he had to remind himself not to touch her hand or kiss her. "Thank you for coming," she said. Her eyes spoke kisses.

"I'd do anything for you," he said, a flood of emotions boiling between them. She reached out and they shook hands, enjoying the lingering touch of one another. "I hardly know you," she said in a very quiet voice, "but I sure like you a lot."

He wanted to say something clever, but the words stuck in his throat. "Me too," was all he managed. He took a deep breath and watched her walk away.

ANN Breaking News with Allison Miranda

ALLISON MIRANDA: We have this breaking story from the Atlantic Hotel and Convention Center. ANN has just learned that a floor vote has taken place. I repeat, a floor vote has taken place, and the ten-amendment limit is no longer in effect. Here is our reporter in the field, Peggy DeMetrio, with the latest developments. Peggy?

PEGGY: It's an incredible scene here, as you can see and hear in the background. The main hall is in sheer bedlam as delegates are trying to out-shout and out-shove one another in order to be next to speak. This is a severe defeat for the center moderates as the radicals of the left and right combined to ignore Committee and simply threw out the limit. So far, 26 amendments have been submitted and many, many more are on the way, including: mandatory school prayer; outlaw divorce; death penalty for abortion; life in psychiatric prison for gays and lesbians who do not repent; evolution teaching outlawed; funds cut off to universities that do not establish creationism centers. And here are a few from the left: Civil rights status for gays; death penalty for child abuse; no death penalty but life in prison without parole for capital offenders; civil rights status for mothers of young children so they can get jobs, training, and the like. The list gets longer by the moment. These delegates may eventually say enough and close the Agenda. It's clear now that many of the delegates who ran for their office under the Congressional Act of Convention simply lied about their agendas. Stealth candidates, you would call them. In the meantime, things are rough on the floor. I have seen several floor fights—fisticuffs—in the past hour.Under the same Congressional Act, these delegates are immune from civil proceedings, so I don't know how order can ultimately be kept here. Back to you, Allison.

CHAPTER 30

That afternoon, while he worked in the I.G. office, David's collar com sounded, and he pressed it. "Yes?"

"Captain Gordon." He didn't recognize the woman's voice. "You know me." He shook his head, exchanging puzzled looks with Jankowsky. "You were just at my house in the country."

Tabitha Summers! "Yes, I remember," David said sharply, giving Jankowsky a thumbs up, and switching to the privacy of an earphone. "Speak to me, Miss Summers."

"I heard about Ib."

"Yes, Lieutenant Breen and I went to visit his wife earlier. Hala is—"

"I'm there now."

"I see."

"Hala and I spoke. She's getting out of town with the kids. But I want to see you. I have something."

"Stay put. Don't say any more."

"Yes. Line's probably tapped. I ought to know, with my years in the business."

David rose. "Sir, it's Summers. I think she has the list."

Jankowsky whistled. "Jeez, you don't stop for a moment."

"Where do I take her? She needs to get safe quick, seeing what happened to Ib."

"Bring her around the back. It's the only sure thing I can think of just now."

David drove as fast as he legally could, arriving at the Shoob house in less than 30 minutes. Tabitha Summers stepped off the curb to meet him. He saw her—grim, wearing an off-mauve raincoat, tattered white sneakers, a scarf, and God knew how many sweaters to cover her thin frame. "Get us out of here," she said slamming the door. She buckled up. David saw no signs of surveillance as he pulled out. "What have you got?"

"The list you're after. Ib snatched it from the carousel. He was afraid the wrong people would get it. Like a fool, I let him talk me into keeping a copy. I kept it stored off-line."

"Did you bring a hard copy with you?"

"Are you serious? I e-mailed the file to your boss inside an easter egg." She meant a hidden computer file that, if its secret key was triggered, opened to play out some visual surprise, usually something goofy and fun; in this case, not.

"Are you going back home or do you feel you need protection?"

"I'd rather go home than anything, but I'm afraid to. Besides, I have work to do."

"You're retired."

"No more."

David ushered her into the I.G.'s office. After a five minute conversation, Jankowsky forwarded her easter egg program to Tony Tomasik and led them around the back to the Task Force. After they stepped through the security measures, Tomasik welcomed her. "Miss Summers, thanks for coming."

"I can't shake this nagging feeling that Uncle Sam needs me. Again."

"What do you propose to do for us?" Tomasik asked.

At that moment, Jankowsky showed the printout to David. On it were several prominent names, including General Robert Montclair at the Atlantic and the motor mouth of off-the-chart right-wing causes, retired General Felix Mason. Tomasik exclaimed as he read the list. "Two dozen names," he counted. "Prominent generals, admirals, senators, businessmen, wow." David noticed tears in Tomasik's eyes.

"The President needs to get this," Jankowsky said. He waved it angrily at Tabitha. "Why have you held on to this?"

"Nobody would have believed me if I'd said anything," she said calmly. "Look what happened to Ib."

Jankowsky nodded grimly. "I'll walk this up through channels right to Norcross."

Tabitha rubbed her hands. "You need more than just the list. Ib had some really hot documents stashed somewhere. You guys got a computer here?"

"Do we ever!" Tomasik said.

"Let's find those documents!" Tabitha enthused.

Tory slept over at David's place.

After dinner, they shared a bottle of Cabernet Sauvignon, and fell asleep on the living room floor. Toward midnight, they woke up and made love. They went to the bedroom around 2 a.m. and lay quietly together, listening to each other's breathing.

David pondered that it was scary to fall in love with a woman who'd had such a tragedy at 14. She must have been a very wild child. He could understand how some guys would not know how to relate to her, maybe seeing her as an empty vessel or something, some stupid carnivore mating standard. Her tragedy made her all the more unique to David. Yes, he must wait and be sure he would not regret having children. Then again, might they not fall out of love in two or three months? Might she move on or he move on? He stroked her cheek lovingly, grateful that she was not Kristy. Maybe the fact that she was so different, and yet so wonderful, would make her extra special for him. He'd wait and see. He could feel her puzzlement; then she responded by planting a tiny, loving kiss on the palm of the hand that was stroking her cheek. How funny this was, to be able to communicate in a language of kisses!

In the morning, because they were running late, they took separate cars—Tory to the convention center, David to the small back street that housed the I.G. office. He watched her, both waving, as she sped off in the half-mist, half-drizzle that threatened to be a rainy day. David shaved, donned his fatigue uniform and side arm, and drove to work.

"Morning, Sir."

"Morning, David. You look rested." Colonel Jankowsky had shadows around his eyes and a light beard stubble on his cheeks.

"I am, Sir. Have you been here long?"

"I stayed all night."

"Oh, no, I should have—"

"No, no, it's fine. You should get your sleep if you can. I don't sleep so well lately. Miss Summers has been on the machine all night."

Jankowsky nodded. He put a finger to his lips, reminding David that the task force's existence was unknown to most of the staff; and those who knew didn't realize its true nature; most thought it was just a library unit. "C'mon, let's walk over."

A light rain dripped in the alley as David and Jankowsky hurried to the task force office. Through the usual security checks, up the stairs they went, emerging into the odd atmosphere of chapel, library, and high-tech.

The atmosphere was sepulchral. It looked like a place in which light had not shone for 100 years. The usual cipher clerks and other mystery persons walked about silently. Near a computer terminal in one of the larger rooms, which echoed when people spoke, were Summers and Tomasik. The blinds were drawn, and one of the fluorescent lights flickered steadily and jarringly. Tomasik was in fatigues, wearing an o.d. T-shirt. He sat on the edge of a desk, wagging his short legs back and forth, black jump boots looking shiny and massive. Nearby sat Tabitha Summers, swathed in sweaters and gaunt with concentration. At the sound of voices, she removed her headset and rubbed bleary eyes. "Hello, Colonel. Did you bring me some coffee and donuts?"

Jankowsky looked perturbed. "I'm sorry, Miss Summers. I was on the other side, waiting for the receptionist to arrive. I would have gone, but I had to watch the store."

"Oh never mind," Tabitha said, "I need sleep more than I need donuts."

"We have cots up here. We can put you in an empty room," Tony said.

"We can send someone to get clothing, toiletries for you, " Jankowsky added.

"Thanks," Tabitha said, "a cot sounds good right about now, but I don't have time." She yawned.

"You heard about Consiglio?" Tony asked David.

David nodded. "I guess that eliminates one mystery candidate from the blank spot on top of the list."

"That leaves plenty of candidates," Jankowsky said. "What do you think, Tony?" He turned to Tomasik with an unspoken part of his question.

Tomasik shook his head and made a sure face. "That was no weekend patriot action, any more than Cardoza getting it. I'll lay odds it's our cabal."

The list, David thought. A cabal. In America?

Tabitha laid her goggles aside and tousled her hair with her fingers. "I'm going to stretch my legs a bit. That diner you mentioned sounds good. I'll get a cup of coffee."

"Did you learn anything?" David asked as Summers rose reaching for her raincoat.

Jankowsky spoke for her. "Did she! Huh! She broke through CloudMaster's defenses. Made the machines at NSSO and the Atlantic think she was the third machine that sits at the White House. Brilliant, huh? She's had full access to their net for hours."

David said: "What do you think, Miss Summers? Why did they pull the machine from you? Who's using CloudMaster? And how long before they're on to you?"

Tabitha regarded him with a smile that wasn't a smile. "I've just had a few hours—twelve hours—to play with it. I'm not sure. I do know that they're running some kind of enormous econometric program on two CloudMaster machines at once. Who is they? I'm not sure. They have their own top secret network, and it's not tied to the Pentagon. The acronym is OIB, and I was able to figure out from context in the message traffic that it stands for Operation Ivory Baton."

"See here," Tomasik said, waving a long print-out before David's face. Tony read in a frustrated voice: "It's just gobbledygook. OIB/H, OIB/A, OIB/17."

"Wait," Tabitha said. She sat down at her terminal again and spoke to it without using the headwalking gear. Masses of program code streamed by until she stopped it. "There, look! I knew I'd seen those OIB's embedded somewhere. OIB-FED-R ... Those are result codes. The machine chews off a humongous amount of data, swallows it, digests it, and spits up a result. They've managed to combine the weather modeling with an econometric model plus some code of their own. I can tell, because when I was in deep, I could see the data streams coming in from around the country, huge amounts, from cities all over—Cincinnati, Seattle, San Diego, you name it. And it's all headed for their system in the Atlantic Hotel."

Jankowsky said: "I'd never have believed it, but it's a clincher. This is not some vague and idle threat. We were looking for only one man, Hamilton, to try and interfere with the convention. Instead, it's the 3045th, either working directly for Montclair, or else using him as a Trojan Horse. Montclair may be working for Hamilton, or even someone else we don't know about. CON2 is falling apart, and whoever these bastards are, they're planning something. They're probably getting ready to move soon. I've got to see General Billy Norcross again. He'll go straight to the President. These people have to be stopped."

What if it's the President? David thought. What about Norcross? Carberry? We could start becoming afraid of our own shadows before this is over.

"I'll go to the Pentagon with you," Tabitha said. "But first my coffee and donuts."

"Go ahead," Tomasik said. He sat by the terminal, which she'd left in deep entry mode. "OIB-FED-H. OIB-FED-L. OIB-FED-A. They are result codes," he mumbled thoughtfully, "of some conditions they have programmed in. From the way it looks, I'd say they have something running that they think will predict the fate of—something? the United States? their plot?—from one moment to the next, based on a million variables, not unlike the weather program or a modern econometric data modeler."

"Damn!" Jankowsky said. He started to put his scarf on. "I'll see Norcross immediately."

Tabitha could be heard, past the sentry at the door, clattering down the stairs on hard heels. The steel-plated security door made her footfalls echo.

"Hey!" Jankowsky exclaimed waving her umbrella. "She left without it."

"I'll catch her," David said. Jankowsky tossed the umbrella. David caught it and started after her. He had to wait a moment before the upstairs sentry could open the security door for him on its smoothly oiled steel hinges.

As he went down the two flights of stairs, he heard

Summers' feet crunching on gravel already, gone from the building. Then he heard a car racing by. Then silence.

He came to the last set of stairs and noticed the bulb was burned out. The lower stairwell was shrouded in darkness. There should have been another sentry—momentarily, blinded by rainy daylight shining through a door that was six inches ajar and shouldn't have been, David stumbled and dropped the umbrella. Catching his balance, he looked.

He glimpsed the sprawled Army private. He had a bullet hole in the middle of his forehead, as though they'd shot him—silencer, David thought—just as he opened the door to peer. Then where was Tabitha Summers?

David took his 9 mm. automatic out of its holster. He clicked the safety off, raised the gun so it rested on his shoulder, and stood with his back to the steel outer door. Rain beat down in sheets now, sending in cool air. Pushing lightly, flattening himself into the shadows as much as possible, he opened the door another inch.

And another inch. There, sprawled in the gravel in the gusting rain, her legs bent at an unnatural angle, lay Tabitha Summers. From the broken limbs and the bloodied head, they'd run her down. It was no longer they now; it was Operation Ivory Baton; it was the 3045th and whoever had brought that dinosaur back from extinction. He was about to rush out to the mangled body in hope of administering CPR, when the sound of a car engine racing caught his attention, just enough to make him freeze. He heard brakes, a squealing of tires. He managed to push enough of his face through the opening in the door, without opening it any further and giving himself away. He could see out with one eye, in the opposite direction, away from Tabitha's body, toward the wide open parking lot. Framed by a backdrop of store windows, of red and blue neon, he saw a dark car. It was hard to see, with the downpour, but there was something familiar about that car. There. Two men sat in the front seat and looked toward the Task Force in anticipation. One was blond, preppy, with steel rims; the other dark, dark...oh yes, he'd seen those two before someplace, but where?

David's heart began to pound as an idea formed. It was a horrible idea and it caused him to remain frozen another moment, staring. He could make out the men in the car. It was the same car he'd encountered at the Naval Observatory the night Ib was kidnapped. One, the driver, had a dark complexion, with mud-colored eyes and a brownish tongue whose tip protruded like a lizard's. Riding shotgun was the young blond man with the steel rimmed glasses and the friendly smile that began to look downright dangerous, maybe even insane, when you looked at it several times. Just now the blond man was beginning to smile broadly, his eyes lit up with anticipation.

"Oh no!" David yelled. He turned inside to run upstairs. He slipped in a puddle of the sentry's blood and fell on the body. Springless bones and rubbery meat cushioned his fall. He scrambled to his feet and, slithering again, made it to the stairway. "Hey!" he yelled.

He made it up three or four steps when the blast caught him and threw him head over heels.

The first blast exploded under the stairs. The massive wood stairwell tilted toward David, forcing the blast upward, and saving him from the main thrust of the explosion. Deafened, he was blown backwards. The blast swirled around and ahead of him, pushing the steel door open so he flew out onto the gravel in the driveway on his back. The building wall stopped the stairwell, preventing it from landing on him outside. A split second later, as he lay on his back, about to black out, he saw the force of the second blast. Unlike the first blast, which exploded vertically, the second went off horizontally and radially. It occurred on the upper floor, blowing the beautiful stained glass windows outward in a fireball, ripping the building's structural walls, collapsing the roof inward. Then something hit David, and the snapshot faded. His last thought was of Tory.

PART III

THE GENERALS OF
OCTOBER

CHAPTER 31

Maxie eased her gray Porsche through the early morning traffic and drizzle. Parking in the nurses' parking lot at Walter Reed Army Hospital, she sprinted through the first rain drops to get to the entrance. She burst into the orderly room and stepped to the mailboxes. Rifling through a handful of memos and envelopes, she asked the duty NCO: "Are we flying anywhere special today for this alert?"

He shook his head. "Not that I know of, Ma'am. But the choppers are feathering and you're asked to—"

"I know, I know," she said pushing through the double doors to the pad area.

"Oh, Captain Bodley?"

She stopped with one door half closed on herself. "Yes?"

"There was a call for you from a Doctor Van Meeuwen. He asked that you call him today. Says it's urgent and you must call him immediately."

"Thanks." She let the doors close behind her. And no thanks, she added mentally. She went to the check-through window, where she showed her I.D. and the orderly checked out her flight uniform from its locker. The pockets were stuffed with potent drugs from morphine to atropine, and a lot in-between, only to be used in a life and death emergency. She'd already begun to think of applying for the Nurse Practitioner program, which required a master's degree in nursing, and which would allow her to be the lead nurse on her flight. She donned the flight suit, hanging her stethoscope around her neck and putting the pistol harness on over her suit. Then she went outside, where three of the 55th's three choppers stood throttling low in a fine drizzle. They were three stories up on a concrete flight apron marked for the three aircraft—orange circles with an X in each circle. Army chopper pilots these days were commissioned rather than warrant officers. Climbing up into Flight 1, she saluted the flight commander, Major Fred Chavez, and his copilot, Major Tom Dash. Four other nurses were in the chopper's roomy interior—a utilitarian, Army-flavor aircraft, pistachio green rather than the olive green on the outer hull, with black stenciled warning messages about bumping heads and securing objects for flight. The nurses had grown close during their training and deployment, and they greeted Maxie as a team member, which always gave her a secret tingle. Only the head nurse, Major Nancy Ilitch, frowned slightly because Maxie was a few minutes late, though not enough for a verbal warning (her nth). "Good afternoon," Ilitch said caustically, pulling in her double chin and making angry red lipstick.

"I'm sorry," Maxie said, "traffic." Not quite true, but screw the old hen.

"We are inventorying pharmacopia, Captain. Care to join us?"

One of the other nurses, Captain Irma Dagdagan, handed her a small box of vials—adrenalin syringe packets, to inject directly into the heart of the cardiac arrested patient. Each nurse had to count hers, and match the numbers with the printout in the box. It was part of the ritual at the start of every twelve hour shift.

Maxie started checking the packets one by one

against the list, and Ilitch's scathing attention went to other matters. Maxie caught a gleam in the edge of her vision. She glanced right, and found the gleam to be in the eyes of Major Tom Dash, who sat sideways in the copilot's seat doing a preflight checkout with Major Chavez. Tom smiled at her, nodded, friendly, and she ignored him. Inwardly, however, she thought: Zap! She'd had her eye on Tom since she'd first seen him—a friendly dark-haired man who looked lean and adorable in his snappy uniform. Secretly, she'd been jealous of Tory.

Maxie had been thinking—maybe Tory was right. Here she was liking this handsome pilot who seemed interested in her, and already all her ingrained instinct was kicking in to deny herself this affair because he wasn't right for her or not good enough. Almost in tears, she was angry at her Mother and Father, who'd schooled her most rigorously in their Expectations of a Southern Lady and the Heir to a Fortune, Not To Mention a Legacy Centuries Old: Officers before and after the English Restoration; officers on both sides of the Revolutionary War, marching around with their little flutes and drums; colonels on both sides in the Civil War; and of course heroes in every war since. If she became a thorough bitch, tore up her pedigree, and mailed her gold credit card back to Father and her DAR membership to Mother, would they get the message? Would they still love her if she weren't a marionette? Could she still love them, once she cut the puppet strings? If she had a serious relationship or even married a fellow like Tom Dash?

CHAPTER 32

Still burning, confused, and passionate from her night with David, Tory found a parking place two blocks from the Hotel. It was just beginning to rain, and she held a newspaper open over her head as she ran through the early morning twilight. She saw the National Guard checkpoint ahead and started to fish out her I.D. At that moment a pair of National Guard MP's in rumpled fatigues, their white helmets scratched and dirty, trod by. Judging by their dingy boots and footsore slog, they'd probably been on duty nonstop for days. They both saluted. "Morning, Ma'am," one said. "You with the Regulars inside?"

Lowering the newspaper, she returned the salute. "Yes, I am. But I'm not playing cop today. Computer jockey."

"Oh," they said, impressed.

"I see those boots," she joked; "about due for retread."

"You said it, Ma'am." "You got that right, Ma'am."

"Where are you from?" she asked.

"Virginia, Ma'am. He's from Bristol. I'm from Roanoke."

"Tourists in Washington."

"Right. My mom runs a little store back home, and

she needs me to help. Ol' Snuffy here, he's got three kids and a delivery route."

The other added: "We can't wait to go back home."

The first added: "Nobody ever asked us our opinion. Hell, we're just privates, Ma'am. We swore to uphold the real Constitution, not any new phony one."

"I hear you guys," Tory said.

"You have a nice day now," the one said.

"Be careful, alone out here like this," the other said.

"With you guys to watch the store," she shouted after them, "I'm not afraid!" But she feared for all the Snuffys out there. They grinned, waved, and lumbered off along the endless twirls of concertina wire, rifles slung.

As she neared the MP check point, a dark humvee pulled up, and three burly young men with gym bags got out. She looked the other way, pretended not to see them. They pretended not to see her, and no salutes were exchanged. Football player big, they trudged through the checkpoint with a brief show of ID. Tory gave it a moment, then followed. As she signed in, she noted their unit on the lines in the sign-in log above her own: 3045th MI. The two soldiers at the booth were female. She asked superciliously: "Who are the hunks?"

The two women exchanged glances. One said: "Ma'am, excuse me, but them boys got somethin' downright dead cold by they hearts, if you know what I mean." The other one said: "I'm married, but even if I weren't they just got this look that, I dunno, you look in they eyes, you be scared."

Tory entered the lobby and tossed aside her wet newspaper. She had made it on time. Lots of noise came from the Assembly Hall that stuck out from the three towers the way the U.N. General Assembly Hall stuck out from its single tower in New York. The scene she encountered was disturbing and disgusting. Somebody kept banging a gavel, to no avail. There was a pounding of fists on tables, a raucous noise and counter-noise, as if the delegates were animals. These were the brilliant minds, Tory thought, who claimed they could do better than Washington and Madison and Hamilton and Franklin in Philadelphia during the long hot summer of 1787 (Jefferson being in Paris as U.S. Ambassador to France, but about to return and do his part by penning the Bill of Rights). The Second Constitutional Convention was fast becoming a laughing stock and an object of derision across the country;the 900th amendment was being introduced—something about sending all immigrants of the past 25 years back to their countries of origin, and closing the borders permanently. The unarmed private security guards with limited authority, hired to maintain order in CON2, had already lost control as shoes and empty, greasy paper lunch sacks flew through the air. Two delegates argued on the verge of a fist-fight; since the delegates had complete legal immunity, they could not be arrested. In one corner stood a group loudly and constantly yelling things from the Bible; in another stood Hare Krishnas, chanting and ringing bells. Each group had been invited there by one or more delegates, and could not be removed for some technical reason. In the hall outside, in the gray area between private security's jurisdiction and General Montclair's, two drunks lolled on the floor, one in a pool of reddish-clear wine vomit. Trash was strewn everywhere. Tory shook her head and took the elevator downstairs, where the heavy CloudMaster machine newly assigned to the Atlantic had been mounted on a concrete base.

Jet met her there, glad to see a friend. "Ma'am," Jet said, "there are more and more strange rumors flying around. There's been another murder, this one an OCP Congressman from Samoa." Tory was sick of the war of words, sick of the twisting of words, sick of the sickness America had borne for so long, and wanted only to fly away to a tropic island with this wonderful new man in her life, David Gordon. For a moment, assaulted by the bedlam that confronted her, she closed her eyes and allowed herself to regress a few hours. There was David, in her bed, looking sleepy and vulnerable, like a beautiful tiger, powerful but innocent. Her heart melted as she clung to the image, wanting to possess him, to surrender to him and conquer him all in one passionate embrace. The memory of last night rose in her like the smell of rose petals in a summer rain. If he wanted to be with her again, she was ready.

Colonel Bentyne stopped by. She'd only met him a few times. He was a chunky, red-faced man with an odd smile that looked uncomfortable. He wore thick glasses, and his starchy fatigues looked too big on him. He also had tiny sores around his lips, which he'd treated with a glossy cream of some kind, Army-issue, generic, gleaming yellow. By contrast, his teeth were nice and white; hand him that much. "How are you, Breen?"

"Fine, Sir." She had to remember that this man was going to write her review for the CON2 period, and it would stay in her file forever, and one point less than a perfect score was a negative signal to some future promotion board not to advance her. After shaking his hand, she secretly wiped her hand on her pants. "It's the best thing," he was saying. "Get everybody consolidated here. You'll like it here. It's a very exciting time, and it's an interesting place to be."

"It sure is, Sir," she said. "It's an historic moment."

"Staff meeting at five this evening, my suite on the 36th Floor. You'll get to meet Colonel Bronf, the Chief of Staff. General Montclair might even poke his head in."

"Yessir, I'll mark it on my calendar."

"Very good. We're staffing up here, and I expect you'll be supervising about twenty people for me. Big shop. Combined Admin, Data Processing, Medical Support Services, you name it." He noted her corps insignia on her lapels and winked. "Just the job for an MP officer, eh?"

"Yessir. I feel right at home." After he left, Tory went to the office canteen and washed her hands and face in the little corner convenience sink.

Jet nudged her. Jet had that pixie smile, with slight overbite, and a twinkle in the eyes. She held up a big cookie with chocolate frosting and sugar sprinkles. "Ib's favorite," she told Tory. "I just thought you might need something sweet and gooey."

Tory snatched the cookie. "Do I ever. Gimme that! Is there any coffee here?"

"I made you a pot. Looked like you'd need that too."

CHAPTER 33

Maxie had just finished her part of the drug inventory inside Flight 1 when the radio crackled. Major Chavez, the pilot, had a brief conversation, then turned and hollered: "All Up Alert. We've got a live one." The engines throttled up and the airframe began to tremble. The nurses quickly secured loose items that bounced around on the curettage counter. All together, they turned off the lights and flipped the counter up, locking it secure. Then they strapped in. As Chavez and Dash prepared the roaring, straining helicopter for flight, the rest of the air crew hurried on board—a flight surgeon, two physician assistants, three EMT's, and two flight crew. The EMT's had smuggled in coffee and donuts, which they handed out after they'd all strapped themselves into seats and benches. "Where are we headed?" someone asked.

"Don't know yet," someone else said. "There's a new plume of smoke down there." Several arms reached out and fingers pointed toward the northwest part of the District, past Rock Creek Park, toward a settlement of old brownstone townhouses jammed daintily together in tree-lined neighborhoods. Maxie sipped her coffee and watched disinterestedly, ignoring the smell of sugar and fat emanating from the donuts. Ilitch's red lipstick had parted into a circle of enormous size, as the woman stuffed in an eclair the size of an eyeglasses case. Ilitch's eyes became correspondingly large, almost desperate, slightly crossed, as if they wanted to meet around the back of the eclair. And she wondered why she had three chins. Maxie resisted the urge to giggle quietly. She wished she had a camera.

"Bomb explosion," Chavez announced on the p.a. "Some secret Army installation just got the patriot treatment. They've got burns, amputees, stack of bodies. Better inhale those donuts. This looks like a busy day."

Slowly, Maxie remembered that—wasn't that the part of town where David worked? Silence reigned in the ops bay as they finished their coffees and stared out of the windows. Maxie saw tall flames rising from one building, smoke from the building beside it whose roof had fallen in. Civilian police cars and ambulances were there. Chavez's voice crackled on the intercom: "Few survivors below. Flight 1 is going in. ETA in two minutes. Flights 2 and 3 are turning back to base. Be advised, that's a highly restricted area down there. Don't talk with anyone."

CHAPTER 34

David groaned as he came to lying on his back. For some glacially long seconds, he thought the flashing colors in his mind and the screaming of sirens were the same thing. Then he began to untangle his senses. The colors and the screaming separated, the colors giving way to a grayscale landscape painted in drizzle, while the screaming turned into sirens. The screaming also turned into the feeble cries for help coming from the second building further away, which had not directly suffered the blasts, but must have partially collapsed and now was in danger due to spreading fire.

David shook his head as he sat up. He touched his forehead and found it slippery. He saw blood on his fingers. The scab on top of his head was intact. Beside him was a pile of bricks where Tabitha Summers's body had been, and he guessed she must be under there. No way she could be alive. A fire engine was trying to get into the alley, but was blocked by debris. Jagged, scorched timbers stuck out of heaps of broken masonry. Combs of lath and plaster were scattered about. Concrete blocks revealed teeth of torn rebar.

David heaved onto his stomach, then did a pushup to get onto his knees and palms. He remembered the urgency of Tomasik and Jankowsky—dead now, along with Tabitha, gone also the list of names, and how many other innocent people. He remembered the blond-haired man and the opaque-eyed shadow in the driver's seat, and suddenly had a sense of desperation. Whoever they were—whatever Operation Ivory Baton was—they were killing everyone connected with Ib Shoob's discovery. And that meant that he, David, was next. Perhaps he was the only one left alive who knew. He rose, swaying, and pushed down his uniform. The raincoat, although filthy, had only a small tear. His car was down the street on the other side. People were running to aid him, but he yelled. "Go help the ones inside! There's a woman's body under the bricks here." Civilian paramedics offered to help, but he brushed past them. A thick gauze pad got onto his forehead somehow, and he waited a moment while someone wrapped his head. "Just a grazing flesh wound," he heard. "Get that cleaned out and stitched up. You okay, bud?"

"Thanks," he whispered. He accepted a drink of cranberry juice. Never during those two or three minutes did he sit down. It started raining again—a fast, straight rain from a bright sky—and he welcomed the cooling water that dribbled through the heat and pain on his forehead and swept the mud from his coat.

He turned onto the side street just as the first military vehicles arrived. Combat soldiers in full gear jumped out and began forming a perimeter. As David turned the corner onto the bigger street where his car was parked, and crossed to the other side, he began to think that he'd be able to get away. Just keep walking, walking, walking, hands in pockets, don't look left or right. He heard the sound of a helicopter and looked up. There, flying at 2000 feet, he saw three dark choppers flying in a row, each with big red crosses on white square backgrounds. The rear two choppers swung to one side, still in line, turned slowly, flew away. As he walked, David spoke Tory's work number into his collar com.

She answered: "Yes?"

"Tory."

"David!" She sounded pleased.

"Something terrible has happened."

"What!"

"The place I work has been bombed. Everyone is dead, including Tabitha Summers."

"Oh my God."

"I'm not badly hurt, and I'm walking away. I saw some of the guys who did it. I think. I recognized one man I saw the night Ib was kidnapped. Pleasant preppy blond guy. The other was in Top Five. Reminds you of a lizard. You remember, the guys in the police sketches."

She cut to the area of her main concern. "How badly hurt are you?"

"Another scrape on the head, like last time. I'm coming in to see Carberry. We were betrayed from up top, I don't know by whom. Someone or some group high up in command. In case I don't get to him, you do the same. One of us has to reach Carberry. Tell him to watch out for Operation Ivory Baton. Montclair is in on it. So is Felix Mason. So are two dozen other important people whose names I don't remember just now. It's on the list, which Tabitha had and which is now lost. See if you can get Jet to dig it out of the system. It's got the names of all the important conspirators. They killed Consiglio and Shoob. I've got to talk with Carberry, get him to call off the convention. See if you can get to Carberry also. CON2 must be canceled. Stopped dead. Killed." As he stumbled along, he could see the rest of it. There were people waiting in the wings, just waiting for the right moment to step in and take over with a Constitution of their own.

She shrieked: "David, please take care—"

"I love you, Tory. I'll see you in a little while. I'm coming over there." He cut her off—turned the button off because her hysteria cut his heart. He stepped off the curb and crossed the street. There was his car. A row of dark green Army and dark blue Air Force MP squad cars cruised by with flashing lights and screaming sirens. Inside sat MP's and Air Police in fatigues, holding shotguns. Civilian police cars stood parked with flashing lights, apparently told not to go any closer. A row of Army field ambulances crawled in—olive boxes with white squares and red crosses, their windows and headlights covered with steel mesh. Their headlights were round and yellow, trailing wisps of rain and fog, sallow candles in a funeral procession.

As he approached his car, David fished out his keys. They jangled familiarly and reassuringly. He'd get in and drive away and start making a list of the names he remembered. He put the key in the door and started to turn it.

"I wouldn't."

He looked up.

There was Mr. Blond with the steel rimmed glasses. His cherubic face was wreathed in a smile that wavered between childish delight and ice cold insanity. "It might explode if you turn it on, Captain Gordon baby."

"What do you want?" David felt a numb matter of factness. Of course they'd come for him. He suddenly felt tired; felt the smash he'd gotten to the head; swayed a little.

"My colleague and I," Blond said indicating with his thumb the reptile man who stepped out of a doorway, "want to save you so we can ask you some questions. If you run or yell, I'll shoot you in the neck and you'll never walk again. One way or another, I will drag you in for questioning."

"I'm a U.S. citizen. An officer—"

"You are a dupe of the corrupt and evil forces that took over our country many years ago. Since you don't know any better, save your breath. Now walk with us."

"Where are you taking me?"

Mud-Eyes managed a faint smile. His voice was raspy, as if coming from a leathery throat. "We heard you talk with your little chickie. You want to go to the Atlantic Hotel? Why not let us chauffeur you? A free ride to see Colonel Bronf."

"And who the hell is Colonel Bronf?" David muttered as they herded him along. People were running past them toward the ruins and fire, and ignored the three men. Then he remembered—it was the sweaty, cigarette-smelling, balding little assistant chief of staff he'd met while working on the Corcoran case. This lizard-man had been in Bronf's office that day.

David echoed the hotel provost marshal's complaint. "I thought nobody ever got to see Colonel Bronf more than once."

And Mud-Eyes said: "You just got lucky, asshole."

CHAPTER 35

Tory took Jet aside. They were alone in the basement room with CloudMaster. It was cool and semi-dark in the room, but Tory knew the cameras watching over CloudMaster scanned every person, every face near the precious machine, so she whispered: "Jet this is very important."

"Oh, okay, Ma'am," Jet said in bright puzzlement, looking at Tory's fists clawing into her uniform at the shoulders.

"Jet, Tabitha Summers was just killed."

Jet's expression flew apart. "Oh no."

"Listen carefully. Captain Gordon is out there walking wounded, trying to get a message to Carberry. I'm going to find Chairman Carberry and give him the same message in case David doesn't make it."

Jet wailed in disbelief: "Why...?"

"I'm going to find Carberry and talk to him. I want you to start looking for a copy of Ib's list of the conspirators' names."

"But I've been looking everywhere!"

"I know. Keep up the good work and don't lose hope. The list has got to be in the net someplace, and we need to get it to Chairman Carberry or General Billy Norcross."

"I'll do my best," Jet said. "Good luck, Tory." It was the first time she'd ever called her immediate supervising officer by her first name. Tory was grateful for the personal gesture. They shook on it.

"Good luck, Jet. If you find the list, call me right away."

As Tory looked for Chairman Carberry, CON2 was on break. The corridor around the main hall was jammed with delegates, security personnel, members of the press. Tory threaded her way through. She sidled into the hall to the podium area. A young page told her that Carberry had gone back to his hotel room, Room 1861 in Tower One, for an hour.

After a moment's hesitation she decided to go up directly, rather than call first. She had no idea how she would broach the incredible subject. She entered a quiet, carpeted corridor on the eighteenth floor, found Number 1861, and knocked.

The door opened, a thick voice said "Yes?" and there he was, 6-5, 240 pounds, former halfback in pro football, ex-Air Force officer, retired senator, active on the boards of a dozen corporations, linchpin of CON2, and a pivotal figure in American politics. She stood flabbergasted for a moment, shocked that he had no bodyguards.

"Yes?"

"I'm sorry, I have something very important to tell you and you've got to give me a minute of your time," she blurted.

He narrowed his eyes suspiciously. Then he pulled the door open. "Come on in." He hopped slightly with each step to move so large a frame about. She'd had no idea he was so big. To millions of Americans he was a strong, fatherly voice, a face both powerful and kind. His features, a racial cocktail, were mahogany-colored and handsome. "Want a cola? What's on your mind?"

"Thanks, no. Well, I don't know exactly how to go about this—"

"You'll have to be quick, because I'm due back—"

"Okay. I think there is a plot against CON2."

He sat down, tired. "Why doesn't some general tell me that, if it's true?"

"Because—" she choked up. My career will be down the drain and I'll have nothing again.

He stared at her.

She felt a wrong chemistry and blurted: "Because there is evidence that General Montclair wants to destroy CON2. There was a computer file, and we had written evidence, but it was destroyed in an explosion—"

He popped a soda can that made a fizz. "You are either out of your mind or very courageous, or both. Are you a flying saucer nut too?"

"There have been disappearances, murders, disturbances. Your own assistant was just murdered. Chairman, you've got to believe me. The military, I don't know why, is against you and they'll do anything—"

His eyes widened. "Yes, I know that. Do you think I'm blind? These fertilizer patriots killed Vern. Their purpose is to intimidate me to stop CON2, which I shall not do. But these conspiracies gives me a damned headache. When will you people ever—?"

"Sir, I'm not making this up."

He smiled broadly, and for a moment she was lulled by that smile's warmth. "Okay." The smile thinned. "Enough." Anger seeped into his tone, and the eyes blazed. "Young lady, do you have any idea what thin ice you're on?" His words whipped around her like cat-o'-nine-tails. "Do you have any idea of the scope and the concerns and the delicacy with which I have to weigh every action I take and every word I say? I have to be careful of every nod, every glance, every betrayed emotion. You know why? Because this convention, if it is to work, has to be a hundred per cent free of influence from the established government, executive, judiciary, and legislative; and especially the military! General Montclair was hand-picked by General Norcross and the President of the United States to head the task of protection for me and my convention. Do you know what my inclination is? To ask you to hand over your gun. To call Montclair and have him come over personally, arrest you, and throw you in jail."

Tears stung her eyeballs. "I wish you would not do that." She felt herself badly failing here, and unable to save the situation.

He rose and jabbed a huge finger in her face. "I'll tell you what I'll do. I'll think about it. Out of all this stuff that's going on, reshaping this country, I will take a few minutes over the next day or two to deliberate within myself if I want to help you finish ruining your career or not."

"Yessir."

"This could mean the end of your career. You hear me?"

"Sir?" Her knees knocked together. "I hope I'm wrong. I felt I had to warn you. I have a friend who—" She started to tell him about David and the Task Force, but he wouldn't listen. He moved toward her, waving his arm dismissingly. "You poor crazy woman. Get out of here and hope I decide to forget this conversation. Go!"

Tory walked out woodenly, pulled the door shut, went to the nearest ladies' room, began to cry. Then she vomited. For a moment she felt utterly beaten and helpless. Then she remembered David. And hoped Jet had the file she needed. Her duty was not done. She was needed in many places, and she shoved the bathroom door open in a running start.

As she did so, her com button sounded. "This is Dispatch. Lieutenant Breen?"

"Yes?" She felt a thrill of fear.

"Colonel Bentyne orders you to report to the Provost Marshal's office right away."

"Sure—what's up?" Tory's heart began racing.

"You'd better come up here, Lieutenant."

"All right, I will." She forced a bright tone. "Connect me with Computer Ops?"

"I'm sorry."

Tory rang off and tried Jet's personal com. The dispatcher cut in again: "I'm sorry, that unit is out of circulation."

"Is it broken?"

"I have no information."

Tory slowed to a walk. "I'll be up in a minute," she lied. She needed time to think. Was she imagining things? Had she really just spoken with the former Senate Majority Leader and put her career on the line? Surely this was a bad dream and she'd wake up any moment. She felt again the terrible sense of loss when she'd been 15. Could she endure ruination again?

But she had sworn to do right for her country, for the Constitution. Did she trust David enough to believe him? Could this be a lie, a cruel hoax? She pictured David walking down a rainy street with blood on his forehead, and realized she loved him. She would do as he asked. There was no mistaking the tone of menace in the dispatcher's voice.

There seemed to be a lot of activity in the common areas of the hotel. Burly young men in distinctive blue-and-yellow camouflage uniforms waited in knots here and there, at corners and elevator doors. No females in that outfit! They wore subdued rank markings and carried weird assault guns that might have been designed by insect engineers. Some had unit patches on the right shoulder, indicating past combat service. All wore airborne-qualified patches.

As she waited for the elevator down, she glanced outside hoping to see David. She saw only coils of barbed wire, parked trucks, troopers with rifles. The sea of olive green was spattered with endless repetitions of the words military police in black letters on white background, as in some schizophrenic dream.

In the elevator, she took out her 9 mm. automatic, checked the clip, and put the gun back in her holster. She checked to make sure she had extra ammo on her belt.

She met Jet in the doorway of the computer center. Jet looked scared as she shoved a piece of paper toward Tory. "That's part of the list. I was printing to a spooler file when they cut the power off. It's back up now, but I lost the rest of the file and all my other work."

"Thanks," Tory said. She glanced down the list, saw Montclair's name on it among others. That was all she needed for now. "Keep trying," she ordered Jet. "Keep trying until you find the rest of that list!" She hugged Jet briefly, then ran.

"Lieutenant Breen," the dispatcher said from her collar com.

"This is Breen."

"Request status."

"I'm near the elevator on the first floor. What is the emergency?"

"You will be given that information by Colonel Bronf."

Tory remembered Colonel Bellamy, the Provost Marshal. She hadn't met him, but David had told her about him. If there was anyone left who might help, it had to be Bellamy. She had part of the list now. Someone must believe her. The MP station and patrol desk were on T-3-12 on the way to Bronf's HQ. She noticed in the lobby an MP sergeant she knew, and waved. He waved back, looking puzzled at the informality. She motioned, and he met her halfway. "Hi," she said, "can I borrow your baton?"

"Sure, Ma'am," he said cheerfully and gave her the baton. She gripped the solid, heavy weapon in both hands, hefted it, tested the feel of its side-grip. The elevator opened for her as she walked toward it, as though some unseen eye guided it. She was alone inside as the door closed. Her mouth felt dry and her heart beat strongly as the elevator began its quiet rumble upward. Her stomach felt giddy, as though she were weightless. She held the baton in both hands and looked up as if she could see through the elevator roof toward her fate. "Lieutenant Breen, status please."

"I'm on my way up." Something was wrong here. All the buttons from Floor One through Floor Thirty-Five were lit up. As she passed each floor, the light in that button dimmed momentarily. Someone had rigged the electronics. Was she trapped in this elevator? Would they take her up to the forbidden floors? Maybe they already had David up there.

Impulsively, she poked the baton against the red STOP button. The elevator shuddered to a halt. The cage rocked. The shaft echoed loudly with an emergency bell.

"Lieutenant Breen," a man's voice said. "What are you doing?"

"What are you doing?"

"I asked first."

"This is Colonel Bronf. I am giving you a direct order to report to me personally on the Thirty-Fifth Floor immediately. Do you hear?"

"Yessir."

"Or it's curtain time for you and the Army. Release the STOP button."

She reached over, held the button, tried to think for a moment.

"I order you to release the button."

When no thought came, she pulled. The bell stopped, and the elevator moved.

"Very good," Colonel Bronf said.

The Nine button flickered. Then the Ten button.

"Keep coming," Colonel Bronf coaxed.

Eleven. Twelve.

Impulsively, Tory jabbed the STOP button again. The elevator stopped. It rocked gently. The emergency bell again filled the elevator shaft.

"Lieutenant Breen!"

The door opened, and Tory stepped out into the lobby. Startled Navy and Air Force clerks looked up from behind the thick glass of the patrol desk. Tory stepped to the window. "Where's Colonel Bellamy?"

A Navy dispatcher, a slab-faced woman with kindly eyes behind thick lenses, looked panicked. "They have him upstairs," she whispered. "Get out of here because they're coming to get you next."

CHAPTER 36

Flights 1, 2, and 3 of the 55th Aviation Battalion (MAES) sat alert and ready on the flight pads atop Building 4 at Walter Reed. Maxie, in full flight gear except for the helmet, hurried down a first floor corridor in search of cigarettes—followed by the wide-eyed gaze of staff and patients alike—when Paul Van Meeuwen grabbed her by the arm and yanked her into a semi-dark alcove. "Maxie!"

She gulped air, trying to get her breath. "What—?"

"Maxie!" He gripped her arms painfully and shook her. His face was contorted with need and desperation. "I've been calling and calling. Why haven't you returned my calls? You know that wasn't me the other night."

She tried to push him away, got one arm free. "Paul, you bastard, let me go."

"Maxie—"

"I've had it, Paul. I'm not taking any more of your baloney. I'm a lady, dammit."

"I demand you talk to me, bitch!" He grappled with her, trying to regain a hold of her other arm, the one with the gun strapped under it. She twisted to one side, repeatedly slapping his hand away. She had a wiry strength, and suddenly she saw him, as Tory had—a weak man, a bully, a charmer, a selfish boy who had never grown up. "Maxie, please, I promise—"

"No! Let go. Paul," she said through gritted teeth, looking right and left in the dim area, noting that passersby were beginning to notice, "you can't go grabbing people. You can't have your way. It's over between us." She grew frightened, seeing rage in his eyes. He reddened and his jowls shook as something built up inside of him.

She tried to back away.

He put the fingers of one hand around her neck and squeezed, while raising the other fist way back and up high as if gathering to strike a blow that would surely kill her. The desire to kill radiated from his crazed eyes.

Breaking through the chains of paralysis, seeing stars already because the blood flow was impeded in her neck, she kicked her steel-toed paratroop boot against his shin. Turning slightly, she raked the boot's outer edge down along the shin, and stomped on the arch of his foot.

Van Meeuwen yelled, and his fingers loosened from her neck.

She kicked him on the knee, and he went down with a grimace of pain, holding his knee with both hands. In her anger—a complete rage, directed not only against him but against her parents, against the whole world that kept molding and compressing her into shapes that brought only pain—she pulled out the 9 mm. automatic and pointed it at him. She wanted to yell "If you ever bother me again, I'll blow your ass off!" but the words would not come out. For a moment she wanted to pull the trigger. She caught herself, enraged to the point of shooting this awful man, becoming guilty of killing someone, and ruining her life in the process. She couldn't do it. The gun faltered and Van Meeuwen's scheming eyes were upon it, no doubt thinking how he could turn the situation to his advantage. A grin was actually beginning to spread around his coldly handsome features as he realized her helplessness.

Lights were going on, and she heard feet approaching at a run.

Van Meeuwen rose limping, straightening out his long white coat. He took control with a cruel, bullying tone of efficiency and command in his voice. "You won't get away with this." It was the Reasonable Doctorly Tone.

"Get away with what, Paul? Self defense?" she asked bitterly.

"I am going to destroy your life and your career," he said calmly, as if offering a lady a chair to sit on. He held on to the wainscoting and hobbled, grimacing.

"What's going on here?" a voice yelled from the corridor.

Swiftly, Maxie pressed the button that dropped the clip out of her gun. She slipped the clip deftly in her pocket. In the same motion she tossed the empty gun high in the air so it would arc down toward him. "Here, Paul, catch!"

Van Meeuwen reacted by instinct, catching the falling automatic to his gut with both hands in a beautiful football move, with a little sideways dance step and all, before he grimaced and caught himself again on the wainscoting. The gun sat idly in his hand, pointed in her general direction as he squinted down at his knee and gasped with pain.

At the same moment, Maxie threw herself on her knees. She extended her arms in a crucifix, knees spread, sprawling backwards not quite falling. She wailed as loudly as she could: "Please, Paul, don't shoot me. Don't kill me. Don't rape me. I'm not the one who stole your drug money. I would never report that you killed those patients. I'm innocent! Oh please, don't do it. Spare me! I'll never tell anyone about the bodies."

The lights went on fully, and there was Maxie on her knees, pleading loudly, and there stood Paul Van Meeuwen, sheepishly holding the gun. And there came two MP's in full regalia, drawing down on Van Meeuwen. "Hit the floor!" one bellowed hoarsely. "Drop the gun and dive!" the other yelled. "Down or I'll shoot to kill!" Hammers were cocked with loud clicking noises. A heartbeat away from death, Paul dropped the gun. Before it hit the floor, he did. The two MP's manhandled him. One had a boot on his neck and pointed a gun at his head, while the other handcuffed him. Paul had a distinctly painful, unhappy, and very scared expression. Served him right, Maxie thought.

An elderly doctor helped Maxie to her feet. "Are you all right, my dear?"

She eyed the brigadier general star on each collar tip and realized it was the Chief of Surgery, Paul's topmost boss. "Yessir. He was going to kill me." Which was true. She could explain the details later. "I'm glad you all came to rescue me."

The general grunted. "I've had doubts and questions about this man all along." He turned and said to the MP's: "I want this man taken to the psychiatric lockdown and held for examination. Put him in a straight jacket."

Maxie said: "Sir, I'm wanted on the flight deck. It's an emergency. Can I be excused? I'll file my report as soon as I'm free from duty."

"Just leave your name and ID with the MP's," the general said, noting her unit insignia. "Good luck to you, young lady." He shook her hand. "We're all so proud of you!"

Maxie's last view of Paul Van Meeuwen was his crushed expression as he was led away under heavy guard. He was handcuffed and hobbling; the MP's still had their guns drawn, no doubt ready to shoot him at the slightest sign of psychopathic violence. She trotted back toward the elevator. Dammit, and now she couldn't make it to the PX in time! What a pain in the rear, this Van Meeuwen. In a corner stood a couple of grizzled old retired soldiers, white haired and gaunt. They wore hospital jammies and were on crutches. One ancient veteran was just about to peel a brand-new pack of unfiltered Camels with shaky fingers. Maxie waved a fifty dollar bill in his face and grabbed the cigarettes at the same time. "Here's your fifty bucks. Gimme them."

The old man smiled toothlessly as he took the money. "I was just about to quit smoking."

She ran to the elevators. "Thanks, you are a gentleman!" she yelled over her shoulder.

"I can get you another pack anytime!" he yelled after her. "Anytime at all!"

Within a half hour, she was airborne along with the full flight team on Flight 1. All three choppers were sent to a terrible accident at a munitions depot just outside Washington. It had been the main depot for small arms and training explosives for the entire region. Four city blocks were flattened and there were many casualties. They worked with civilian paramedics on the ground and bundled about fifteen badly burned workers for transport in land ambulances to a nearby civilian hospital. Maxie worked hard, ignoring the smells of various things burning, and the screams of the burned. Her flight suit was covered with stains—blood, plasma, tar, ashes. And tears.

On the flight back, as afternoon turned into evening, Tom Dash made his clumsy, shy pass. Maxie was still in the bloody flight suit because she felt cold; it was drafty in the chopper. One of the other nurses had stripped down to her fatigues and T-shirt and was putting on clean flight overalls she must have brought with her. Another sat huddled in a blanket, looking as though she needed to sob but couldn't—a new nurse, young, just out of school. Maxie, who had nearly ten years' hospital experience at age 30, put her hand on the girl's shoulder and stayed with her a bit. Tom stepped into the rear section holding a cup of coffee and walked directly over to Maxie. "Excuse me, Ma'am, but do you have any sugar?" He outranked her and could have called her Lieutenant. Maxie felt utterly charmed inside.

"Why yes, Major, I believe I know where some is. Why don't you go back up front and I'll find it and bring it to you?"

"Thank you." He sort of made a little bow and went back to the cockpit. Irma Dagdagan winked at Maxie and tossed a couple of sugar packets through the air. "Go get 'im, Maxie!"

"What ever do you mean?" Maxie said. She went forward and handed Tom Dash his sugar. "There you are," she said.

He seemed tongue tied. "Thank you very much."

The pilot, if he cared, did not pay any attention. Goggled and helmeted, he drove the craft on at a steady clip under mixed clouds toward the blinking red eye of Washington's Monument. Maxie took a deep breath and blurted: "It's so neat up here! Sometimes I think I might just go to flight school. What's this button? And that light?" Tom Dash lit up, overcoming his abashedness, and launched into a delighted lecture about the control panels. Maxie watched him as he spoke. He seemed so different from Paul. More like David. Maybe a little shyer. Rock solid under the surface, handsome, and tending to blush when spoken to. By the time they landed on Building 4, he asked to take her for pizza and cokes. "—When this is all over," he added.

"I think that sounds like a fun idea," she said. The pilot turned on the P.A. "Got bad news for you, gang. We're back on Alert status. There's chaos in the streets, and we're gonna be on standby all night." A chorus of groans arose. "Sorry about that," the pilot said in a black humor, turning off the P.A. with a flick of a gloved thumb. Tom whispered to Maxie: "Looks like that pizza will have to hold a while." She squeezed his hand and beamed. "I can wait." The look in his eyes said that he could too.

🌍 **ANN Breaking News with Allison Miranda** ⚡

ALLISON: And now this development in our breaking

story at the Second Constitutional Convention. Peggy DeMetrio is at the Atlantic Hotel & Convention Center.

PEGGY: Allison, night has fallen. I'm on the corner of Connecticut and Wyoming Avenues, about a block from the Hotel Atlantic, and as you can see and hear, I am watching an endless line of military vehicles stream past.

ALLISON: What are they? Ambulances? Humvees?

PEGGY: Not ambulances, nothing with flashing lights and sirens. Just an endless stream of olive-drab trucks with dark bluish camouflage splotches, an occasional humvee, and more trucks.

ALLISON: Does it appear they are bringing in supplies or troops?

PEGGY: Allison, a moment ago, three Army medevac choppers with big red crosses on white backgrounds pounded by overhead. They had red crosses on their bottoms and sides, and I can see from here that they are landing on the roof of Tower 3.

ALLISON: Excuse me, Peggy. We have a bulletin from WCCR's John Bell inside the Atlantic Hotel and Convention Center. Let's switch to John.

JOHN: I'm in the Press Room on the third floor of Tower Two, and we're detained here, so it seems, or maybe a better word is contained, we are contained here. There's plenty of coffee, they brought in donuts, we can go to the bathroom, and they've told us if we want to we can leave the building under escort but we cannot, I repeat, cannot, get back in. Most of us have elected to stay in here, hoping for a briefing from General Montclair.

ALLISON: John, any word from General Montclair what's going on?

JOHN: Not a clue. I'll sit tight and give you a heads up when and if something more happens.

ALLISON: Thanks, John. Good luck. Peggy has just signaled from the street near CON2. Peggy?

PEGGY: One of the Army Air Evac helicopters now takes off from the roof of Tower Three and appears to head toward Bethesda. I'm told it's eerily calm along streets outside government office buildings, most of which have lots of lights lit. The Capitol, where both houses of Congress meet every day when they are in session, is quiet. I'm told there are lights on in the Dirksen and Rayburn office buildings which house, respectively, the Senators and the Representatives. Neither building is more than two minutes away from the Capitol by underground railway. Wait a minute. Oh my God. Oh. Oh.

ALLISON: Peggy, you're breaking up. Peggy? Can you hear me? Do we have—? Yes, we have—

PEGGY: Allison, I see an unbelievable scene out here. While the two other Army choppers took off, I just witnessed an apparently unrelated event. A carload of black motorists passing through a checkpoint have been hauled from their car by men in blue-

and-yellow camouflage fatigues. The commandos wrestle with these four or five big men, who may have been drinking. Now there is a fight and clubs swing and, oh my God, several shots. Several shots!

ALLISON: We hear popping noises. What's that? What is it?

PEGGY: Shooting! There is shooting over there. We are flat on the ground now, to avoid getting hit. The camera woman and I are okay so far. The motorists aren't resisting, they are down on the ground. The shooting has stopped. Someone, an officer, is running. There are people running. I have to question how disciplined some of these shock troops really are! Now a second one of the Army choppers makes a wide circle and appears headed in this direction. Maybe to pick up wounded. I hope nobody just got killed over there. Yes, one chopper is landing in the middle of the intersection and the noise is so loud. Can you still hear me?

ALLISON: We've lost contact with our Peggy DeMetrio. Please stand by... Stand by... Stand by. I think we're getting something. Peggy? Ah—Peggy, you're coming in choppy. Are you still outside the Atlantic?

PEGGY: Allison, we were cut off for a few minutes because of the most incredible thing. Commandos in blue and yellow fatigue uniforms tried to stop these Army medics from treating the motorists who'd been shot. They also started to arrest me. Finally, a doctor, a colonel, ordered the commandos back. The other chopper has taken off and the commandos have returned inside the hotel. The flight doctors and nurses are from Walter Reed Army Hospital. I spoke with Captain Maxine Bodley, 55th Aviation Battalion.

ALLISON: We'll roll that footage now, Peggy.

PEGGY: Captain Bodley, what is the status of these casualties? Can you tell us?

BODLEY: Two of the men that we flew out have major trauma. We stopped the bleeding, treated for shock, and put them on life support when we loaded them up. These other two we'll patch up and turn over to the National Guard MPs shortly. You'll have to call Walter Reed for further info.

PEGGY: Captain, can you tell us about—?

BODLEY: (half in the chopper, one boot dangling) We're taking off now. You'd better get back. This prop wash will mess up your hair.

CHAPTER 37

Maxie pulled her dangling foot into the chopper as the flight chief closed the door. On the floor strapped into a gurney was a motorist who had been shot. The flight surgeon and several nurses worked on him. As the chopper climbed, Maxie held on and strapped herself in. Flight 3 was right behind them, and Flight 2 was a knot of flashing aviation lights far ahead. There was a bucking sensation—air pocket, she thought—and the technician holding an IV slipped. Maxie intercepted the falling bag of glucose with its piggy back drip, and raised her hand to put the bags on the pole. At the same time, she heard screaming and realized it was the people around her. A bright light surrounded them. Maxie felt cold air blowing around her, up into her helmet, making her jacket rattle. The chopper yawed, making her feel seasick. No time to feel seasick. As the chopper pitched forward, she cast a terrified glance toward the cockpit. The plexi panel on the left was gone. The pilot sagged in his seat, head hanging over the edge at an unnatural angle. Maxie hung on to a brace as the chopper bucked and kicked violently. She started forward to help. The pilot was dead. Tom Dash desperately struggled with the controls. And losing. There was a crash; something hit the chopper; her last view was of city lights far below coming up fast. She began to blank out, hearing distant explosions. The last thing she heard was a chopper hitting pavement very fast.

ANN Breaking News with Allison Miranda

ALLISON MIRANDA:The Pentagon will neither confirm nor deny that at least one tank battalion from Virginia is being moved closer to Washington. Earlier in the day, stations in Maryland and Virginia had picked up local stories of tanks on flatbed trucks passing on the highways headed toward the nation's capital. Those stories are now being picked up by news services. We hope to bring you more information as it becomes available.

This just in. Metro police report that two U.S. Army air evac helicopters from the 55th Aviation Battalion with doctors and nurses on board were hit by ground fire, possibly one rocket, maybe two. Police say at least one chopper, possibly both, plunged from a one mile altitude, killing everyone on impact. Emergency crews on the ground are sorting through the wreckage, while police are searching for those responsible. Pentagon sources are withholding identification pending notification of next of kin.

CHAPTER 38

Tory started toward the stairwell to escape from Tower Three. With Bellamy captured, and David who-knew-where, she had only one recourse left now. She must make her way to someone higher up—General Devereaux! She had part of the list. Jet could show that the confession dated from just before Vice President Cardoza's murder. She only hoped that when Jet found the full copy directory, the confession and the full list would both be in there under the same creation date.

The open elevator still rang and she knew if she got into it, she'd be on her way to Top Five. As she approached the stairwell door, she heard the thud of heavy feet as the 3045th's goons crashed down the stairs to get her.

She ran toward the stairwell on the other side of the tower. At that moment, another elevator door rumbled open. A buzz cut commando in blue-and-yellow fatigues stepped out. Tory whacked him on the forehead with her baton. He staggered back into the elevator. The stairwell doors burst open and a half dozen football player sized bodies exploded into the lobby. Fluorescent light glittered on blue-black gunmetal. "Don't shoot," someone shouted, "we want her alive!" Tory jumped into the elevator and mashed the button for the garage below. A man large as a refrigerator stuck his shoulder in and pushed against the door to keep it open. His head looked like a fuzzy blond boulder. His muscular arms were bigger than Tory's legs. "Lady, please," he said in the sweetest voice. "Be reasonable."

"I'm real sorry," Tory said. She whacked him on the skull with the baton, making a ringing sound. He sank down as his eyelids fluttered, and lay prone on the elevator floor.

Another bison tried to climb over his semi-conscious compatriot. Tory hit him also, then shoved both of them away with her booted foot. As the door closed, a hand managed to insert itself. She whacked it, and the hand was withdrawn with a bellow.

Then the elevator quietly chugged downward. If they could control it like the other one, Tory thought, her goose was cooked, her turkey was plucked, her chicken was airborne, whatever the expression was. She bit her lip with cold hysterical humor and laughed at the passing number-lights: 13, 12, 11...

Luckily, it seemed they couldn't control the elevator completely, because it hurtled downward with a mind of its own. Realizing that she might have a chance, she relaxed a bit and shifted from panicked paralysis back to a kind of adrenalin overdrive.

"Lieutenant Breen," Colonel Bentyne said, "stop. We must talk. We have a misunderstanding." Tory fought the ingrained discipline in every cell of her body not to obey her superior officer. She disconnected the com button, dropped it on the floor, and ground it with her heel. At that moment, the man on the elevator floor groaned and started to sit up. Tory tucked the baton under one arm and drew her gun. "Down you go," she said. Her boot nudged the back of his head. "On your stomach, hands behind." He joined his hands on the small of his back. She put a boot on the back of his neck, the gun in back of his head. "Don't breathe."

"They'll hang you!" he raged, but made no move to resist.

The elevator door opened. She said "sorry" and whacked him on the temple just to stun him. She pulled him out enough so his legs kept the door open. She threw the baton aside and ran.

She heard barking. Oh God, she thought, they are bringing dogs in. The dogs barked and bellowed madly in the stairwell. Instead of running up the ramp that would bring her outside Tower Three, and surely into the arms of the 3045th, she ran along the twilit utility road in the underground garage, toward Towers Two and One. She had been a first string runner in Army Olympics at Ft. Constance, Texas a year earlier. Her jump boots were well broken in, and she picked a durable, near-sprinting stride. She stopped to take off her fatigue shirt and cap, and threw them over a wire fence among dumpsters, leaving her upper body comfortably clad in sports bra and olive-drab T-shirt. The castoffs might draw the attention of her pursuers and their dogs for a few minutes. They would think she'd climbed over the fence and into the storage areas that loomed shadowy beyond. The dogs would bark and sniff a minute or two after her scent. Upon reflection, she tossed her gun and gun belt over the top too. By now the gun was a liability. Better not give someone an excuse to shoot her. She pulled the blousing off her trouser bottoms and let the trousers hang over her boots. As she ran, she shook her hair loose. She figured she could pass for a civilian technician of some sort. A moment later, she passed a power company utility truck with orange cone. The driver must be upstairs. Over the tailgate hung a man's light blue short-sleeved shirt. She snagged it as she ran past, and put it on. Far behind, she heard shouts and barks. A laboring humvee bristling with shotgun barrels roared distantly as troops pressed the search for her.

She passed the elevators of Tower Two, and could see the end of the road a thousand feet ahead. As she neared the elevators of Tower One, she heard voices and ducked behind a car. Three men and a woman, middle-aged overweight delegates, hurried out of the elevator discussing how best to escape the hotel compound on foot. When they were past, she ran to the elevator door. Just as she touched the button, she heard the ear-ripping bellows of a huge dog in the elevator—must be one of the M.P.s' German shepherds! The animal kept barking—no, roaring—savagely.

She sprinted around the corner and up the stairs toward street level. She heard vicious barking, a scream, some yelling, then more barking. Through a narrow aperture between stairwell and elevator shaft wall, she saw that two commandos and their dog had cornered the four delegates and interrogated them while they stood with raised hands.

She emerged at street level in the circular concourse before Tower One. From the curved sidewalk, with its waiting area and taxi stand, broad stairs led up to the sheltered entrance and inside to the concierge desk of Tower One. She walked slowly, feigning casualness, to blend into the crowd. She saw delegates in suits and military people in uniform, but also men and women in work clothes, so she wasn't noticed for the moment.

What she noticed, however, was that civilian trucks, buses, and cars were being routed out of the area. There were shaven-heads everywhere, heavily armed, in their blue-and-yellow fatigue uniforms. The reservists were being funneled out through several small gates ringed with barbed wire. Oh God! Officers were walking around circulating photos of herself, Tory saw. Desperately, she hunched her shoulders and stayed in the shadows of the great building, trying to think of an escape while danger grew with every lost minute.

CHAPTER 39

Rims and Mud-Eyes took David's gun. Rims stomped his com button to pieces on the sidewalk. While Rims covered with a gun, Mud-Eyes cuffed David's hands behind him. David closed his eyes in pain, as the cold steel closed on his wrists, and at the violation of his dignity. The two pushed David into the back of an MP car and jumped in on either side of him. A shaven-head driver sped them with lights and sirens along the highway toward the Atlantic Hotel. City lights glowered in the fog along the Potomac.

The car roared on squealing tires into the bowels of the parking garage. They shoved him into a service elevator car that smelled of army blankets and machine grease, then rode to the 35th floor of Tower 3.

Colonel Bronf was a cold, ruthless inquisitor. "Captain, let me make something clear to you. There are two reasons why I don't totally step on you right now for refusing to talk. One, we lose whatever information you have about the conspiracy against us."

David laughed. "You see the legitimate United States government as a conspiracy against you?"

"Spare me your senseless humor. Two, because we are collecting bargaining chips here. Delegates are primo, of course. Bunch of little shits like you might serve as pawns if we need to do a prisoner exchange."

"Unbelievable," David said. "Listen, you guys can still quit this before it—" A huge hand slapped him across the temple from behind, and he blanked out. He was dimly conscious of being led and manhandled down a series of corridors, into a big room with a wooden floor, smelling of old socks.

Rims and Mud-Eyes were gone. A pair of young shaven-heads with fanatical eyes and inhuman strength were in charge. They handcuffed him to a steel railing that ran the length of the wall under a row of windows overlooking Washington. A plastic bottle of water and a box filled with cheez-drip cracker snacks were left nearby. They seemed to want to be kind. A young man asked very earnestly: "Are you liberals ready to repent and change your ways?"

Liberals? David felt puzzled. What?

"Any time you want to repent and join us, you can do that," another said. "They might even let you be an officer with us."

After the two boys left, David turned to the other man chained about twenty feet away. "Colonel Bellamy!"

"Oh, Gordon! They got you too. They got you after all. But you're alive."

"I tried, Sir." He told Bellamy all that had happened. "You were right, Sir."

Bellamy nodded. "I wish I'd been wrong. Oh yes,

there are big names in this. It's a small group, but they have billions of dollars, and influence everywhere. Some of the top people in industry, government, you name it."

David felt sick at heart. He thought of Tory, and hoped she was okay.

"They've got Carberry in a room here on the same floor," Bellamy said. "By now I think he is ready to renounce CON2 and reverse his position, but not for reasons these dickheads want. Ironic, isn't it? After all we went through to convince him? Now it's too late."

CHAPTER 40

Tory fought a sense of panic as the men in yellow-and-blue fatigues closed in around her. They hadn't spotted her yet; had not identified her in the crowd; yet. There were hundreds of people, civilian and military, and it would take a while to sort through all of them. She estimated there were maybe fifty of the commandos, busy herding their armed regular military counterparts out through the barbed wire gates.

Tory knew it would be minutes before someone compared her face with one of the broadsheets; minutes before the yelling, the pointing, the scuffling that would quickly end in her detention. And in her pocket was the most deadly list of names in the world. Half of it; Jet was still looking for the rest—if the 3045th hadn't gotten to her already.

She looked longingly up into the gray-wet sky. Scudding ash-colored clouds suggested freedom. The air smelled wonderful, the way it must in the last minutes for a condemned person. The three towers of the Atlantic Hotel & Convention Center loomed sullenly, their glassy surfaces hard and cruel. She looked down in disbelief at the scene in the concourse outside Tower One. Civilians were being herded out one gate, uniformed men and women in regular green fatigues out several other gates. Civilian traffic—a flower truck, a U.S. Mail truck, taxis, buses, a food delivery semi—was being hurried out through the zig-zag tank traps. Commandos holding assault rifles appeared on the walls of the concourse, on the lower-story window sills, on the steps leading to the lobby in Tower One. Most people maintained a stunned silence; others exchanged rumors and opinions. Out of all of it she gleaned a pastiche of untruths and half-truths: two big generals had a disagreement and one was taking over the convention complex; there had been another political murder and the complex was being sealed until the murderer was caught; a plot by liberals was being foiled; a plot by radicals was being foiled; and so on.

Tory did not have time to speculate. She was desperate for a way out. Then she spotted a group of scraggly looking enlisted persons in rumpled fatigues, unarmed, and shuffling along. From the sniffles, crutches, bandages, and coughing she realized immediately it was the daily sick call. Her gaze darted a few meters ahead, where she spotted the deuce and a half that would take the dozen or so troops to a dispensary in Rock Creek Park. Perfect! If they didn't look at the sick troops too closely, she'd make it out of here and into General Devereaux's headquarters. Sidling through the crowd, she joined the tail end of the shuffling group. She quickly read they were all strangers to each other, and nobody questioned who she might be. Several commandos laxly oversaw the group; the commandos treated the sick soldiers with extra contempt. None of their number presumably would lower himself to display such weakness. What an arrogant bunch, Tory thought as she mussed up her hair and tried to look under the weather.

In pairs, the sick soldiers clambered up into the back of the 2 1/2 ton truck. Tory joined them, huddling under the canvas roof that stretched over steel ribs. There were four rows of hard green benches, in pairs facing each other. The two rows along the middle were back to back.

"All right, load 'em and roll!" shouted a commando outside.

The tail gate slammed shut, and there was a rattle of chains. The truck's engine coughed into life. A canvas flap slipped across, closing the back and making the truck bed dark. To the front, another canvas separated the bed from the cab. The rear of the cab was open, and she could see the outline of two regular-military reservists—a driver and another person, perhaps his assistant or his supervisor.

"Did anyone check these turkeys out?" someone yelled in an authoritative voice.

Tory's heart leapt into her throat.

"We took a head count, Sarge."

"You counted sixteen, but my list says fifteen."

"I mighta counted wrong."

"Have him turn off the engine. I'm going up in back."

"Okay, Sarge."

Tory bit her lip. She stayed huddled, not knowing what to do. There were a few really sick troops around her; a woman doubled over holding her stomach; a thin young Puerto Rican with sunglasses in the gloom, head back and mouth open in sleep; several unhappy looking boys with casts on legs or arms. And Tory.

The chain rattled, the tail gate crashed down, and

the canvas was torn aside. Three commandos stood on the steel bumpers looking in. Two held Uzis; the middle one, an NCO, peered around with a sharp, suspicious gaze. His lips moved as he counted silently. Tory cringed as his violent eyes raked the troops, closer and closer to her.

A voice shouted outside: "What's the holdup?"

"We got a miscount on the goldbricks," the NCO yelled inside the truck.

"Move them over to the side. You can count 'em there."

"Yessir," the NCO yelled. "Okay boys, let's move these turkeys like the man said." The three men jumped down.

The truck coughed into life, shuddered, and began to roll. Then it stopped again, jerking its passengers. The inside smelled of burned motor fuel. The air brake whistled. "Now what the hell?" someone said.

Tory's heart beat so she could feel it. Her mouth was dry. She heard footsteps, conversation, a muffled curse, as someone stepped onto the running board to look into the cab, check out the driver and the other man. She heard the NCO's sharp voice. That man wasn't about to let up in his pursuit of details. This truck was not going to roll out of the complex until he'd checked and double-checked his list against the bodies on board. The NCO shouted: "OK!" Tory could feel the vibration as the sergeant jumped clear. The air brake whipcracked again, the truck lurched, and they moved forward with clattering engine.

Tory sized up the situation. In less than a minute, the truck would stop on the sidelines. The head count would take another minute. She edged closer to the front and looked at the cab. Army combat field vehicles were capable of being reconfigured in any number of ways. This truck, outfitted for hot Virginia summer days and not yet converted to winter hard-top, featured a canvas cab with plastic removable windows. The side windows in the cab were in, but the rear window was not. It was now or never.

As the truck already slowed, Tory brushed the canvas aside and swung herself, in one smooth motion, through the foot-wide gap between cargo area and cab. The driver just happened to apply the brakes at that moment, and her momentum carried her jarringly into the front seat. Didn't this thing have seat springs? She braced herself against the dash to break her momentum. For a moment, she had to catch her breath.

Neither the driver nor the other young man betrayed any emotion. The driver said softly: "Lady, where the hey did you come from?"

"Don't give me away," she begged in a whisper.

Their hard, angry faces did not register any change in expression. The shiny, opaque surfaces of their sunglasses did not hide the resentment they felt toward the commandos who were treating them like third-class citizens. Not only were they not part of Montclair's elite; they were reservists, weekend soldiers. No matter that most weekend soldiers carried years of valuable experience and mature work habits; such subtleties would be lost on the blue-and-yellows.

Tory sat between them, trying to be as small as she could, chin tucked in. They could not guess she was an officer, and she decided to leave it that way. "Guys, please don't say anything or I'm cooked. These are really bad guys, and I've got to see General Devereaux."

"Who?" the passenger, a corporal, asked.

"She means that old guy from Iowa," the driver said. The driver looked like a tough kid, with brawny arms and part of a front tooth chipped off.

The corporal stifled a laugh. "The old man with that voice?" There was respect in his tone.

The driver spat out the window. "Yeah. Old guy's been in every war you can think of. Been shot, pissed on, puked on, crapped on, killed and come back to life. Still swears like a freaking grunt. You a friend of his, lady?"

"My grandfather was his best friend. In 'Nam. Rocky Devereaux came back. My granddad didn't."

"Holy shit," the corporal said.

The driver ground out in a harsh, low voice, never losing his veneer of toughness: "Here, pull this over your freaking head, lady." With an oil-stained, calloused hand he covertly extended an old arctic cap with wool flaps on the front and sides.

"Thanks," she whispered. She pulled the cap on, smelling in it his sweat, his tobacco, his brawls, his curses, his hard work keeping this 2 1/2 ton behemoth moving.

"Pull over here!" shouted another commando.

"These blasted muckers," the driver said, slamming gears. The truck lurched forward, leaving rubber, and then jerked to a halt. The engine idled.

"Tom," the corporal said, "keep your cool."

The driver relinquished his grasp on the door handle. He'd been about to jump out and have a go at someone. "I hate these guys," he said.

"Another thirty days in the stockade," the corporal singsonged softly.

"Especially that son of a bitch out there with the ugly face." He glared at someone.

"Especially him," said the corporal. "You know he's a fool, and it's not worth messin' up on fools. Don't get us all into trouble, Tommy. Just shut up and sit still. We'll meet these assholes in a bar some night, guaranteed. Then we'll do it our own way, brass knuckles and all. These bastards'll never know what hit 'em, and we'll be gone when they wake up in the hospital." The corporal laughed. "Ma'am, ya gotta please excuse us, it's been a rough day, and we don't speak English none too good even when things are going okay."

"I cannot screaming wait," said the driver, gripping the wheel, staring at the man he disliked, and rocking back and forth in his seat. "I cannot screaming wait."

Tory said: "Guys, I've got to get to General Devereaux. These guys are plotting to take over the country, and Rocky Devereaux will know what to do."

Someone in the back shouted: "There's fifteen of them. Fifteen. Gotta send you back to kindergarten."

"I counted sixteen."

"You counted yourself, Grabowsky." Tory heard boots on gravel as men jumped off the rear.

Tory took a deep breath, closed her eyes, and counted the butterflies in her stomach as a man approached the cab shouting: "Get the truck outta here!"

Tory let out a big gust of air and opened her eyes. Saved?

She heard the gate slam, the chain rattle. Tom made one slamming motion after another, releasing the air brake with a whine, revving the engine, cranking the big steering wheel around. The truck careened back into line and followed a caravan of civilian trucks. They were among the last to get out. Already, commandos were closing makeshift wood-and-wire gates to separate the convention center from the outside world.

"Thanks, guys," Tory said as they rolled down a free and open street.

"Anything to piss them dickheads off," the driver said.

"Where you going, lady?"

"Rock Creek Park."

"We'll have you there in a minute," the corporal said.

"Oh shit," the driver said. As the truck slowed, Tory saw the traffic jam ahead. They were halfway between the convention complex and the park. At Dupont Circle, traffic was in chaos as a column of military vehicles headed toward the convention center, while dozens of civilian and military police cars blocked cross traffic. She looked over a sea of flashing dome lights from the relatively high vantage point of the canvas-shrouded cab. "They're turning us around," the driver said.

A policeman in yellow slicker waved them by. The driver leaned out and shouted: "I got sick people in back there."

"You can take them to Walter Reed," the cop yelled. "I don't have time to argue. Keep moving."

"Aw F—" the driver started to say, then kept his upper teeth clamped on his lower lip in an endless f-sound.

Tory quickly calculated: That would take her several dozen blocks out of her way, but it opened endless possibilities. Still, she must personally deliver this scrap of paper to Rocky Devereaux. She reached into her right front pocket and felt the oft-folded wad of paper there. This was her mission now: get directly to Devereaux and personally hand this list over to him, and nobody else. She took the paper out, lifted her right trouser leg, and tucked it as far down into her thick wool o.d. sock as she could, until it was snug under her boot.

"You want to get out here?" the corporal asked. "Maybe you can walk."

"That's a good idea," she said.

The driver jammed on the brakes.

Someone behind them honked.

"Gotta make up your mind!" the corporal said, holding the door open and half-stepping out onto the running board. He grinned as if they were old friends.

"Good luck!" the driver said.

It was the first time she'd seen him smile, a faint flicker of humor in a mean young face.

Several horns blared. Cops stepped in on all sides. "Get that truck outta here!"

"Thanks guys," Tory shouted and jumped onto the wet, slick pavement.

"Good luck!" the corporal said good-naturedly, looking baffled.

The truck roared into motion and thundered away, leaving a cloud of blue-gray smoke. Then a thousand civilian cars and trucks took its place, and Tory hopped up onto a curb. She had almost no money—just a crumpled five dollar bill—no I.D., but Rock Creek Park was still blocks away. Already she could see a United States flag luffing on its mast outside Devereaux's command post in the tent city.

The sky turned blue-black angry, and the air smelled of impending rain. Tory felt raindrops on her bare neck as she hurried along. Past Dupont Circle, the sidewalk was clearer of pedestrians. Traffic on the street seemed to be moving again, albeit slowly. She was well past the barricades and police cars, thinking only of what to say to Devereaux now that she was so close, when she heard squealing tires.

She turned, then froze. Two police cars mounted the wide, empty sidewalk, one behind her, the other in front. The cars rolled to a stop and their doors opened. Tory had time to realize that she could not escape. There was a six foot retaining wall, topped by a steep embankment, on her right. On the left was the street, filled with rushing traffic. By the time she'd taken all this in, there were a half dozen uniformed police officers around her. All of them eyed her with anger and hate, as though she'd done something terrible. It all happened so quickly, she hardly had time to gather her thoughts and protest.

Sprinting lightly, she heaved herself over a low wall, dropped about ten feet through some tree crowns, scratching herself, made a bone-jarring landing on a grassy hill, rolled down another ten feet, and sprinted across the back lawn of a hotel.

She could hear policemen and women hollering as they climbed over the wall. Several bodies made thudding sounds, but they sat still in shock for a few moments before trying to run after her.

On her long legs, Tory ran as she had that day so many years ago on the sand in Imperial Beach, with death and horror a few feet behind her.

Through the lobby.

Phones were just ringing, and people in ritzy

security jackets were innocently lifting their lapel coms.

She was out the front door when the first shout rose in the lobby.

A police car was screeching around the corner up the street.

Tory ducked through an alley of bushes, ran blindly on the other side of the sidewalk, a blur to startled pedestrians who glanced through the bushes.

She ran until the sounds of pursuit dwindled behind her.

Then she walked.

A ragged figure, no longer a military officer but a street person, she wandered tiredly in the direction where she knew her only hope lay. She could try calling General Devereaux, but surveillance was so sophisticated that she knew if she even touched an electronic gadget of any kind, there would be cops of every stripe on her. *Of all the tumult taking place at the convention center, why me?* She knew the answer: Bronf and Bentyne and the rest of them needed scapegoats. Having the authorities chase her would buy them an hour or two of time while they finished taking the entire CON2 hostage. The incredible horror of what was happening would begin to dawn on the media, the White House, the Congress, the general public sometime today when they figured out what the generals were up to.

Tory's path kept taking her to roadblocks. If she tried to pass any of them, she'd be taken into custody. The day quickly passed, heading into afternoon. She used her crumpled five dollar bill to buy some cheap but filling fast food from a burger joint. She chewed hungrily in the shadows while police cars prowled past. They were looking for an attractive female Army officer, not a ragged tramp.

Finally, toward evening, she found the break she was after.

Tory walked slowly along a wet sidewalk illumined by occasional street lamps. She'd done her crying by now. A bath would take care of her image. She'd soon be back in her Jaguar, flash ten credit cards, and—but why even think about it? She had a mission to accomplish.

It was only a matter of time before she wound up in another police station, and then in the hands of Montclair's people. She came to an intersection in a middle-class neighborhood, mixed zoning with gas stations on opposite corners, a dark and shuttered church on the third corner, and a small strip mall on the fourth. As she stood contemplating what opportunities this might present, she noticed a police car rolling to a stop at the light as it turned red.

Instinctively, she drew back into the shadow of a tree.

The cop noticed her and stared, but did not do anything.

Then she noticed the markings: It was a Military Police car, so this was not his jurisdiction. Then she noticed the shields on the front and back bumpers: "Iowa Proud And Ready: Your Army Reserve Dollars At Work."

The opposite light turned from green to orange. The MP noticed the change and got ready to drive on.

Tory ran into the street waving her arms and

yelling. The MP stared at her, open-mouthed. He started to roll forward, but she ran in front of his car. He braked to a halt. She whooped and jumped up and down. He opened the door and rose out of his seat: "Lady, are you nuts?"

"Yes! I'm having an emergency, and you are the most beautiful man on earth."

"Ma'am," he said in a hushed voice, tucking his chin in, "if you need a taxi or something—"

"No, no, I need you to drive me straight to General Devereaux right now."

He grinned. "Yeah, and I'm Popeye, and you're Olive Oyl."

"No, I'm Tory Breen."

"Who?" His face darkened.

She waved the list that the generals in the hotel wanted to kill her to get. "I am a personal friend of General Rocky Devereaux. Here is a list of the conspirators who have taken over at the Atlantic Hotel—"

"Ma'am," he said in a totally different voice, "Drop that piece of paper. I want you to raise both hands and step away from this car."

"It's an important list."

"Drop it."

She did, and the paper fell down. The wind fluffed it up and it started to roll in ungainly barreling motions. It dawned on her he might be one of them. Her guts froze and she began to tremble. His eyes glittered with deadly plans. He had a .357 Magnum revolver pointed straight at her heart as he stood in a shooting stance. "I want you to walk slowly over here and lie down on the ground." With a free hand, he jiggled the car's spotlight, which shone on the ground. "If you make a wrong move I will shoot to kill. This is your only warning."

Tory swallowed hard and moved to comply. The list was floating down the street. Better that he shouldn't get it.

"Lie down."

She lay down on the wet street, smelling stray gasoline and tar, feeling water soaking into her already soggy clothes. Nothing mattered anymore; she'd done all she could. Her fate, and the list's, were in other hands now. The MP kept the gun pointed at her while he called in on his com button. There was a short, whispered conversation she could not hear. She heard him exclaim: "He will?" He paused. Then: "Put him through."

After a silence, the MP said: "Lieutenant Breen." He held his ears as if they hurt.

"Yes?"

"Ma'am, that was General Devereaux." He squinted and tossed his head in a quick motion.

"Oh, you got through?"

"Yes Ma'am." He grimaced, holding his palms to his head.

"What did he say?"

"He said do you have dark reddish hair. I said yes. He said did she say she has a list. I said you said you do. He said bring that woman here now, Specialist, and guard her with your life. So I guess I owe you an apology, Ma'am." He holstered the gun and helped her up. "I'm truly sorry." Poor guy, he trembled. "Where's the list?"

"That's it down the street there, that tiny speck."

He ran after it. For the first time in a while, Tory laughed.

⊕ ANN Breaking News with Allison Miranda ⚡

ALLISON MIRANDA: There is so much news coming in right now that our servers have trouble keeping up, and we have every available reporter working around the clock to sort the different parts of this giant story out for you. Here is just one of a thousand news stories we are triaging for you right now. This is the American astronaut Linda McGregor, aboard the German orbital shuttle *Deutsche Raum-Hansa R.S. Horizont* speaking a few minutes ago:

LINDA: We are 300 miles above Kansas at night, moving rapidly east into the Ohio Valley area. It's an amazing sight below. Because a major power outage of suspicious origin has crippled most of the U.S. and Canada, it is pitch dark on the continent below. Only the capital still seems up and running, probably on Civil Defense backup power. The other urban centers are blacked out, but they seem to be glowing with a dim orange light. Our pilot, Klaus Gittermann, radioed Transit Control in Mannheim about it, and they in turn queried Houston. It turns millions of ordinary U.S. citizens, who are so worried and scared about the developments in Washington, have gone to their local places of prayer to hold candle-light vigils, or are just standing outside their homes holding flashlights and candles. There are so many millions of these tiny lights all across America, that they are visible from outer space. It looks to us like a dim glow of hope during a very dark hour indeed.

CHAPTER 41

While Bellamy dozed near the window, David found a com button lying loose and dusty in a corner. He tried it out and—wow!—it worked. He tuned in to radio news, careful that nobody saw him with the button. Bellamy looked bruised and had a sprained ankle. David wasn't anxious to get the same treatment.

He listened with the button to one ear. The only stations on the air were those broadcasting local feeds of ANN News. Generally the tone was not the hyped up sound of news anchors talking up a story; rather, it was the subdued, shocked tone appropriate to events like wars or assassinations. The anchors were as scared as everyone on the street.

In a far corner of the room, amid blankets and a coffee pot, several of the young commandos liked to hang out and rest during their breaks. They had a small black and white t.v. set plugged in, ancient, with bent rabbit ears, which they kept having to adjust. At the moment, several were admiring their handiwork via a local news program. It was an image of what was happening at that moment in the Second Constitutional Convention, and David and Bellamy managed to catch glimpses.

The assembly hall looked a lot different now that the regular Army MP's had been replaced, and the drunks chased off. There were no more delegates urinating in hallway corners or trading favors for bribes. The corridors surrounding the assembly hall were thronged with young men in blue-yellow camouflage fatigues. They brandished assault rifles, wore full combat gear, and appeared utterly dedicated to the cause they'd trained for in the Texas desert. The thousand delegates were seated inside, some talking earnestly among themselves, others staring numbly at one of history's unexpected twists. A woman was seated at a table on a low stage near the podium, formerly reserved for Chairman Carberry. She was sleek, dark-haired, well coifed and manicured, in a stylish dress. Very business-like, she spoke in a crisp, well-enunciated voice with the barest hint of a drawl that could be from anywhere in the South or the Midwest. As she spoke, she held aloft a Bible. Her face seemed emotionless. Each carefully, coldly enunciated syllable, spoken in a near monotone, sent ice water down David's spine. "It's quite simple," she was saying as she waved the book in the air. "All you have to do is sign this book and you can walk out of here, having done your duty. You just sign this book and you can leave because your job here in Washington will be completed, a job well done. The only Constitution to come out of this Convention will be a Biblical one, and I am asking you to sign the inside of this book I am holding, indicating your support for the New Constitution, One Nation Under God. If you do not comply, you will eventually be freed, but you will be held here at the convenience of the acting government of America Under God as long as we find necessary, which could be a while." Sure enough, David watched a stream of these foundering fathers file lamely to the table to sign, eager at the promise of escape.

"They've taken over CON2," Bellamy said, shifting painfully. His ankle looked swollen, and he favored that leg. "I wish we were far away from here, because when the shooting starts, we're gonna be right in the crossfire."

Sure enough, about three in the afternoon, a group of commandos came in with ammo boxes, heavy machine guns, and a canvas bag of bayonets. A half dozen men unscrewed and removed the broad windows. Preparations for battle, David knew. The cold night air teased at him, blowing the drapes in and out. The distant sounds of the city rose up, traffic, an occasional horn, almost like normal. Each commando knew what he had to do, and there was little conversation. Under heavy guard, David and Bellamy were led out of the former gymnasium, across the hall, and locked in a small office but not shackled. The only furniture was a small table. The parting word from a darkly grinning young man as he jangled keys was: "If you're smart, you'll stay in there and when you hear shooting, lie down flat." He put a Bible on the table. "You'd better think about surrendering to Jesus, because you'll want to go to heaven when hell breaks loose."

"Oh great," Bellamy said when they were alone. "You should make a run for it."

"Not if it means leaving you here like this."

"Don't be stupid. I can't run. I'd get us both killed. Maybe you could get away. Bring back help when all this is over. If the building is still standing."

"It will be standing," David said. "They don't want to shed any more blood than they have to. The delegates are worth gold—as long as they hold them, they can probably hold off the entire Army."

"Just think," Bellamy said. "if they capture CON2, they can claim they are saving the country somehow. That's the kind of thing that's gone on for centuries in Latin America. They could "—his face darkened as a new realization sank in—"they could reject both the old Constitution and the one coming out of CON2, and substitute one of their own."

"Not a happy day for democracy. Or for our hides."

The concrete corridor outside rumbled with the passage of booted men carrying equipment. "They must have been planning this for years," Bellamy said bitterly.

As darkness fell, a sickly calm descended. It reminded David of visits to an aunt when he was a boy, an aunt who had been dying of Alzheimer's in a desolate old-age home. Nights there had the same depressing, wrenching hopelessness, a diseased peacefulness.

David heard occasional laughter as the commandos of the 3045th prepared to offer their lives, fanatical young men dedicated to the incomprehensible cause of wrecking democracy to impose moralitarianism on others. David checked the com button for any voice mail, especially from Tory. He was disappointed, then worried, and finally relieved to find no messages from Tory. Had something happened to her? Should he call Jet? Better not. The skinheads might find out. To think that she might be in this same building, and he could not get to her!

About two hours after dark, David and Bellamy heard distant explosions, seeming to move closer. David remembered the Civil War—a previous time when America's children had turned on each other in a blood bath. There was a stirring among the young commandos. Not laughing anymore. Soft talk. Sincere prayers. More explosions—closer yet. Quick boots as men moved into position. Clicks of steel muffled by canvas as slings tapped against rifles.

There was a particularly loud blast. A massive explosion. It shook the walls and rattled windows throughout the hotel.

Bellamy said after a moment of analytical silence: "The power stations. Somebody is knocking them out. We'll be on emergency generators before long."

CHAPTER 42

Specialist Owens drove Tory to Rock Creek Park, where thousands of tents reminded her hauntingly of another terrible time. Maybe Union troops had camped there long ago. Owens's car inched through checkpoints manned by Iowa reserve infantry, and he parked it among military vehicles. An adjutant led them to Devereaux's large tent. Tory had a sense, somehow, that ghosts watched in the faintly foggy air, this dark night in the hollows of the park. She walked among canvas walls and parked infantry vehicles, past shadowy sentries who were little more than a cough or a glint of steel or the glow of a cigarette in gloom.

General Devereaux's headquarters consisted of several large, dimly lit tents joined in a cross shape with connectors to other tents all around. Inside, the floors were raised wooden slats over nylon tarps. Rows of desks were empty, except one occupied by a night clerk. The long tables with their rolled charts and maps were quiet. Gas-burner stoves hissed comfortingly, and the air had a dry smell of books, hay, and machine oil. Rocky Devereaux came forward with his hand extended. A cigar loomed in the other hand. "Hello, what have you gotten yourself into?"

He pumped Tory's hand. "I want to hear your story—the whole thing, beginning to end. I have the feeling it's going to be a long night. Trust an old warrior's sixth sense."

"Sir, this is Specialist Owens. He did a remarkable job out there."

"Specialist, I am personally giving you a commendation and a promotion. Step inside the office and see the Command Sergeant Major. You are now a sergeant." He stuck out his hand. "Congratulations."

Owens stammered: "Sir, that's—why, I'm—my wife will be so—"

"What do you want, a parade? Go see the sergeant major, sergeant."

"Yessir." Owens shook Tory's hand. "Good luck, Ma'am."

She squeezed his hand. "Good luck, Sergeant Owens. I'm glad I'm the first person to have the privilege of calling you that."

"Go on, Sergeant Owens," Devereaux said. "I'm glad to be the second."

"Thank you, Sir." Owens saluted and hurried off.

The General led her to a separate wing of this tent headquarters, to a large office with desk, long table, wall map of Washington, and chart-easel. "Sit down," he ordered. He called for refreshments, sat behind his desk with his feet up, and sucked on the cigar.

Tory handed him the list.

Devereaux put on his reading glasses. He shouted over his shoulder: "Bielicki!" As Devereaux read, a young infantry major rushed into the office. "Yessir!"

"Bielicki, this is a list of the names of some of the people who have decided we need to be saved from ourselves. I want you to make me a copy, just a hip pocket kind of thing. I want you to put the original in the safe. Then I want you to start broadcasting this all over the world. Don't stop."

"Yessir."

"First, I want it to go on world wide military communications. Then I want it to go to every news station in town, with a press release from me saying this is a list of conspirators against CON2 and against the people of the United States, drawn up by Vice President Cardoza an hour before he was murdered by agents of the people whose names are on this paper."

"Yessir!"

"Write it up. Send it out. Keep sending if it takes all day and all night. I want everyone on earth to have those names so they can't cover this thing up any longer."

"Yessir!" Bielicki saluted and jogged away to another office.

"Now I want to hear your story," Devereaux said. "First you'd better take a shower, put on some dry clothes."

A female sergeant took Tory to a tent reserved for women, where Tory took a hot shower. The sergeant had the quartermaster issue her a sweat suit that fit her fairly well, though it was a little baggy in the hips. Tory regarded herself in the mirror and realized she must have lost ten pounds today. The sergeant poured Tory a cup of hot tea, wrapped a blanket around her, and escorted her back to the General's office.

Devereaux listened with half-closed eyes, nodded occasionally, and did not betray any emotion until Tory had poured her heart out.

"Okay," Rocky said, cigar clenched in his teeth."You want to surrender to me?"

428

"I guess so," Tory said. Her heart was on an elevator, going down.

"Okay, I'll take you into custody." He winked. Reaching into a desk drawer, he pulled out an old .38 Special in a chapped holster. "Go get some rest, okay? There are some cots in the orderly room. Blankets. Take what you need. Be ready when I need you."

Ten minutes later, in a darkened room under an Army blanket that smelled vaguely of floor polish, Tory's thoughts raced and she could not sleep despite her tiredness. Mentally, she still ran for her life. As she lay in the dark, she listened to her heart beat. She heard the hiss of a gas burner and watched the flicker of its glow under the shadowy canvas ceiling. She drifted into a half sleep in which she could almost hear the neighing of long-ago Army horses. She smelled cigar smoke, maybe General Grant's, amid the sweet smell of oats.

"Lieutenant Breen!" a man said. "Lieutenant Breen! General Devereaux wants to see you right away!" Tory swung out of her bunk groggily and rubbed her mussy hair. The man speaking was elderly, with white hair and round glasses, as he held out a clean fatigue shirt, a folded field jacket, and a helmet. "Hi, I'm Joe Ciampi. You remember me from the Pentagon last week?" She did—the tall, rumpled command sergeant major who'd seemed more like a tailor or bookkeeper than a warrior. Ciampi continued: "One of the lieutenants looked in his duffel bag. We figured you'd like to be in proper uniform to go back to the hotel."

"Back to the hotel?" Tory asked. A pain, like pliers

twisted tightly, grabbed her gut. "He's going to send me back?"

"Not exactly," the sergeant major said gently. Tory donned the shirt, jacket, and helmet, and followed Ciampi out of the orderly room. Instead of MP insignia, the shirt lapels bore crossed infantry rifles. Devereaux was on the phone in his office. "Hello, General Montclair?—Yes, how are you? This is General Devereaux, 399th Infantry Division.—Glad to hear it.—Fine, fine. Hey listen, I've got one of your lieutenants here in front of me.—Breen—Told me a godawful story.—What's that?—No, she's been disarmed.—No problem at all. I've got four guys holding her down. She's got a kick like a horse, that girl. If it's okay with you, I was gonna toss her in my car and stop by.—That's right, maybe you and I can chat and sort things out. That okay with you?—Great. I should be there in about an hour. What's that?—Sure, front steps of Tower One." He hung up. Another phone blipped, and he picked up. "Devereaux.—Oh, Ernie. How are you?—Yeah, Joey says hi. Hey, remember that little chat we had the other night at poker? You were right. Montclair is an asshole—yeah, you win; will you take a check?—Same to you, buddy.—This might be it. I'll see Montclair in one hour.—Okay, buddy, break a leg.—Yeah, yeah, same to you." He hung up and noticed Tory: "Ready to roll?"

"Sir?" She felt her teeth chatter.

"Stop shaking, Lieutenant. If you're in the Army, you get paid to be bored most of the time but scared shitless at least once in your career."

Joe Ciampi brought coffee and donuts. "Rocky, want me to come along on this?"

"Naw. You hold the fort. If I call you, get Colonel Bibbs out of the sack, but I think we've got all the bases covered." He frowned a moment, then added: "Joey, I need to speak with Senator Carberry."

"I'll see what I can do." Moments later Ciampi popped back in. "The cellnet is out of the loop, and the land lines are down."

"Dammit," Devereaux said. "I know they've got a field phone someplace in there. Could you see if you can raise Montclair's staff? Who's the Acting?"

"Someone named Colonel Bronf," Ciampi said.

"Get me Bronf," Rocky said, rubbing his hands together in cruel anticipation. Tory saw a look in his eyes that suggested he might order steak sauce with his request.

"Yessir." Ciampi hurried out of the room.

Minutes later, the phone blipped. Devereaux picked up. "Yes?—Colonel Bronf? This is General Devereaux. I need you to get me in touch with Senator Carberry.—What's that?" He gripped the receiver in both hands and hollered into it: "—Chuck your chain of command.—You hear me?—Are you deaf or something? Chuck you and chuck your chain of command. You get a runner up there to Carberry on the double"—he looked at the receiver and said in amazement, "that hair ball rang off on me!" He slammed the phone down. "Who else do we know in there?"

Ciampi suggested: "How about Bellamy, the Provost Marshal?"

"See if you can raise him."

"Sure, Rocky." Ciampi spoke softly into the phone, then waited for his request to be forwarded through the Emergency Satellite Command. Devereaux, waiting with his phone, put his palm over the speaker. "Breen, have some coffee. You're shivering." He moved his cigar around, rose, and went to a closet. Out came a long, wool Army greatcoat with Iowa markings. "Put this on. I hate to hear your teeth rattle like that."

Tory put the coat on. "Four stars on each collar end. Have I been promoted?"

Devereaux pointed his cigar at her. "You might get there one day."

Joe Ciampi came back. "You got it, Rocky. Bellamy's on the com."

"I'll talk to him. Bellamy? Yes, this is General Devereaux. What the hell is going on in that building? What? Oh for Chrissake. Have they lost their minds? Years ago, I'm afraid. Builds up like ring around the tub, you see. Can you move around in there? No. You what?" He put his palm over the phone. "His ankle's bent or broken or some damn thing. He's got someone with him. A David Gordon."

Tory jumped up. "My David Gordon? Is he all right?"

Rocky said: "I got a Lieutenant Breen here who wants to know if Gordon's in one piece." He nodded to Tory. "He's fine."

Tory sped through a series of emotions, from rejoicing through fear, to mortal concern for David. Rocky, however, appeared to see things differently. "Okay, if you got a bum leg, then Gordon can do the walking. You know where Carberry is? Then get him to the tenth floor service elevator in Tower 1. Tape his big goddamn mouth shut if you have to. I don't care how he feels about his little pet convention; we can't let these buzzards have him. We've got to get him to the White House so he can issue a statement and cancel this godforsaken stupid idea. You think you can do it? You gotta do it. You have no choice. I am giving you an order, Colonel. You get Carberry to that spot as fast as you can, and I don't care if you have to kill everyone in the hotel to do it, yourself included. Just so Carberry comes out alive. Got it? God bless you, son. And tell David Gordon there's a girl here named Tory who's waiting for him. If I know young men, the boy will carry Carberry in his arms if he has to. Hang on a sec." He handed the receiver to Tory.

"David?" she whispered into the phone. "David?"

"Tory. Darling. I love you."

"Oh, I love you too, David. Are you okay?" She choked up. "I want you back in one piece—do you hear?"

"I'm gonna do my best."

She sniffled. "That's not good enough. I'm giving you an order, do you hear? I don't care if you're a captain and I'm just a lieutenant. I'm wearing four stars here, come to think of it. I love you and I want you back here because maybe we can sorta hang out, you know, get married, adopt a few kids. Want to do that?"

After a moment: "I've been meaning to ask. Tory, will you marry me?"

She froze, smiling coldly, feeling threatened. He was saying that now, but afterward…it would be like the others. "Yes?" she whispered.

His voice sounded distant, but full of passion and desire: "I fell in love with you, Tory, right there while those idiots were waving smoky weenies."

She laughed warmly at the memory, then choked

up at the terrifying physical distance between herself right now and the man she loved. "I love you, David." There, she'd said it. There wasn't just the possibility that he'd leave her, but that they might never see each other again if something happened to one or both of them. And there was always that lingering iota of doubt because of what they'd talked about in Arlington. Things were happening too fast, and she decided it was silly, under these dangerous circumstances, to worry about getting hurt again in romance. "Yes!" she said firmly, "I want to marry you." Her voice cracked with a sob she fought to keep in: "Come back in one piece, please."

"I promise."

"I'll hold you to it." She repeated her unanswered question: "Are you okay?"

"Yes. A little bruised around the edges of my ego, that's all. That general there with you—he's on the level?"

"I can vouch for him," she said. She thought of Granddad, and Vietnam. "He's our only hope. He and General Norcross."

"Okay, Tory. I've got my orders. I'm getting out of here, and I'm bringing Stan Carberry with me. Mouth taped up if necessary. I'm going to think about how I want to share a pillow with you tonight, and we'll just talk, talk, talk all night like a couple of love birds."

David always had that sense of humor, she thought. "I want you here in my arms, David Gordon. Do you hear me? As soon as you can. I want you here." Tears rolled down her cheek at the thought she might not see him again. Through the blur, she noticed Devereaux and Ciampi had left the room, probably to give her some privacy.

Shortly, Rocky Devereaux strode in. "Breen, you were right. Those idiots are trying to bargain with the White House right now. Not another minute to waste. Let's go!"

Joe Ciampi brought a .45 caliber antique with canvas holster and belt. He offered it to Tory. "I won't need this tonight, but you might."

"Thank you." It was all the words she could get out. She belted it on.

Devereaux said: "I hope granddaddy is watching, because he'd be mighty proud of you."

At that moment, the lights went out. There was a tangible sigh as computer systems shut off, lights faded, generators died. A blackness descended, silvered by moonlight. Gas heaters guttered eerily. Tory heard distant explosions.

The phone blipped, and General Devereaux picked up. "What the hell is that?" A minute later, he hung up. "That was the Pentagon. It's gone a step farther again. A couple of generals in the hotel have started a coup d'etat. They're not just out to kill CON2. They're taking the country over. At least that's what they think, before I wrap my hands around their stinkin' adams apples. Those sounds are the main power lines and road intersections getting blown up by these altar boys from hell. So far, the President is still safe, and General Norcross will join him at the White House."

CHAPTER 43

After speaking with Tory, David felt a warmth inside that was quickly replaced by yearning. He might never see her again. He might not get out of here alive. What irony, to have met someone like Tory who'd turned him inside out, and now this.

Bellamy's expression mirrored frustration. "I wish I could do something more than sit here waiting to get an artillery shell down my neck."

"There is something you can do, Sir. You can help me plan a way to get Carberry out of the hotel."

Bellamy shook his head. "You're nuts. The place is crawling with rock-heads."

"They're plenty busy, and they'll be busier yet when the war gets closer."

Bellamy thought for a few minutes. "You know," he said, "I know a few quirks about the hotel. Look here, on every floor there are maid cupboards. Know what those are? The maid wheels her supply cart down the hall, and uses her master key to open all these little doors in the walls. She puts new supplies on the shelves—towels, linen, soap, you name it—and then she moves on. Each of the master suites has one, that can also be opened from inside the bathroom. What if we—?"

Together they hatched a plan. When they were done, David said: "Granted, it's dangerous as all get-out, but it's better than sitting here."

"Remember one thing," Bellamy said, "I've never seen one of these troopers alone. I think they make them travel in groups to keep the brainwashing active. One individual alone might start thinking, God forbid. Two individuals might start conspiring. What I'm saying is that it's only a matter of time before someone stops you and asks where your unit is. Or asks to see your I.D. What are you going to say then?

"I'll figure something out." He picked up the Bible the skinheads had left for him. Thoughtfully, he tucked it under his arm.

Bellamy, using a nail file he'd found, laboriously and painstakingly unscrewed the lock on the door, pausing every few instants to listen for footsteps. All one heard was the slamming sounds of artillery. "Who is shooting at whom?"

"I don't know, but our friends here will be busy enough," David said. The door swung open, and he poked his head out. The gloomy corridor was lit only by battery-powered emergency lights. The atmosphere was almost holy, almost serene, except for the clicking noises in the window-rooms across the hall, where weapons were being taken apart and oiled for a last time. "Good luck!" Bellamy said.

David shook Bellamy's hand and started down the hall. A cool wind gave him a taste of freedom, a false sense, he knew, but an enjoyable difference contrasted to sitting in that room. The first stop was the laundry area down the hall, exactly where Bellamy had said it would be. David pawed his way through several gurneys until he found blue-and-yellow camouflage fatigues that roughly fit him. He was athletic and slim enough that it would take a few moments for someone to notice that he did not have that crazed look in his eyes, and on his lips that all-knowing smurk of the fanatic, his face a radiant mix of ignorance and bliss. He found fatigues; and a cap to hide his scab.

Furtively, looking right and left, he walked down the hall to where Carberry was being held. Twice he passed small groups of commandos. A few nodded and one or two spoke a greeting. He waved the Bible, and they waved back. Naive, unsuspicious boys, they would be like savage dogs if called on; one word from an officer or NCO, and they'd fall on him and tear him to pieces.

Next, he went to the end of the corridor and found the maid's station. The master key would be in there.

Locked. He remembered an old trick. At least they'd left his wallet. He took out his military ID card and thrust it between the door and its jamb. Tight fit, but there was a teeny rattle. As he worked up a sweat, moving the card up and down, he felt the bolt give a little. Standing on tiptoes, and shoving the card down until it frayed, he felt drops of sweat flying away. Then the door gave. The card pressed against the beveled edge of the bolt, pressing it out of its hole. The door swung silently open into a small, dark room that smelled sweetly of bath soap and clean towels. David stepped inside, in a wan emergency light, and skimmed his fingertip along a row of keys as Bellamy had instructed, until he found the right key. He turned off the light and prepared to leave.

As he turned to close the door, a voice pinioned him and a shiver ran through his system. "You there!"

It was a booming, almost hoarse voice. "What are you doing?"

He turned and faced a huge sergeant with a blond haircut and little pig eyes, mouth twisted up at the corners showing yellow teeth.

"I asked you what you're doing, Private."

David remembered the Bible and held it up. "I was looking for more of these."

The giant's eyes became one percent less pig-like; his snarl softened, and the teeth went away. "What is your duty station?"

"Downstairs, Sergeant."

"Where downstairs? Where exactly, Private?"

"Down by the lobby desk, Sergeant. I'm, er, part of the reception group."

"The what group?" The snarl came back, a little. "You look like a bright one, Private. Got some education?"

"Yes."

"That there book will see us through what's coming, but right now you hie your behind to your station and stand by your pals, you hear me?"

"Yes, Sergeant. Thank you."

"If I see you wandering around by yourself again, I'm going to have a serious talk with your boss." The sergeant went one way, and David went the other. He had no intention of going anywhere but to the suite where Bellamy had said Carberry was being held. There were no guards in the hall in front of the suite, which first made him think Bellamy was wrong. Then he heard shouting inside. He recognized Carberry's voice; after all, everyone in the world had been listening to it for the last few weeks. He heard several men trying to reason with Carberry about something. David also spotted a doorway marked Utility nearby.

When he got to the nearest stairwell, he grasped the handle and looked around.

He was alone in the hallway. Quickly, he grabbed a supply cart—abandoned when the civilians had turned control of the hotel over to the military—and wheeled it down the halls. He found what he wanted in a large utility room: a long brown folding table, heavy, about six feet long, wood on top, with metal legs. Also in the room were a stack of dusty-violet hotel table cloths and a cardboard box full of Gideons. He straddled the table over the cart, then loaded the cloths on it. He emptied the box of its Bibles and stacked them visibly. Unless he met the same NCO again, the Bible ruse might work at least one more time.

Gritting his teeth in fear of being challenged again, he wheeled the contraption out into the hall, right into a group of passing commandos. They stopped, stared at him, and he at them, and then they stared at the Bibles. "Right on," one of them said, and resumed walking.

David wheeled his rig to the wall outside the suite, against the small maid's door for putting towels in the bathroom closet on the other side of the wall. He'd figure something out. One step at a time now. Quickly he opened the table cloths and spread them so they covered the table and hung down to the floor. He placed the Bibles on top to anchor them.

Then he heard voices.

He ducked under the table. There, he broke into a sweat.

Footsteps drew near, vibrating the floor.

He smelled the dusty carpet by his face, felt the vibrations in his frame, and felt helpless. He tried to control his loud, ragged breathing.

"Hey, this is different," said one man, slowing, close to the table.

"Don't loiter here," said another. "We've got a job to do, and that's all."

"Don't even slow down. This is forbidden territory," said a third.

Their footsteps fell away, and David let out a breath of relief. With his sleeves, he mopped sweat from his forehead. It was stuffy under the table. He wasn't particularly cramped, but it was only a matter of time—minutes perhaps—before they discovered him. They might take him out and shoot him, given they were capable of anything.

In the quiet, he heard Carberry speaking angrily far away. That would be in one of the bedrooms, perhaps; certainly not in the bathroom, and the maid's cupboard opened into the bathroom. David pushed the table about a foot clear of the wall. He reached up and stuck the key in the maid's door.

The noise reverberated, and he froze.

Carberry was still talking. Good. The noise might be loud in the hallway, but it would not be heard past the bathroom in the suite. He listened; no footsteps audible. As quietly and quickly as he could, he turned the key. The wooden door, which was about two feet square, whispered open a few inches. It was a simple wooden affair on two hinges; no springs involved.

Hearing footsteps, he closed the door and froze again, then ducked behind the table. Fear made him stiffen helplessly. He nearly peed. Then he thought of Tory. He must make it through this. He must look into her eyes, hold her hand, kiss her rich mouth again.

Seconds later, several men passed by, carrying something heavy.

When they were gone, David opened the door. Could Carberry get through there? He was a big man. The cupboard was about two feet deep. Inside were a few towels, bars of soap, a bottle of shampoo, plastic cups wrapped in sanitary paper; that was all. David inspected the shelves. There were two of them, heavy wood; after a moment's panic, he realized the cupboard was modular. The shelves could be removed by pulling small metal studs out of the frame on either side under each shelf. David swept the towels, the other items, and the two shelves under the table beside him. So far so good.

Someone had entered the bathroom and stood there humming to himself, with only the flimsy innner door separating them. David was afraid to move, lest the slightest rustle give him away. He heard urine tumbling into water. Heard a zipper. Water flushing. A door open and close. Silence.

The inner door was locked, and the key would not work from inside. However, the lock was so simple that David was able to disengage it by pushing the tumbler back with his finger. The door opened a few inches, and David glimpsed the bathroom. Expensive tiles gleamed everywhere, in various shades of luxuriant green, from moss through pistachio, alternating with a background almond. Jesus; what now?

Wait. And hope not to be discovered.

The bathroom door opened and a heavy man entered. The door closed, and David pushed the inner maid's door open an inch. Carberry washed his face at the sink, sighing deeply.

"Chairman!" David whispered as he pushed the door open.

Carberry whirled.

David held a finger over his lips. "I'm a good guy. I'm here to get you out."

Carberry's mind seemed to run a thousand calculations. "If this is a trick—"

"Why would it be? Sir, I'm Captain David Gordon, U.S. Army, and I'm going to ask you to follow me without too many questions. Please whisper and move quietly."

Carberry finished his calculations. He glanced back at the door, saw he had nothing to lose, and said: "You're a hell of an optimist, sonny."

"This way!" David whispered. Carberry heaved himself through the opening. It was a tight fit. David pushed the table away and helped him out on the other side.

Inside, fists pounded on the bathroom door. "Hey! What's that noise in there?"

"Come on!" David whispered. They ran down the corridor.

Behind them came the sound of splintering wood as bodies repeatedly threw themselves against the bathroom door that Carberry had locked for privacy. There were several gunshots. "They've blown away the lock," Carberry said.

"Hurry!" David hoped the bigger, older man could keep up with him. But Carberry had been an athlete and an Air Force officer in his day, and he stayed right behind David. They were running all out, feet thudding in the carpets, arms pumping like locomotive pistons.

"Hey! There they go!" someone bellowed.

Involuntarily, David glanced back and saw a head sticking out of the maid closet.

The door marked Utility was just ahead on the left. "Damn," David said huffing.

"What's the matter?"

David glanced back. The head had withdrawn. "Didn't want them to see—" He pushed the door open. "Follow me."

"Right behind you, Sonny."

David heard shouting behind them, police whistles, running feet. "Carberry got away!" someone yelled. "Everybody, look for a tall nigger and a dirty looking white private."

David let the door slip shut. They were in a janitor closet, attested by mops on the walls and a drain in the floor. A steel ladder embedded in the wall from about six feet up rose into a service shaft in the ceiling. "It's our only way," David said.

They turned a bucket-cart upside down and used it to climb up, David leading. With luck, it would be a minute or two until the skinheads figured out where they'd gone. The path took David into a claustrophobic, chimney-like tunnel.

David heard the door below open. Footsteps milled about below.

He and Carberry stood immobile, hoping nobody would look up.

He held his breath.

The footsteps faded away and the door slipped shut.

Carberry whispered: "They'll be back. They're not that dumb."

"We bought a few minutes. Keep moving!"

They came to a wider service area on the next higher floor, a brick tunnel, painted white. Some inexplicable dusty machines stood against one wall. "Air conditioning," Carberry guessed. "Okay, Captain. What now?"

"We are in the upper portion of Tower Three. Colonel Bellamy and I took a call from General Devereaux at the Composite. We are to rendez-vous with his people in two hours on the tenth floor of Tower One."

"How is that possible? The hotel is sealed off from the world—"

"I don't know, Sir. But right now, we need to get to that spot and hope for the best."

Carberry shrugged. "Not much else we can do."

The tunnel went on forever, but about twenty feet further along they found another steel ladder. "Let's go," David said, climbing on the rungs. "We need to go downward to the lobby level, which connects across."

They climbed down, hand over hand, foot over foot. David heard their breathing, the echoes of their shoes, and hoped the sound did not carry. Someplace up there a light shone dimly down the shaft.

They dropped onto a concrete platform just high enough for a man to stand up in. They were entombed by concrete on all sides except one—a quadruple elevator shaft that dropped 30 floors into the basement of Tower 3. There was no railing, and the drop was dizzying.

"We have to get down to the 5th floor," David said.

"Colonel Bellamy told me the building is riddled with these service tunnels and shafts."

Carberry said drily: "It appears we are completely out on a limb here. Or is that a ledge?"

"Unless we can ride down on top of an elevator," David said. "Only I've never done anything like that before. I've jumped out of airplanes, but nothing like this."

"Did I mention that I have fear of heights?"

Just then the shaft began to hum. They flattened themselves against the wall. David could not help notice the mix of fear, courage, and determination on Carberry's face as he squinted upward into the path of a descending elevator. A wall of cool air moved down and enveloped them; then the car passed on silently oiled wheels. Its back was turned to them, so the doors would open and close on the opposite side. David's eyes followed the car as it sped downward; he could hear men talking inside; heard the name Carberry. He looked at the Chairman, who looked grim. "They'll be looking for you everywhere," David said. "We have no choice. Did you notice? There is a platform on top of the car for a workman. If we can hop across, and if nobody is in the elevator—" (Carberry rolled his eyes up at these ifs)—"we can ride down and then make our way across." He added: "Are you airborne qualified? It would help."

Carberry closed his eyes as if in pain—or prayer. "Okay," he said, visibly gritting his teeth. "Okay, Captain, you crazy son of a bitch. Oh God, why do I let myself get talked into things like this?"

"Sh!" David said. "Here it comes, back up. We'll wait until it comes down again. We can listen and maybe catch it when nobody gets on."

The car sped silently past, apparently empty.

It stopped a few floors above, took on a noisy load of passengers, and started down again. "...Loose in the building somewhere, and we have to find them. Can't let Carberry escape or else..." The elevator trundled past, its sound gritty because of the weight its pulley wheels exerted on the steel cables dangling in the shaft.

Twice more the car made the trip, each time ferrying more troops downstairs to search the corridors. Each time, David and Carberry lay flat and held their breath, afraid their breathing or their pounding hearts could be overheard.

Then there was silence. A faint wind whistled in the shaft, bringing in a smell that cut through the machine oil and raw steel—a smell of freedom, an aroma of open skies and fresh air. "We can't sit here all night," Carberry said.

"Here comes."

The elevator rose to the 29th floor and stopped. The doors slowly rumbled open, but nobody appeared to get in.

"Now!" David said. He propelled himself off the edge, leaping about three or four feet, and catching the heavy cable. It was more rusty than greasy to the touch, but he felt like kissing it. Carberry landed shakily, rocking the empty car with his huge weight. The door rumbled shut. "Down, down, down," David whispered.

"Shh!" Carberry whispered back.

"Oh no," David whispered. The elevator started to rise. Faster and faster. Wind rushed through his hair and filled his clothing. They were going to die. He knew it. Faster and faster. The car was rushing headlong straight up, for a collision with the ceiling. They'd be squashed like bugs. David closed his eyes and hung on to the service bench until his knuckles whitened. The thick, rusty cable crackled and grumbled near his ear. Out of control. Everything was out of control. He was clinging to a postage stamp about 35 stories off the ground, headed for a final bloody slam of destiny.

David felt the wind rushing through his clothes as the elevator speeded upward. Numbers—black, on white squares—flashed by: 32, 33, 34. Abruptly the ride ended. Weak and limp, hanging on to the bench, David saw the number 35 and realized they were at the top floor. Their shelf was about six feet from the naked, raw concrete and steel girders of the roof of Tower 3.

The elevator door rumbled open, and several pairs of feet pounded inside. "Sir," a man said, "General Devereaux is on his way here with a column of mechanized infantry."

"That old fool."

"He wants Carberry."

"Carberry is loose in this building, and I want him too. If we can't have him alive, then I want him dead, but I want the corpse in our possession, do you understand?" The door rumbled shut, and the cab started downward.

"Yessir."

"It's vital to our operation. Meanwhile, I'm going down to meet Devereaux."

"Sir, there is no time. Your broadcast is set to begin in a few minutes."

"That's fine. I want to give Devereaux one chance to join us. At his age, they're usually the last to hear about a new idea that makes sense." The men in the car laughed—deep, hearty, mean laughter that was so close David realized if he sneezed they'd lift the flimsy grating, see him out there, and that would be the end. He lifted a finger to his lips and looked at Carberry. The Chairman hung on in terror as the car plunged through space, leaving their stomachs a few floors behind.

CHAPTER 44

Tory sat with General Devereaux in the lead one of fifty infantry vehicles or LXs, each with ten soldiers and light equipment. The vehicles were rugged and utilitarian inside. The men sat on canvas and steel seats. The cockpit up front had two high-backed seats and glittered with red lights. Slit-like windows of bullet-proof glass ringed the bulkheads at standing eye level and kneeling eye-level. Radio equipment occupied a wall niche. Tory and the general sat in the front pair of seats. The two young infantrymen they displaced sat on their backpacks in the aisle. Each vehicle had exit hatches high middle right and in several low areas where men could egress, crouching low, to avoid flying bullets.

The column passed through hastily thrown up checkpoints manned by National Guard and Reserve personnel, visible to Tory through mesh-covered windows. At several checkpoints a similar scenario played out. A sentry challenged: "Who are you?"

The vehicle commander shouted: "399th Iowa, the President's."

"Right on, 399th! Go get 'em!"

Within an hour, they rolled through the familiar checkpoint outside the Atlantic Hotel, past Towers

Three and Two. The hotel was surrounded by troops in blue-yellow camouflage, with automatic weapons and NBC masks. They looked ghoulish with their reptilian snouts and large inhuman eyes, Tory thought.

They stopped near the gate where Tory had only yesterday joined sick call in her desperation to escape. Now there was a makeshift barrier of parked cars, piled furniture, and commandeered civilian delivery trucks preventing access to the hotel. A large civilian garbage truck blocked the one entrance through the barrier. The glass entrance to Tower One, raised on concrete steps and tucked between sculpture gardens, was about 300 feet beyond. The garbage truck was apparently fully loaded, for papers and rags hung from its rear loading mouth.

"Wait here," Devereaux told Tory. "Everyone wait. I'm gonna handle this myself." At his wave, a tech opened a side hatch.

Tory's stomach gave a twist. Fifty unmufflered LX engines racketed, and diesel smoke drifted over the sidewalk as she watched. One by one, at Devereaux's order, the engines shut down, leaving an eerie silence. Tory could hear wind blowing among the tires. Flags snapped in the night, high up on the hotel's display masts. She smelled gasoline, grass, something else—food! Gravy, beef, something. Her stomach growled, but her skin crawled more noticeably at the moment.

General Devereaux climbed down the side with surprising energy for a man of his age. He wore a long Army coat with four stars on each lapel. He had an old-fashioned steel pot helmet with four white stars in a horizontal row, front and back. He had a cigar stuck in his mouth, and the .38 dangled in a holster by his right hip.

He climbed down and marched swiftly toward the garbage truck.

Sentries appeared on top of the walls. Rifles pointed at him from the lower, nearer hotel windows. Two men emerged at a crouch, assault rifles pointed and ready to fire.

Tory heard him say: "I'm General Devereaux. You boys stop this right now."

"You can't come in here, Sir," a young fellow's voice quavered.

"Now don't be silly, son, I'm a general. I give the orders and you do what I say. Don't we pay you to do that?"

"Yessir, but—"

"Young man, I didn't drive all the way over here to chat with you. Go get me General Montclair right this instant! I want to talk with him person to person right out here in the street."

"Sir—," the boy stammered.

A short, massive looking colonel appeared from around the truck. Colonel Bronf, Tory realized. She'd seen him go up and down in the elevators. David had told her about him. He was a dark, ominous looking individual. On him, even a regulation Army uniform looked somehow totalitarian, his saucer cap resembling something an SS officer might have worn. And he carried a swagger stick! He moved a gloved hand in a brief but formal salute. "General, my compliments to you."

Devereaux removed his cigar and said: "Are you in the U.S. Army?"

Bronf's lips formed a grim line, and his eye cavities darkened. "Yes."

Devereaux's voice was smooth as an aged whiskey, with just that much hint of warning in it, as he returned the salute. "Well then, howdy, Colonel, my compliments to you. Say, who am I complimenting here?"

"Colonel Bronf, Sir. Assistant Chief of Staff, Security, 3045th M.I. Detachement, Reserve. General Montclair is getting ready to make a radio address and unfortunately is not available right now."

"Colonel, I don't have time to wait around, and what I need is for him to surrender this place to me immediately. Not only that, but I demand that you turn over Mr. Carberry to me personally right this minute, and release all the delegates. Why don't we begin by you dropping your gun on the ground and ordering all these fine red-blooded American boys to throw down their arms and just walk up the street there with their hands up?"

"General, we don't have time to play games."

Devereaux shouted. "You hear me, boys? I represent the President here. On behalf of your Commander in Chief, I am ordering you to throw down your weapons and come out here. You won't come to any harm, I pledge my good name on that."

"General—," Bronf barked, stamping his foot and stepping forward.

The young soldiers exchanged a chorus of boos and pleas with each other.

"You better hurry, boys!"

After another minute it was clear that nobody was surrendering.

"Okay, Bronf, have it your way," Devereaux said and turned.

Bronf stood staring, while Devereaux walked toward the row of LXs.

Bronf shouted after him: "General, it's very important that there be no bloodshed. This is a peaceful and temporary transfer of power until the country can be be restored to order and tranquility."

Devereaux half turned, but didn't stop walking. "What's your idea of order and tranquility? Taking hostages? Terrorizing the entire nation? Why don't you begin by stopping your crazy scheme? You can't win."

Bronf stood silently glowering.

Devereaux raised his hand in a signal, and the engines coughed into life.

As Devereaux climbed up the ladder into the open port, Tory heard him mutter, "Well, we brought our toys." Devereaux climbed down and dusted himself off. The coat flapped, and the .38 swung in its holster. The half-burned cigar had gone out, and he stuck its dark, soggy corpus between two radio buttons on a wall panel. A private pulled the hatch shut and turned the crank to lock it.

Devereaux waggled his finger, and Tory stepped near. "Look out there," he said. As she bent forward, the LX lurched forward. "I had to borrow something from Mark Nash. Remember Mark? Commanding general, 699th Tank Regiment, Reserve, Bangor, Maine? He just happened to have one old M-60 gathering dust in his armory."

At that moment, a blocky tank clattered past Tory's window. It was streaked with mud and dirt. Its barrel was pointed backward and the chassis rocked in rolling motions as it charged toward the garbage truck.

Bronf jumped out of the way just in time as it raged at the truck like a dinosaur, tipping the truck over. Truck and tank disappeared into the darkness. Shots rang out, but then someone must have ordered the young soldiers to cease fire. Bronf! He ran up and down, waving his arms and yelling—probably that there must be no shooting.

"I know what he's saying," Devereaux rasped. "He's telling them we're trying to provoke them. That's a damn lie. I don't want to see a single American boy killed or hurt here on the streets of our own capital."

Careening wildly, the aging tank made a circle under the stairs of Tower One, tearing out aluminum frames and causing picture windows to blow out explosively and then turn to powder under its churning treads. The tank rolled back down the stairs, ran right over the garbage truck which flattened in the middle and bent up at both ends like a banana. The tank then attacked the piled barriers, shoving parked cars out of the way, overturning trucks, and flattening furniture.

"Enough," Devereaux said. "Let's exploit our advantage. Tell him to take off, and tell Mark thanks."

The tank wheeled and raced away into the night.

The LXs lurched forward with wheezing air brakes—directly into the maw of the Atlantic Hotel and Convention Center. Tory hung on to a metal rail and wondered—was Rocky Devereaux insane?

🌐 ANN Breaking News with Allison Miranda ⚡

ALLISON MIRANDA: We briefly stopped broadcasting while we relocated to the emergency broadcast center in an old fallout shelter in the basement of a location I am not at liberty to disclose. I can tell you that we were acting on rumors that commandos were en route to take over the station. We are under heavy police and military security at this very moment. Many of the major transmitting towers in the Washington, D.C. area have been knocked out, and we are transmitting on special Civil Defense bands. We will continue broadcasting as long as we are able.

We'll continue updating you on all the tragic stories pouring in as I speak. There is pandemonium in the Atlantic Hotel as commandos under orders from General Montclair have sealed off all entrances to the building. Trapped inside are most of the delegates to CON2 as well as many members of the press. Details are sketchy.

General Robert Montclair has sent a taped communique, which he asked us to play over the air. After some discussion, our bureau chief agreed to play the tape, only for its newsworthiness, and you will read a disclaimer across the picture, that this is not the official view of either the Pentagon or the White House.

MONTCLAIR: Sometimes in the course of human events, it becomes necessary for people of good moral fiber to stand up against a government that has been taken over by liberals, homosexuals, socialists, foreign agents, and criminal elements. For too long, we solid American citizens have sat back and let crime rule our streets. We have let the greedy rob us in the financial market place. We have been taxed out of our homes. We have sent our children to schools where they were taught they were descended from monkeys, taught homosexual practices, handed needles and condoms and told how to use them. We have had our guns taken away, seen the Bible thrown out of schools, prayer banned, and atheism promoted. Finally, in this hotel, we have seen the death sentence handed to the Constitution. For weeks now, I and my fellow loyal U.S. military officers and a committee of clergymen, business leaders, and elected officials have watched the Constitution gutted. We have watched the compromise of weak and ineffective amendments replaced by a carload of contradictory, radical, and dangerous ideas. They have made their convention illegal and un-American. To all of that we now say, enough. We stand at a decisive cross-roads, and there is no way back. I repeat, no way back. The old constitution became a dead item the minute this convention opened. The convention itself has fallen apart and is incapable of producing a new constitution. In the absence, therefore, of a legal constitution, it is necessary for men of good will now to take charge and put this nation back on course. It is time to produce a carefully crafted new constitution put together by the wisest and most Christian clergy, business leaders, elected officials, and other responsible persons. As we assert our rightful control, we will for a very short time freeze all government activities so that that great task can be completed. I ask you all to join with us in creating a new, free, conservative, non-baby murdering, family oriented, gun-owning America in which those who push drugs, liberalism, crime, abortion, queerness, evolutionism, and other bad ideas will be swiftly and severely dealt with. My friends, your daughters will be safe, you can leave your doors open at night, and you will all be heroes in this glorious quest. The top military figures in the nation are fully on the side of this peaceful action. I now call upon General Norcross and all the members of active duty military to join us in this sacred quest.

ALLISON: There you have it, the taped communique from General Montclair and the Hotel Generals.

We have this important breaking story from Chicago. Police have confirmed that a body found in a parked car in a garage in a very posh downtown men's club is that of Robert Lee Hamilton, the eccentric billionaire who founded the Middle Class Party. Details are sketchy at this point, but Hamilton may have been kidnapped while eating alone in a secluded dining room, as reportedly was his custom. The slaying appears to have been execution style. No further details are available at the moment, but we will be following this major breaking story throughout the day

World financial markets reacted with shock to the ongoing coup attempt in our nation's capital. After a chaotic opening session with heavy volume, the U.S. Securities and Exchange Commission has halted trading until stability is restored in Washington. Around the world, the story is about the same. ANN Business Editor Walter Golob says world commerce is reeling as financial centers around the world are dumping their dollars and central banks are buying dollars in an attempt to shore up the world's currency stability. At this moment, the building housing stock market in Shanghai is actually burning out of control. It was set ablaze by investors angry that the Republic of China has shut down trading; they wanted to move their money from U.S. stocks and bonds into European and Asian securities.

CHAPTER 45

The elevator shot downward and ground to a stop on the 15th floor. The car was locked into position. A bell rang loudly for a moment, boots tromped off, then fell silent. They were alone. In the stuffy silence, they communicated in whispers.

David said: "Down five more floors before we reach the connecting tunnels to Tower 2 and Tower 1."

"Let's wait it out," Carberry said. "I'm so terrified I don't know if I can ever let go of this bench and stand up."

"So far so good," David said. "I'm just glad it stopped moving."

"Could we hop out here? Ease down into the car and split?"

"I wouldn't take the chance." Inwardly, he wondered how they'd get off. Looking up, he saw a service platform, but it was ten feet up and four feet across the abyss. As he pondered this, his hands encountered something hard. He looked closer in the dim light, and made out a hand-held control box on a cable. He lifted it, grinning. "Look, Sir. I'll have you out of here in a minute." The control box had buttons to make it go up or down, faster or slower. A technician was supposed to be able to ride the thing up and down while repairing the pulleys and what not, and he couldn't very well reach the buttons inside. David grinned as he pushed green. The car lurched. "Oh Jesus, My Lord and Savior," Carberry said, looking terrified. Another button, and the car began moving down. Touching a bar on the side made it go faster. But only so fast. Inching down, the car slowly, slowly descended. To the 14th Floor.

"Oh my God," David said looking up. "The door is still open on the floor."

"Hope they don't step without looking," Carberry said as 14 passed by. "Not that I care about them, but if they land on us—"

They just reached 13 when someone shouted above: "Hey! The elevator's gone." Someone else shouted: "Look, there's people on top!" Another voice: "Call downstairs. Get people on every floor, every door. It's them! We got them!" Floor 12 passed with agonizing slowness. A crowbar thrust through the Floor 12 door's rubber center buffers, without effect, and the crowbar withdrew. "We'll get 'em on the next floor," a man said coldly as if hunting squirrels.

"Can't we cut the power?" someone else asked.

"We're on emergency power; we'd cut the lights too. Can't do it."

David had a sudden inspiration. Handing the controls to Carberry, he reached across the roof and grasped an exposed yellow cord, evidently providing power to something. He gave a yank, and the cord came free just as the car reached 11.

The car came to a dead stop.

"You cut the power," Carberry whispered. "Oh God what now!"

The crowbar pried through the rubber again, and

a raw-knuckled hand reached in. David touched the thick twist of exposed copper wire at the end of the yellow cord to the crow bar. There was a popping sound and a smell of smoke. The crowbar fell clattering down the shaft, bouncing this way and that. On the other side, a group of men were cursing and wailing, stung by 220 volts and enough amps to drive a powerful engine.

David and Carberry fumbled the cord back into its connector. There was a burst, a puff of smoke, but thankfully no fuse out. The elevator began to drop again. At the 10th floor, the commandos had the door open and were waiting in a flurry of flashlights. "There!" one shouted. "Hop on and get them alive!"

David kept the elevator moving. There was no escape if they went up—just minutes of agonized waiting for the commandos to come and get them. As the elevator car rumbled past the floor, three men leapt into the void. Two landed on the car, one with his boot on David's hand. A third one grunted, groaned, tried to hang on, and then fell flailing with a long sickening scream that came to a soggy ending many seconds later. David pulled the power cord out of its connector and thrust it against the closer man's thigh. The elevator stopped. There was a rush of smoke, a scream, a stench of burned flesh, and the man collapsed on top of David. The other man had a knife in his hand and was bending over to stab Carberry. As he raised the knife, David applied the power to his back.

Nothing. This time the fuse must have tripped and the elevator wouldn't move. David reached over and slid the knife wielder's gun from his holster. The knife-wielder couldn't quite see in the dark, and kept moving his head, trying to focus on his target. David slid the safety off and shot the man in the torso. Carberry pulled down the sagging body and propelled it on a silent journey into darkness.

"Get some lights in here!" a voice yelled above.

David pulled on a lever that released a mechanical brake, and sent the elevator into a slow, jerky, powerless descent. Carberry tucked the other gun into his belt. Just before the 9th floor, a service shaft opened up. As the men above beamed a light down, David and Carberry leaped across onto a shelf like the one they'd been on near the 30th floor.

"They're in the service shafts!" a voice yelled.

"Smoke 'em out. Get tear gas down there!"

"No, if smoke goes in the ventilator shafts we'll screw up the whole hotel and screw ourselves. We have enough guys. We'll comb every inch of the shafts until we—" The rest of his statement was drowned out as David and Carberry climbed into a different shaft.

"If we don't get away, this is the first place they'll look," Carberry said.

"There should be a shaft crossing over soon," David said, praying Bellamy was right again. Both men continued descending down the steel rungs as fast as they could, into blackness, into blindness, into the unknown.

"I see light below," Carberry said.

Sure enough, they were descending into a brighter area. "It's a ventilation duct," David said as they emerged into a tunnel of blood-red brick, a cross between a catacomb and a baking oven. "We're on the 5th floor." It was one of those moments, like standing in the lobby, when the building's immensity made itself felt. Warm air hovered in the huge corridor. There was a dead light every few feet, but there were enough emergency lights to offer visibility. Beyond the lights was a deadness, a stillness, that signified all extraneous machinery was off. In the tunnel, although a warm breeze lingered, there was no sound of propellers pushing it. The tunnel ran straight as an arrow, and they crossed the five hundred feet into Tower 2. Once or twice they heard voices, and they ducked into alcoves, but the only thing they heard close by—or felt—was a rat or two scurrying around their ankles. Carberry lifted his ankle as though he'd kicked something. "Damn! Time for the civilians to come back with their cats and clean out the vermin."

"More ways than one," David said.

They came to Tower 1. The shaft ran on, but David pointed to a wall stenciled Elevators. "We've got to find a service shaft and go up to the 10th. That's where we're supposed to meet Devereaux's people." He blindly followed the instructions relayed by Bellamy from Devereaux, but how could the general possibly get anyone into this fortress to extricate Carberry?

"Here," Carberry said, lifting a sheet of plywood from a brick opening. It was dark in there, and reminded David more than ever of an oven. Without benefit of flashlights, David reached forward and felt a ladder. He felt a gentle gust of air rise to his face. Smelled musty. Spiders fled from his face. "Careful," David said, "the shaft drops down who knows how far. Nine floors for all I know." As he climbed up the steel rungs, Carberry right behind, David's eyes became accustomed to the dark.

They climbed for several minutes.

After moving forward a few yards, David saw a dim light. "It's another one of those shelves," he said. He had a sense of deja vu as they climbed up there. Again, they were prisoners in a concrete tomb, with only the elevator shaft opening off to one side.

"I hear noises down below," Carberry said.

At that moment, they heard a shout. "Over there. On that shelf. It's them!"

Glancing up and to the right in the four-car shaft, David saw young faces staring at them, insane with hatred. Assault rifles clicked as safeties went off. He and Carberry barely managed to duck out of the angle of fire, pinned on a few square inches.

The shaft filled with noise and acrid powder. The air whizzed with bullets and bits of concrete nicked off the shelf. Several pieces stung David's face, and he covered his eyes. "We can't get back to the ladder, and they'll be at the other door in a few seconds!" he said. He was beginning to think he'd have to let Carberry make a run for the ladder while he offered covering fire from both handguns. That might save the Chairman, he knew, but it would cost him his life.

CHAPTER 46

A wall of armed, ghostly figures in blue-yellow fatigues, their faces alien and their eyes like round, black windows in their gas masks, stood on either side as the column of LXs roared straight toward the tunnel entrance into the underground garage complex.

Tory felt a mixture of hot anger and cold fear as the LXs rumbled around a corner, and down a ramp.

Devereaux pulled his cigar down and twirled it between his teeth. "Goddammit, why is there no smoking in government vehicles?"

"Sir," Tory said, "are we getting into a trap here?" Her fear deepened as the empty concrete field of the vast underground garage came into view. The hotel was on emergency power, and the batteries threw islands of aseptic light amid an ocean of darkness. The parked cars had been removed. To the left along the wall was the Tower One elevator door.

Far off against the right wall, Tory saw a vast array of LXs painted in blue and yellow swirls. Armed men ran away toward the rebel LXs as Devereaux's column screamed down into the garage and took positions. Fifty LXs, Tory figured—500 riflemen. They were well armed. Each LX had at least one top-turret heavy machine gun—but so did the rebels, no doubt.

Dead ahead was a solid concrete wall.

Devereaux told Tory and his NCO aide: "We'll get Carberry out."

Charlie frowned. "How do we get out of here, Sir?" Tory saw what he meant as they rolled forward. Garage walls loomed to their left and ahead. On the right, on the other side of a no man's land about 300 feet across of oil-spotted concrete under sickly yellow illumination, were rows of blue-and-yellow LXs, and beyond that acres of garage with stacked equipment. The ceiling was an impenetrable mass of steel and concrete twelve feet over their heads. Devereaux's LXs filed in until the front vehicle nearly touched the wall ahead. Tory heard engines roar behind as the excess vehicles broke rank to form double and triple parallel rows. The soldiers jumped out and took positions behind their vehicles.

"They're moving a couple of garbage trucks down the ramp behind us!" someone yelled over the mike. "They're boxing us in!"

Devereaux nodded. "Let's not waste any time."

It was a standoff, Tory saw as she clambered out. Hundreds of yellow-and-blue uniformed men took position behind their vehicles. Despite the distance, Tory saw the hostility in their eyes.

Devereaux opened the hatch, jumped out, and relit his cigar. He stayed well in the cover of his LX. From another LX, several men ran at a crouch with weapons and mountaineer equipment. Their faces were painted black, and they wore beanie helmets and goggles over watch caps. "Those boys are some Montana reservists I borrowed, and smoke jumpers to boot," Rocky said. "They go mountain climbing for fun in their time off." They stared as the specialists hurried about their tasks.

"I never underestimate my opponent," Devereaux said, "but I know Montclair's style of leadership. He couldn't lead three piss ants to a urinal."

Tory checked the .45 Ciampi had given her. She knew both sides had rifles whose rounds would go through armor, and whiz around like cleavers in a butcher shop slicing people up.

"We take for granted they screwed up the elevators," Devereaux said, "so we won't push buttons and wait for the elevator to arrive. We'll make our own elevator and go up to the tenth floor. Hold your ears, guys!" He stepped aside and bent away. Tory did the same. She saw a commando tape something to the elevator door and withdraw. There was a bone-jarring explosion. Tory felt as though she'd been punched. Her head rattled and she was deaf. The elevator doors had been blown off. A grenade rolled in. Another tremendous explosion, and the elevator was rubble. Another grenade rolled in, dropped two floors, and blasted the elevator engine.

Two LXs now drove in close to shield the operation so the blue and yellow boys couldn't see what was going on.

Charlie dropped out of a lower hatch on the safe side. "General, it's General Montclair." He handed a field phone to Devereaux, and Devereaux spoke his name, then listened. "Yeah, Montclair, what do you think you're doing? This is all so pathetic. Give up now, and maybe they'll let you off with life. You might even be paroled before you're 90." He listened. "No, that's wrong. The military is not going over to your side. General Norcross is not on your side. You didn't know this, pal, but he just had about twenty admirals, generals, and colonel types arrested all throughout the area. It's over before it begins, pal. Norcross just announced this evening that he will take all measures necessary to put down your rebellion, so why don't you just quit?" After a moment: "What's that? Time for your radio speech? Sure, if ya gotta, ya gotta. Meanwhile, I'll make you a deal. You don't shoot at us, and we won't shoot at you. How's that?" Devereaux's voice rose and he waved his cigar over his head. "I've got tanks, cannon, and jets ready to turn this place into rubble, and I frigging mean it. I am prepared to die here tonight, and I am prepared to kill all of you, and I will get all of us killed, and all of those goddam yuppie lawyers who came here as delegates to this stupid convention, but this will end here tonight on my terms. Do you understand that? No? Stick it up your—" He looked at the phone. "He hung up on me!"

Men with fire axes and hooks pulled out pieces of the elevator carriage, while two men in fire retardant suits sprayed dry chemicals into the shaft. Soldiers laid planks over the gaping hole. The mountaineers stepped onto the planks with their M-16's tied to their backpacks. They attached lineman pulleys to the thick elevator cable, and winched themselves upward. Electrical cables, attached to the climbers' belts, trailed out of the shaft to the nearest LX, whose whining engine powered a generator.

Sharpshooters hunkered just outside the shaft and pointed rifles with telescopic sights and laser targeting aids upward. Tory heard tortured whining and grinding sounds. "Those are electrical drills," Devereaux said. "Our guys are bolting all the doors shut on their way up so Montclair's duds can't mess with them from below. The snipers'll take care of anyone who sticks his nose over the edge from the higher floors." He spat a brown wad that made an LX tire gleam.

Even as he spoke, the snipers took careful aim with heavy rifles and picked off a few targets. Tory watched, queasily, as two or three lumps of blue and yellow matter sailed by toward the bottom of the shaft. Each body made a sound like cracking knuckles when it hit. "We got it under control, General," said a sniper wreathed in gunsmoke.

After five minutes of tortured silence, Tory heard a shout. Men carried into the shaft a plywood platform secured by braided steel cables to a pulley device. They attached the pulley to the elevator cable and ran an electrical cord between the pulley and the LX generator. The empty platform rolled efficiently upward and out of sight. Tory marveled as the operation proceeded with flawless timing. Then she heard shouts, and the generator cut off.

ANN Breaking News with Allison Miranda

ALLISON MIRANDA: The United States is currently undergoing the first military coup attempt in its history. Unknown Army elements have seized control of CON2. The Atlantic Hotel and Conv ention Center is an armed fortress tonight, with thousands of heavily armed commandos inside. They are reportedly holding all 1,000 delegates hostage in the main meeting hall, but they claim some will be released if they swear allegiance to a new Constitution with some Bible connection that is not clear yet.

Chairman of the Joint Chiefs of Staff Billy Norcross has pledged to support the Bradley administration totally and without regard for domestic politics.At the request of President Bradley, General Norcross has shifted his headquarters to the Situation Room at the White House. Norcross is said to have already ordered the arrests of dozens of dissident military officers who are reportedly unhappy both with the old Constitution and with any potential new Constitution that might arise out of CON2.

There are confirmed reports of fighting, with hundreds of casualties, maybe up to a thousand, and the number rapidly continues to grow, along New Hampshire Avenue between DuPont and Washington Circles, where National Guard and Reserve units are trying to hold the line against renegade units trying to reach the White House.

We ask you to bear with us as we continue sorting out the news. Stories are coming in, so many, from all sides, and the situation is so fluid right now, that we are doing our best to keep up.

There is a confirmed report now that early during this coup attempt, two Neptune SuperMarine amphibious attack helicopters with forty commandos being shot down on their way to the White House by Marine Corps forces loyal to the President, using car-mounted machine guns. Secret Service agents with shotguns also participated. Both helicopters crashed and burned on city streets. Observers said surviving commandos were stopped a block from the White House in bloody hand to hand fighting with lightly armed U.S. Marine embassy and White House personnel, some using knives and entrenching tools. All those commandos are said to have been killed or captured. Loyal casualties were heavy.

We cut now to the White House Press Room, where the President is speaking to the nation at this very moment.

BRADLEY: My friends, when I came here three years ago, I came as an old boy from Mississippi at the call of his party and his country. As you know, I quit the Middle Class Party earlier this year when I realized how radical and dangerous its direction had become. I tried to stop this CON2, but the mood of the country was not in my favor, and opportunists in MCP moved quickly ahead with their plans. Now we have a crisis on our hands, but do not worry. I will lead you out of this crisis and restore order. Democracy is in no danger tonight. Our goal must not be radicalism.—but healing, and that is what this Presidency is all about. The people who like to bash me have called me slow, indecisive, and lacking in principles. Everyone wants something done now, without thought or plan. I shall stay here with this government, in this ancient and glorious house of presidents, and defend the American system of government. We have to remember that democracy is a gift we are entrusted from generation to generation, but democracy, like virtue, has many enemies, and each generation must defend democracy in its own way and its own time, or it cannot not pass those freedoms on.

CHAPTER 47

David had his gun drawn as he peeked around the corner on his vulnerable high perch. He saw that the elevator door up one floor and to the right was open and empty. Only a dim illumination came from an emergency light in the 10th floor hotel hallway beyond. David still couldn't believe his eyes. Moments before, commandos had been machine gunning them; then two of the commandos had been shot from below, their bodies had dropped silently into the shaft, and the rest of the skinheads had withdrawn from the open door.

"Don't tell me we have to climb up there," Carberry said dispiritedly, thinking several steps ahead. He held his gun limply at his side, and wiped sweat from his forehead with one sleeve.

David kept his gun trained on the door above, but he peered down over the ledge. Something was going on below. "Hey, this is David Gordon! Don't shoot!"

"David who?" came a voice from below.

"Gordon. Captain, U.S. Army. Under orders from General Devereaux."

"Captain Gordon, Sir! Glad to see you. I'm Sergeant Goldman. Have you got our man up there?"

"Safe and sound."

Moments later, three sooty-faced, grinning men came up the shaft using some sort of clamp device that allowed them to hoist themselves a foot at a time. They had light gear, and small assault rifles strapped close to their bodies in addition to M-16's on their backpacks.

"Mike!" one shouted. David looked up and saw fanatical eyes in the high doorway.

The man named Mike swung a few inches to his left and released a spray of rounds. A commando dropped his rifle into the shaft, then followed in a slow, silent pirouette of death. Acrid smoke drifted in the shaft.

"That was close." The three point men climbed up onto the shelf. They all shook hands. David quickly explained the tactical situation. "They could come swarming any minute," he told them. "Especially that door up there."

"We'll keep our eyes on that door," Mike agreed.

Carberry said: "If I get out of this alive, I'm running for my old Senate seat as an unaffiliated citizen."

Mike said: "Why don't we change the Constitution so this won't happen again?"

"Naw," Goldman said, "forget changing the Constitution, man. That's the whole drill. Leave it alone."

"Heads up!" the third soldier said. A wooden platform arrived, driven by one soldier dressed like the first two, his face also blackened The platform was not quite as wide as the elevator. Mike nudged Carberry: "Hop on there, Sir, quick!" While the big man froze in fear at jumping across the abyss, the three soldiers tied ropes around his waist and shoulders. "Here you go, Carberry. If you drop, we've got you. All you got to do is jump for the cable!"

Carberry rose, flexing his knees. "Well, I'm getting good at this."

Just then a commando face appeared in the doorway above. And another.

"Go go go," Mike screamed, shooting at the commandos.

Carberry jumped, caught the cable, and was whisked out of sight.

Two or three minutes, the platform appeared again with two men on it. "Captain!" Mike shouted. "Now!" Mike and the other man extended their free hands to help him.

David rose and jumped.

As he landed beside Mike, Mike's partner took a bullet in the chest and spun, with a stunned expression, out of sight into the shaft.

The cable swung back and forth. Mike raised an Uzi and sprayed upward. "Take us down!" he screamed into the shaft.

More shots came from above. David heard two bullets sing past his ears. This was it, he thought. I'm gonna die any minute now.

Goldman was hit several times and slumped on the platform above.

Suddenly, there was an enormous explosion. The shaft filled with a blinding, choking white dust that rose in a column and instantly enveloped David. Coughing and gasping for air, David clung to the swaying platform, unable to see six inches before his face. The platform bounced violently up and down as it swung, and he thought with panic of the long drop down into the shaft—to a certain death.

His worst fear was that he might never see Tory again.

CHAPTER 48

The generator in the basement under Tower 1 cut in again like a million dental drills. Hot, sweaty air washed Tory's face—and, she saw, the sooty faces of those around her—as the wooden platform descended. On it hulked Senator Carberry. He looked rumpled, dismayed, and helpless, and Tory felt sorry for him. His gray hair looked mussy, and he teetered as soldiers helped him to the safety of Rocky Devereaux's LX. Devereaux clapped him on the back. "Gonna take you to the White House."

Carberry shook Devereaux's hand and grinned ruefully. "I'm all for that."

Tory glanced nervously over her shoulder as she and the men crowded toward the LXs.

Now that the blue and yellows saw that Carberry was in enemy hands, they began shouting in rage. Commandos jumped over their defensive lines and ran toward Tory's position, firing wildly. Bullets rattled off the LXs' thick hides and gouged holes in the soft concrete walls above.

"In the bus!" Devereaux shouted as he pushed Carberry's huge frame in and then clambered in, Tory right behind.

Machine guns began to prattle as roof turret gunners opened up.

The garage was littered with commandos' bodies. Some crawled aimlessly, too badly wounded to go forward or backward.

Blue-and-yellows had not moved. Officers conferred feverishly and tried to reach somebody, probably Montclair, on a field phone.

Then a cease-fire order apparently stilled the blue and yellows' guns for the moment.

Devereaux waved his cigar. "Bah, Montclair's too busy with his radio program upstairs. He doesn't have time to mess with us, he really doesn't need reports of shooting down here to screw up his day even worse, and anyway, he couldn't lead a squad of vultures to a dead horse."

A young officer ran up. "Sir, the enemy guys are attacking upstairs in the elevator shaft. We've got two or three men trapped up there and I can't get anyone else up this shaft. The assholes are firing from an open bay higher up."

"If you can reach Sergeant Goldman, ask him if he has another avenue of retreat."

Another NCO spoke up. "Goldman is dead, Sir. So is Smith. It's just Mike Lewis and your Captain Gordon up there. They're trapped but they may have a back way out of there. He couldn't be more specific because they could be located, so he's shutting down his com button."

Tory's heart sank. She had so hoped to be in David's embrace just about now. Her disappointment was a body slam, but it was more important David came out of this alive. Better he stay up there, safely hidden, than risk traveling down this shaft.

"Into the LX," Devereaux ordered, and boots thudded and steel hatches clanged. He spoke into his com button. "Mark, are you there? Yo, Mark. We're about ready here." Tory climbed in after him. Charlie pulled the hatch closed. The soldiers had abandoned their equipment in the blackened elevator shaft. Hatch doors slammed shut in staccato array. "Hold on to your socks, everyone," Devereaux said. "This will either work, or we'll be dead. Okay Mark!"

Tory felt a wrenching explosion, as the LX shifted under her. She saw the shocked look on Devereaux's face. She felt a wall of blackness slam against her.

A series of explosions meteored all around, shaking them like rag dolls.

Tory was stunned. Her teeth were shaken, and her vision blurred as her skull danced around on her shoulders while her body sank sideways to the floor of the LX.

This didn't seem right. What had gone wrong? She felt pressure in her eyeballs, as if thumbs gouged her brain, the result of a huge, fatal explosion. Devereaux lay bloodied, mouth open. Tory crawled toward him, but bodies were in her way, and she became dizzy, heavy. Something had gone dreadfully wrong.

🌐 **ANN Breaking News with Allison Miranda** ⚡

ALLISON: We have reports of a massive explosion in or near Tower One at the Atlantic Hotel & Convention Center. We are following, of course, the heroic efforts of a mechanized battalion of the 399th Infantry Division to bring out some of the delegates. There is no word as to their fate in the explosion.

In another continuing story, Pentagon officials have now released the names of the dead in the crash of 55th Aviation Battalion Flight 3. We will have those names for you shortly.

A presidential spokesman says and I quote, We've had personal assurances from the Chairman of the Joint Chiefs, Billy Norcross, that he and the vast majority of the military are behind the president one hundred per cent. This is not a civil war but an armed insurrection by a few people, and we expect it will be under control soon. The President, as Commander in Chief, has declared he will remain at his post in the White House and see this situation to its bitter conclusion, with all the criminals rounded up and America at peace once more. There is no plan to evacuate the White House, or indeed to evacuate the government from Washington, although the members of the Supreme Court were flown to safety. Both houses of Congress are meeting in emergency session tonight and are expected to issue statements soon calling for complete multipartisan condemnation of this outrage.

This late word now from the Pentagon. The Chairman of the Joint Chiefs of Staff, General Billy Norcross, has pledged full support to President Clifford Bradley to end the insurrection of what are now called the Hotel Generals. This would seem to contradict a communique just hours ago from General Montclair that the Armed Forces were fully on his side, including General Norcross and all the top military brass. President Bradley has issued a communique thanking General Norcross for his support, and ordering him and other leaders to the White House for a joint press conference.

You are about to see footage of an apparent night time firefight between insurrectionist commandos and Air Force police on the tarmac at Reagan International Airport in Washington as the Supreme Court justices were about to be flown out of the capital by the Air Force to an undisclosed location. The large shape in the background in this infrared night film is a C-130 cargo plane that was used in the evacuation. The flashes in front are shots being fired. The Air Force reports that the justices were successfully evacuated, at a cost of ten Air Police, and at least a dozen insurrectionists.

CHAPTER 49

As Maxie came to, she tried hard to remember where she was and what was going on. Confused, she struggled onto one elbow. She was in her flight suit amid rubble, and it was drizzling—lightly and newly, for she was still dry underneath. She remembered the fire in the chopper. That had been night time. The flaming machine ahead of hers had plunged toward the earth. She only remembered Tom Dash fighting the controls of her crippled chopper as it leaned to the side coughing smoke.

Now she was on her back and it was daylight. It was raining on her face and she wiggled her arms and legs. No major pain anywhere. She turned her head to one side and screamed. There, in the rubble, sat the decapitated head of Senior Flight Nurse Major Lillian Ilitch. It was wrapped in a towel, still in its helmet, and sat upright on a flat stone. The eyes were closed, peaceful, and she looked very sweet, almost asleep. The red lipstick gave its alabaster paleness a humane color. "Oh my God," Maxie cried, sitting up.

"Hush," said Irma Dagdagan.

Tom Dash leaned close offering a cup of cold water. "We were hit by the same rocket that knocked Flight 3 down," Tom told her as she sipped. "They went down hard. We had secondary damage to the tail rotor and I managed to get us down in one piece a couple miles away. The ship's a complete wreck, though." He pointed across the piles of rubble that might once have been a city block—now resembling Berlin in 1945 or Atlanta in 1865—and there sprawled the broken, blackened wreckage of Flight 1. Fire had turned its big white squares shades of brown, and the red crosses black.

Something whined past over her head, and Irma hugged Maxie to the ground. Tom ducked also, saying: "We're under fire from some strange guys in blue and yellow gear over in that hotel. They seem to be working their way over here, and I guess—"

Maxie gripped his hand. "You're the flight officer in charge now, Tom. Why don't we get the hell away from here? Lead us! Where is everybody?"

He nudged his chin in a direction. She saw several dispirited men and women in torn flight suits. One or two were lying down. One sat up. A fourth sat with his head over his knees, hands clasped above his head in prayer. "That's all that's left?" Maxie said.

Tom had tears in his eyes. "I can't leave them. They're hurt." He swallowed. "I'm going to wait here."

Maxie shook him. "Wait for what? Those maniacs to kill us all? Can the two on the ground be moved?"

Irma spoke up: "They can be moved, if we have stretchers."

Tom nodded. "You're right, I guess." His eyes mirrored disbelief. "But this is America. We're supposed to be rescued."

Maxie pointed at the armed figures scrambling over rubble toward them, 500 yards away if that. "This may be America, but those are idiots."

"Here is a stretcher," Irma called faintly from the hollow in which the wreckage lay.

"Keep your head down!" Tom yelled, taking command. "You people over there, let's go, we're moving out!"

"Anywhere," Maxie said, "just away from this part of town."

The sight of commandos moving in on them was enough to mobilize the survivors of Flight 1. As they moved away in a group, carrying the two wounded (a nurse and a tech), Maxie could hear the commandos looting the burned helicopter, looking for supplies and medicines.

Maxie and her small group emerged from the bombed-out block onto more recognizable city streets. In the middle of an intersection they found several city buses, one of them on its side, and a red fire engine whose tires all were flat. The vehicles formed a rough square, and in the middle hunkered a mixed group of emergency workers. On the ground were more wounded. "What's going on?" Tom asked.

"You can't go any further," a fire captain said. "There's a civil war or something going on. These Hitlers from Hell are trying to take over, I guess, and the roads are all blocked ahead. These people"—he pointed to the wounded on the ground—"were shot trying to get through. I hear there are more people cut off and just trying to get this far."

"We have to set up a triage station," Maxie said. "Do you have a radio?"

"Negative, Ma'am," said a policeman. "We have a

few com buttons among us, but none of them are working. We're totally out of touch."

"We have some small arms," Tom said, "maybe we can break out of here. Bring back help. There must be friendly lines somewhere in the city."

"We've got shotguns and small arms," another cop said.

The fire captain shook his head slowly. "I still have a bullet in me from Gulf II. I never thought I'd be in battle again fighting for my country, least of all in Washington."

A policeman in torn uniform hobbled up on a crutch, one leg wrapped in bloody bandages. "I just took a flesh wound, it's nothing. Keep it wrapped and hope to find some antibiotics. I was a Navy corpsman, Captain. I can help."

"Great," Maxie said. "Do you smoke?"

"No, Ma'am." He looked puzzled.

"Here." She handed him the $50 cigarettes, which she hadn't opened yet. "You hold on to these. If anyone needs one, you give 'em one, okay?"

"Yes Ma'am!"

Maxie closed her eyes for a moment. Religion wasn't something she ever consciously thought about; it was just there, all around. Her family had funded a pew at the chapel at West Point a century ago. Bodleys married, were baptized, and had funerals in the Episcopal church. Bodleys went to religious schools, although some, like Maxie, were expelled for things like experimenting with pot, and went on to other places, but the fact of religion was always there under the surface. Maxie had even as a child known that people forgot about God until they were in severe danger, and she'd considered that hypocritical; so she'd always kept a little reserve back channel available just in case she were on a sinking ocean liner or a plane about to go nose-first into the Himalayas. Now she prayed intently to this old family friend, this old uncle who was just the most powerful and noteworthy of so many Lee and Bodley uncles. After all, with colonels on both sides— "Oh Lord, now I know why you've kept me in luck all this time. There is something you want me to do here, I can feel it in my little old Virginia bones. I guess a person's never ready to stop playin', but everyone's got to go out sooner or later and put some quarters in the meter. This must be it for me. Please, I just met this nice guy here, and—" Her thoughts were cut short as she heard gunfire and shouting.

A fog of gray smoke drifted constantly among the disabled buses and the fire truck. She caught the acrid, distasteful pungency of expended gun propellant. People were running everywhere. Tom took her by the arm. "Maxie—"

Instinctively, she smiled and turned so that she fit neatly between his arm and his side. She felt almost as though she wished he would take her away and lay her down to sleep, as if she were a small child. Then she felt how he was trembling, and she realized that she did not have time to be helpless. She wrapped her arms around him and squeezed. "We're going to be brave, y'hear me?"

He ran his hand up and down her back. The warmth, the pressure, the friction calmed her. "We're going to get through this, Maxie."

She hugged. "We made it through a chopper crash." She looked up, dazzled that he was there in her arms. "Do you like me, Tom Dash?"

He swallowed. "Well, um, like is not the word. I—"

Her lightness was suddenly replaced by a deadly seriousness, a sickening, toxic stew of fear and loss and imminent death. She tugged. "Say it, man. There isn't time."

"I think I am falling in love with you, Maxie."

"So am I. I want you to give me one big old french kiss so bad, but then if I lose you or you lose me, I don't want us to spend the rest of our life remembering how nice that—"

Tom bent over and placed his mouth on hers. His tongue touched hers, stifling the words that did not need to be said in any case. She felt his body with her hands, heaping touches of him toward herself as if gathering in what she could, as if she were a crazy lady with a large bag billowing in autumn wind, to gather petals, to store what she could before a long hard winter. She trembled with passion, just for a moment, because then someone with a voice like a drill sergeant bellowed to nobody and everyone who would listen: "I've got casualties here!"

They stepped in out of the mist, a battered, dirtied, scared looking bunch of kids in camo uniforms. They carried stretchers with figures on them, and the figures seemed mingled with white sheets and great splotches of claret colored blood, almost happy looking in its brightness. And the wounded, how they cried. Screams came from the fog, from voices grown hoarse but unable to stop. She could clearly hear the mixture of fear and pain.

"Who are you?" she said stepping in their path.

A young sergeant said sullenly: "Motor pool unit, Ma'am, active Army. We're just a supply outfit for staff cars over in Foggy Bottom. Didn't even have time to draw our own weapons. They trucked us up here and our truck got blown over before we could get where we was goin'."

"Fine," she told him, "bring your wounded in here and lay them in a row over there." She pointed to a small group of casualties who were already laid out along the fire truck. Irma and another nurse were frantically working on one of them. "Hey, Irma, do you need help?"

"I.V., stat," came the reply. "Need units of blood."

Tom stepped forth. "I'm useless here, Maxie. I'm going to take a few hale and hardy boys with guns and we're gonna try and break through. We'll bring back help."

She nodded. "I love you Tom. For that. And for yourself." She sniffed, and a tear rolled down her cheek. "Let's do what's got to be done. Bring back supplies, blood, ambulances."

He shook his head. "I love you too, Maxie. I don't think you can get an ambulance in here just now. More like they need to bring in paratroopers and infantry to stop these guys. Right now they're just throwing cooks, clerks, drivers at them. Kinda like at the Battle of the Bulge."

"Go, Tom. God bless." She hugged him, then pushed away. She watched as he trudged away with one starved afterglance that matched her hunger, and it was as though he were pulling something out of her heart.

Unnoticed, there'd been a whistling sound, accompanied by a rumbling feeling, kind of like a train going by. Suddenly, an explosion tore through the air a block away, rattling the ground. Maxie felt a mild deafness that would not go away. She could hardly hear her own voice as she stepped around, directing people here and there.

Soon she found herself in an argument with a Marine Corps lieutenant colonel in dress uniform, whose nameplate read Myers. Myers had been in a staff car, headed to a briefing at the Pentagon, when he and his driver had been cut off in a guerrilla ambush and forced to run for their lives. He was a lean, well-exercised man of about 35. He wanted to round up all the intact Army personnel and form a perimeter.

"What do you normally do, Colonel?"

"I run a computer lab."

"Well, I work in the medical field, sir, and if you try to form up a unit here, you're going to draw fire down on us. I don't want that."

"Captain, there's no time to argue!"

"Just my point." She waved up the littered street, toward a destination unknown. She shook her head. Looked the other way, toward the foggy oblivion from which the wounded had staggered, and where she could hear light gunfire. "Leave me a few people with side arms and take the rest back there."

Myers furiously looked around at the cover afforded by the vehicles. "Captain, goddammit, just this whole setup is going to draw fire."

It was a circular argument, they both knew. There was no time.

"Do what you want," she said. "This is a field hospital right now, and I'm running it. Now either help carry bodies or get the hell out of my way." She left him standing there and moved on to direct the work of two civilian paramedics who had found a box of I.V. supplies in the fire truck. Myers' words drifted after her: "I'm sorry, Captain, just sorry. If I can help…"

She snapped back: "Do what I told you. Leave me about four or five men with rifles or side arms and collect who you can. You can form up a perimeter line about a thousand feet away. If you get hit, hold out as long as you can. Retreat slowly if you are overwhelmed. That will buy time and I may be able to get the patients out before the devils overrun this position."

"Yes Ma'am!" the colonel said, saluting the captain. He turned and briskly, with new purpose, waved his arms and directed men to form around him. Bewildered, and somewhat sullenly, some did; others had to be coaxed.

Maxie forgot to return the colonel's salute, because she was surprised at how easy it was to direct people once you had their attention. She barely had time to wonder if the thing she'd told him to do would be a good one. She'd made it up in her head, mainly so he'd go do something and not be a pest. Then again, maybe he was the type of man who, once he'd been given direction, knew exactly what to do.

Within an hour, the situation changed again. They were still stuck, out of communication, with men and women dying for lack of replacement blood. But now the first doctors appeared. Navy people. One was a young woman, a lieutenant commander, the other an older Afro-American admiral who specialized in urology at Bethesda Naval Hospital. Both were in civilian clothing; they'd been on their way back from a Bible club prayer breakfast in Maryland, had gotten lost because some of the streets were closed, and wound up running for their lives as Colonel Myers had. The gray-haired black gentleman approached, directed to her by various persons, and trailed by the woman. "Hello, I'm Rear Admiral Stintonburger"(so she understood the name through a bunch of shouting and gunfire)"and I wonder if I can help."

"Me too, I'm a resident in dermatology."

The admiral said: "We're told there is some fireball nurse in charge up here. We'd like to report in for duty." He was looking over her head, barely seeming to notice her.

"That would be me," Maxie said. "Hell, I'm just a captain. You want to be in charge?"

"No way," Stintonburger said with a twinkle. "You seem to have things well organized."

"We're short on everything except casualties," she told them. "Commander, you organize a triage function. I've got to get some more organizin' accomplished. Admiral, you're the chief medical officer here." She saluted, and he tossed one back. She told him: "Anyone gets out of line, you shoot 'em, y'hear?"

He saluted again, laughing. "Aye aye, Ma'am." He and what-was-her-name hurried off to do as she'd told them. Her worst blinding worry right now was the lack of supplies. She called Irma over. It was late afternoon now, and the light was beginning to fade quickly. "Irma, can you get some of these people who are just lightly wounded, and train them? You know, the basics. Stop the bleeding, clear the air passage, do CPR, treat for shock, wrap 'em and hold 'em until more can be done?"

"Sure, Max. You're doing a great job here." Irma briefly clasped Maxie's shoulders with her hands. Irma was no bigger than Maxie, and had a beautiful Filipina face with exotic eyes and smooth butterscotch skin, and thick rich black hair. "You know what it is, Max?"

"What's what? I'm hungry."

"That too. What's what is why you're so intimidating. It's the flight suit."

Maxie looked down at herself. "Yeah, now that you mention it. I always thought this thing was kind of really cool. All these pockets. But then you—"

"I don't have the commanding manner," Irma said grinning. She turned and headed toward a group of wounded men sitting indolently, in shock, around a steaming coffee pot. They'd lit a small fire between some stones. Wouldn't hurt any, Maxie thought, after briefly considering. Then her attention turned elsewhere. "Food. Where are the cooks here?" Two young men stepped forth. "You guys. I know there is something to eat somewhere nearby. You guys find it and serve it to the rest of us."

They looked at each other.

"It's better than hanging around. And it's a direct order. Now march!"

Time was flying by in the constant hubbub. They were a growing concern, with at least a hundred people of all ages and sizes and in all kinds of uniforms or the lack thereof. After dark, they received a small group of tourists from Japan. Six men and their wives, she figured. Three of the men and one of the women were medical doctors. Maxie made the Sign of the Cross. Their English was reasonable—they were on vacation from Kyoto, they said, and under the circumstances would be glad to help. They were hopelessly lost and cut off from the hotel rooms, one of them said.

"Honey, that describes just about everyone in

Washington today except our friends from hell, who are hopelessly lost and cut off from their minds." She pointed at new casualties staggering in from the night. "Just grab them as they come. Stop the bleeding, clear the airways, do what you have to do."

About mid-evening, four young Navy corpsmen carried in a stretcher. Maxie looked at the man on it and realized it was Colonel Myers. Horrified, she held her hands to her face. She'd sent him out there. She turned to the closest corpsman. "Is he—?"

"He's dead, Ma'am. Took shrapnel in the stomach and chest. The other side's been firing those Long Toms over the city. They're mostly firing at Rock Creek Park, but every once in a while a round goes astray. Are you Captain Bodley?"

"Yes."

"He did tell me before he went, to warn you, that the hotel soldiers are sending out snipers throughout the city, to harrass and interdict."

"Thank you."

The body of Myers, and his bearers, disappeared into the night as blur after blur of activity surrounded Maxie. The two cooks she'd sent out had returned with two cooler cases full of freshly made hamburgers and french fries from a fast food restaurant. The place had been closed, the power off, the doors locked, the help run away, but the two cooks had known exactly what do to. She clapped them on the shoulders: "You men have saved the day!"

One hamburger was about all she could handle right now, and she ate it while directing surgery by lamp light over a young man who had lost most of his left arm. He was in shock, and the wound had to be washed out, the arteries sewn up by the admiral, and the stump wrapped in gauze.

All through the night, Maxie kept thinking of Tom Dash, each time she had a moment to breathe, to think, to be herself. She ached inside, thinking that something might have happened to him.

The Japanese decided to try their way out. Another Japanese tourist had come along, a senior honcho with a big car manufacturing company. He'd spoken authoritatively about getting to the Japanese embassy and that it was not too far away.

As the night grew late, there seemed to be a lull. Occasional rounds still poured in over their heads, in the direction of the Composite at Rock Creek Park. Small arms fire rattled irregularly in the city, but the intervals were longer. Maxie sat with Irma, sharing coffee that the two cooks had made especially for them. An Army Infantry sergeant had just arrived to have a bullet removed from his side. He sat with them, a sandy-haired man of indeterminate age. Battle, Maxie figured, seemed to put a patina on everyone, especially the men, so they all looked dirty and tired and unshaven. Their hair was short and mussy and ranged from dirty brown to dirty black, with the occasional dirty blond thrown in. "Do you ladies know if we're gonna get rescued here?" he asked softly, looking strained in his bandages. He had a field jacket draped loosely over his otherwise bare upper torso, while his lower half wore boots and fatigue pants.

Maxie shook her head, looking at the sky. While it remained foggy on the ground, the sky was clear in patches, but mostly it was filled with big bruised billowing clouds the color of ashes. "I keep thinking a whole bunch of parachutes will suddenly float down. Paratroopers, to save us."

The sergeant smiled as he accepted a bit of coffee from Irma. "Well, Ma'am, I think in these desperate times those fat old generals don't want to lose their best aces in the hole, if you see what I mean. First place, how'd they know if they send in a battalion of guys, that they won't turn and go over to the other side? Second, if you got troops you know is loyal, you wait, you don't just throw them at the problem, you wait until daylight and check it out from the air and plan your next chess move. I'll bet them boys in the park is all pulled out right now. Them a-holes, if you pardon my French, they's lobbing artillery at a bunch of empty tents. All them good reserve troops is just holding the line until they can bring in some fresh regulars from places like Fort Riley and Fort Campbell, not to mention Fort Hood and Fort Polk, places like that. And Marines from Camp Lejeune and Camp Pendleton. That's gonna take a few days, and meanwhile we's out here swingin' in the breeze."

"So what's your plan?" Irma asked. "You're wounded. You can bag out if you want."

The sergeant nodded with a wry grin. "Can't win for stayin', can't win for leavin'. I done made up my mind. I'm gonna pull out with the next little batch o' boys that's going. We got hit pretty hard up there, you seen Colonel Myers take it up front real bad. I think you ought to pull outta here with us, Ma'am," he said, addressing Maxie.

"That would be impossible. Half these people can't be moved, much less walk. If we move, they die."

The sergeant's grin evaporated. "Ma'am, what's

you gonna do if them lucifers comes through the rubble at you?'

"We're no threat to them. We'll negotiate. We'll fix their wounded too."

The sergeant rose, shaking his head. He seemed to have inner thoughts that he felt were best kept close to his heart. "Next time I got a holy moment, I'm gonna say a prayer for you ladies."

"If you get out," Irma said, "send back blood. Lots of it. And antibiotics. Tell them we have people who need medevac. Couple dozen MAES units would be in order."

"I promise I will, Ma'am."

"Good luck," Maxie said.

"Thank you, Ma'am."

Maxie watched as the sergeant and a tall black man, very dark-skinned, with long bare muscular arms, gathered a small group about them. There were maybe a dozen, Maxie figured, all with minor wounds, but all with rifles and able to walk. They looked like a painting of cossacks in their torn, baggy, and ill-assorted uniforms. A few had helmets; the rest wore a wild assortment of hats, including one or two with russian-style fur caps with dangling furry earmuffs.

A light drizzle began to fall. Maxie forgot about the sergeant and his men. She jumped up and organized a group to spread tarps between the fire engine and a school bus. About 25 men actually managed to right one of the busses. They got the lights to work inside, and busily swept glass out the doors.

Maxie was just helping a woman with a leg wound to hobble toward the newly promised sanctuary of the bus, when shots rang out, then screams, and then there was silence. Someone bellowed with outrage.

The lights on the bus went out. Someone ran past Maxie, and she asked: "What's going on?"

"Snipers, Ma'am. They just killed the two men cleaning up the bus."

Maxie's heart sank. She let the woman at her side hobble off to a crowded group sheltering under the tarp. As drizzle gathered in her hair and started to run down her face, she thought about crying. But nothing came out. This was far from over, and she couldn't let herself cry until it was over. "Everybody! Listen up!" she cried in her loudest voice. "Spread the word. Keep a low profile. There are snipers all around us out there. No lights, you understand? Not even a cigarette." She thought she was being ignored, but then she saw men whispering to each other, gesticulating, looking over the protective vehicles with wide, scared eyes. No lights, she thought; they'd have to operate while one person held a poncho to ward off the drizzle and to keep the glow of their battery lights from attracting more shots. Thank God for the fire engine. She hoped its batteries would sustain her lights until dawn.

Casualties kept straggling in. Stretcher cases, who were usually far worse, came in intermittently. As she was working on a man with a gaping stomach wound, trying to stop his bleeding and pack his intestines, and knowing he would probably die soon, she noticed a very tall black man with glistening skin and long muscular arms. He caught her eye and wandered over dully. "All dead, Ma'am."

"The sergeant?" she asked without ceasing to work.

"All dead. And the Japanese. Slaughtered. It's sniper alley out there, Ma'am. I'm the only one of the boys that got back here." Tears ran down his face.

"Go get some coffee, and then come see me. I have work for you," she said firmly.

He began to cry even as he answered: "Thank you, Ma'am. Thank you." He covered his face with his palms and turned away, doubling over. She noticed he had a wound in the side, but was too preoccupied to check on it.

Thinking of Tom, probably buried in the same pile of bodies somewhere in a lake of muddy water and smashed concrete, she knew why she wasn't crying. She was saving it all for when they brought her the news. She could handle anything until then, anything!

A while later, the man with the stomach wound expired. Maxie had stayed with him, and she held his hand until it began to grow cool in the clasp of hers.

Someone brought her a cold hamburger, and she ate it without wondering where it had been or if it was still safe to eat. She cleaned out a shallow grazing wound on a man's forehead and was stitching it up, when she looked up. It was just in the first light of dawn—where had the time gone?—when she looked up because Admiral Stintonburger was calling out to her. He was leaning over a patient and held his hands up in their bloodied surgical gloves. When she looked more closely, in slow motion, she noticed that he had a hole in the middle of his forehead; he collapsed before her eyes. She cringed inwardly, but kept working. Several people ran to help the doctor, but she could tell from here he'd died almost instantly. The young dermatologist threw her scalpel down and began to scream hysterically. In and out, her wailing, like some sort of crazed calliope, until two other young military women embraced her and comforted her. Maxie finished her procedure and left it for a corpsman to clean up and bandage the patient. She walked over and put her arms on the doctor's shoulders. The doctor was pale, and trembling; her eyes looked away and she seemed to be unable to focus. "Doctor."

She looked at Maxie. "I'm sorry, I—what?"

"You're going to have to pull yourself together. You are now the only remaining medical officer. There is a lot of work to do, and no time to waste, do you understand?"

"Yes."

Maxie motioned for the two other women, lightly wounded, one a driver, the other with a Navy commel detachment, to stay with the doctor and keep her together.

Then someone else motioned for Maxie to come quickly.

The shot that killed Irma had arrived stealthily, sometime during the night. As a dingy light filtered down through a pearly sky, someone had found her flight-suited body sprawled face down in a muddy puddle. She'd been hit by a high velocity, high caliber slug of some kind, right through the center of her torso. "Oh no," Maxie said feeling hysteria pressing at the trapdoor, "oh no." She singsonged, rolling the body over. "Irma, oh no, please no…" Irma had long grown cold. Maxie kissed herself on the hand and then touched her fingertips to Irma's closed eyes. "Put her with the others," she told the onlookers as she rose blindly and staggered back toward the center of the encampment.

She walked in among the wounded and slumped down with her back to the roof of a fallen bus. Several of the patients touched her, having nothing else to give but their thanks and affection. Then she noticed, next to her, a very handsome young man. He lay on his back, covered by a blanket, and he was looking at her with alert eyes. "You okay, lady?"

Maxie nodded, wiped something away from her nose. That seemed to make her able to talk again. "Yeah. How are you?"

The boy looked into the sky. "I can't move my legs. I was able to move my arms until a little while ago. I have a bullet somewhere near my spine. Am I going to die?"

"No."

"I have a wife. She's real pretty. We have a baby on the way. I want to see that baby."

"You will." Maxie slid her leg under his neck and gently lifted him toward her, so that his head was supported by her knee, and his back lay in the V of her folded left leg. She put her left arm around him and held him close to her. With her right hand, she reached under the blanket and found his hands. They were dry and chilly. "Can you feel that?"

He smiled broadly. "I feel something warming my hands."

She grinned joyfully. "That's wonderful. There is hope, you see. Okay, I'm going to take a little rest for a while. We'll keep each other warm."

"You can have a corner of this blanket."

"Thanks, but I'm warmly dressed. What's your wife's name?"

"Yvette." He spelled it out. "We were thinking if the baby is a girl, we'd call her Yvette Junior. And if it's a boy, Yves."

"Sounds good to me. What's your name?"

"Tom."

She closed her eyes and felt a dullness, like wet concrete, sliding down her brief glimmer of happiness. "Tom who?"

"Tom O'Leary. I'm from Bristol, Virginia."

"I thought I heard a little Virginia drawl in them thar words, my friend."

"You got a good ear, Ma'am. You must be from around there."

"I am."

"Say, are you still holding my hands?"

"Yup. Got a firm grip on 'em, right here." She pulled tightly on them.

"I can't feel them anymore. I wonder if that's 'cause you let go."

"I'm not letting go of you, Tom O'Leary. We're in this together."

As dawn grew fully around them, there was a long silence as though the world had died and must be resurrected. Someone was rumoring that a cell phone had been found in a ruined civilian automobile. A call for help had been made to a civilian operator in Delaware using a credit card. The phone was being brought to the encampment and given to Maxie. The shooting grew distant, or was that because she was nodding out, her head against Tom O'Leary's. She could hear rain dripping someplace, but it was almost dry in the lee of the bus.

Just as she was falling asleep, something terrible tore at her ears and pressed her against the bus. Dully, she opened her eyes and looked around. "What was that?"

"Wow." Several men rose and stood pointing toward the northwest. "Damn. Look at that."

She still held Tom O'Leary in her lap, and she

shifted slightly to change positions. Her leg threatened to go to sleep. "You okay, Tom O'Leary?"

"I'm fine, Ma'am. You're keeping me nice and warm. What was that noise?"

One of the men answered: "Huge explosion over there by the convention center. Maybe them crazy bastards blew themselves up in the hotel."

"And the whole friggin' CON2 with it," another said.

"Good riddance," another said.

"It's going to be over soon," Tom O'Leary told Maxie with utter assurance.

CHAPTER 50

Tory coughed. For a moment she panicked. Her eyes were glued shut and sightless, and she touched them fearfully to see if she'd gone blind. She heard moaning as she sat up. She rubbed her eyes, removing a sludge of blood, oil, and dust. Her ears still rang from the explosions that had rocked through the underground garage. Now, as she and the others slowly picked themselves up battered and with bleeding nostrils, she began to blurrily see again. Nobody in her vehicle had been killed.

Then Tory began to hear gunfire. She peered through a wire-guarded window and saw small arms tracer fire coming from the rebels, who seemed to fire into a brightness in the dust.

Rocky Devereaux jabbered on the phone. His nostrils were clotted with blood, his forehead was bruised, and he had machine oil smeared on one cheek.

The haze of white dust drifted so thick she could barely see. The blast had moved LXs around like toys, and blue-yellow commandos began to pick themselves up from the garage floor. The indistinct brightness grew. Clouds seemed to drift about.

People in Tory's LX shook their heads, wiggled a

503

finger in an ear, tapped a forehead, squinted. The air conditioning seemed to have cut out, and the air was thick. Devereaux shouted: "Mark? You out there?"

Then—the ground started to shake. Tory felt her teeth rattle. What now? Would she live to see David Gordon again? She clung to a metal shelf with both hands as her body got shaken around like a reed. The vehicle itself started groaning in protest, and loose panels inside vibrated loudly. Objects fell from shelves and crashed to the floor.

"My God! Look!" someone shouted.

The dust outside the portholes began to drift clear. Tory saw now what the brightness was: Devereaux's men on the outside had sapped a 50-foot section of the garage wall, and daylight streamed in through the drifting dust.

A huge mass hovered somewhere in the mist, and the mist lightened as daylight penetrated through a fine powder of concrete gone aerosol in the explosion. It seemed to be a constellation of glaring round lights.

A monster shape loomed up, then rolled over the rubble and into the garage, almost too big to fit: an "Ike" MBT-2010 Eisenhower main battle tank with 175 mm. gun, a rack of missiles, a Vulcan III gatling gun capable of firing thousands of rounds per second, two mortar tubes, a flame thrower, and two Winchester rapid-fire armor-piercing cannons. The leviathan's quad turbo-nitro-diesel engines howled and whined with dinosaur glee. The long barrel had pointed backward as the tank crunched through the broken walls—now the tube swung from back to front; the tank never even faltered. The twin Winchesters rapid-fired, tearing lightly armored rebel LXs like paper. Rebel gunners fell by their weapons.

Other commandos scattered, dropping their light arms as they ran. Those who were too stubborn to quit died in the next few dozen seconds.

Another tank rolled in behind the first.

And another. The ground shook. The floor of Tory's LX chattered audibly, and fallen objects bounced around.

Like primordial giants, the Ikes rocked and rumbled over the mound of wall-debris. Everything shook. The rebellious commandos turned from their intended attack on the Iowans and shot at the tanks. The air filled with fireflies as the Vulcans opened up. The commandos became a bloody soup, washed against the opposite wall in a tangle and mangle of boots, helmets, and bits of yellow and blue cloth. Another Ike rolled in, and another.

One rebellious officer ran into the open, knelt, and aimed a shoulder-fired rocket. Before he could fire, an Ike's main gun coughed. The tank rocked gently and kept coming. Where the officer had been was a patch of dusty daylight. The officer and his rocket had been pulverized. There was a hole in the garage floor. From a hole in the ceiling hung a five or six ton palm tree upside down in a dusty glow of lobby daylight. Its thick trunk came to rest standing up on the garage floor, while its car-sized rootball rained fine soil down in a rain-like torrent.

In all, six MBT's drove down the line of commando LXs. It was not a battle but a rout. It was over in about five minutes. Their Winchesters barked. The rebel LXs, and anyone foolish enough to stay in them, became burning junk. Vulcans stammered in smoky bursts. The tanks continued on their foray, and reduced the 3045th's supplies and vehicles to blazing cinders.

Devereaux made fists and laughed. "Great day for the Irish! Charlie, roll this contraption out! To the White House! Get General Norcross's office on the horn!"

The loyalist LXs wheezed into racketing life and started to move.

Devereaux stuck the cigar in his mouth. "Okay! Let's go!" An aide placed four-star pennants to flutter on the fenders of the LX. "On to the White House!"

Tory felt grateful to be alive. She held on with both hands as the vehicle surged forward. Devereaux said into the phone: "Nice job, Sherwin. I need an escort, how about it?—I've got this guest on board, by the name of Carberry, ever hear of him? He's anxious to join up with the President.—What's that?—Three Ikes?—How I love thee. Be sure and have them run with their turrets turned backward or the boys in the White House will think we're coming at them. And thanks!" As he hung up, Charley handed him another phone, and he spoke briefly with General Norcross.

"Young lady," Senator Carberry told Tory, "I owe you the deepest apology. Believe me, the President and I will have a long chat, and I will mention your name specifically." He added: "I take it Captain Gordon is your—?"

"I'm in love with him," Tory stated. "We're going to get married."

"He's a very heroic young man."

"How is—?"

"He is alive, last I saw. I'm afraid it was touch and go there. You'd better pray."

"Thank you." There must be hope! She held her

hands over her face and felt faint as she thought about the possibility of his dying. How could her luck always be so grim? God, what have I done to deserve this? Some voice inside her protested at that thought: Why must I always think the worst? I deserve better!

Devereaux hung up. "Norcross is with the President. They managed to pull in some reserve units, Marine guards, odds and ends, and they just barely fought off a dickhead attack. Now they've got troops rolling in from everywhere, and the situation is still fluid, but I think we'll get it under control." He added. "There is one thing that puzzles me deeply. Why did these guys go out on a limb like this? It couldn't just be that Mason and Montclair have flipped their wigs. There has to be something more."

"A foreign power?" Carberry wondered out loud.

"I dunno," Rocky said. "They have to be waiting for tactical and strategic support from someone, somewhere, but who or what?"

"A nuclear device," someone suggested. "A secret weapon?"

"Oh God," Devereaux said. "Get me Norcross again. I'd better make sure he's thinking the same as we are."

At that moment, they crossed one of Washington's major traffic circles, Logan Circle, and Tory had simultaneous views down two broad avenues. The noisy, bumpy, smoky LX made it hard to see straight and she held on for dear life, but stared out in fascination. It had rained lightly during the night. The slick streets reflected a cold, pearly morning light. The early sun hid behind quilted clouds charcoal-brushed, in other areas milky white. Distant landmarks—the Capitol

Dome, the Washington Monument—poked through surly fog.

Vermont Avenue was littered with bodies and overturned vehicles near Logan Circle. Cars sat at odd angles, and a tank burned orange-red framed in black smoke. A skirmish line of infantry moved at a crouch toward the Atlantic Hotel and Convention Center, whose blackened walls and window-holes billowed with smoke as guns fired.

New Hampshire Avenue, which also crossed at Logan Circle, was still aflame with battle. Two old M70 Abrams tanks just then fired. They rocked on their carriages and spouted balloons of gray smoke. A second later, plumes of dirt erupted several thousand feet down the street.

Tory's convoy screamed down a long avenue lined with fresh military vehicles on either side. Untested soldiers awaited their turn at battle, holding their M16's while crouched behind vehicles. Every face was taut with fear and curiosity. Quite a gauntlet for the commandos to run on their way to the White House, Tory thought.

"Yessir," Rocky was saying. "I'd get the FBI, the CIA, everyone on it. Something more is going to happen. I got a nose for it. This just can't be all there is. They would have never—Yessir. Thank you."

Apparently satisfied with that conversation, Devereaux lit his cigar, popped a ventilator hatch to let out the smoke, and settled back.

Tory peeked again. Smoke still drifted on New Hampshire Avenue. She saw exploded LXs, tanks, and trucks. Nurses and doctors in field gear triaged the walking, the wounded, and the dying at a field station that consisted of three assorted civilian ambulances and a furniture van. American flags flew everywhere. Sullen, handcuffed prisoners in blue-yellow fatigues were herded into buses. Young GI's moved about their tasks with glum efficiency, but cheered and made victory signs when the LXs passed.

A half dozen MEAS choppers flew overhead, fast, in formation, rooftop level, and Tory thought of Maxie. She called via com button.

"—is Captain Bodley," said a familiar voice. Just then something exploded near Maxie. There was a steady noise that sounded like bees buzzing, or was it devils shouting in hell?

"Maxie, it's me, Tory. Where are you?" She pictured Maxie, stethoscope around her neck, hair flying.

She sounded sad or tired. "Someone just handed me this phone. All our com buttons are out. We need ambulances, nurses, doctors, major medevac."

"I'll tell General Devereaux."

"Who? Tory, where have you been?"

"In the hotel with the 399th."

"I heard about that. Figures you'd be there. Driving the front tank, no doubt." Tory heard machine gun fire on Maxie's end. Three loud crump blasts followed one after the other.

"LX's," Tory corrected. "What are you doing?"

"I'm standing here in the rain, up to my elbows in blood, and brains, and mud, trying to tape this guy's chest back together so he can be moved. The other one here has both legs off, but we taped up the stumps, and wrapped him ready to roll." Now Tory understood the chorus from hell: it was the moaning and screaming of wounded soldiers in agony, some dying, all terrified. Maxie said: "My chopper was shot down last night. The sons of bitches keep shooting our choppers down. A sniper picked off another one of the nurses during the night. She was my friend."

"Oh Maxie, I'm so sorry." Suddenly she realized the hell her friend must be in.

Maxie's voice was all energy, white-hot, almost inhuman. "I'm down to one doctor and she's half out of it with shock. Meanwhile, our guys are getting creamed over here. The streets are all screwed up, and we can't move the wounded out to Bethesda and Reed. I love ya, Vick. If we get out of this alive, let's disco."

"You'll get out alive," Tory said. "I love ya too, Maxie."

"Thanks. If you meet a guy named Tom Dash, and if I don't get out, tell him we'll have that pizza some other time."

"You met a guy? A nice guy?" Tears were streaming down Tory's face as she tried to keep up a false cheer.

"Yes. He's a nice boy. Last I saw he was trying to lead a bunch of wounded guys out of here. I sure hope they all make it through. This whole thing is such a bummer, Tory. What a drag. I don't even have time to cry."

"Did you dump that snake oil doctor yet?"

Her voice came with a throaty little chuckle. "He's in a straight jacket. That's another story."Maxie's voice suddenly dropped. "Oh Tory."

"What?"

"This boy just died on me. His name is Tom O'Leary. I thought he was going to make it. He was doing so good. I am holding him here in my arms." There were five more crump sounds, a long rattle of machine gun fire, and the continuous wailing of wounded. "Bye, Tory. I've got some badly hurt GIs here. We need help. Send us transportation! Send us cover and get us out of here!"

"I'll tell General Devereaux. Where are you?"

Maxie told her, and Tory explained to General Devereaux. Rocky spoke hoarsely on the radio. "Mark? Goddammit, where are you?—Listen, Mark, we got some Army nurses in trouble on the corner of—what's that?—I can't! Come on, I'm busy headed for the White House. I'll send twenty LXs and three Ikes, it's all I've got handy. Do me a big favor, old buddy, drive your tanks over there and cover my boys and those nurses. Anyone you see shooting nurses, back a tank over him a couple times, do you hear? Call Conrad MacIntosh and have him run some trucks over to help those nurses. They've set up a temporary field dispensary between some wrecked buses. Got a bunch of wounded soldiers need to get to a hospital." A minute later, the three tanks, and most of the LXs following Devereaux's, peeled off one by one, each making a snappy turn with a big roar and a gout of black diesel smoke, and speeding away down a side street. Tory prayed they'd get there in time to save Maxie from harm.

CHAPTER 51

While the dust was thinning out, and before the commandos overhead could start shooting, David and Mike Lewis jumped off the platform, landing on another tunnel mouth a floor below.

"We've got to go up and check on Goldman!" Mike insisted.

"Agreed," David said. "Let's go." They found a perpendicular cross-shaft and climbed up a set of metal rungs. They found Goldman dead of a single shot to the heart, and pulled his limp body back into the shadows. "We'll send someone for him when it's all over," Mike said.

David picked up Goldman's assault rifle and ammo pouches. Hearing voices, he sprayed the door above with bullets. Another body dropped down into the shaft, and he felt an insane craving to kill all these shaven-heads.

Mike spoke into his com button, but there was no answer. "That explosion must have knocked out my com. They can't send anyone up here for us. Their priority is to bring Carberry to the White House. Is there another way out of here?"

David shrugged. "You got me. This place is a nightmare of hidden service tunnels." He pointed behind him to the shaft. Mike gave Goldman's body a pat on the shoulder, a farewell ruffle, and slid past David. "Hurry, man. Let's get out of here."

As David and Mike started down into the utility tunnel, the sounds of battle erupted from the elevator shaft behind them. They heard what sounded like cannon fire and rockets exploding, and exchanged puzzled looks. The sound was as if an ammo dump was in the process of blowing up. Whatever it was, the thought mirrored in their eyes as they exchanged worried glances, it could not be good.

No time for worry now. Their first order of business was to escape before commando search teams found them. Their second order would be to hide out until it was safe, or, if possible, to escape from the hotel and get to friendly lines.

Cautiously, sometimes a step at a time, the two men advanced. Often, they heard the voices of their enemies just feet away through a thin wall or around a corner.

A new sound began to be heard: the muffled slams of exploding artillery shells. The hotel was being shelled from outside. Each explosion echoed in the tunnel walls and echoed back and forth like an evil whisper.

Smoke drifted lightly and ominously in some parts of the airconditioning system. The one thing David dreaded most now was being caught in a massive conflagration. If the hotel went up in flames, most likely he and Mike would die quietly and insidiously of smoke inhalation. The flames might never even reach them.

"That smoke is getting worse," Mike said, coughing, as they walked through a brick tunnel whose floor was so thick with dust that it was like walking on sand.

David raised his hand and listened. "It's quiet out there," he whispered.

Mike's eyes were upturned and wide in his dirt-streaked face. "Yeah. We must be in a quiet part of the hotel." The artillery barrage continued outside, but the babble of voices between explosions seemed to have evaporated.

David pointed to a laundry shute stenciled 10th Floor. Red water pipes for fire emergencies flanked the laundry shute. Creeping carefully along the wall, they came to a service entrance. The door also read, in larger letters, 10th Floor.

Just as David was about to reach for the door handle, the door slammed open.

A group of commandos burst in from the outer corridors, fleeing in panic, but they still had their weapons. They spotted David and Mike and raised their weapons to fire.

David pulled back against the wall, just in time to avoid a hail of bullets that flew past and knocked chips off the bricks. David felt the sting of brick debris on his face and brought the assault rifle up. He sprayed the exposed commandos with about thirty seconds of unremitting fire, barrels blazing, and watched them drop.

Mike had been hit. Covering, David dashed out to the fallen man and sat down. He cradled Mike's head on his lap. Mike had difficulty speaking, but he mouthed a word and twitched a finger, pointing to a fatigue pocket. He looked up with huge, imploring eyes and his mouth was open in one unrelenting gasp for air.

David probed in Mike's pocket until he touched something—he knew instantly what Mike wanted. David pulled out a photograph of an attractive red-headed woman with frizzy hair and a playfully crooked smile. Two tow-headed boys of eight or nine were in the picture, one on either side of her. David felt Mike's hand on his wrist in a grateful grasp. David held the picture in front of Mike's face. "She looks like she has a nice sense of humor," David said. Mike seemed to want to talk with the woman. Mike moved his eyes, as if he were staring at the picture through a false light, a smoky room, and unable to make out clearly, but struggling—as David held the picture up, Mike made a brief croaking noise and grew still. He did not become heavier, nor more limp, just—he was gone. David, placing his emotions in a temporary holding basket like a letter to be answered later, tucked the picture in Mike's pocket and rose.

Four commandos sprawled lifelessly in the thick dust. Only one of them still moved, moaning and feebly trying to raise one hand.

Quickly, David went through the dead men's packs, until he found a spare blue and yellow uniform. He donned a camouflage cap, and donned one of their shirts, only buttoning three or four buttons. Under that, he still wore the Class A uniform trousers and black shoes in which he'd reported to work. He wanted to be ready to toss the commando uniform off if he had to, in case friendlies started shooting at him.

David checked the wounded man, but he was dying, and there was nothing David could do for him. The man had two bullet wounds to the mid-torso and already had lost a lot of blood. His eyes were glazed, and his body was limp. Still, he moaned faintly.

David grabbed the man's wrist and lifted. With great effort, he got the limp figure over his shoulders. He felt warm blood running down his legs as he carried him out into the hotel corridors.

As David staggered with his load, the scene outside was pandemonium. They were in a wide main corridor in the middle of Tower 2, from the looks of it. The carpeted floors were littered with debris. Here and there were upturned maid service carts, broken ammo cases, a sock or a cap or a boot. The corridor had the acrid smokehouse stench of cordite, and a thick pall of smoke hung motionless, thicker in some spots than in others. From broken doors and windows, fresh air blew through as if he were outside. The corridor ran out in each direction toward a T-intersection with the floor's outer perimeter corridor.

Seeing several of commandos repairing a machine gun in a hall niche, David put the dying man down and told them: "Call a medic."

He did not stop to ascertain if they obeyed. They made no sign that they recognized him from the alarm, but concentrated on their deteriorating situation. What had happened? David wondered. Why had their leaders gone out on a limb like this, when the situation must have been hopeless from the beginning?

Rather than try the elevators are out, David decided, better to try for an exit stairwell.

He stopped to let several commandos pass carrying a large mud-colored container of mortar rounds, each man holding one handle of the heavy box. They headed toward the outer walls, which, David saw as he drew near, were pocked with holes. The thick concrete had been hit by so many shells that, in places, one hole overlapped another. Each hole was about a foot in diameter. That was some strong concrete, David thought, luckily, or the whole building would have started to collapse by now.

The rounds still came in, sporadically, and each time, the walls shook and emitted a gout of shattered concrete and drifting dust. A shell exploded not far away. A group of commandos operating a machine gun at a window hardly seemed to notice as they kept firing into the city. The window had long been blown out, its frame gone to the very floor. A fresh wind blew in.

The rest of the outer corridor of the hotel was equally a disaster. The carpets were covered with blood, dust, and debris. Bodies lay everywhere, sometimes several in clumps, in that bilious blue and yellow camouflage cloth. Sometimes the dead men had the courtesy to lie face down as if asleep. At other times they lay sprawled and grimacing. One corpse's face had been peeled off leaving only one eyeball and grimacing teeth.

David was dead tired, but he thought of Tory and was anxious to get out of the hotel. Again and again, the floors shook as tank and artillery fire hit the hotel. Windows rattled.

Through a particularly huge hole, David glimpsed an astonishing sight. The city of Washington was a battleground. Thick dirty smoke roiled in the streets, punctuated here and there by the flash of a rocket of the wink of a tank muzzle. Lots of objects burned. As he watched, a tank tormented in a narrow street by snipers shoved an accordion bus out of its way, turning the bus into a shattered v-shape. The tank climbed over the bus and rolled away, raking the houses on either side with machine-gun fire. Finally its turret swung around. Rocking on its chassis, the tank delivered a shell whose explosion sent a Civil War-era brick building down in a shower of dust. This, in downtown Washington.

The commandos David encountered did not look dispirited, but there was something seriously bleak about them, and he heard them speak of a betrayal—he wasn't sure what, and he did not stop to ask for details.. The halls were strangely empty, littered with clothing, bandages, empty shell casings.

David found a stairwell and bounded down ten flights of stairs, at one point climbing over a slippery pile of dead commandos. In the lowest stairwell, he found the door lying down and a path open out of the hotel. It led across a lawn, where bodies lay, wet from the rain. It led to a shattered wall, part of which had collapsed inward, revealing the city beyond: acres of rubble, a no-man's land.

David thought of making a run for it, but decided against it. Too risky. And he still had something important left to accomplish. For a moment, he still contemplated fleeing. It looked inviting, but no thanks. In the distant drizzle, he glimpsed the broken body of a downed helicopter with Red Cross markings. The chopper burned with black oily smoke rising from its trashed interior. David heard gunfire from above and saw bullets bouncing off the water-soaked walls. He turned away and went back into the bowels of the hotel.

David made his way toward Tower One through corridors littered with bodies and wreckage. His passage was brightly lit by morning sunlight that streamed through shattered skylights. The sweet, damp wind blew in freely.

He found that the lobby was obliterated. The glass ceilings were gone, and it was raining on the flattened tropical garden. The marble floors were heaved up and broken like brittle candy. A huge Canary Island date palm hung upside down into a hole in the ground, and David could see daylight on twisted vehicles in the garage below. Thick diesel smoke, tainted with a medley of acrid smells, rose from the garage in a column to heaven, dissipating in drizzly sky like an offering.

Outside, artillery still fired steadily. Fighters ducked from rubble pile to rubble pile. The floor shook every few seconds as a new shell landed.

David headed upstairs, using an unscathed inner stairwell. He found his way to Tory's former work place. Emergency lights still burned along the way. He came to the restricted rooms that contained CloudMaster. Kicking the door in, weapon ready, he was surprised to see a smallish figure busy in a room marked Data Processing. "Hello?" he said pushing a disangled door in and stepping over a pile of crumbling drywall. The figure turned, and he instantly recognized her. "Glad you're alive!" he said.

"Captain Gordon!" said Jet Steffey removing her head walker's gear.

They shook hands, then hugged. She grinned pixielike. Her butterscotch face was smudged, but her eyes twinkled undaunted. "Didn't know you were still around, Sir. Where've you been?"

"It's a long story. Still working?"

She sighed. "Yes, I couldn't get out. I called home and my husband took our baby to my mother's, so they're safe. I figured I might as well keep busy, though everyone else left. I promised Lieutenant Breen I'd look for Ib's file. With Tabitha gone, she wanted something to show Carberry. It's probably all too late now, huh? How is she?"

"She's with General Devereaux," David said. "Find anything yet?'

"Yes. Take a look at this." She turned the screen slightly so David could see better. David leaned forward and looked at a handwritten document. He stared at it, using a small hand-shaped cursor to "tug" the image around on the screen. There were several pages of neat handwriting, with many words crossed out and replaced by other words above them. "What is this, Jet?"

"It's the document Ib found. The one he wanted to give you the night he was kidnapped."

"Huh? Who wrote this?"

"Robert Lee Hamilton, Sir. Ib says he did a hand-writing analysis. This is the document Vice President Cardoza was about to deliver to President Bradley. Now you see why he was murdered that night in Washington State, and these generals made it look like a militia plot."

"I still don't get it," David mumbled, but it wasn't true—the awful realization was already dawning on him. As he came to the beginning of the document, it stared him right in the face. There, printed in bold letters across the top of the page, were the words: "Constitution of the United States of America."

The words that followed didn't seem quite right.

Then he remembered: he'd heard these words spoken in the hotel before the insurrection.

Jet spoke the words out loud. "This is the constitution that the generals wanted to institute to replace the old Constitution."

"I'll be—," David muttered. "Those sons of bitches, excuse me."

"Hamilton wrote this over a year ago, Sir. He was not only in it with them, he betrayed everyone—he was the leader."

"And he's dead," David said, "murdered. What does that mean? Someone bumped him off as payment for failure? Because this whole thing is clearly a failure? Or does someone want him out of the way because there is another plot?"

She handed him a set of head walking goggles and explained: "There is more, Sir. The CloudMaster in the hotel is down. I've found one cable connection still up, and I managed to network into the machine at the White House. I'll show you what I've found."

David put on the goggles. Instantly, he found himself in a fantastic landscape of cyberspace, a city of the imagination, peopled by blurs and shadows as in an architect's rendering of a building as yet unbuilt. "You don't have to do anything, Sir. I've installed us in tandem, so anywhere I go, you go." David found himself riding with her in a surreal taxicab of sorts. It was black, white, and gray, but he almost could have reached out and touched the dash. Only there would be no dash. It was all a metaphor.

"I wish Ib could be here to see this," she said. David found himself being transported along a street. Traffic whizzed all around them, and at one point he almost physically cringed because a huge truck bore down on them and lunged away at the last moment.

"What was that?" he asked.

"A file packet," she said. "We're in the data stream, sorta. Actually, the data is a river under our feet, so to speak. Everything here is a metaphor."

"I remember that from the previous tour," he said. The cars and so on were analogs of the data in the stream below. That way you could track the message packets.

"Watch where we are going," Jet said. Her taxi turned a corner into a huge warehouse with ornate neo-Roman pillars on either side of the entrance. David found himself leaning into a turn that never actually happened. "We were never allowed up here before, Sir. We ran the system from the CloudMaster hardware downstairs, but we never got near the application programs. This is the program, Sir, that I believe Ib and Tabitha and who knows how many other people were killed for. And there is something else."

"Tabitha mentioned this Federov program," David said. "I'm confused. I thought we were looking for a list of names."

"That too," Jet said nodding. "I'm sure Ib had this all figured out. It's too bad they got to him—he might have prevented this entire tragedy." The taxi glided under a sign, FED-OIB-A, and into a large, semi-dark bay a hundred feet on a side. Embedded in the walls were moving pictures of large masses of people waving little books. "It's Algeria 1990. The scenarios aren't lit because the program isn't working on that module. In Algeria, during their first free elections ever, the people voted to get rid of their new secular

Constitution and replace it with the Koran. They voted for fundamentalism over democracy. I know this now because I've cruised up and down here all morning checking these modules out. Each module has a view-me option that tells the user about itself. There's one for Hitler coming to power after being elected in the Weimar Republic, one for Lenin, one for Athenian democracy being destroyed by demagogues in the 400's B.C. There's one thing that puzzles me." David watched as they coasted to a halt just before a brightly lit bay introduced by the words: FED-OIB-N. "I don't get it, Sir. What's N?

Gunfire rattled far away. It went on for some time, while David and Jet explored the Federov application program. David was astonished by huge conceptual relays linking the entire nation in a web of fiber-optics. He and Jet sat parked on a virtual hill overlooking a city, no, a nation of lights, almost like a couple parking. Only he and Jet sat silently, each preoccupied with personal thoughts, when shouting broke David's reverie.

His shoulder was roughly shaken, and he jerked the headset off. There stood Colonel Bellamy, grinning broadly. He was accompanied by a squad of New Mexico reserve infantry. Bellamy said: "It's over. We've stormed the assembly and the skinheads surrendered. There's a few more on the roof of Tower 3. And there's still fighting near the Mall, but we're cleaning it up." They all cheered and shook hands.

It was beginning to end, then, he thought, and his knees felt weak. He thought of Mike and hoped his comrade was still alive. And he thought of Tory, suddenly, very clearly, and realized after all they had been through there was nothing that could stop them from being together—certainly not a horrific mistake she'd made as a neglected and distressed child. He loved her more than he could ever have dreamed of loving Kristy. He would marry Tory. He would! It was firm in his mind now—not a shadow of a doubt.

Only Jet stayed in the world of metaphor. Suddenly she said: "Captain Gordon! Come here quick! I've got it! I know what's going to happen! This isn't over! It hasn't even started yet!"

ANN Breaking News with Allison Miranda

ALLISON MIRANDA: We have several stunning developments. Chairman Carberry was rescued from the Atlantic Hotel in a daring raid by reserve generals acting against the so-called Hotel Generals. A battalion of the 399th Infantry Division broke out of the hotel complex and headed for the White House after freeing CON2's chairman. Hostage negotiators report dramatic news in the standoff with the Hotel Generals. Generals Robert Montclair, Felix Mason, Louis VanOort, and several others reportedly have committed suicide. Informed sources say the generals realized all hope was lost when General Norcross sided with the President and ordinary soldiers did not join their commando units. They claimed Norcross had been in the plot with them, but changed his mind at the last moment, a charge the Pentagon vehemently denies. Information is extremely sketchy at the moment, but we are told the Hotel Generals ordered their commandos to shoot them rather than face trial in this coup that seems to be unraveling. The commandos were allegedly told to douse the bodies in gasoline and burn the bodies on a hotel rooftop. Heavy smoke is pouring from the top of Tower Three. A spokesman for the commandos of Unit 3045 says they will release all the delegate hostages unharmed, along with a number of uninvolved military personnel. Among the released were a number of lightly injured personnel. About eighty commandos are said to be still holed up in Tower Three, demanding free passage to the fundamentalist dictator General Alberto Shopenhauer of Colombia.

CHAPTER 52

Tory's LX was stopped at several checkpoints. "Sir, tell your tankers to keep their barrels pointed backwards if you're going toward the Capitol area," an MP major told General Devereaux in a tone that suggested he said this for the hundredth time, "because we have sniper teams on the side streets. Anyone who points a gun the wrong way within a mile of the White House takes a rocket, no questions asked!"

They got as far as the Reflecting Pool, only on the strength of Devereaux's fluttering pennants. There, they had to get out and walk the rest of the way through cordons of civilian and military police.

Tory saw a White House blacked out and glowering in patchy dawn light. A circle of tanks and trucks surrounded the outer sidewalk. Rifle and gas mask carrying members of various uniformed police and military services formed a human shield many bodies deep all around. A Marine Corps unit had hastily deployed several field pieces on the lawn, Tory assumed to protect against air attack. Sandbagged machine gun positions were all around. Helicopters circled overhead. In the clouds, jets circled slowly sounding like knives on grindstones.

Tory clambered out of the LX with Peggy, General

Devereaux, and Senator Carberry. If Carberry felt any apprehension about meeting with a President with whom he'd differed publicly on so many issues, he did not show it. Tory felt embarrassed to be at the White House in her disheveled, dirty uniform, with an infantry officer's too-large shirt

General Devereaux negotiated with a stern-faced Marine colonel who kept shaking his head. Devereaux waved his cigar. The colonel took Devereaux's .38 Special and frisked him and Carberry. Devereaux's eyes were big as masher marbles when he handed over his precious relic. Tory was patted down by women Marines, her .45 taken. The weapons were tagged, to be stored for later return.

Secret Service agents led Carberry, Devereaux, and Tory into the White House through a heavily guarded entrance, along carpeted corridors, to a large reception room gorgeously paneled in walnut. There, President Cliff Bradley and General Billy Norcross held court. The two leaders shook hands with well-wishers and thanked those who had come to stand or die. Tory sensed nervous levity amid a general impression that the coup was about over. Only Rocky Devereaux looked worried as he paced dourly and tried to figure out the poker hand he'd been dealt.

Tory shook hands with President Clifford Bradley and decided he wasn't what the press and the talk shows had made him out to be. He was big, he had a strong grip, he had keen eyes, and a gentle smile. She felt self-conscious about her lumber jack appearance, but he patted her hand warmly and said: "I'm grateful and you will all be invited for a big thank you dinner when this blows over."

Tory glowed. "Sounds great, Mr. President."

President Bradley and Senator Carberry warmly shook hands. Then they moved together toward a table of coffee and danish as though they'd always been friends. An aide followed them with a hand phone. "Mr. President, it's the U.S. Ambassador in Berlin. He says it's extremely urgent."

"Ask him if it can wait until afternoon. We have a lot going on here."

The aide spoke with the ambassador, then said: "He says you must speak with him privately. It's extremely sensitive."

"All right," the President said with a sigh. "I'll grab some coffee and danish here, and talk for a moment with Senator Carberry, and then I'll take it in my office."

Many people swirled around in this victory galaxy, military, FBI, Secret Service, White House, Congressional leaders like Senator Wayne Nichols and Representative Norm Delano. General Billy Norcross, hailed for siding the military with President Bradley, stood with his aides. Tory heard talk of Norcross as President Bradley's running mate in the next elections, which the Middle Class Party now looked sure to win.

Tory found herself a glass of cola and put some ice into it. It was the first cold drink all day, and she relished it. Next in her priorities, she approached a secretary and borrowed a com button. She was anxious to call David, but afraid the call might enable the commandos to find him. Perhaps if she asked General Devereaux?

She found Rocky Devereaux holding his cigar in one hand and a cup of coffee in the other. He stood in the entrance to General Norcross's office down the hall from the Oval Office. The office had a beautiful blond oak door with inlaid geometric figures. The door stood partly open and Rocky was regarding a large painting on the wall behind General Norcross's desk. "Mighty nice," he was saying, "mighty nice." It was a painting like those one saw in the Louvre—Napoleon, on a rearing stallion, waving a scroll of laws in one hand and a sword in the other. All around his steed, humans and goddesses engaged in a scene part battle, part orgy, and part symposium.

Tory turned to the larger room again, sipping her cola and feeling exhausted. Overwhelmed. She wasn't sure which more than the other. As her gaze roved, she noticed two naval officers chatting with two secret service agents over coffee and danish. The naval officers were in dress uniform, which surprised her. One was a boyish young blond with steel-rimmed glasses. The other was a kind of dour, ugly man of uncertain race who had the flattest, meanest, brownest eyes she'd ever seen; he seemed to frequently lick his lips with the point of his tongue. A repulsive man. Mud-Eyes. She averted her eyes.

Tory's borrowed com button beeped. "Excuse me," she told Devereaux.

"Sure," Devereaux said, eyeballing a table full of food outside. He sidled out.

"Tory, it's David!"

"David!" she squealed. "Hi! Oh God, I'm so glad to hear your voice!"

"You're okay?"

"Yes. Are you okay?" She made slight jumping motions. "Is it really you?"

"Yup. You sound like an angel from heaven. I'm tired, hungry, and scared. Where are you?"

"I'm in the city net with Jet. We're in CloudMaster,

chasing down Operation Ivory Baton. The program is still generating strange new output. Where are you?"

"I'm inside the White House."

"You're joking."

"No. We brought Stan Carberry to the President."

"Oh good. I think it's about over for the 3045th. You know what, though."

"I love you very much. What?"

"I love you very much too and would like to play some more monopoly. Meanwhile, Jet's driving down this alley here, and there are suddenly N's all over the place. You know, we thought this was something Montclair and his bunch were running. Now I'm not so sure."

"What do you mean, David?" Her eyes again drifted through the throng, past chatting generals, admirals, and senators, to the two naval officers. Hadn't David mentioned the men who'd kidnapped him? Men who looked like those two? A preppy blond and a mud-eyed lizard man?

The two men stood isolated and drank coffee, and even though they might conduct brief, smiling, shallow conversations here and there, exchanging congratulations, they remained observers who were not really part of the scene.

Something is wrong here.

In the same moment, Tory noticed President Bradley walking past toward the Oval Office. He carried coffee and a danish and looked so sad and weary, poor thing. Steel Rims and Mud-Eyes sipped coffee. They looked this way and that, and then exchanged flat glances with each other.

Oh no.

David said: "This guy Federov, an old Soviet, wrote a book on all the ways democracy will destroy itself. Algeria, '91; Russia, '17; Germany, '33; you name it. Someone wrote up a huge program, using a Harvard econometric program and a Navy weather program as some of the main processing engines...."

Heart pounding, heart pounding. Mouth dry.

"...Basically, the program runs a million factors through its sieves and filters and spits out scenarios for how close the U.S. is to any one of those outcomes. Right now, we're getting a strong reading about something called N—but we have no idea what it means." As he prattled on, Tory glanced at the throng around the coffee table while listening to David.

Steel-Rims and Mud-Eyes, the two phony Navy captains, suddenly walked by right in front of her.

God, no.

They didn't see her standing in the open office door as they walked past in the direction the President had gone, toward the Oval Office.

They are following him.

David's beloved voice faded into elevator music as her mind raced, as her thoughts trying to overcome a pounding sense of shock. Something was, like, really really wrong here.

To kill him.

What else could it be? Suddenly the details didn't matter. In an eyeblink, she realized that Devereaux had been right. This conspiracy had unguessed dimensions. The events at the Atlantic Hotel and Convention Center had been a sideshow. The main event was about to take place.

Must reach the President before they do.

"Love you, I'll call you back." She dropped the com button and started running.

She grabbed General Devereaux, making him spill his coffee. "Go round up Secret Service guys, tell them the President's in danger."

She ran out into the corridor.

Everyone was so intent on guarding the outside that almost nobody at the moment was thinking about guarding the innermost inside.

In the hallway, as she glanced toward the celebratory crowd, she caught a brief glimpse of General Billy Norcross. He didn't see her. In fact, he was so aglow that he didn't seem to see anything at that moment. It was just a glimpse of him, like a fawn in a car's headlights, and she had no time to look another second, but he drifted toward his office with a look of ecstasy. The glow of empire was in his eyes. He looked far beyond America, far beyond humble and homespun democracy.

She bolted toward the right, down a long empty corridor.

A man in a suit stepped out of an office and she grabbed his lapels. He looked alarmed and grappled for her wrists. "Secret Service?" she asked, noting a badge on his belt.

He nodded, started to grab her.

She shook his hands away. "Two men are on their way to kill the President. Follow me."

They ran down the hall together. "You said two of them?"

Tory nodded, and he drew his gun as he spoke into his collar button: "Echo Breaker, Echo Breaker! One Seven Emblem, One Seven Emblem. We have two tigers headed for Location One! I repeat, two tigers.

Probably armed! Wearing Navy uniforms. Echo Max, Echo Max!" As they jogged side by side, he continued speaking with other agents.

Tory and the agent rounded a corner and slowed to a halt. The closed door of the Oval Office was straight ahead. On the ground sprawled two Secret Service agents in suits, a man and a woman. Blood puddled around them, and their dead eyes stared straight up. Their chests were so mangled with a flurry savage knife wounds that flesh and cloth mingled in a bloody stew. How had the killers gotten knives past the check points outside?

Tory and her companion threw themselves against the door. It was locked.

The agent shot the handle off and he and Tory crashed into the room together.

As Tory's momentum propelled her staggering across the room, she glimpsed a horrific scene. The impostor Navy captains had the President on the floor between them. Steel-Rims tired to work a nylon garrotte with formed handles around Bradley's neck. Bradley had one hand inside the garrote and was fighting for his life. Mud-Eyes pulled on Bradley's obstructing hand, but Bradley was strong and was hanging in there, and Mud-Eyes raised a fist to punch Bradley unconscious. Steel-Rims changed tactics and pulled the garrotte to tow the President over his knee and break the President's spine in a thorough execution.

As Tory recovered her balance, Mud-Eyes's fist froze in mid-air as he turned and looked over his shoulder. Steel-Rims continued his frenzied assassination with gritted teeth and diamond-bright eyes. "Take them!" he shouted hoarsely.

Mud-Eyes moved like a lynx. He threw a thin dagger of composite materials that had, like the garrotte, escaped notice by metal detectors outside. Tory's Secret Service companion staggered back as the object embedded itself in his chest, and he collapsed helplessly. His gun fell. Tory, charged with adrenalin, caught the .357 magnum revolver before it hit the ground.

She fell backwards over his body, awkwardly, but landed rolling.

Steel-Rims gave the President a karate chop across the neck. She heard a crackling noise, and the President's head lolled to one side. His eyes slowly rolled upward and his mouth grew slack.

Mud-Eyes came at Tory. He had a composite knife in each hand and a deadly plan written in his eyes. She fumbled for a solid grip on the gun.

He and she were both moving very fast. Her brain, processing even faster, agonized at the minuscule differential between his running speed and her lifting speed.

She turned to face him, but could not raise the heavy gun fast enough.

Mud-Eyes hit her like a concrete mixer, knocked the wind out of her, but as she flew backwards, she squeezed her hand, felt the resistance against her trigger finger, and heard the explosion of the .357 magnum round, muffled by his body. She hit the hardwood floor and slid.

She rolled as she landed, and Mud-Eyes rolled with her, as if they were embracing. Only he was too weak for embrace now. Too weak—the knives slipped from his twitching fingers.

His eyes opened in shock as she involuntarily lay in this obscene embrace with him while he died in her arms. She lay on his chest, face to face, close enough to kiss. Repulsed, she watched blood fill his mouth, stirred by his flickering tongue. The blood bubbled up and drooled down one cheek making black puddles on the carpet. His reptilian eyes gave her a lingering starving look as though he longed to eat her.

She screamed and flailed away from him.

Steel-Rim had a satisfied grin as he pulled the limp President over his knee. He twitched the garrotte to get a new, tight fit around Bradley's neck and finish him off. Steel-Rims's face seethed with white-hot concentration as he gathered the strength of every muscle to give a tremendous yank that would break the President's spine.

Tory advanced on him with the revolver in both hands. The gun bucked as it barked repeatedly, deafeningly. She walked closer and emptied the gun into Steel-Rims's chest. Acrid gunsmoke drifted around her face, making her eyes tear, but she fired repeatedly in a dull, even rhythm. Each time, Steel-Rims's body jerked..

Steel-Rims's facial features slackened in a look of surprise, then regret. His arms faltered and he looked down at Bradley as though he loved him.

Then he looked up at Tory dreamily. She kept firing until nothing more happened. The clip was empty and the last shot, dead true between the eyes, shattered Steel-Rims's head and spattered the carpet and the front of the President's desk gray-burgundy.

Tory fell to her knees and embraced the dying President.

There was a terrible silence.

Then, all through the building, telephones began ringing.

🌐 ANN Breaking News with Allison Miranda ⚡

ALLISON MIRANDA: Pandemonium has broken out in the White House. Because of the news blackout inside, we have been unable confirm or deny a rumor floating out that the President has either been killed or is seriously wounded. An Air Force air-evac helicopter that sits round the clock on the White House roof helipad for just such an emergency is now powering up its rotors. Our correspondent says he can see dozens of armed men streaming into the White House—Wait, we have this phone contact now—it's with someone inside the White House—it's with the office of General Billy Norcross—and here is General Billy Norcross, speaking to us live from the White House, and maybe he will help make some sense of this chaos and pandemonium.

BILLY NORCROSS: I'm in charge here.

CHAPTER 53

Maxie was numb with exhaustion. The smell of drifting gouts of gunsmoke mingled with a still-subtle, but growing, stench of decay from bodies and body parts outside the perimeter of trashed vehicles at her medical station. The orderlies carried bodies to a spot in back, among some rocks. They'd long since run out of body bags and were simply stacking the bodies in a cleft among boulders piled up during recent construction. They first stripped uniforms from the dead to make bandages.

A constant stream of walk-in casualties flowed in. There appeared to be many sniper-trained commandos; several of Maxie's patients with minor injuries hid between the vehicles and scanned the horizon, ready with rifles to shoot back if they saw any more snipers. Explosions pounded steadily as tank and artillery fire rocked the city. Maxie was busy and tired, and by now ignored the constant rattle of machinegun fire, along with the popcorn-popping of small arms. Occasionally a rocket or a large shell pursued a slowly shuddering, maniacally whistling path to its target. Sometimes the impacts were far away, slamming air and ground alike. Sometimes the impacts were closer, deafeningly so, and sometimes tiny gravel fragments landed on the buses nearby and peppered Maxie's skin.

Numbly, Maxie kept on with the work. She was now the only nurse left. The woman doctor had disappeared; probably run blindly into the hazy light, staggering among rocks until someone picked her off. Maxie directed triage while her corpsmen stabilized whom they could. The corpsmen directed a small volunteer crew of brave souls to carry away those who were beyond help.

Suddenly, the rattle of gunfire grew close and intense. Men in the compound shouted and ducked for cover. Bullets whined past overhead, some slicing through the thin skin of the buses. Other bullets shattered the safety glass and sprayed the compound with stinging but harmless fragments. "Keep your eyes covered!" Maxie yelled as she ran to look. She threaded her way among men and women most of whom were on their knees and elbows, with their arms wrapped over their heads and their foreheads to the ground. "Stay down!" Maxie yelled as she stepped forward and into the crack between two buses that lay overturned, back end to back end. Glass fragments exploded around her, and she shielded her face. Her hands were bloody, but she ignored them. If the final attack was on, how could she evacuate her station now? Whom to take, whom to leave? She decided that she couldn't leave anyone behind, so they would all stay, she with them.

Hands reached out to help her, to pull her into the safety between the buses. A dead man lay sprawled in the center; there was no time to move him, so he lay on his back, legs spread, one hand on his blood-soaked fatigue uniform chest, the other stretched high over his shoulder as if he were doing the backstroke. The two remaining men wore flak jackets and helmets. They had several small ammo boxes and some loose ammo in a pile. She picked up the dead man's M20B2 field rifle, smelling the oil and burnt powder in it, and crawled forward with the two soldiers flanking her. Might as well die fighting, she thought. "What are they doing?" she asked.

"Ma'am, they're not shooting at us. Frank here caught a stray round. They're shooting over our heads."

Maxie peered out and glimpsed a startling sight. The low horizon, seen from her position, swarmed with men in blue-and yellow camo. Some wore helmets; others caps; and some showed their shaven heads. They popped up and down, firing their rifles. Out of sight, they appeared to have some field artillery, for she could see the gouts of smoke and hear the explosions as the shells streaked into the sky.

She pulled back in. "I have decided we are not going to evacuate."

One of the men was an older NCO. "I would suggest we stay put, Ma'am. We've got too many wounded. We'd be walking into the line of fire."

The other, a younger NCO, agreed. "They're not worried about us, or we'd be goners already. Please, let's stay put."

Maxie closed her eyes and sighed with relief that they agreed, though she couldn't admit that to them. Her relief was short-term, however, for in another second an explosion rocked the ground and showered dirt and glass on them. Maxie and her companions ducked down so hard she tasted brownish-red soil in her mouth. It caked her lips. She grimaced. Explosion after explosion rocked the ground. She held her rifle tightly.

"Let's pull back!" the NCO said as the wrecked buses around them began to bounce on the rolling earth, threatening to roll over and crush them. Maxie and the two men scrambled to get clear. She stumbled repeatedly as the ground bucked under her.

"Look!" someone cried. "Jets!"

Maxie looked up and saw the distant flashes of silver as five Air Force jets peeled away. The last two of their rockets were still flying, directly toward Maxie it seemed, and she was too fatigued to react. Instead, the rockets streaked overhead and exploded in the front lines of the mutineers.

"That's our side!" someone shouted, and everyone cheered. Sporadic fire still came from the mutineers' line, but the milling bodies were gone. Maxie scanned their position but could not see a single man moving. The air above their position was filled with one huge thunderhead cloud of gray smoke.

"Look over there!"

Maxie and everyone around her turned to see several tanks roll up the road toward the field station, coming from the direction in which the Japanese tourists had been killed.

"I hope they're ours," someone said.

"I have a feeling they are," said the tall black man who'd nearly been killed the night before. He grinned from ear to ear, despite the pain of his wounds. "But them ain't all tanks!"

"Earthmovers," Maxie heard someone exclaim. For every tank there were three huge yellow bulldozers, each the size of a small house. Must be ten of them, Maxie thought. Just three tanks? Another man said:

"They're civilian, like you see at the city landfill. What the—?"

The main battle tanks moved past Maxie's position, blazing with machine guns and rockets as they rolled. Every ten seconds, each tank would buck as an artillery round left its muzzle with a groaning noise and a puff of smoke. The tanks were aiming at objectives over the horizon.

Meanwhile, the 50-ton earth movers swung into action, pushing boulders and the debris of shattered buildings out of the way. "I know that song," someone said. "They are clearing a landing strip. Jesus, look, five minutes and they've cleared a football field."

One minute Maxie just heard the clattering of tanks and earthmovers.

The next minute she heard the thunder of rotors and the sky suddenly filled with black shark shapes. No, olive-drab attack helicopters. The sky was black with them, flying in a wide sweep formation ten across, several deep, stacked in layers so they could fire simultaneously. But they weren't firing anymore. The horizon just beyond the station was taken; they'd hold their fire for the next objective. Most of them flew on, but several circled for a landing on the newly cleared ground.

A cheer suddenly rose. Men and women raised their arms, waving. For in the sky, headed directly their way, was a long line of smaller choppers, and Maxie recognized their shapes and their sounds. They were MAES units, probably two or three dozen flights, like a hundred insects growing larger every second. Maxie swayed on rubbery legs and felt ready to just sit down and roll over and go to sleep. She still carried the rifle slung over one shoulder. Her job was done. Soon, she would have a double martini and go to sleep.

One by one, the medevac helicopters set down on the clearing just created by the earthmovers, which were moving back toward the safety of the city. Each MAES flight kicked up a cloud of dust as it set down. The nearest one was close enough that the wind of its rotors sent up a cloud of grit that stung Maxie's face and burned one eye.

A man jumped out. The pilot. He ran like a maniac, throwing his headgear aside as he ran toward Maxie. He grinned widely as he ran to her.

Tom Dash.

She let him take her in his arms. She wrapped her arms around his sinewy ribcage. She felt like going to sleep with her head pressed safely against his chest. He held her close so she smelled the aviation oil and the cleaning fluids in his flight suit. And his spicy aftershave.

Maxie wanted to talk, but she couldn't. She looked up at her tall aviator in disbelief. Wave upon wave of relief pounded over her like an ocean. He looked so crisp and healthy and handsome! His teeth shone like ivory, and his eyes looked wildly humorous and happy. A flood of sound from all those high-powered engines threatened to overwhelm her.

Somehow, Tom stepped aside and she faced a group of stern old men in heavy combat gear, who for a moment all looked like her father. She thought they were going to yell at her and ask why she had not used her gold credit card. What made it worse was that they all had lots of stars on their helmets, or colonels' eagles at least. A four-star general, saluted her. "Ma'am, I'm looking for a Captain Bodley."

She nodded, licked her lips. Swallowed hard. She wanted to start crying, and some of her facial muscles were trying to start that, but couldn't. She remembered she'd saved all her crying for the death of Tom Dash, but here he was alive, and now she could—when it was convenient and not terribly inappropriate—weep for all the dead and wounded here. At the same time she felt she should smile brightly, perhaps serve a cookie or some tea. So nothing came out. She felt Tom's arm over her shoulders, pulling her close. He rocked her gently against his side.

A three-star general said: "We're looking for some Army nurses, Ma'am."

The four-star general prodded gently. "I'm General MacIntosh, Ma'am." He looked around and his face seemed to become a dark shade of gray. "My God, what a place of hell this is."

"The stink," one of the generals said, looking ready to gag.

"We have a lot of dead people here," Maxie said. "We also have a lot of wounded who need urgent help." She pushed Tom gently away. She needed room to breathe. To think. "I'm," she started. Then she pushed the rest of the words out: "the only nurse left. I'm Maxine Lee Bodley." He looked stunned, so she added: "Sir." And she added: "I'm turning it over to you right now." She added a salute.

MacIntosh saluted again. "Thank you. Well done. Where are the rest of the nurses? The doctors?"

"They're all dead, Sir."

General MacIntosh turned a deeper shade of concrete, almost olive green. It took him some seconds before he could speak, and then, as dozens of men and women carrying stretchers and rescue cases jumped down out of the MAES choppers and came running full tilt, he could only say: "Oh God, I am so sorry."

ANN Breaking News with Allison Miranda

ALLISON: We have a remarkable story for you amid these many remarkable stories.

ANN has just learned that the former Second Lady, Meredith Cardoza, has issued a statement. She is currently at a U.S. Naval facility in Newport News, Virginia, where she was flown from the aircraft carrier U.S.S. Jimmy Carter.

Mrs. Cardoza says that, in the hours following her husband's murder, her life and the lives of her children were threatened if she spoke out about what she knew—what her husband had told her—about the conspiracy hatched by billionaire MCP founder Robert Lee Hamilton. We have some details now.

Mrs. Cardoza says she eluded Hamilton's security teams and flew to Rome, where she sought asylum at the Holy See. Vatican and Italian authorities worked frantically to secure the family while avoiding terrorist incidents caused by the U.S. insurrectionists. Under Papal diplomatic portfolio, and accompanied by heavily armed Italian Carabinieri in armored cars, the family were taken to Rome's Fiumincino International Airport under cover of night. While an Italian Air Force troop plane flew toward Spain on a decoy mission, the family and their guards were smuggled out of Italy on an Israeli El Al Airbus 9900 and flown to the Ivory Coast Republic in Africa, where Mrs. Cardoza and her children received asylum on property owned by the Archdiocese of Djibouti. For the past nine months they lived here in secret, guarded by Ivory Coast special forces.

Mrs. Cardoza alleges several recent plots to kill her, all of which failed. Her children are safe at an undisclosed location in France. She says it was her duty to return to the United States and help bring the renegade generals to justice.

President Bradley has issued a statement welcoming Mrs. Cardoza's support, and has asked all American citizens to work toward seeking a peaceful resolution to this second U.S. civil war.

CHAPTER 54

As Tory held the unconscious President, alarms and sirens went off in cacophony. Feet thundered in the halls on all sides. The doorway filled with bodies and brandished steel as men and women fell over each other to reach the President. Tory thought she was about to die in a hail of bullets from all the weapons aimed at her head. Then someone screamed: "Two men! Two men! She's not one of them."

"She shot them." "She killed them."

"Clear the deck! Clear the deck!" a hoarser voice bellowed, and a Secret Service agent holding an Uzi muscled his way in.

He in turn gave way as Navy paramedics pushed in with a stretcher.

For Tory, the next few minutes with their shouts and shoves blended in a kind of wet, warm hell. The President's body was removed from her embrace. She raised her hands to her eyes and cried. Hands on her shoulders squeezed and comforted, and as she recovered, she realized it was Devereaux on one side and Carberry on the other.

"He's alive but barely!" a paramedic yelled hoarsely.

"We have a pulse! We have a pulse!" a female nurse yelled.

"Open the airway," the hoarse voice boomed. "It's crushed. I'm cutting now. Cutting!"

"Chopper!" someone else screamed, "Chopper!" as Tory heard the deep throb of a powerful helicopter on the roof.

"Tape, use tape!" the nurse yelled. "Pressure! Stop the bleeding. I'm going to intubate. Oxygen! Over here!"

"Move! Move! Move!" a man waving an Uzi hollered to other men with Uzis. "Cover! Cover! Cover!"

Tory sniffled and rose in the ungainly crush of bodies. The many people crowded into the Oval Office moved as one, causing some of them to stagger against each other and crash against chairs and tables but they quickly lifted the President, now strapped in and taped up and tubed in and cut open, hand over hand to several Navy air crew in white bubble helmets and olive-drab flight suits waiting just outside the door.

Tory told Devereaux: "General Norcross is behind all this."

Devereaux nodded grimly. "Norcross. He was the final, core layer of the conspiracy. He found out about the plot to take over CON2. He let Montclair and Mason and the others think he'd back them, then he switched sides at the right moment. He had this planned with split second timing. Think of it—as the coup is put down, more uncertainty and terror as the President is murdered by unknown assassins. Coming to rescue us from all that chaos is Billy Norcross, America's Napoleon. Think how close he got!" He chewed on his cigar for a second or two, said "harrumph" to clear his throat. "Your grandpa'll be proud of you. God knows I am." He started toward the door. "Come on, we have to find General Norcross."

Devereaux pushed through the crowd of dazed, jabbering men and women and strode down the corridor. Tory followed. Devereaux said: "Now I see why Jankowsky's Task Force was bombed. Norcross was using them to try and learn if anyone was on his trail, and when the Task Force and Tabitha Summers got too close, Norcross's people terminated them. It was Norcross's people who killed Shoob, not Montclair's bunch." Devereaux stuck the cigar in his mouth and, with his fist, pounded on Norcross's office door. "God dammit, Norcross, open up!" He turned to two open-mouthed agents and said: "Bust this door down. Now!" When they stared at him, he bellowed: "Right now, boys." A phone kept ringing inside.

It took the two big men several lunges, and still they had to shoot off the door handle, before they got inside. General Billy Norcross was not in his office. A side entrance stood ajar. As they entered the office, Tory heard ANN on a radio:

🌐 ANN Breaking News with Allison Miranda ⚡

ALLISON MIRANDA: We seem to have lost contact with the White House. Minutes ago, we were speaking with General Billy Norcross, who told us that he has taken charge of the White House. A moment ago, as the news was unofficially spreading that an assassination had been averted and the President is alive, I repeat, the President is alive though his condition is not exactly clear at this moment, our line to General Norcross's office went dead.

From outside, the White House seems to be in pure chaos. An unknown body on a stretcher has been lifted onto the rooftop helipad by a frantic cluster of man, and the standby air-evac chopper is just now lifting off, apparently toward Bethesda Naval Hospital. Secret Service agents have begun sending people outside the building under armed guard. We have absolutely no idea what is going on. Hello? Hello? General Norcross?

CHAPTER 55

Devereaux ignored the anchorwoman's voice. He and Tory stared at the painting of Napoleon. "Look at that," Tory said. The Napoleon on the white charger in the picture seemed to have manic eyes as he directed the carnage of battle all around him. He waved a white scepter. "The Ivory Baton!" Tory said. "OIB-FED-N. Norcross or Napoleon, take your pick."

"What are you mumbling about," Devereaux said. "C'mon, we've got to catch Norcross. Oh why in the hell did those morons take my gun?"

Together, Tory and Devereaux rushed out Billy Norcross's private side entrance.

As they pushed through the crowd of stunned news people and men with assault rifles outside, he explained: "That guy I was just on the phone with? My people are on their way to capture him—the commanding general of something called the 9595th M.I. (Reserve) over in the Virginia woods. Another bunch of closet goose-steppers from the Wild West. Wanted to know if I work for Norcross and if he should begin the attack on the other side of the city. That was Norcross's other hidden ace. Good thing we just cut his flank off." They hurried across the lawn after the fleeing Norcross. A Marine briefly tried to stop them, but Devereaux, cigar butt gritted between his teeth, lifted his shirt collar ends and flapped all eight stars; the boy dropped back looking pale. The jog took them around the side to a small exclusive gravel parking lot hiding under huge pine trees. Devereaux tossed his cigar stub aside. "Listen," Tory said. She heard the slam of a car door.

"There's the son of a bitch," Devereaux said, pointing to a shadow in an expensive car. "The emperor." Tory moved to arrest Norcross, but Devereaux shook his head. He stopped to light a new cigar. "Wait a moment or two. Let's give His Imperial Highness a minute alone." Instead of a car engine starting, they heard a muffled pop. Devereaux said, "Jeez, he didn't waste any time."

As they neared the car, Tory smelled a whiff of gunpowder. The air was squalid and gray and filled with burning, but this was an exquisitely specific smell. Tory pulled open the passenger side door. Sitting crumpled against the driver side door was General Billy Norcross. In his left hand, clutched to his gut, was an ivory baton. His right hand loosely cradled the service revolver with which he'd ended his life. The man who would be emperor had his head tilted against the window. His mouth and eyes were open in a vacant expression. Blood, bone, and brains dribbled down the window from the open bowl of his skull.

🌐 **ANN Breaking News with Allison Miranda** ⚡

ALLISON MIRANDA: As we were led to believe in the last hour, we now know that indeed there has been an attempt on the President's life. That attempt failed, and the saga of the Hotel Generals has spun out a few more surprises.

The President is alive at Bethesda Naval Hospital and is expected to recover.

The Acting President is Rep. Norm Daley of Washington State, Speaker of the House.

General Billy Norcross, the apparent author of this coup attempt, committed suicide minutes ago outside the White House.

Acting President Daley has appointed Rocky Devereaux, an Iowa realtor and Army reservist, Acting Chairman of the Joint Chiefs of Staff.

President Bradley's two would-be assassins were shot to death during the assault, by a female U.S. Army officer of the Military Police Corps, we are told.

In an up-to-the-minute poll, more than 90% of American voters appear to favor Cliff Bradley if next year's presidential election were held today. We believe that is the highest approval rating a sitting U.S. president has ever received.

Reaction to Meredith Cardoza's statements has been overwhelming. After Mrs. Cardoza accused MCP leaders, including the late Robert Lee Hamilton, of murder, conspiracy, and treason, all but a handful of the elected MCP officials have resigned from the party and said they will form a new organization, the Stability Party. MCP offices in at least 14 states have been sacked and burned by angry mobs. There are reports that at least two state MCP officials, in Maryland and Oklahoma, were dragged into the streets and killed by lynch mobs.

CHAPTER 56

It was sunny, not too cold, the kind of Sunday Tory loved, a last Fall day before the golden leaves fell and the dark months of winter settled like a blanket. She would also be glad when this morning was over with, for the White House lawn was covered with flags, bands, people in uniform, families, Congressmen, Supreme Court Justices, and more families. Civilian police and state troopers from as far away as New Jersey, Pennsylvania, and North Carolina were on the streets to help keep order. The only military units in sight were two or three marching bands. Congress had quickly passed, and the President had signed into law, the so-called Roman Law, which forbade the presence of any military leader in the city at the head of his forces. This was similar to a famous law the Roman Republic had enacted after tossing out the last Etruscan emperor in 519 B.C. That and a consular system of government with checks and balances had delayed the republic's becoming an empire and a totalitarian state for five centuries.

Before the parade, hundreds of neatly uniformed military personnel and their family members milled about. Tory pressed as close to her love as she dared. She introduced him to her grandmother, who had come especially to Washington for today's ceremony, a white-haired woman in a buttoned up dark blue coat, who rarely smiled and wielded her black handbag as though it were a weapon. She did seem to like David. Maybe that was a good sign.

Tory did not fully trust that David would remain hers. I've had too many failures at love, she thought, but here I go again. He kept giving her looks that made her feel warm inside. Their hands were clasped together, and on them sparkled a pair of gold wedding bands that Maxie had borrowed from First Lady Mrs. Bradley, whose daughter was about to get married soon. Maxie had promised to return the rings shortly, when David and Tory had a chance to buy their own. Mrs. Bradley had been more than happy to help out. Maxie had arranged a brief ceremony at the White House late last night, with a hastily summoned Air Force chaplain officiating and Maxie and Tom Dash as witnesses. The big family wedding ceremony could come later, Tory and David thought. They were just happy to be husband and wife. Tory had to admit that she still felt some tight little band of fear inside; how could something this wonderful last for her? When all the excitement died down, would he get cold feet and—no, not David. She squeezed his hand, and he glanced at her with a little frown, then a look of understanding, at her uncertainty. He squeezed back, and she glowed inside.

White House tailors had sewn their new insignia of rank on last night. Effective last midnight, she was a captain, he a major.

"I want to take you away from here," David

whispered in Tory's ear. She whispered back: "I just want to go someplace and hold hands with you." Briefly, he squeezed her hand, in the secrecy between their bodies, and she squeezed back. Even that was beyond regulations for two officers on parade at the White House, but today who was really checking?

Maxie brought a nice-looking tall man in dress Army uniform. "Hiiiii y'all." Slash smile, small nose, smoky voice; but the sunny blonde hair was tamed with hairpins; and the lovely eyes had shadows, not enough to dull the glow of her personality, but those eyes had seen young people die. She hugged Tory. "When do we disco?"

"How about this evening?"

"That'll work," Maxie said. She whispered: "You like Tom?"

Tory examined Major Tom Dash. Of course Maxie would meet someone with a name like that. He seemed friendly and gentle enough, with just that aviator's thrust of chin, and that doctor's wrinkle of brow, as he and David were comparing notes about some man thing—how many pounds of thrust in an F-1 or some such thing, how many cannons on an Elizabethan barkentine. She told Maxie: "So far, I don't see the ego."

Maxie punched lightly with a white glove. "Never again."

"You're off to a roaring start, Max."

"My parents agreed to throw a big wedding next month. Everyone on Earth will attend. I know this is the man for me." She must have thought of past personalities, for her eyes slitted with anger and she made fists. "I'll never again let a guy be so mean to me."

"If you forget, I'll send you to Dr. Van Meeuwen."

"Oh look," Tom Dash said, putting his arm around Maxie as she pressed against him, "isn't that Allison Miranda of ANN?"

Indeed, Tory spotted the ANN news crew moving about, interviewing people. There were two camera persons and the unmistakeable attractive, dark-haired Allison Miranda. "They're coming our way," Tory said.

"Isn't she just gorgeous!" Maxie enthused.

"Hi," Allison smiled excitedly as she came toward Tory with an extended microphone in foam wind cover. "Aren't you the M.P. officer who saved the President's life?"

"Er," Tory began as cameras surrounded her.

Soon, uniformed personnel were called into formation, and civilians were gently herded behind rope enclosures.

A drum began its deep, measured tolling. An eight-person color guard with the U.S. flag and other banners moved onto the now-cleared lawn in synchronized steps. Ahead of them walked the Master of Ceremonies, a tall Army major with drawn saber raised before his dark blue dress-uniform shoulder.

The President and his wife stood at a podium, flanked by senior members of all three branches of federal government. Also present on the stage were Meredith Cardoza and her three children; and the top flag officers of each service, the Joint Chiefs, with their new Acting Chairman, General Rocky Devereaux.

Two bands waited, one at either end of the stage: a Navy brass band; and an Army fife and drum corps with antecedents in Revolutionary War times. Drums pounded and brass blared while the M.C. and his assistants formed the honorees into a long straight line, a motley of beautifully tailored dress uniforms representing all services. A Coast Guard admiral, master chief petty officer, and a U.S. Navy Muslim chaplain stood with Ibrahim Shoob's family at one end of the line. An Army Command Sergeant Major, a Colonel -rabbi, and a colonel waited with Solomon Goldman's wife and children. Similar clusters of bereaved families and military representatives stood in for Jankowsky, Tomasik, Lewis, and so many others. The M.C. escorted Tory to the podium, where she sat between Mrs. Bradley and General Devereaux. The new Speaker of the House, Representative Daley of Washington State, who had briefly assumed the role of Acting President of the United States while Cliff Bradley was in a coma, sat nearby. He was a dour man, resembling those old busts of Roman city fathers. He always wore black suits and never smiled. Life seemed for him to be one long funeral. He held on his lap a plain wooden box the size of a jewelry case.

The music fell silent and President Bradley opened with some brief remarks. There would be other ceremonies, and other bereaved families to be honored, as things were sorted out and fallen heroes buried, before this blot could pass into history along with the Civil War. Bradley singled out Tory for intelligence and heroism, and she didn't really hear the words for her ears were singing, with a rushing like waves on the shore. In the crowd, smiling, Grandma winked, and Tory winked back. Her next assignment was Command and General Staff College, and after that the sky was the limit. Rocky had told her: that star—maybe more than one—might end up on Breen shoulders yet! Loaded with medals, including the

Legion of Merit for Valor, Tory sat down. Mrs. Bradley put a gloved hand on Tory's sleeve and whispered affectionately: "The President, the Speaker, and a number of other people will put strong letters in your record." There was a round of cheering, and a brass rendition of The Army Song, for Tory.

Meredith Cardoza, in a firm, clear voice spoke about the necessity to forgive, and about the healing process that must now begin, the sooner the better. It would be the best tribute the nation could give her late husband.

One by one, the high muckity mucks made speeches.

Then the award ceremonies began. The Joint Chiefs walked along the line of honorees returning salutes, pinning medals, shaking hands. With them walked old sourpuss Congressman Daley, holding that small wooden box as if it contained the ashes of a loved one.

Uniformed soldiers carried satin pillow displays, one pillow for each type of medal—and the pillows were crusted with many medals. Today General Devereaux handed out many Purple Hearts for those wounded in action. Tory watched as the group moved to Colonel Richard Bellamy, and then to newly created Marine Corps Warrant Officer Marguerite "Jet" Steffey. The family of each person killed in action received a pillow full of medals, and lengthy condolences. Tory thought Hala Shoob would collapse as the generals and NCOs surrounded her; yet Hala stood with grim pride and accepted Ibrahim Shoob's medals in recognition for his heroism and sacrifice.

The generals and admirals, along with President and Mrs. Bradley, Congressman Daley, and other officials, moved into position near the color guard. A Marine solemnly escorted Tory behind them. The M.C. called out: "Your attention please." It grew very still. Just one drum made a very tiny beat, one stick tapped against one rim, softly.

Everything happened in slow time, solemn time, military time. The M.C. marched in dignified, gliding steps toward Maxie. Maxie stood between her mother and father, who beamed proudly. Maxie's uniform gleamed with the medals she'd just had pinned on. The M.C. approached Maxie; halted facing her close up; spoke a few words with her; and then about faced. Tory watched the look of puzzlement, or horror? grow on Maxie's face. Maxie stepped to the MC's right, slightly forward. Then, in step, they marched toward the color guard—two tiny figures on that green expanse.

The ticking of the drum stopped. It was very silent, like the silence of death, Tory thought, the stillness of tombs. Only the wind moved, ruffling the old officials' white hair, and the colorful regimental parade flags, some heavy with more than two centuries' battle ribbons. Maxie was one tiny, unwavering figure in that sea of colors.

"Lieutenant Colonel Maxine Lee Bodley, United States Army Nurse Corps," said Representative Daley, "on behalf of the Congress of the United States, I am privileged to offer you our sincere thanks. You represent not only yourself today, but all the nurses of all wars, all the women in our armed forces, all the daughters of America. I am proud to be able"—he opened the wooden box, assisted by Mrs. Bradley—"to present you today"—he draped the blue ribbon around her neck, with a medal that hung just over her bow tie—"with the Congressional Medal of Honor for remarkable valor in the face of enemy fire, and for service to your fellow soldiers and to your country above and beyond the call of duty." He read from a slip of paper: "With snipers killing fellow nurses around you, and your safe retreat advised, with casualties piling up, you did single-handedly establish and keep operating an emergency triage facility between several burned out city vehicles. While battle raged back and forth for many hours within yards of your position, while ordnance continually passed within inches of your person, you kept treating the wounded, thus saving many lives. When the last remaining medical officer was shot dead, you directed emergency surgeries. When bandages ran out, you used parts of uniforms. In the end, you were able to orient loyal armored, transportation, and infantry units that not only secured your position, but in fact led to a decisive maneuver in outflanking and isolating the disloyal forces who soon after surrendered. The Nation is grateful." He shook Maxie's hand without a change in his dour death mask and stepped back.

The M.C. raised his saber and bellowed. "Present—Arms!" The Joint Chiefs of Staff—and everyone else present in uniform—turned to salute the medal itself—and by default the woman wearing it—while the Army's Old Guard fife and drum corps played The Battle Hymn of the Republic. Tory, at attention and saluting, noticed Maxie and Devereaux were the only two persons who remained dry-eyed. How did they do that?

Then it was mercifully all over, and people were dispersing. Maxie and Tom came over, and Tory's and David's families mingled. Maxie had her arm around Tom's waist, and today nobody seemed to care about decorum. Tory felt David's hand reach for hers, and her fingers wriggling with his in a loving squeeze, and she almost, almost felt like letting go, like trusting him, loving him, which she wanted so badly to do.

"Let's flee this place," Maxie said. "I implore you. If I see another medal—"

Tory breathed a big gust of relief. "Yes, let's get out of here. You always know such fun places to go around town, Maxie, and maybe this time we can go without a big scene, what do you think?"

"I hope I don't have to spend the rest of my life saluting everybody," Maxie said.

Tory said: "Knowing you, it'll work out somehow."

Tom said: "Y'all, Maxie was talking about these wild discos and watering holes."

As Tom spoke, Tory noticed for the first time a bit of a countrified drawl, very soft-spoken.

"We're gonna party tonight," Maxie said pressing a white-gloved hand against Tom's chest, briefly putting her cheek against his shoulder. Her face had a happy glow.

"And I'm gonna teach you how to fly," Tom said putting an arm around Maxie.

Tory thought if you hurt her, I'll teach you how to fly. But he had gentle eyes; like David, and a sweet smile. And he did carry on a very nice, if rather shy, conversation about his father's ranch, and how he'd studied forestry but always wanted to be a pilot.

While he spoke, Tory noticed Maxie darting off and getting in a big conversation with David's mother and sisters. Maxie shook their hands and nodded, and they put their heads together in an exchange information. Soon they were all nodding. Probably trying to establish that they are Bodleys eight places removed on the Warington side, Tory thought as she sighed and listened to some more of Tom Dash's wonderfully sweet prattle. But, as Tory learned soon enough, that little anthropological conniver, Maxie, had something very different in mind. Or maybe not so different, depending on how one saw it.

🌐 ANN Breaking News with Allison Miranda ⚡

ALLISON: With the regular national election results now tabulated and final, the President of the United States is Clifford Bradley and the Vice President is his running mate, Meredith Cardoza. In all, Bradley and Cardoza's American Moderate Party, the largest of the moderate centrist parties, won the executive branch and majorities in the legislative branch by landslides of 43 states and a 66% majority of those voting. Over 90% of the eligible population voted, as a result of the extensive voter registration and education drives conducted by political and patriotic organizations after the collapse and disappearance of OCP and MCP, the demise of CON2, and the reaffirmation of the Constitution of 1787. Fringe parties including the Democrats and the Republicans shared less than 5% of the vote.

EPILOG

FT. RILEY, KANSAS

Major David Gordon, Executive Officer of his battalion in the 1st Infantry Division, was working at his desk at Fort Riley when a young buck sergeant tapped respectfully on the door and said something.

"Huh?" David's mind was awhirl with parts requisitions, courts martial orders, and all the other bric a brac—his Ft. Lewis company XO days writ large. It was the same stuff—just more of everything.

"Yessir, excuse me for interrupting, but he said put snap into it, Sir." The sergeant grinned cautiously, ready to be reprimanded.

"What are you talking about, Sergeant?"

"Um, Sir, there is a very, er, … four star general outside waiting for you in a staff car. I think your wife just had a baby."

"Oh." Surprised, not about the baby but about the general, David grabbed his garrison cap and raincoat and rushed outside. He wore fatigues and combat boots. He bolted down the stairs to a waiting staff car flying red pennants, four golden stars on each pennant. Inside sat Rocky Devereaux in his Class A uniform, chewing gum, and looking impatient.

"Sir! I didn't know you were—"

"I wasn't, but get in. We have someplace to go." As David slid into the back seat, he shook hands with Devereaux. "I have to sign out of—"

Rocky had a phone in his hand. "Who's your G-1? I'll give him a call." While David answered, he interrupted to bark at the young female sergeant driving. "Young lady, does this car have a siren?"

"N-no Sir?"

"Oh hell, and hell again. Okay, drive as fast as you can without getting us killed. We need to be on the airfield in ten minutes so my pal here can catch a hop. The major has some important people to see, not the least of which is David Allan Gordon Jr., currently not quite one day old." He winked at David, with a smack of chewing gum. "I have the plane on hold for you, don't worry. There's a pissed off Navy Admiral on board—just give him the finger for me, will you?"

David was pleasantly surprised, even shocked. "I didn't know you were on post today. Actually, this is an overwhelming surprise."

Rocky winked as the car lurched around a corner. "That's number one in strategy, son—keep them off balance. I get to go to a parade now and then. Keeps the back stiff, the chin firm, the abdomen concave. You'll be wearing birds on your shoulders before long."

"Yessir, I hope so."

"We'll get you fixed up on a division staff for a year

or so, then get your own battalion command. Infantry, of course. Maybe one day you'll be in my shoes, God forbid." He laughed harshly for a moment, then softened. "That's one hell of a sweet gal you married, David."

"Yessir, I think so."

Devereaux looked out the window to hide his facial expression. "Her granddad was my best friend. He died in my arms. In a way, it's lucky he didn't live to see how his son turned out. They're a fine family otherwise."

"Yessir."

"I know I don't need to ask you for any promises. I know you're taking good care of her. It—it means a great deal to me."

David offered his hand. "Sir, if I may, I'd like to offer you my handshake on that, and a gentleman's word."

Devereaux's handshake was strong but, for once, he had nothing to say, and looked fixedly out the window.

Walter Reed Army Hospital, Washington, D.C.

David rushed through the hospital's front entrance, signed in, and pinned on a visitor badge to be with his wife and son.

First he stopped in the hospital gift shop and bought a little stuffed bear, making sure it was from the baby-proof section, and hypo-allergenic. Devereaux, chewing his gum, had suggested this while seeing David off on the Navy Learjet. "Works every time," Rocky had said, "but make sure the goddamn thing says hypo-allergenic, or those women will be all over your back. They'll have no mercy, you know. Everything's gotta be hypo-allergenic these days."

"There you are!" said a woman's voice as he rushed out of the gift shop, "I thought I'd catch you here."

He turned. "Maxie!" She looked cute in jeans. He hugged her.

She hugged him. "Congratulations!"

"Thank you!"

"Guess what? I'm pregnant!"

"You are?"

She jumped up and down squealing, and he was glad she wasn't in uniform, wearing her Congressional Medal of Honor. "Yes! Yes! Tom is just out of his mind with happiness!"

"That's great, Maxie. I'm happy for you both."

She put her arm around his elbow and towed him firmly along. "C'mon. No time to waste." She pressed a button, and immediately, both elevator doors opened—of course, if Maxie needed an elevator—and lights blinked frantically as if the two elevators were competing for her attention. Maxie towed him into the closest one. The door rumbled shut and the elevator climbed. "If I have a boy, then he can come over and play with David. Dave? Davy? Nah, he's gonna be a David, like you." Her smile crinkled so that the freckles on her nose ran together. "Tory had a long discussion about that the day after you two met. She really, really liked you right from the first moment. She said you were a David, and I definitely agreed."

David nudged her. "You set us up." He added. "Thanks."

The elevator opened, and Maxie again towed him

along. People looked at David, who trailed the little blue bear, and smiled. "You should see the glow on your face," Maxie said. "Wait until you see Tory!"

They raced down a hall, barely registering the women patients and their nurses. They turned into a corridor that had a sign, "Private."

Maxie said: "There were so many doctors on rounds here this morning they had to bring them in the room in shifts."

It was quiet here, and peacefully gloomy. Most of the rooms were empty. Only one middle-aged female nurse, a lieutenant colonel, nodded distantly as she passed them in the corridor.

David and Maxie entered a room with lights on, and there were three people in the room. David's sister Dora lay in bed, smiling happily and proud at her success.

"Look at the little bear. How cute!" Dora said.

David gave Dora the bear.

Tory, wearing jeans and a sweater, stood beside the bed holding a bundle in a white blanket. Tory had an inner glow as she turned to show him his son. At first, though, he had eyes only for her. She looked more beautiful than ever. It was something his Dad had once told him long ago, that a woman never looks more beautiful than when she is out and about with her new baby. She was tall, and dark-haired, with that pretty, solemn face.

Her eyes glowed with love, and her lips trembled as she whispered: "I never thought I could ever be this happy."

She offered him his son.

David regarded his son in utter amazement and helplessness. He'd seen all of Dora's and Elaine's children as babies, and they all looked alike. Devereaux had said: "At first you won't feel a goddamn thing, just numb, especially when you think of the bills. When they hand him to you, take him and make all kinds of noises. Don't worry, he'll grow on you. Soon you'll be as crazy about him as you were to get married in the first place. I have five kids—I should know."

"So this is my son," he said, shaking his head in amazement as he held the tiny bundle, who weighed less than eight pounds and was blissfully asleep. The child had pink skin and dark hair. David held him and swayed gently with him. The baby yawned, smacked his lips, and kept on sleeping. David marveled at how tiny his hands and fingers were.

"He looks like you," Dora said in her loud, direct way.

"He's going to be hungry again in a little while," Dora said, absently holding the blue bear. "Why don't you give David Jr. to me and you two can go down the hall and hold hands? Mom and Elaine just went to the flower shop and they'll be back soon. Tory's grandma went with Maxie's mom to the cafeteria for coffee."

David kissed his son lightly and handed him into his sister's capable arms. He bent over and kissed Dora on the cheek. "Thanks, Sis. This was wonderful of you."

"Don't just thank me," Dora said. "Thank the woman who made it possible in the first place."

David turned, and Maxie looked embarrassed. "Oh come on, it was just a few little eggs. I've got plenty to spare. Actually, now that I'm pregnant, I'm glad to know they really work." She winked, stood on tip-toe, and gave David a hug.

Dora cooed to the little boy, who was biologically a Bodley on the direct side; though Maxie's dad's lawyers already had a ream of papers to prevent David Jr. from laying any claims on the Bodley estate, though nobody expected David and Tory's son to be such a bad sport.

Tory took David's hand. It was her turn to tow him away.

Maxie called after David: "The President has promised to be his godfather, and Vice President Cardoza his godmother. Meredith—that's her first name—just loves kids. Turns out she is a sixth cousin of mine on the Bodley side. She's a Warington, and they are related to…"

"Maxie," David heard Dora's firm voice, "come here right now, please, and get me some water…and then I would like you to sit down quietly here beside me and hold the baby."

Alone, David and Tory walked down the empty, silent corridor. She held his hand in hers, and walked with him down the long shadowy corridor to an exit door that said not to open except in emergencies. Outside, the sun had come out and a light wind blew the rain drops on the glass dry.

She looked demure and feminine in her dark button-up sweater and white blouse with tiny blue flowers stitched along the collar. David held her tenderly, with his palms around her delicate ribs. He would have kissed her, but she seemed in that push-away mode she sometimes still had. She patted both hands lightly on his chest and wriggled her fingers nervously. She reached down and took his hand, with the wedding band, and raised it up so their wedding bands touched firmly. She squeezed his hand between hers.

He wanted to ask: are you still unsure about marrying me? Are you still afraid to be rejected? He took her hands in his, and pulled them to his chest.

Neither spoke, except for this language of hands.

He was barely taller than she, and she looked up into his eyes. Her eyes were bigger than ever, moist, dark, full of secrets, of fears, of questions. Her lips moved as if to speak, several times, and each time she looked away, and then beseechingly into his eyes again. "Tory—I will never—"

She listened vulnerably as he spoke.

"I will never leave you and our son."

She flickered alight in stages as her uncertainty dissolved.

She answered him with a sparkling glance. Then she rested her forehead heavily against his chest in final, complete, relieved trust.